JOEL

JOEL

Escape from Abuse

Ted Louis

iUniverse, Inc.
New York Lincoln Shanghai

Joel
Escape from Abuse

Copyright © 2005 by Ted Louis

All rights reserved. No part of this book may be used or reproduced by any means, graphic, electronic, or mechanical, including photocopying, recording, taping or by any information storage retrieval system without the written permission of the publisher except in the case of brief quotations embodied in critical articles and reviews.

iUniverse books may be ordered through booksellers or by contacting:

iUniverse
2021 Pine Lake Road, Suite 100
Lincoln, NE 68512
www.iuniverse.com
1-800-Authors (1-800-288-4677)

ISBN-13: 978-0-595-36378-0 (pbk)
ISBN-13: 978-0-595-80815-1 (ebk)
ISBN-10: 0-595-36378-4 (pbk)
ISBN-10: 0-595-80815-8 (ebk)

Printed in the United States of America

CHAPTER 1

I was orphaned at the age of 14. My parents were killed in a plane crash returning from Saudi Arabia where my father worked for ARAMCO as a petroleum engineering project manager. They were on their way back to the US on one of their two required exits from the country each year. I was in boarding school in the US because teenagers were not allowed to remain in Saudi for middle and high school. That didn't really bother me because I didn't like living in Saudi anyway. It was so unbearably hot and gritty where my parents were stationed.

My world was turned upside down by their sudden deaths. I was an only child as were both mom and dad. They always told me I was the best birth control device known to man. I knew they were kidding because mom had a hysterectomy a couple of years after I was born. My grandfather on mom's side was my nearest kin so I ended up living with him. I never knew him very well before the accident. We had only seen him on holidays because my dad's job took us out of the US for long stretches at a time. He was nice but a distant and pretty straight laced person. He was, however, a genius when it came to managing money. He had one serious fault in my mind. He was very stingy handing out any money for me to spend.

The airline company flying the plane my parents were on settled for a fairly large sum of money as compensation for their deaths. Of course, granddad was in charge of it until I reached majority. In the four years that elapsed before I turned 18, he had managed to double my nest egg. With my parents estate, insurance policies that they had plus the company policy, and the airline settlement I was worth over $7.5 million when I was entitled to the money.

I decided to allow granddad to manage my assets until I finished college but did insist on a larger allowance to enhance my lifestyle and get a BMW. I did not live extravagantly but did have a decent apartment within a short distance of the college.

School had always been easy for me. I graduated from high school when I was barely 17 and finished my Ph.D. in Computer Science at 23. I had taken dual masters programs in Finance and Computer Science. I figured I needed to learn how to manage my money after I left college. I also spent as much time with granddad as possible learning from him how to preserve and increase my money. I learned as much from him as I did in any of my Finance classes in college. I was saddened a year after I left college when he passed away. Between the two of us, we had managed to increase the size of my nest egg to just over $26 million. Although I was granddad's only heir, he left all of his estate to various children's charities which surprised me no end.

I took a job out of college in 1988 with a high tech consulting company in San Antonio. This was convenient for me because my parents had a very nice home that I had inherited just north of SA in the hill country. Actually, after working there for a couple of years I had purchased the majority interest in the firm and now not only worked for the firm, I also directed its running. I hired an office manager who took care of the day to day operations of the business. I only managed consulting projects that were either interesting or challenging.

Although I didn't need to work, I guess the work ethic that was ingrained into me from my earliest childhood would not let me be a playboy.

I had been with Alamo Consulting Consortium for about 4 years when I was roped into helping coach a little league baseball team by one of the policemen that I had met while doing a project for the San Antonio Police Department. Jack was persistent in his pestering of me until I consented to help. This had been my major social outlet for the past two years taking up most of my free time during the season. I always had a soft spot for kids and after my initial reluctance to become involved I thoroughly enjoyed my interaction with the team.

It had been a long time since I had played any ball although I had played all through boarding school and on an intramural team in college and if I do say so myself I was not too bad. I never played any of the glamour positions just mostly outfield and some second base. I was quick and had a good arm and wasn't afraid to take a hard slide. Not too bad with a bat either, but definitely not pro material.

It was about the middle of the little league season one afternoon when I got to the ballpark early to get all of the equipment out of the shed and ready for the kids to arrive. I noticed there was one kid sitting in the stands already waiting for the game to start. I waved and gave him a smile as I passed. He just looked at me showing no emotion, not returning my wave. I was familiar with most of the kids that attended the games but I had never seen this one before. "He must be new to the neighborhood," I thought.

He looked like any other kid you might see hanging around the area. He was wearing a tee shirt that was about two or three sizes too big and his blue jeans had the required rip in the knees. His sneakers were standard fare. The laces were untied and spread open.

"God, how do they keep from tripping on those laces?" I muttered to myself.

Soon the kids arrived and the game got underway. The guys played really well but unfortunately our team lost by one run in the final at bat. They were all pretty bummed out. As much as we tried to tell them that the most important thing was that they played their best it was still disappointing to them when they lost. I gave all of the guys a coupon to redeem at the McDonald's down the street for whatever they wanted which helped to heal their wounded prides.

I had worked this out with the manager of the McDonald's that whoever brought one of my coupons in they could order anything they wanted and I would pay for it. This was one of the small extravagances I allowed myself. The kids that played on our team were some of the less fortunate and I sometimes think that this was the only substantial meal that some of them got. I always got a chorus of "Thank you, Coach Johnson" whenever I handed out the coupons. This scene always choked me up because I knew that they sincerely meant and appreciated it.

By the time the game was over and the kids all rushed off for their treat it was beginning to get dark. Jack went off with the kids to make sure that they behaved while I was left to get all of the equipment put away in the shed. As I locked up and turned around to survey the area to make sure that I had not missed anything, I noticed the same kid I had seen earlier still sitting in the bleachers. He had not moved since I first saw him.

Seeing no equipment that I had missed in my quick look around, I walked over to the bleachers where the youngster was sitting. "Hi, did you enjoy the game?" I asked.

He just looked at me as if he didn't understand what I was saying. I tried again in Spanish and then in German the only two languages that I had a passing acquaintance with. There was still no response.

Although it was getting dark, I took a closer look at the youngster and noticed that he appeared to need a bath. His clothes were not any dirtier than many kids who had been playing outside all day. His hands however looked like he had been digging in the dirt.

"Don't you think that you had better start home? Won't your parents be wondering where you are?" I questioned not knowing if he heard or understood anything I was saying. His only response was to lower his head and look at his shoes.

"Are you hungry?" I asked. He looked up slightly and I noticed that there were the beginnings of tears in his eyes. From this, I surmised that he was hearing what I was saying but for some reason did not or could not speak. I held out my hand inviting him to come with me. My intentions were to take him to the McDonald's where I could ask Jack what we should do with him. "Come, let's go to McDonald's," I said to him.

Instead of taking my hand, the boy stood and walked a little closer to me but stopped short. As he did so, he stepped more into the lights shining on the field which I had not yet turned off. I was able to get a better look at him. He appeared to be about 11 or 12 years old and quite short maybe 4' 6" or 8". His skin had a yellow cast to it that I had not noticed when I first saw him in the daylight earlier. His light brown hair was cut short and not too professionally. It looked more as if someone had taken a pair of scissors and whacked at it. His features were regular but not what you could call handsome, cute maybe. Probably his best feature was the color of his eyes which reminded me of the color of the water off the Florida gulf coast. I think they call it azure blue or something. Anyway, they were light blue with a hint of green.

I turned and started toward the pole where the light switch for the field lights was. As I reached the pole and took out my key to open the box to throw the switch, I looked back to see if he was still there. He had stepped down off the bleachers and had followed me staying about 10 feet behind. Taking this as a good sign, I decided to walk down to McDonald's hoping that he would follow me. I didn't want to scare him by trying to get him into my car.

It was less than a block and on the other side of the street to the destination I hoped he would follow me to. I kept looking around to see if he was with me. He maintained his roughly 10 foot distance but was following. I wondered what would happen when we had to cross the street as I reached out and pressed the button to change the light so we could cross. I prayed it would stay WALK long enough for him to cross behind me. To try to encourage him I walked more quickly as I crossed hoping he would try to maintain the same distance. He did.

I walked to the door of the fast food place not knowing what I would do if he would not close the gap between us. As I opened the door, I felt something push up against me. When I looked around it was as I had hoped the boy. I said as I looked down at him, "Let's get you something to eat. What would you like?"

Remembering his dirty hands I said, "I need to wash my hands, how about you?" Getting no response, I herded him into the restroom. I wet my hands and was about to dispense some soap when he stuck his hands under the water also. I let him soak his hands under the water for a while before dispensing a lot of liquid soap into my hands and taking his into mine scrubbing them in an attempt to wash some of the accumulated dirt off. I gave up trying to get all of it from under his nails. Taking a paper towel, I wet it and made an effort to wash his face. By the time we were finished he was at least more presentable.

When we went back into the dining area and I looked around for Jack he was nowhere to be found as were all of the team. "Well I guess I'll just have to wing it," I thought. "I'll have to call him later." It was not unusual for the team to be gone by the time I got there. They could inhale their meals in what seemed to be an instant. I sometimes wondered if the food even made it to the table before it was gone. Jack usually stuck around until I arrived unless he had something he had to do.

If the boy would not speak, I wondered what I should get him to eat as we approached the front of the serving line. When the teenager at the cash register asked us what we wanted, I decided I would just get a couple of Big Macs, fries and a couple of large chocolate shakes. From the look of the boy's head nodding up and down I could tell this was alright with him. When our order was ready, I carried it over to an empty table and set it down. It was barely on the table when he grabbed one of the hamburgers, tore off the wrapper and took a huge bite.

"Slow down, I don't want you to choke," I chuckled. "There's plenty of food, don't worry." I watched in fascination as he demolished his burger in about six bites, then started on the Biggie fries and the shake. I hadn't unwrapped my sandwich and had only taken a few sips of my shake when he looked up at me and then at the other Big Mac. I hesitated for a moment before I shoved it toward him. He quickly had it unwrapped and began his second attack, but this time he ate it in a somewhat more leisurely fashion. I nibbled a few of my fries and then pushed them toward him. He looked up and then quickly began to devour them as well.

"You wait right here, I have to see the manager and pay my bill. Okay?" I said as I got up. I caught Larry's attention and asked him what the damages were for the team's eating frenzy. I wasn't too surprised when the total for the 16 little eating machines came to just over $150. It usually ran about that after each game. I didn't care. I could easily afford it and it gave me pleasure doing it. I paid the bill and started back to the table then I turned back and ordered two of the "fried pies".

As I sat down at the table, he was just slurping the last of his shake. I handed him the pies and he gobbled down the first and looked at me before I nodded and he consumed the second as well.

"Where do you live?" I asked. Getting no response I continued, "Are you new to the neighborhood? I haven't seen you around before." He shook his head to indicate I think that he didn't live around here. I wasn't really sure. At least I thought he could hear me or was very good at reading lips. I decided that I needed to call Jack to see if he knew of any reports of a missing kid.

I took my cell phone and dialed Jack's number. It rang three times before he picked up. "Hi, Jack, it's Crane," I said. After we exchanged pleasantries I continued, "Do you know of any reports of a young boy about 10 to 12 years old being reported missing or having run away?" I went on to describe to him the events surrounding the youngster I was now sitting with. Jack did not know of any but would call in to police headquarters and find out since he was off duty for the rest of the weekend.

Five minutes later, he called back and said that they did not have any missing persons report for someone matching the description I had given him. He suggested that I try to get the kid to lead me to his home or failing that to take him to the police station and turn him in. I quickly rejected the second suggestion. I could not bear the thought of the kid being locked up over the weekend until some Child Protective Services official could get there to process him probably on Monday.

"Hey, little buddy, let's go see if we can find your home. We can't stay here all night," I said. "Do you have a name?" getting no response I continued after a few seconds, "I have to call you something. I guess I'll just call you Boy until we find out what your real name is. Is that alright with you?" He didn't answer but did give me a brief smile that made me want to give him a big hug, but I resisted. I sure didn't want to frighten him away.

I got up from the table and started to the door when he threw his arms around my waist and held on like he was afraid I would abandon him there. Although it made walking somewhat difficult, we finally managed to get back across the street and to my new BMW that I had just picked up two weeks ago.

"Well, what am I going to do with you? Will you tell me where you live?" He just squeezed me tighter as an answer. "It looks like I'll have a houseguest for the weekend. I'm sure not going to turn you over to the police tonight," I snickered. I opened the passenger door to my car and attempted to peel Boy off my side. He reluctantly released his grip on my waist and allowed me to put him in the seat and fasten his seatbelt.

We quickly made it to Loop 410 and then to 281 north. The BMW wanted to stretch out but I held it in somewhat control only traveling at 85 after we left the city. I turned off on 306 and then wound my way through some of the side roads that people from the more civilized areas would not even consider a good cow path. When we finally reached the gate to my property, I activated the electronic gate to allow us entry. My house was located on thirty-five acres near the top of a magnificent hill with stunning views of Canyon Lake and the whole canyon area all the way to the dam. This was my parent's vacation house. They had been very prudent having mortgage insurance on the property so that when I inherited it, it was free and clear. It was much too big for a single person as it was over 4800 square feet with four bedrooms and five baths. Even though it was too big, I could not convince myself to sell it and move closer to my work.

Boy's eyes were almost popping out of his head all the way from San Antonio. He had the most disbelieving look on his face as I drove into the three car garage alongside my Land Rover. I got out of the car and went around to his side of the car and opened the door. He was still in shock so I released his seatbelt and pulled him out of the car setting him on his feet. He immediately threw his arms around my waist again, but this time those beautiful eyes had fear showing in them.

"Nobody is going to harm you," I whispered to him as I led him to the door into the back hallway of the house. "Would you like something to drink? A Coke or Seven-Up or Dr. Pepper is all I have."

Not getting an answer, I led him to the refrigerator and opened the door. I reached in and got a Dr. Pepper. He released one arm from around my waist and grabbed a Coke. I popped the top on my can and took a swallow. When I looked down, he was holding his can up to me as if to say "open it". I popped the top on his can and steered him to the couch in the family room and turned on the TV. As we sat down, he released his hold on my waist but sat as close to me as he could.

Being this close to him in a closed environment I realized just how long it had been since he had bathed. He was a little ripe. I hadn't noticed it as much in the car with the windows down as I like to ride or at McDonald's but now it was very noticeable.

"Boy," I said, "you need a bath! As soon as you finish your coke we'll find you something to wear and then you need to climb into a shower."

Finding him something to wear in this house was not going to be easy. I'm just over 6 feet tall so I knew nothing that I had would fit him. Well maybe a tee shirt would serve as pajamas until we could get his clothes clean. One of my tee's would probably come down to his knees because I like to buy them at least one size larger than necessary. Then I remembered that the last time Jack and his family were visiting a couple of weekends ago his youngest son had left a pair of shorts, a tee shirt and a pair of briefs. He had ridden home in his bathing suit and had left the clothes by mistake. I think that kid would forget his head if it were not attached. The clothes might be just a little big but they would fit better than one of my tees.

When "Boy" finished his coke, I reminded him he needed to take a bath. I led him to a bathroom in one of the spare bedrooms and showed him where the soap, shampoo and towels were and made sure he knew he was supposed to use them. I told him he could stay in the shower as long as he liked but that I expected him to be thoroughly clean when he came out. I placed Timmy's clothes out for him and told him I would throw his dirty clothes in and start them washing as soon as he was finished.

About twenty minutes later my young guest appeared all fresh and clean. I had not thought about providing a comb or brush in the bathroom until he showed up with his hair in a mass of tangles. I quickly remedied the situation and soon he looked like a nearly normal boy. The yellow cast of his complexion was even more noticeable now that the dirt had been washed off. It seemed a little strange to me but not knowing anything about his background or ancestors I pushed it to the back of my mind.

"Come here young man. Sit down beside me here on the couch," I said to him.

He ran to the couch and jumped on it landing right next to me pushing me about six inches to the right. "Whoa!" I chuckled. "Do you feel better now that you are all clean?" He just looked up at me and smiled the first really big smile I had seen from him. Timmy's clothes as I had expected were a little large but not so much that they were hanging off him. In fact, I had seen some kids intentionally wear theirs as baggy or baggier. "We need to wash your own clothes so that you will have a change. Let's go do that now."

I got up and went to retrieve his clothes, but as I did, I had him clinging to me again making it difficult to walk. "It's alright son, I'm not going to leave you. I'm just going to put your dirty clothes in the washer. Do you want to help?" I asked.

I could almost detect a nod of his head.

We grabbed his dirty clothes and headed for the laundry room. As I turned the dial on the washer and added a good amount of detergent to the tub, he took the clothes and stuffed them into the washer. Again, he turned his face up to me and gave me another full smile. This time I took a good look at those beautiful azure eyes and was surprised at what I had not noticed before.

I guess I had never really looked at him in full light, but when I did, I was shocked to see that the whites of his eyes were also yellowed. This started my mind spinning. "What causes the eyes and skin to turn yellow?" I thought trying to remember the health classes I had taken so many years ago. "OH my God!" it suddenly dawned on me. "He could have hepatitis of some kind. If it is I hope it is not the catching kind," I prayed inwardly.

One of my friends and neighbor here at the lake was a well known San Antonio pediatrician. "Please let him be at home this weekend," I said to myself.

"Boy, I have to make a phone call. Would you like a dish of ice cream while I make the call?" I said and without waiting headed to the refrigerator knowing young boys appetites. "I have Chocolate, Vanilla or Butter Pecan. Which do you want?" I asked as I got down a large bowl from the cupboard and a couple of spoons from the drawer. I also retrieved some chocolate and butterscotch syrup in case he wanted to make a sundae.

"Help yourself to as much as you want of any one or all of them," I said as I place the three half gallon cartons of ice cream on the counter and lifted him up onto one of the bar stools.

I picked up the phone in the kitchen and dialed Sam's number. Dr. Samuel Greene is a jolly man. He stands about 5' 3" and probably weighs around 250 pounds. He is great with kids. I have been at his place when his grandkids were there with their friends and he was the center of attention of all the kids. You could tell from his eyes as he looked at them that the kids were the center of his universe.

Thank goodness Sam answered the phone. "Hi Sam, this is Crane Johnson. I got myself in a situation and I would like to impose on you if I could," I started. I explained the situation as succinctly as I could without leaving anything important out.

"Yeah, it looks like you do have a situation there," Sam almost snickered. "How can I help?"

"You know I'm not a doctor but from what I can remember from health class, this kid shows all the symptoms of hepatitis. Could you possibly take a look at him to see if there is any imminent danger either for him or for that matter me?"

"Crane, you know I don't usually make house calls, but for you I will make an exception. I'm here alone this weekend anyway. Carol went to see the grandkids in Houston. I tell you what, break out a bottle of that 'Clos du Bois' Merlot and I will be there in ten minutes."

"I have it chilled to a perfect 65 degrees and I'll open it and let it breathe until you get here. Thanks, Sam, I owe you," I said.

True to his word, Sam showed up almost exactly ten minutes later. "Hi Sam, come on in," I said as I let him in the back door. "The little guy is in the kitchen eating some ice cream."

"That's a good sign. Usually hepatitis patients have a suppressed appetite. Has he eaten anything else?" he asked.

I related the stop at McDonald's as we started for the kitchen. "Hi, Boy, this is Dr. Sam. He wants to take a look at you to see if you are alright," I said, introducing my neighbor.

"Crane, pour me a glass of that Merlot while we wait for this young man to finish his ice cream," Sam said as he put his medical bag down on the breakfast bar. He drew a deep breath taking in the bouquet of the wine and then took a sip and savored the rich flavors of this exceptional California wine.

Our guest finished his ice cream and Sam convinced him as only he could do to go with him into a bedroom to be examined. It seemed like they were in there forever, but in reality it was only about twenty-five minutes.

Sam came out of the bedroom smiling with his arm around Boy chatting to him. Boy still was not saying anything.

"I don't think he has hepatitis," Sam indicated picking up his unfinished glass of wine. "Why don't you go watch some TV young man, I want to talk to Crane for a minute, okay?"

Boy looked to me and I nodded. He shuffled into the family room and picked up the remote and started surfing the channels.

"Crane, did you see the boy with his shirt off?" he asked me. When I shook my head no he continued, "He has been badly beaten on his back, buttocks and upper thighs. I put some antiseptic salve on the welts and I'll leave a tube of it for you to use tomorrow morning. There are also indications that he has been sexually abused. His anus is swollen and appears to have some tearing that has partially healed. I didn't do as intrusive an examination as I'll need to do to determine the exact extent of the abuse, but I'd like for you to bring him to my office on Monday and I'll do a much more thorough exam.

"I can see no physical reason for his inability to speak. His throat and voice mechanisms all appear to be in good health. There is some redness at the back of his mouth which I would be willing to bet was caused by forced oral sex.

"Crane, how did you get messed up in this?" he asked. "I will have to file a report of the suspected sexual abuse to the state. You know I'm required to report anything I see."

"Why is his complexion so yellow if you don't think he has hepatitis?" I asked somewhat confused by what I had just heard.

"It looks like his kidneys may have been bruised when he was beaten and may have nearly shut down. The liver may also have been bruised and not functioning properly. One or both of these conditions could be a cause of the yellowing. Keep track of his trips to the bathroom to see if he's producing any urine. If he's not, let me know tomorrow morning and I'll talk to a colleague of mine who runs a private dialysis clinic. I'll get him in to do a quick dialysis to keep him healthy until I can run a complete blood workup on him. I'd also like to do an MRI and CT scan on his abdomen to see if there is any other damage when you bring him in Monday. If you can have him there at 8:30, I'll see him before my other patients.

"Okay, let's see what we can do with the rest of that bottle of Merlot," Sam chuckled. "Also we need to discuss the legal ramification of you keeping this boy here for the weekend and my treating him without parental permission. Both of us could be in deep shit if we're not careful.

"I know a lady who works at CPS and lives on the other side of the lake. I think we should call her and get her take on what we're doing. I think I have her home number in my PDA. Let me check.

"Yes, here it is, Theresa Shannon. I've treated some kids under her supervision before. She seems to really care about her charges."

"You go call her and see if she can come over here either tonight or tomorrow morning and advise us. I'll go check on Boy to see how he is doing" I said as I indicated the phone in the kitchen.

I walked back into the family room and saw Boy sitting on the couch watching a breaking news report on one of the local channels. Just as I walked in to sit down the news reporter started speaking about one of the many shootings that occur in the city it seems like on a daily basis. I didn't pay much attention until Boy suddenly uttered the first sounds that I had heard from him. It was a high pitched squeal almost above my hearing range.

"Wha…What's wrong?" I stammered. As I reached out to him, he curled up in a tight little ball and started sobbing, tears running down his cheeks like a waterfall. What the reporter on TV said started to register since it was apparent that is what had set Boy off. The report was about a man suspected of shooting his wife in their home at least six times in the face and head before taking off. When I looked at the TV they were displaying a picture of the house and an address of the crime scene that I knew was about a mile from the little league field where we had played that afternoon. The TV indicated that the police thought that the incident had occurred sometime around noon based on some neighbors' reports but had not been reported to the police until nearly 8PM.

I pulled Boy onto my lap and started to rock him back and forth as I stroked his back. "It's okay, you're safe. No one's going to hurt you. You're okay. Don't worry I'm here." I nearly started to weep as well as the hurt that Boy was feeling seemed to invade my soul.

I was still holding and rocking him when Sam came into the room and said that Theresa would be here in about 30 minutes. I told Sam to go release the gate so that she would be able to get in without buzzing us.

When he came back, I told him what I suspected about what had set Boy off. "I need to get hold of Jack to see if I can get some more information on the crime that the TV had reported. He may be able to get more details that aren't available to the general public and possibly the names of the people involved. I think that those people might be related to our young friend. Will you hold him while I call Jack?"

Not waiting for an answer, I struggled to my feet still holding Boy. I nodded my head to Sam for him to sit down and then handed Boy to him. I rushed to my bedroom and grabbed the phone and dialed Jack's number.

"Come on Jack, answer the phone!" I impatiently muttered at the phone. Finally, a young voice I knew to be Timmy's answered the phone. "Hi, Timmy this is Crane Johnson. Is your dad there? I need to talk to him, please."

Timmy said that he'd go get his dad. It seemed to take forever for Jack to come on the line. When he did, I related to him what I thought about the crime and the possible relationship of the victims to Boy. "Jack, can you find out the names of the victims and any other information that might be useful in identifying Boy?" I asked almost pleading.

Jack said that he would try to get as much information as he could but it might take a little while. I asked him to do his best and to call me no matter what time it was.

The minutes seemed like hours as we waited for Theresa to get here and Jack to call back. I nearly jumped out of my skin when the front door bell rang announcing that Theresa had arrived. I was just opening the door to let her in when my phone rang. I knew it would be Jack calling back.

CHAPTER 2

"Hello…Oh, hi, Jack" I said answering my phone. "Thanks for getting back to me. Theresa Shannon from CPS is at the door. May I call you right back? Thanks!"

"Come in. You must be Theresa Shannon. I'm Crane Johnson. Please come into the family room. Dr. Sam is in there," I rambled as I extended my hand to her and invited her into the house.

After greeting Sam, Theresa sat down on the couch next to him and Boy.

I said, "I need to call Jack back to see what information he's been able to discover. Sam, will you fill Theresa in on what you know of the situation and I'll fill in any of the blanks that you can't."

Walking swiftly to my bedroom, I dialed Jack. "Jack, sorry about having to get back to you like this, but things were getting a little hectic just when you called. What were you able to find out?"

"Here it is in a nutshell," he started. "From what I can figure out, the boy in your house could, and I must emphasize could, be the son of the murdered woman you heard about on TV. It appears that the husband killed her after a violent argument that had been going on for several days according to neighbors. Several of them saw the husband speeding away from the house around noon or thereabouts.

"Something that was not on the news and is being kept under wraps is that there were three young boys locked in a closet in a back bedroom. It appears that they were all undernourished and had been subject to physical if not sexual abuse. All of them were covered with bruises and scrapes.

"The neighbors also reported that there was another son who was not in the house when the police arrived. There are indications that he had been locked in a shed in the back yard. It looks like he was able to dig his way out of the shed through the dirt floor. The police are looking for the boy now."

"Okay, do you have any names? Anything that might identify the young man I have here? I asked when he paused for breath.

"The name of the boy that they are looking for is Joel, Joel Andersen. One of the neighbor kids reported seeing Joel at the front door of his house screaming as if he were in extreme pain and then suddenly stopped. Other neighbors said that they had seen Joel walking down the street in what they described as a trance or daze early this afternoon and they had not seen him since," he concluded. "That's all I can find out right now. I'll keep in touch with the investigators to see what I can glean and if there is anything significant, I'll be in touch. Right now, I'm going to bed. It has been a long day and it is getting late."

"Thanks, Jack! I really appreciate this. I owe you big time. I'll talk to you tomorrow," I said ringing off.

I walked back into the family room just as Dr. Sam was wrapping up his review of the situation with Theresa. "I'm sorry to have been so rude leaving you like that, but I needed to get the information that Jack had that might pertain to this situation. It might not, but it sounds to me suspiciously like it does," I said before relaying what Jack had told me.

They both listened intently until I finished. I had deliberately delayed the inclusion of the name that I believed deep down belonged to the boy that Sam was still cradling in his arms as we talked.

Finally I couldn't hold back any longer on my desire to confirm or deny the name of my young guest. "Jack told me that the name of the missing older boy was Joel Andersen." With that announcement the boy in Sam's arms let out another high pitched squeal that so startled me earlier. He began sobbing almost hysterically again.

Sam made every effort to comfort the boy and at the same time asking him gently if his name was Joel but received no response. "Crane, I believe we should put this youngster into bed. He needs to get some rest. I'll give him a light sedative to help him get to sleep. Theresa, you did not see or hear me say that, right?"

The good doctor struggled mightily to get up without dropping the boy. He normally has a hard time getting up from my couch without the added burden of 60 or 70 additional pounds.

I could barely keep a straight face as I led him and his charge, still in his arms, to one of the spare bedrooms directly across from my bedroom. I retrieved Sam's bag from the kitchen counter and brought it to him before leaving the room.

Theresa began as I entered the family room, "If that boy really is Joel Andersen, then I am somewhat familiar with the family. Although it is not one of my cases, one of my associates was telling me about an Andersen family that had been put on watch for possible neglect of four young boys. The family had been interviewed at least twice, but nothing overtly demanded that the children be placed in protective custody. She was suspicious that there was an unhealthy atmosphere for the children but was not in any position to have the children removed just because she had a bad feeling about the home environment.

"It's too late to do anything tonight. But, I'll be back tomorrow after I have contacted Joyce. She's the case worker I mentioned. If the other three children have been taken into custody, she will be made aware of them for further processing. I can't say right now what will happen to your little friend after tonight. Just watch him like Dr. Sam suggested and we will see what tomorrow brings."

Theresa was gathering up her things when Sam came back into the room. "He's sleeping quietly now. The sedative should allow him to get some needed rest. Perhaps we will know more by the time he wakes up. I'll fill out the suspected abuse forms you gave me and have them ready sometime tomorrow morning. I guess our priority after making sure that he's safe and healthy is to determine just who he is for sure. I think that we are all fairly certain that we know his name. We do have to confirm it before any substantial steps are taken. Let's all get some sleep. I don't think there's anything more we can do tonight and besides I'm beat."

"Thanks so much for all of your help, both of you. Sam, I'll call you in the morning after the little one wakes up and let you know if his kidneys are functioning. Theresa, it was nice to meet you. Call me any time if you get more information," I said as I saw them both out the front door.

I buttoned up the house for the night and set the alarm before I looked in on the sleeping boy. He looked so peaceful lying there with the silvery moonlight providing just enough brightness to see him. Turning to my bedroom, I glanced at my alarm clock. "Good God, it's almost 1AM. No wonder I'm so tired. This has been a long and certainly not a normal day."

Leaving the door open to my bedroom in case he started to get restless, I stripped out of my clothes, threw them in the hamper and then slipped between the sheets of my king size bed. I don't think I had been in bed five minutes before I was dead to the world.

It seemed like I had just gotten to sleep when I awoke with a start. I listened carefully but heard nothing unusual. Looking at the clock, I saw it was nearly six o'clock. I started to roll over when I felt something in bed with me. Since this is not a frequent occurrence, it nearly scared the crap out of me. I quickly turned on the bedside lamp to see what it was. Squinting against the bright light assaulting my sleepy eyes, I saw that the object was Boy (Joel?) curled up in a ball in the middle of the bed. "Oh, shit!" I thought. "Here I am, naked as a jaybird in bed with a pre-teenage boy whose name I don't know for sure. Christ, what would CPS or the cops say about this?"

He did look so peaceful lying there that I couldn't help but lean over and give him a light kiss on the top of his head. "This kid is getting to me," I thought and quickly got out of bed and went to my dresser to retrieve a pair of pajama bottoms. I slipped them on before crawling back into bed without disturbing him.

Surprisingly I went back to sleep and when I next looked at the clock it was almost eight. Rolling over I saw that he was awake sitting up in the bed staring at me. "Good morning, little one," I said through a sleep haze. "I don't know about you, kid, but I have to pee bad!" I swung my legs over the side of the bed and walked quickly to my bathroom to do my business when I felt him behind me pushing against my leg. "Do you have to go too? I guess that there's room for two. There has to be because I can't wait." I moved to one side of the toilet and let my stream loose. He hesitated briefly before pushing down his borrowed underwear and began urinating. I watched closely remembering that Sam had asked me to see whether and how much urine that Boy produced.

Men have this unwritten rule that they don't look at another's penis when they are taking a piss, so it was hard to watch him pee. But I did, and was pleased to see that he produced nearly as much urine as I did. His did have a much darker color and had a noticeably strong and unpleasant odor.

"Let's get our hands washed and then I'll see what I can rustle up for our breakfast," I said as we finished.

As he turned around, I noticed for the first time his back and the horrible weals and welts. "Oh my god, how could anyone do this to you?" I sobbed dropping to my knees. "I can't believe that anyone could be so cruel." Tears began running down my cheeks as I got a better look at the damage done to his back. My stomach felt like it was going to turn inside out and I could feel the acid pushing up into my throat. I swallowed hard trying to recover from this atrocity I saw in front of me.

"Let's go get some of that salve that Dr. Sam left," I choked out. "Then go put on some clothes while I throw on a robe." I could hardly see through my tear filled eyes to apply the ointment to his injuries, but did manage to complete the process.

Thank goodness my housekeeper had been grocery shopping this week. She makes sure that I have enough food to feed an army all the time. For once, I was glad that she kept me so well supplied. I pulled some sausage links out of the refrigerator along with some milk, orange juice and syrup. I decided to make waffles.

I have an old waffle maker that must be almost as old as I am that makes four six inch square waffles at one time. I dug it out of the cupboard and plugged it in to begin heating up. After putting the skillet on the stove and adding a pound of the sausages, I mixed up the waffle batter. I'm a real gourmet, I used a mix that only requires you to add the liquid and presto you have the batter. I took my pastry brush and liberally painted the heating surfaces of the waffle iron with oil. This thing is so old that it predates Teflon but it makes the greatest waffles. I poured in the batter and began setting the breakfast bar with plates and utensils. I also put the syrup into the microwave and heated it up. I hate to have cold syrup on my hot waffles.

All this time Boy was sitting there watching intently. At least this morning he was not as clingy and allowed me to move around without him being wrapped around my waist. I guess he knew that I was not going to abandon him. The sausages and the first batch of waffles were ready almost simultaneously. I drained the meat and set it on the bar and then carefully peeled the waffle from the iron before buttering it and pouring in the batter for the second batch.

I cut the waffles into the four sections, placed them on the platter and set them on the table.

"Dig in or I might eat them all," I laughed. He took me at my word and stabbed two of the waffles and six sausage links. Smothering both of the waffles with butter and syrup, he began attacking his plate like he hadn't eaten in a week. "Slow down, nobody is going to take it away from you. There's plenty more to come."

I ate one of the waffles that were left on the plate and a couple of the sausage links. As I picked up the platter to go get the other waffles, he stabbed the remaining one and plopped it on his plate. When I returned with the fresh batch, he just smiled up at me with syrup and butter dripping down his chin. I reached over with my napkin and wiped his chin. I caught him between fork loads.

I got one more waffle and two more links and he ate all of the rest along with two large glasses of milk and a large glass of OJ.

I was just putting the last of the breakfast dishes into the dishwasher when the phone rang. It was Sam.

The first thing he said, even before hello, was, "How is he this morning? Has he gone to the bathroom yet?"

"He appears to be just fine this morning," I replied. "His appetite is good and he did pee." I went on to describe the color and odor of the urine to him. Sam was not too happy about my description but said he was glad that he had started passing urine. He said that the dark color in the urine could be from blood as a result of the bruised kidneys but would need a sample to be sure. It could also contribute to the strong odor. When he asked me if I had a small glass bottle with a lid, I knew what he was leading up to.

"Yes, Sam, I know what you want me to do. And yes, the next time he goes I'll be there with the collection bottle. Damn, now I know why I didn't go into nursing," I chuckled at the image in my mind.

I found the bottle that I told Sam I had and washed it with soap and water. Then I filled it with water and placed it in the microwave and turned it on for a couple of minutes in an effort to sterilize the bottle. After the water boiled for a minute, I carefully removed it, dumped the hot water out and sealed it with the cap.

I had just gone to check on Boy when the phone rang. Seeing that he was napping on the couch with the Saturday morning cartoons on TV, I returned to the kitchen to answer it.

"Hello."

"Good morning, this is Theresa Shannon. How is our little friend this morning?"

"Oh, good morning, Theresa, he's doing fine. He's eating like he's been starved and he's producing urine so that is one less worry."

"Good, I've talked to Joyce this morning and she's taken the three other suspected siblings into protective custody. She would like to meet with your boy to see if he is the missing son. Would later this morning be alright?"

"Yes, I think that would be okay. How about 11 o'clock? Do you think it would be possible for her to bring the other children just in case Boy is actually Joel? It might also help him to recover his voice if he knows his brothers are safe. Let me know if she can bring them. I'll have my house keeper fix us some lunch and we can eat out by the pool. It is turning out to be a gorgeous day for a picnic."

"I'll check with Joyce but I think she will be agreeable. Eleven I'm sure will be fine."

I hung up the phone and checked on Boy again. He was awake and engrossed in the cartoons so I didn't bother him. I picked up the phone again and called Mrs. Ramirez to see if she could prepare a picnic lunch for us even if the other boys could not come. I don't know what I would do without her help. She had been taking care of my household every since I moved to the San Antonio area out of college. She cleaned the house, did my shopping and even fixed meals for me two days a week. The way she looked after me you would think she was my surrogate mother. She readily agreed to fix the picnic only asking how many people she should prepare for. When I told her that there would possibly be four young boys she laughed and said she had better make extra.

I went in and sat down beside Boy. He looked up at me and as I really looked at his eyes for the first time today, they seem to me to be less yellowed than yesterday. I hoped that I was not just wishing it to be so.

"We're going to have some visitors later this morning," I started. "The lady that was here last night and a friend of hers named Joyce are coming to see you. Is that alright?"

He gave an almost invisible shrug and went back to watching the cartoons but did slide closer to me leaning into my chest. I put my arm around him and leaned down to kiss the top of his head. His only response was to snuggle closer to me. We sat that way for probably an hour when he slipped off the couch. He grabbed my hand and pulled me toward one of the bedrooms. I had a feeling that he needed to take a bathroom break so I forced a detour to pick up the bottle that I had sterilized to carry out the good doctor's instructions.

It was a bit awkward but we managed to get a sufficient sample for the analysis. His urine was still as dark and strong smelling as earlier so I capped it as quickly as I could. I rinsed the outside of the bottle and dried it, took it to the kitchen and wrapped it in foil before placing it in the refrigerator. That sounds gross but it's what the doctor ordered.

Since it was only 10:30, I decided I should give Boy a tour of the outside of the house. So far he had only seen the interior. I opened the sliding patio door and motioned for him to follow. I never get tired of the vista that unfolds out my back door. Boy stopped frozen just outside the door not believing what he was seeing. I believed that what had mesmerized Boy was the panorama until I looked down at him. To my surprise what had stopped him in his tracks were the hill country pests, the nemesis of every gardener…deer.

There were eleven deer chewing up what was left of some very expensive landscape plants that I had installed earlier in the year. Boy's eyes were fixed on them I'm sure because he'd never seen them before or at least not so close up. When I realized this, I placed my arm around him and nudged him further out onto the stone patio toward the deer. As we approached, they lifted their heads and looked toward us but did not move away. The closer we got the more of their attention was focused on the two of us. When we were about 8 or 10 feet from the closest one, it started moving slowly away. This started the whole group sauntering off to wreak havoc on new pastures.

After the deer were out of sight, I led Boy around the rest of the back of the house. We toured the pool and hot tub area as well as the steep set of steps leading down to the lake front. By this time it was nearing 11 o'clock so we started back to the house to wait for our guests. Since I had not heard back from either Theresa or Joyce I did not know if the other possible brothers would be coming but was hoping that they would show up.

As we entered the house, I heard the buzzer for the entry gate go off. The security camera at the gate showed that it was Dr. Sam. I did not realize he was going to be here but I was glad that he was. I pushed the button to release the gate and at the same time I saw on the camera two more vehicles approaching. One I recognized as Theresa's car from last night. The other I just assumed was Joyce's SUV.

As I walked toward the front door to greet our guests, I motioned Boy to my side and put my arm around him before proceeding to the door. Dr. Sam was the first to arrive on the front porch where we greeted him. He shook my hand and extended his to Boy who surprisingly took it and shook it giving Sam a weak smile. Next to arrive was Theresa and the scene was repeated. Finally, a rather large woman both in height and girth approached and introduced herself as Joyce Gehrig.

"Hello there young man," Joyce said brightly to Boy. "It is a pleasure to meet you. I hope that you had a pleasant sleep. You're looking well today."

"I've brought the other children, but would like to visit with this young man before we introduce them," she directed to me. "Theresa will look after them for a few minutes while I spend some time with him."

With that, she placed her hand on Boy's shoulder and led him around the corner of the house toward the pool.

I walked with Theresa to the SUV to check on the kids that had been left there. To my surprise, the three children in the vehicle consisted of a boy who appeared to be about 6 and what I'm sure was a set of twin boys who were maybe 9. It was obvious to me just from looking into their eyes that they were Boy's brothers. They all had the distinctive azure colored eyes that were so noticeable in Boy. Or maybe I should start calling him Joel.

CHAPTER 3

❦

The three boys simultaneously released their seat belts and began clambering out of the SUV. First out was one of the twins wearing a red shirt and immediately turned to help his younger brother step out quickly followed by the other twin wearing a blue shirt. After all three had exited, they stood in formation almost as if for inspection. The youngest was cute as most kids his age are but the twins were drop dead gorgeous and as identical as any two humans could be. Both Theresa and I literally gasped as we got a good look at them. It took a moment before either one of us could find our tongues.

Theresa recovered first and asked the youngest "What's your name?"

"Timothy Jay Andersen, but I like to be called TJ," he replied startling both of us with his adult like answer.

"Hi, TJ, it is nice to meet you." Turning to the twin in the red shirt, she asked what his name was.

"Lawrence Jay Andersen, but I like to be called Larry," he replied in the same manner as his younger brother.

Not to be outdone the other twin in the blue shirt responded "Leonard Jay Andersen, but I liked to be called Lenny."

"Come on guys, let's go get something to drink," I said as I turned toward the house. Theresa followed me as she wrapped her arm around TJ and ushered him into the house. Larry and Lenny followed making several detours to inspect the fountain and other landscape details in the front of the house.

When we got all three of them to the kitchen, I opened the refrigerator and told them to help themselves to the soft drinks. It is a good thing I wasn't standing in front of them or I might have been trampled.

TJ turned to me and asked "Do you have any chips?"

I choked back a snicker at his boldness but replied "Of course I do, TJ. But I don't want you to eat too much and spoil your lunch. We are going to eat soon," I went to the pantry and retrieved a package of potato chips and one of pretzels and placed them on the breakfast bar before opening them.

The kids were just beginning to stuff their mouths full of chips when Joyce entered through the patio door with Boy in tow. The boys at the bar all turned in unison and jumped down from the stools and ran for Boy and began hugging him. All three of them were talking at once and asking questions. It looked as though Joel (I'm sure that is him now) was trying to speak but nothing was coming out. He was becoming more frustrated and I saw the tears of joy at being reunited with his brothers being replace with tears of frustration the more he tried to talk.

Seeing this I went to him and wrapped my arms around him, looked into his eyes and softly whispered in his ear that it was all right. I picked him up and carried him to the couch in the family room with the other three kids following so closely behind that I could feel them rubbing up against my legs. When we sat down TJ crawled up on my lap with Joel and kissed his brother on the nose. The twins sat on either side of me wrapping their arms around all of us. I kept repeating softly to him "It's okay! It's okay! You're alright. Your brothers are here. You're safe now. No one is ever going to hurt you again. I promise, I promise."

I hadn't noticed but Dr. Sam, Theresa and Joyce had all followed us into the room and were gathered around watching. As I looked up, I couldn't see them clearly because my eyes were filled with tears that were streaming down my cheeks. "What are we going to do? What is going to become of them?" I asked to no one in particular.

Before anyone could answer, the back door opened and my housekeeper charged in carrying a large basket which I knew had to be our picnic lunch. Mrs. Ramirez, Hildy Ramirez, is not what you would expect from someone with an Hispanic surname. She is actually third generation German-American having grown up in New Braunfels. She married a Mexican-American which is the reason for the Ramirez last name. Her long grey-blonde hair is tightly braided and wrapped around her head like a halo. She is tall, nearly six feet, and big boned but not fat. Her heart is pure gold, but she looks like she could snap you in two if she had a mind to. When she enters a room, you have no doubt who is in charge.

Setting the basket down on the kitchen counter, she strode into the family room. "Now, who do we have here?" she asked looking at the boys surrounding me ignoring the adults.

"The little one on my lap is TJ. Joel is the other one. The twin with the red shirt is Larry and the one in blue is Lenny," I told her.

"Oh you guys are so handsome. You look good enough to eat," she beamed which got an unexpected reaction from all the boys as they jerked back as if she was actually going to eat them.

Hildy just laughed and reached into her pocket and brought out a tissue and wiped the tears from my eyes and cheeks. I had forgotten that I had been crying. As I said, when she enters a room she dominates it.

"Come on boys, I need some help with the food in the car. The faster we get it unloaded the quicker we'll get to eat. TJ, Larry, Lenny can you help? Joel will you help also?" she queried.

The boys all jumped down from the couch and followed her as if she were the Pied Piper. Soon each of the smiling boys returned carrying a portion of our picnic. Hildy was the last in holding up one of her delectable three layer chocolate cakes and a half gallon of vanilla ice cream. She put the ice cream in the freezer and the cake on the counter before directing the boys to take their burdens out the patio door to the large table at one side of the patio.

"We'll be ready in about ten minutes," she said over her shoulder as she closed the door.

It was only then that I realized that I hadn't introduced the other guests to her. "Oh, well, we can take care of that over lunch," I thought rather embarrassed at my oversight.

True to her word, almost exactly ten minutes later Hildy stuck her head in the door and announced lunch was ready. Turning to me, she said, "We need another chair for the table. There are nine of us and only eight in that set. Grab one of the kitchen chairs and a couple of those large cushions so we can get TJ high enough to reach the food."

I did as I was told. Upon reaching the table, I was amazed at just how much food she had prepared. There were two large platters stacked high with sandwiches, one ham and the other ham and Swiss cheese. A large bowl of warm German potato salad (my favorite), one of cole slaw, a Dutch oven full of ranch beans, a plate heaped up with a variety of cheeses, chips, dips, ice tea, soft drinks along with a full compliment of condiments. There was barely room for us to put our plates.

After we got TJ settled onto his throne, we all sat down and started filling our plates and passing the items we could reach. I took this opportunity to introduce Theresa and Joyce to Hildy. She already knew Dr. Sam.

Hildy made sure that the boys got their plates filled to overflowing before she was content to fill her own plate. I must say that even TJ did a yeoman's job of polishing off nearly as much food as his older siblings.

Not a lot of conversation took place until everyone's stomachs were almost full. All the adults pushed their chairs back and groaned at the amount of food we had eaten. There was very little food left in any of the cutlery. The mountain of food that I thought I would be eating on for a week had dwindled to perhaps enough for a light supper.

Hildy stood up and asked "Who's ready for some chocolate cake and ice cream?"

Naturally every one of the boys raised their hands and all but Joel hollering "Yes! Yeah! Oh, boy!" You would not have thought they had eaten a couple thousand calories just minutes before. The adults on the other hand all politely refused.

"Larry, Lenny can you help me?" Hildy asked. Getting a positive response, she turned and went back into the kitchen followed closely by the twins.

I couldn't believe the size of the cake slices on the plates that the twins returned with. She must have cut half of the cake in four pieces. Then on top of that, there was what looked like a pint of ice cream piled on the plate. We all just chuckled and shook our heads as Hildy returned with two more plates laden down like the ones the twins carried.

As soon as the plates were placed on the table all four of the boys dove in like they hadn't eaten a thing.

"God," I thought. "I'd have to swim an extra hundred laps to work off all those calories."

"Hildy, will you watch the boys for a while? I think the rest of us have some things to decide," I said.

Dr. Sam, Joyce and Theresa all followed me back into the house. Before anyone could even sit down I asked, "What is going to happen to those boys? God, you can't send them to an orphanage or a group home. The worst thing that could happen to them is to be separated. I can't let that happen."

Joyce started "Well they can't stay here. They…"

"Why not?" I interrupted before I even thought about what I was asking.

"You are a single man. That's why. It is just not done," she answered giving me a strange look as if I were totally stupid.

"If I were a single female would that make a difference?" I retorted with more vehemence than I realized.

"Of course it would. You just don't put young children, even boys with a single male. It's just not done," she repeated.

"What? Do you think I would molest them? Good God, what kind of monster do you think I am? I could never hurt a child," I said becoming very emotional. Turning to Sam I asked "Sam have I ever given you any indication that I'm a pedophile? Or some other kind of creature that could harm a kid?"

"No Crane, all I have ever seen in you is joy when you have been around my grandkids. I have never seen you happier than when you are playing with them. I have even mentioned it to Jack Hogan your policeman friend. He is of the same opinion that I am. You are not a threat to any child, boy or girl. He said that he is amazed at the rapport that you have with the little league team. The boys on the team all seem to adore you. It is the highlight of their day when you can give them individual attention. I would trust my grandkids with you any time and never bat an eye."

"Thanks Sam. I appreciate the endorsement," I blushed at his words.

"If it were possible to have the boys stay with you how could you take care of them? You have to work. Who would be here to be with them after school and to send them off in the mornings?" Joyce asked.

"No, I don't have to work," I said. "Maybe I should give you a better idea of my financial situation. This house that sits on 35 acres of prime land is free and clear. I own 80% of a very successful consulting company that generates over $200,000 after taxes for my use. That does not count the consulting fees I receive for projects I personally manage. Last year that amounted to slightly over $150,000. And I don't work full time at it. My investments, according to my financial adviser's last statement, total well into the millions.

"So you can see I don't have to work. I work because I want to and to have something to keep me occupied.

"As far as having a female around to provide the motherly touch, I'm sure that I can convince Hildy to accept my offer to move into the apartment over the garage to become my fulltime cook, housekeeper and nanny for the boys if they are allowed to stay."

Joyce looked a little taken aback when I finished. Turning to Theresa she said, "What do you think? What are the possibilities of getting Judge Frank and our supervisors to buy into this?"

Theresa was a little surprised at my rattling off my financial status so openly. Although I live well, I certainly do not live up to my income. Finally she said "I don't know but I think we can make a case for Crane to seek custody of them at least temporarily. I have the authority to issue emergency temporary certificates for foster parents and I am very tempted to do just that.

"Just look out the patio door at how happy the boys are together out there in the yard, it seems a shame to take them back to that 'group home'. The conditions and atmosphere here are one heck of a lot better then they are there. They certainly appear to have taken to Hildy. Look at them!"

"I think we should ask the boys if they would like to stay here at least temporarily don't you?" Joyce offered.

Everyone nodded their heads in agreement. "Crane, ask Hildy to bring the boys in and let us talk to them while you convince her to live here at least while the boys remain. Okay?" Joyce directed.

I did as I was asked. It was not hard to convince Hildy to stay. She was living in a mobile home that was over 20 years old and on its last legs. She had also formed an attachment to the boys in the short time that she had been around them. As I was talking to Hildy, we heard the boys loudly proclaim their desire to stay here. Their big question was if they could go swimming.

"Well it looks like things are settled at least where the boys are concerned," I chuckled. "I don't have any swimming trunks for them but I can get some this afternoon. All we have to do is go to the mall."

Hildy and I went back into the family room and I was about to ask what the decision was when Theresa spoke up, "I'll have to get some forms from my house to fill out the temporary foster home certificate. I should have it completed and back to you by around 5 this afternoon. It will allow you to have custody for up to two weeks or until the Family Court rules differently, which ever comes first. It will give you the authority to seek medical attention for them in case it's required. CPS would have to approve any charges that exceed the limits in the foster home certificate. If you want to try to keep the boys longer you'll have to undergo a thorough background investigation that, believe me, is VERY intrusive."

"Now on another matter," Joyce started, "the boys don't have any clothes other than what they have on. The police won't allow anyone into their house to retrieve anything until the investigation has been completed. That could take up to a week before they are finished."

"Don't worry about that," I said almost choking. "We will head down to Crossroads Mall and I'll get them everything they need. We'll leave just as soon as you give us the okay. Also, Joel will be undergoing a series of medical procedures Monday morning to determine the extent of any sexual and physical abuse. I will personally see that any test that Sam even remotely considers necessary will be done and I guarantee that the bills will be paid."

As soon as everyone was satisfied that we had taken care of all the details Theresa, Joyce and Sam left for their homes with Theresa promising to get my temporary certification prepared and delivered to me before nightfall.

Hildy and I herded the boys into the Land Rover and headed back into San Antonio to get them outfitted. There is no way I could give a coherent account of our shopping spree. It was the first time I had ever had four rambunctious boys in a mall. TJ especially seem to have the uncanny ability to melt into the background every time my attention was diverted from him. I swear he was 6 going on 15. I spent most of my time hunting him down and getting him back to the group. Hildy was fantastic in equipping the boys with clothes for every contingency. I don't know what all I signed for. I just know that the total for our shopping spree came to $2,554.91. I think it could have been more but we were running out of room to stuff it in the Land Rover.

The twins and TJ were chatterboxes all the way back to Canyon Lake. All four of the boys could barely contain themselves digging through their packages and holding various items up for all to admire. Joel was still the only one who was silent. It was killing me and I could see that it also bothered the other boys. I could even detect some moisture in Hildy's eyes as she looked at him.

By the time we reached home everyone was exhausted. "Okay guys, let's get all of these packages unloaded and into the house. We have to figure out where all of you are going to sleep until Hildy's apartment is cleaned up and ready for her. Larry and Lenny do you want to share a bedroom?"

"Yes!" they answered in unison.

"And for the time being, Joel, would it be alright if TJ shared your bedroom?" I asked.

Joel nodded and gave his youngest brother a quick hug.

"Okay, Joel, go show TJ where to park his stuff. You other two take the bedroom right next to Joel and TJ's. Hildy, that leaves the other one for you for the time being. Why don't you go get some of your stuff from your place and I'll lay out some chicken so we can barbeque when you get back.

"Alright guys, hop to it. Get your new clothes put away and get into your swim suits and we can all get wet. Go!" I told them.

The evening went by very quickly. The boys swam and horsed around in the pool until almost dark. I didn't last that long. After about an hour, I retired to a lounger and just enjoyed their endless energy. Our dinner on the patio turned into another one of Hildy's feasts. The boys topped off their meal with the rest of the chocolate cake and some more ice cream left over from lunch.

"Hey guys, everyone into the showers to wash off the chlorine and get into bed. It has been a long and busy day," I ordered around nine o'clock.

Thirty minutes later I was tucking in the twins. "Good night boys! How am I going to tell you guys apart? I guess we'll just have to get you name tags to wear," I laughed then kissed each one on the forehead. Although I said that in jest, I could not detect even the subtlest difference between the two. I knew this was going to present a real challenge.

Joel and TJ were snuggled together in the queen size bed in their room when I entered. I kissed both of them on the forehead as I had done the twins and told them good night before going into my own room.

Although I hated it, I decided that sleeping in the nude would not work with the house full of people. Reluctantly I retrieved a pair of pajama bottoms and slipped into bed.

"God, what have I gotten myself into this time? Am I capable of raising these kids?..." I fell asleep asking myself one question after another.

CHAPTER 4

Sunday started out much like Saturday had. I awoke to find Joel in bed with me and to my surprise so was TJ. At least this time I had pajama bottoms on.

"This cannot go on indefinitely," I thought. "I'm sure that CPS would have some serious reservations."

I slipped out of bed and into the bathroom for a quick shower. The boys were still sleeping as I returned dressed for the day.

Hildy was already up working in the kitchen preparing for the onslaught that was to come as the boys woke up. It was a good thing too. The scrambled eggs, bacon and pancakes were ready barely in time when four ravenous boys hit the breakfast bar.

The rest of the day went pretty much the same. Hildy seemed to spend all day preparing food for the hungry hoard. Swimming occupied the boys when they weren't eating or chasing the deer that were again attacking my landscape plants.

From time to time during the day each of the boys would wander over to where I was and give me a hug or squeeze my hand usually without saying anything. I still couldn't tell the twins apart. My mind was in turmoil. I was beginning to love all of them and at the same time the logical part of my brain was telling me not to let myself get too attached. I wanted them to stay with me but I was afraid. Not that I couldn't provide for them, but I had doubts as to my capability as a parent to raise them. "Is love enough to be a father for four growing boys?" I asked myself. "What if the state won't let me? Do I really want to take on the responsibility?" All the questions I asked myself last night in bed came rushing back through my mind.

After lunch on the patio and the same questions going over and over in my mind, I couldn't take any more. I went into my study to look up my lawyer's home phone number. I needed some of his advice and counsel. Calling him at home and on Sunday is a little unusual but that's why I pay him a retainer. Carlos Martinez is one heck of a contract attorney. Our consulting firm uses him for all of the legal/contract work.

I found his home number and dialed hoping that he would be home. He answered on the fourth ring.

"Hello."

"Hello, Carlos. This is Crane Johnson. I really hate to bother you on Sunday but I need some advice."

"Hi, Crane. No problem, I was just sitting here watching a football game on TV. My Oilers are getting whipped as usual. What can I do for you?"

"I need the name of the best Family Practice attorney in the state preferably one that is Board Certified. Do you know of any in the area?"

"Off the top of my head I can think of two that I would recommend. Let's see, the first would be Lewis Angel. He practices out of Houston. The second would be Benjamin Cross. He has his practice in Austin. Both of them are first class and you will pay them accordingly. Do you mind me asking why you are in need of this specialty? The last time I checked you were still a foot-loose bachelor."

"Thanks for the names, Carlos. You wouldn't believe the predicament I am in the process of getting into. If I told you, you would probably recommend a psychiatrist. Believe me I have considered it myself. Once I get things firmed up I'll need to consult you on other matters and I'll fill you in at that time. Thanks again for your help! I appreciate it. I'll see you soon."

As I hung up I thought to myself, "You know a good shrink might not be a bad idea."

I was brought out of my musing by the gate buzzer. I flipped on the security camera and saw it was Theresa. I released the gate for her to enter. She was bringing the temporary foster parent forms. She had left a message yesterday saying that it would be today before she would have them ready. That was okay with me. I just needed the paper work before I took Joel to see Dr. Sam tomorrow morning. I wanted everything from now on to be nice and legal. I didn't want anyone to be able to say I didn't play by the rules.

I met Theresa at her car and took the papers from her. She couldn't stay so I went back into the house to check on the boys. They were entertaining themselves in the pool playing a spirited game of tag.

After a while, they got tired of their game and hopped out of the pool. Thank goodness they dried off before they rushed into the house to see if Hildy had a snack for them. It had been at least an hour since their last meal. Joel emerged from the house carrying a plate with probably a dozen or more cupcakes on it in one hand and a large glass of milk in the other. The three other boys followed behind carrying their own glasses of milk looking longingly at the plate their brother was carrying. They sure seemed to have made themselves at home.

When they finished the cupcakes, I asked Joel to come to me. He was a little hesitant at first but then came over to my chair and sat down on the edge.

"Joel, I think that you know I would never do anything to hurt you, but I need to gather some information from you in order to hopefully help you regain your voice. Do you understand?" Getting a nod I continued, "Do you know what happened at your house on Friday."

Again a nod but his lips began to quiver at the same time.

"I know this is very difficult but please believe me I am only trying to help, okay?" I said. Another nod but this time I could see the tears beginning to well up in his eyes.

"Did you see your dad hurt your mother?"

Now the tears really started to flow and he was wracked with sobs. I put my arms around him and clutched him to my chest all the while stroking his back and just let him cry it out.

After about five minutes which seem to me to be a half an hour his sobbing let up.

"Did your father see you?"

A nod in the affirmative confirmed my worst fears.

"Did your dad say anything to you?"

The tears began again, which indicated to me that the father had probably threatened the boy. This time the other boys noticed that Joel was crying. They had been too busy chasing the deer earlier to notice what was going on with Joel and me until then. They all rushed to us and threw their arms around Joel and asked him why he was crying before turning to me and asked the same thing. I couldn't give them an honest answer because I didn't know how much they knew so I just told them that Joel was sad about a private matter. They would understand some day. Although I got some strange looks from them, my halfhearted explanation seem to satisfy them for the moment.

"I think that I had better talk to Dr. Sam about finding a good child psychiatrist for Joel," I thought. "Maybe I'll find one for myself too."

I told the kids to go play because Hildy would have supper ready for us in about an hour. So if they wanted to swim again they had better do it now. Joel was smiling again as he and the others dove into the pool and started the game of tag all over again. I decided that it looked like too much fun not to join so I dove in right after them.

We played tag and I gave them lifts up out of the water so they could cannon ball back down and splash the others. One at a time they climbed up on to my shoulders playing king of the hill until the other boys knocked both the king and me, the hill, over. I was grateful to Hildy when she announced that supper was ready.

The boys rushed to the table and were about to sit down when Hildy told them in a very firm voice that they were expected to wear a shirt at the table. They were a little startled but when Hildy gave an order there was no arguing. In a flash they made the trip to their rooms, put on a shirt and were back at the table waiting for me to do the same.

"I'm going to have to go grocery shopping tomorrow," she laughed as I returned to the table. "I know it was just last Thursday that I restocked your pantry, but it is almost bare now. I hope there is enough to make breakfast otherwise you might have to stop at a restaurant on the way to see Dr. Sam tomorrow."

"That's probably not a bad idea anyway. I want you to go select all the furniture you are going to require for your new apartment bright and early tomorrow. Right now all there is in it is just a lot of odds and ends. I don't think there's anything in there that's worth saving. You know the type of furniture I have in this part of the house. I want what you pick out to be of comparable quality. Understand?" I stated. "When the boys go to take their showers we can go up to the apartment and check it out. I haven't been up there for several years so I don't really know what condition it's in."

As it turned out the only furniture in the apartment that was worth saving was and old iron bed that Hildy just loved and a wooden table and four chairs that she wanted to keep and refinish. Her father had been a furniture maker so she knew all about taking care of stuff like that. She saw beauty in it that I couldn't. The stove and refrigerator seemed to be working as well as all of the plumbing. The place did need a thorough cleaning but that was to be expected after not being used for at least 10, maybe 15 years.

The boys were just finishing their showers when Hildy and I returned to the main house. They came running out of the bedrooms all at the same time making me wonder if they had taken a group shower. They looked so cute in their new pajamas.

"Come here guys, I need to talk to you for a minute," I said as they piled onto the couch. TJ crawled up on my lap since the other boys and I were occupying the whole couch.

"Tomorrow we have to go into San Antonio so that Joel can be checked out by Dr. Sam. I know the rest of you were examined by the CPS doctor so you don't need to see him unless he thinks it's necessary. We have to be there at 8:30 and it takes about 45 minutes to get there from here so we have to leave early to make it on time. Also, Hildy says that you guys have eaten all of the food in the house so we have to eat breakfast on the way. Is that okay with you?"

Getting affirmative verbal responses from three and a definite head nod from one, I guessed that the decision had been made.

"This means we have to get up real early if we are going to make it for Joel's appointment and get you guys fed. So, Hildy and I will get you up at about a quarter to 7 because we will have to be on the road by 7:15. Guess what? To make all of this happen you have to go to bed early. I think 8:30 is about right. You have time for one TV show and a snack before bedtime."

They reacted better to the snack than to the early bedtime, but agreed grudgingly.

It was difficult dragging four sleepy boys out of bed the next morning but we did. Teeth brushed, faces washed, hair combed, dressed in their new clothes and they were ready to go. I loaded the twins in the back seat of the BMW with TJ in the middle. Joel was in front with me holding his "sample" as we took off almost exactly at 7:15. The planning skills I had mastered managing computing projects for ACC had finally paid off in "real" life.

We gobbled down our breakfast at McDonald's on the way to Dr. Sam's office. I had never been to his office but was familiar with the area so I was able to find it without too much difficulty. Finding a parking spot was more difficult. I finally found a place about a block and a half away.

Just at 8:30 we arrived at Dr. Sam's office. His nurse took the sample and started to usher Joel and me into the examination room. Before leaving the other three boys in the waiting room, I gave them strict orders to act like gentlemen until I returned. It was not my intention to stay throughout Joel's exam but I didn't want them to act up while I was gone.

"Good morning, Sam," I said extending my hand to him.

"Morning, Crane and to you too young man," Sam responded shaking my hand and then Joel's. "I believe that Crane's told you what we're going to do today. Is that right, Joel?"

Getting a brief nod from Joel he continued, "I'm not going to hurt you, but some of the test I have to run on you are a little embarrassing and may even be a little uncomfortable. When you're done here, I'm going to send you to another place where they will take some x-rays of you so that I can tell if you have any injuries that I can't see from the outside. Is that okay?"

Another nod from Joel before Sam continued directing his remarks to me, "Crane you're welcome to stay if you like but Joel might feel a little uncomfortable with you here."

"Thanks, but I think the other three need my supervision more." Walking over to Joel, I put my arm around him and whispered in his ear, "I love you Joel. Let Dr. Sam run his test on you. I'll be right outside with your brothers." I gave him a light kiss on the forehead before heading out the door.

When I entered the waiting room, I expected to see three very impatient boys. Instead, they were all engrossed in the games and books that Sam kept around for his young patients. They were surprisingly good all the while Joel was being examined. I was the one who was impatient or would have been if TJ had not crawled up on my lap and asked me to read a book to him. I never enjoyed Dr. Seuss more. His warm little body leaning into me just seemed to melt all my troubled thoughts away. The twins occupied themselves by playing with every game in the room at one time or another.

The examination door opened right at 9:00 and Joel rushed out, piled into my lap with TJ throwing his arms around my neck and burying his head on my shoulder. "Are you okay?" I asked somewhat surprised. "Dr. Sam didn't hurt you did he?" A shake of his head was reassuring to me.

Dr. Sam appeared and handed me a paper with the name of a radiology clinic on it and told me to take Joel up there and they would perform the MRI and CAT scans that he had ordered. "From the exam I just performed I can find no additional injuries than those I found at your house on Friday night. We will have to wait for the result of the blood and urine tests. Those results should be available probably by Wednesday noon. One test I'm having done the results won't be ready for almost a week. I'll talk to you about that later, Crane.

"I think the most upsetting thing I had to do to Joel were the photographs. They were necessary to document the abuse and to file with the required forms."

"Is the radiology clinic expecting us this morning?" I asked. Getting a nod from Sam I called to the twins, "Come on, guys. Let's get Joel's tests taken and then I'll take you all to a place that serves the best sticky buns and hot chocolate in San Antonio."

With that, all of their ears perked up and they all but ran out of the office. Thankfully, the clinic we had to go to was on the sixth floor of Dr. Sam's building. The MRI and CAT scans took about 45 minutes from start to finish. By this time, it had been just over two hours since the boys had eaten so we headed to Liza's Bakery for the sticky buns.

The boys' eyes bugged out as they got a look at the five inch square buns covered in gooey caramel and layered with whole pecans. A true dieter's nightmare. I opted to have only the hot chocolate which was served topped with whipped cream and a sprinkling of cocoa.

I had just started to enjoy my drink when my cell phone rang.

"Hello."

"Hi, Crane. It's Jack Hogan. I have some news for you."

"Jack, it's good to hear from you. I hope that your news is good."

"Well, it could be. We have arrested the boys' dad. He was picked up in San Marcos trying to rob a convenience store. What could be bad news is that when he goes to trial for the murder of his wife the boys might have to testify. Have you been able to determine if any of them saw anything?"

"Yes, I believe that one of them has some relevant information," I said trying to shield the boys from the substance of the conversation.

"I think I understand. Is that person Joel?"

"Yes."

"That could complicate things if he doesn't recover his voice. Well, we'll have to deal with that when the time comes. I'll keep you informed if there are any new developments. You do the same, okay?"

"Yeah, I'll do that. Take care, Jack. I'll see you Friday for the ballgame. Goodbye!"

The boys were finishing up their snacks when I finished the call. Their faces were smeared with caramel from ear to ear which matched their smiles. I was able to clean their faces of the caramel with a dozen or so napkins dipped in a glass of water.

"Why don't we go down by the River Walk? We are only a couple of blocks from it. Have you ever been there?" All of them shook their heads no. "Well this is going to be a treat. There are a lot of great things to see and there are some really good Mexican restaurants. Maybe we will eat lunch here too. Stay together, I don't want you to get lost or fall in the river."

The boys had a ball and they were well behaved for their age. I think we looked at every shop, restaurant, hotel and they even tried to go into a bar. The highlight of the morning was a trip in one of the guided tour boats that ply the river from end to end. The guide gave the history of the River Walk and pointed out the historic sites along the way. The boys were fascinated.

By lunch time the boys and I were exhausted. We were lucky to find a Tex-Mex restaurant that had a balcony overlooking the water. All the walking and sightseeing had given everyone a ravenous appetite. Basket after basket of tortilla chips and salsa disappeared down the throats of four hungry boys. I must say I got my share of chips as well as dirty looks. It was during this carnage that I heard the first sound from Joel other than sobbing or the high pitched squeals. It sounded like he said "Yum". I don't think that the other boys noticed and I was not really sure that I heard it. I hoped that it was a good sign. Maybe I'll have a continuation of the talk I had with him yesterday.

Our lunch completed, I said to the boys, "I need to stop by my office to let them know I won't be in the rest of the week. Do you want to see where I work?"

A chorus of "Yeah" was all that was necessary and we headed back to the car.

Our office was on the northwest side of town near the USAA complex. It took a while to get out of downtown. The noon time traffic is always bad.

The boys were fascinated with all of the personal computers that we had in the offices. I guess the only ones they had seen were those in the schools. We had computers for each of the 31 associates in the office.

I checked with Carol our secretary to see if I had any mail or messages and then went in to see Foster our office manager to tell him I wouldn't be in this week.

"Foster, if you need to get in touch with me the best way is to use my pager. You know my cell phone doesn't work at the house, but the pager will get me any place in the US."

After briefly filling him in on the situation, I gathered up the boys and headed home. This had been a long day already and it was only two o'clock.

Not surprisingly, Hildy had baked some peanut butter cookies when we got home. Just as the boys were reaching for the cookies, Hildy held up her hand like a traffic cop. "Ahem! Isn't there something you boys forgot? Like washing your hands?"

All four scrambled for the bathrooms and in a flash they were back displaying their now clean hands to Hildy. After receiving her okay, they began stuffing warm cookies into their mouths. While they were washing their hands, Hildy had set out four large glasses of milk which also quickly disappeared along with a half a dozen or so cookies each.

After the feeding frenzy calmed down I said, "Joel, I'd like to speak to you if I might? Larry, Lenny, TJ, you guys go get your swim suits on and go out to the pool. Stay in the shallow end until Joel and I get there. Understand?"

Three heads nodded and took off for their rooms to change.

I took Joel under my arm and led him to the couch. "I'm very proud of you the way you handled yourself through all of those test. I hope you never have to do that again.

"We started to talk yesterday about your dad, remember?" I barely detected a nod of his head against my chest so I continued, "Your dad has been arrested for trying to rob a store."

With this disclosure, Joel started to weep softly. He didn't notice the other boys racing out the patio doors to the pool. Neither did the boys pay any attention to us.

"Joel, I want you to believe me when I say you are safe with me. I will never let anyone hurt you ever again. Did your dad ever hurt you?"

With his head buried in my chest, I was just able to detect a nod.

"I know this is difficult, but it is necessary to find out as much information about what your dad did to you as we can. Did your dad threaten to hurt you if you told anyone about what you saw at the house Friday?"

Another nod from Joel served as an answer. I thought I also detected a very low sound coming from him that sounded something like "uh huh" but I wasn't really sure.

"You know that your dad can no longer hurt you now don't you? He is in jail and is going to be there for a long, long time.

"Did your dad whip you and make the marks that are on your back and thighs? Did he also do other things to you that you didn't like?" I didn't know how to phrase that any more delicately.

Joel sobbed harder but nodded his head.

"You are safe with me. I love you and will protect you with every resource I have. I want you and your brothers to stay with me for a very long time."

Joel threw his arms around my neck and kissed my cheek while the tears streamed down his cheeks. My eyes were also filled with tears. We stayed that way for a few minutes before I suggested, "Let's go get our swim suits on and join your brothers in the pool. I think they are tired of playing in the shallow end. We have about an hour before Hildy will have dinner ready."

We played in the pool until Hildy called us to dinner. She insisted that we all shower and dress before we were allowed at the table. She is going to be a great influence on the boys and on me also.

Bedtime came too quickly for the boys but with Hildy's firm hand, they all went to bed. I tucked the twins in and kissed them on the forehead. I still could not tell them apart.

Joel and TJ were curled up together as they had been the previous nights. I arranged their covers before I kissed them as I had the twins.

I watched the news and caught the story about Harry Andersen being arrested in San Marcos. The police were also charging him with the murder of his wife in San Antonio. A gun similar to the one used to kill her was recovered at the scene of the robbery.

I hit the bed shortly after the news was over. The same questions that had postponed my sleep last night and the night before visited me again tonight but with a vengeance. Only questions, no answers. Sleep finally came although fitfully.

CHAPTER 5

"MOMMA! MOMMA! DON'T! NO! NO! DAD NO! AAAHHH!" I was up and out of bed as if I had been shot out of a cannon. Running across the hall to Joel and TJ's bedroom, I entered the room and flipped on the light. Joel was sitting upright in bed, eyes wide open with tears running down his cheeks. TJ was propped up on one elbow staring at his brother.

I rushed to the bed and sat down next to Joel putting my arms around him and cradled him to my chest. As I stroked his back, his breathing became regular and when I looked down at him, his eyes were closed and he appeared to be sleeping. I held him a few moments longer before I laid him back down on the bed. I'm sure that he had been asleep through all of this.

My next concern was TJ. He still appeared to be shaken by what had just happened. "Come on TJ, let's go get a glass of milk, okay?" He took my extended hand and I led him to the kitchen.

At the bedroom door we ran into Hildy who was coming to see what all the commotion was about. She followed us to the kitchen. The concern on her face was readily apparent as I explained what had just happened. She took charge and began fixing some cocoa for all of us putting miniature marshmallows in TJ's cup.

TJ sat on my lap and drank his cocoa. By the time he finished he had calmed down and was getting very sleepy. I stood up and carried him into my room and placed him on the bed. Saying goodnight to Hildy, I climbed into my bed and kissed the top of TJ's head before rolling over and tried to go back to sleep. Sleep was illusive for nearly an hour as I mulled over the events of the night. It was 3:30 the last time I looked at the clock.

My alarm jolted me out of a fitful sleep at 7:00. TJ was curled up in a ball snuggled against my back. I hated to get up but I knew this was going to be a busy day. I reluctantly got out of bed and into the shower. After my morning ritual I slipped on a pair of chinos and a polo shirt and headed to the kitchen for a cup of coffee.

Hildy was already up making biscuits and sausage gravy along with scrambled eggs for the boys. I grabbed a biscuit and a cup of coffee before going into my study to plan out my day. My list of things to do today grew in length the more I became convinced that I would try to get long term custody of the boys. First on my list was to call Joyce, but that would have to wait until the CPS office opened.

With my plan of action completed, I returned to the kitchen to join the boys and Hildy for breakfast. It did my heart good to see the boys eat. I'm sure that Hildy will be going to the grocery store a lot more often. When the feeding frenzy had subsided, I told the boys to go wash up and brush their teeth.

It was at breakfast that I got my first clue as to how to tell the difference between the twins. I hadn't noticed before but Larry was right handed while Lenny was left handed. So as long as they were eating I could tell them apart. I also noticed that they rarely said anything directly to each other. This struck me as being a little odd since they both carried on conversations with TJ and Hildy and tried to include Joel.

"Guys, I want you to help Hildy clean out her new apartment this morning. Her new furniture is supposed to be delivered this afternoon around 2 o'clock," I told them as they came back into the family room dressed for the day. "This afternoon I think we will have time to swim and maybe go out on the lake in my boat. Do you think you might like to do that?"

Getting the expected response, I said, "Go tell Hildy you are ready to help her clean. The quicker you get done the sooner we get to go boating."

At 9 o'clock I dialed Joyce's number on the card she had given me. "Joyce, this is Crane Johnson. I have a few questions I need to ask you," I said when she answered.

"Good morning, Crane."

"First, do the twins and TJ know what has happened to their mother?"

"Not that I know. I never told them anything except that their parents couldn't take care of them for a while. That may have been 'a little white lie' but until everything gets straightened out I thought it would be okay."

"Should I tell them what is really going on? I think it would be the best but I don't want to mess anything up. I have already determined that Joel knows. Actually, I'm sure he saw what happened."

"Oh, my god! How did you find that out?"

"I asked him a few yes/no questions. Also, he had a nightmare last night and screamed out in his sleep."

"Okay, use your best judgment as to how and when you tell the boys about their mother. Just do it as gently as you can. I know it's not going to be easy."

"Second question, what should I do about their school? I don't think it would be advisable to go back to their old school. Everybody there probably knows more about the situation than the boys do and they might be subjected to humiliation."

"You're right about the school. The schools there in Canyon Lake are pretty good from what I hear. If you are planning to try to get long term custody of them that's where they should be enrolled."

"You read my mind. That was my next question. How do I get the process started to be qualified as a foster parent or foster home or whatever the right term is?"

"Well there are a 'couple' of forms to fill out and then there will be an extensive background check. I'll have Theresa drop them off to you this evening. I had a strong suspicion that you were going to ask so I have already started some of the preliminary steps. Theresa told you the other day that the investigation would be very intrusive. I hope you are up for this."

"I am. The only blotch on my record is I was once ticketed for speeding several years ago when I was in college just after I got my first car. Since then my record is both clean and boring. You already know a lot of my financial situation but my accountant will be able to provide much more detail. If you would like to save Theresa a trip around to this side of the lake you could fax the forms to me," I said giving her my fax number.

"Oh, that would probably work out better. I'll fax them as soon as I get off the phone."

After saying our goodbyes, we hung up. Check one item off my list.

Next on my list was a call to Jack Hogan. I dialed his number at police headquarters.

"Hello, is Detective Jack Hogan there?" I asked when the phone was answered.

"Yes, just a moment. I'll get him," the voice said.

"Detective Hogan, how may I help you?"

"Good morning, Jack. It's Crane."

"How are you doing? Have the boys driven you to drink yet?"

"No, they haven't yet. In fact they have been extremely well behaved."

"Give them time. Timmy has his good and bad days. Right now he is having his bad days. Anyway, that's my problem. What can I do for you?"

"Well, I was wondering what has been done with the boys' mother. Has the body been released by the coroner?"

"I was talking to the detective in charge of the case just a few minutes ago. He said that the autopsy had been completed so I would imagine it could be released if anyone claimed it. Why, what are you planning on doing?"

"Well you know I never got to bury my parents after their accident. There were not enough recognizable remains from the crash so everything was buried in a mass grave. That has always bothered me. I want the boys to have some closure. I know it's going to be painful for them now, but in the long term at least they'll have been able to see her one last time and say goodbye."

"You know she was shot several times in the face and head don't you?"

"Yes, I heard. I also know that they can do marvelous things to repair damage so as to make it all but invisible."

"That costs a lot of money to have that done by skilled undertakers. Are you willing to do that?"

"Yes, I am. I think this will help me as much as it'll help the boys."

"Okay then, I'll call the morgue and tell them that the body is going to be claimed by her sons' foster parent. Do you know which funeral home you are going to have take possession of the body?"

"Yes, I'm going to contact Broadmohr. I know them by reputation and I think they can do what I want. Thanks, Jack. I appreciate what you've done. By the way, do you have any objections to me using you as a reference on my foster parent application?"

"No, I don't object. Do you really know what you're getting yourself into?"

"No, I don't but I've got my mind made up."

"Okay, I'll see you Friday. Bye, Crane."

"Bye, Jack."

Check another item off my list.

The call to Broadmohr went very well. They said they would pick up the body this afternoon and then let me know when and if the repairs could be made to it. They agreed to pick out a casket in the middle price range and to arrange for a plot in a local cemetery.

One more item checked off the list.

Next, I got the number of Benjamin Cross' law office in Austin from information and called the number. His secretary answered and asked me some preliminary questions about my proposed business with her boss before I was finally put through to him.

"Mr. Cross, my name is Crane Johnson and I would like to retain you to help me get custody of four young boys. My lawyer recommended you as one of the best in your field and I want the best."

"My, you are direct Mr. Johnson. I like that. What makes you think that you need to utilize my services?"

"Well, from my reading of the CPS workers here I get the distinct impression that they don't take kindly to a single male seeking custody of any child let alone adolescent boys."

I went on to describe the circumstances that led me to have temporary custody of them and my desire to make the arrangement permanent.

"I see, Crane. Although there is no legal prohibition against you seeking custody, the courts are not inclined to grant such a petition. If you can pass the background check, I think we can make a strong argument for such a petition. I like cases like this. They challenge the courts to do the right thing and not to be bound by old outdated precedence and prejudices. They also challenge me. I am not cheap. I bill at $750 an hour. My junior partners bill at lesser rates and they will be doing a lot of the ground work and research. You can probably count on at least 200 hours of which about one quarter will be my time. Do you still want me to proceed?"

"Yes, I do. I'll have my accountant send you a check for $10,000 as a retainer so that you can begin to represent me. I figure that is about 10% of what your bill will be. I hope that we never have to go to court but I want to be prepared in case we do."

I went on to detail how I could be contacted also who my accountant and business partner were.

Another item checked off my list.

No sooner had I hung up the phone than I heard Hildy and the boys come into the kitchen for their morning snack.

I made one more quick call to a testing service to set up an appointment for the boys to be tested tomorrow morning. As I grabbed another cup of coffee from the pot, I asked Hildy, "How are you getting along? Are they helping or hindering?"

"They are doing great. They have been busy as little beavers. We're almost finished. I just need to scrub the floors and vacuum the carpets and I'll be done," she replied. "I'll leave them with you while I finish the last little bit if you don't mind."

"No, that'll be fine. I need to have a talk with them anyway. One I am not looking forward to," I said getting a strange look from all of the boys. "You guys finish your snacks and then come into the family room."

The boys all had serious expressions on their faces as they entered the room.

"Please sit down. TJ, come sit on my lap. What I have to tell you is not easy to do. You have been told that your parents cannot take care of you for a while. At least that's what everyone except Joel has been told. While that's true it's not the whole truth.

"Before I go on I want you all to know that in the few short days that I've known you I have grown to love you as if you were my own sons and I'll always feel that way. You're always welcome in my house and I want to be sure that you know that.

"The bad news that I have to tell you is that last Friday your mother was hurt very badly. In fact she was hurt so badly that she died." At this point, my voice was shaking and my chest was so tight that I could barely get the last sentence out. That was rather blunt but if I had not just come out and said it I probably would not have been able to get it out at all.

The reaction of the twins and TJ was not unexpected. All three burst into tears and started sobbing uncontrollably. I clutched TJ tightly to me and Joel, bless his heart, did the same to the twins. I was so proud of him I wanted to hug him as well but TJ was my first concern at the moment.

Perhaps ten minutes later the crying began to subside. I'm glad I had thought to bring a box of tissues in with me earlier. It came in handy to dry all of our eyes and blow our noses.

"Can you listen to me now? In a couple of days we're going to have a small memorial service for your mother. You'll be able to see her for one last time before she's buried. I know this is going to be difficult for you. It's all right to feel sad. It's even all right to be mad. Don't try to hide your feelings. If you feel like crying go ahead, it's okay. If you want to talk to me or Hildy, we'll make time for you. You are the most important things in our lives right now."

The boys had nearly calmed down by the time I finished. The twins looked up at me and in unison said, "How?"

I looked at Joel and asked, "Joel is it alright with you if I explain to them what I believe happened to your mother?"

The tears started streaming down Joel's cheeks but he nodded his head to indicate that it was okay.

Clearing my throat I started, "Last Friday you were locked in a closet of your house weren't you?"

Getting nods from three heads I continued, "I think that you also heard several loud bangs or what you may have thought to be firecrackers. Those were gunshots. They came from a gun your dad fired at your mother. That is what caused your mother's death. I am so sorry, but that's what happened. Joel saw it happen and was threatened by your dad. That shock of seeing your mother killed and the threats from your dad to him if he ever told anyone about it is probably the reason that Joel can't consciously speak. I think the term for it is hysterical aphasia. The last bit of bad news, I swear, is that your dad has been arrested and is in jail."

The reaction of the boys to the news that their dad had been arrested was not what I expected it to be. The fact was they did not react at all. It was as if they didn't care. This prompted me to ask, "Did your dad ever harm you in any way?"

TJ was the first to respond. "He used to whip me with his belt when he was drunk. I didn't like that 'cause I didn't do nothing."

The twins chimed in that he used to hit them every time he came home drunk.

"Did he ever do anything besides hit or whip you?" I asked.

One of the twins, I think it was Larry, said "He tried to make me put my hand in his pants once, but I ran away and hid. And sometimes he used to stick his hands down our pants and play with our pee pee." The other twin nodded in agreement.

"Thanks, guys. I think the people from CPS will probably want to talk to you about this sometime. I want you to know I am very proud of you for telling me about it. I can assure you that will never happen to you again as long as I have anything to say about it," I said with as much conviction as I could muster.

"Joel, you are safe here. Your dad can never harm you again. However he threatened you, it's over. He'll never get out of jail and be able to harm you again," I said looking him directly in the eyes.

"Okay, let's get our swimming suits on and swim for a while. I think we have about an hour before Hildy will call us for lunch," I barely got that out of my mouth before they were all off to the bedrooms. Oh, the resiliency of youth!

We swam and enjoyed each other's company for over an hour. I tossed the boys so they could cannonball each other and played what was becoming their favorite water game; king of the hill. They soon wore the hill down and I had to sit on the side of the pool and watch them play.

Soon Hildy called us saying that lunch would be ready in about 20 minutes and she expected us to be dressed when it was ready. It looked like a flock of ducks hopping out of the pool and rushing to the bedrooms. I made a quick call to the marina to have them prepare my boat so that we could take it out later this afternoon.

"Have you boys ever been fishing?" I asked. They all shook their heads no. "Well, this afternoon after Hildy's furniture is delivered we'll go to the marina and try our luck with the fishing pole. I've asked Darrell at the marina if he'd go with us and show you all how to fish the right way. It's been a long time since I've been fishing so it'll be good to have someone along who knows what he's doing."

The furniture was delivered right on time and set up in less than half an hour. We were on our way to the marina shortly after 2:30. Since I didn't have lifejackets that would fit the boys, I rented some from the shop there. The fishing poles were also rented.

We slowly motored around the lake for the next three hours. Darrell had as much fun as the boys trying to teach them how to cast their lines. Not too many fish were caught but we did have a lot of laughs. The boys all looked sad as we coasted into the marina, but brightened when I told them we could do it again this weekend. We turned in our poles and lifejackets and then piled into the Land Rover for the trip home.

Hildy was not too impressed with our meager catch. Since there was not enough fish to feed us all she said she'd make some gumbo with it. She shooed us all out of the kitchen and told the boys to go get a shower taken because they all smelled of fish. She didn't tell me but I clearly understood the order also applied to me.

Shortly after supper, the busy day began to show on the boys. They all sat on the couch with TJ on my lap leaning against me just relaxing and watching TV. As soon as it started getting dark outside I said, "I think you guys have had a full day and need to get some sleep. Tomorrow is going to be busy also. In the morning some people are going to come and give you tests to determine if you have any learning problems and to assess where you should be in school. In the afternoon we're going to go to the school and see about getting you enrolled. Everybody off to bed. I'll be in to tuck you in a little later. Say goodnight to Hildy, then hit the sack."

I went to see Hildy to let her know what was going on tomorrow. She was anxious for me to see the apartment now that she had time to get it set up the way she wanted.

As we walked around her newly furnished apartment it became apparent that the place could stand a good coat of paint. When we had originally looked around, I guess we were more intent on the furnishings. "If you'll pick out the colors that you'd like, or wallpaper if that's what you want, I'll get someone in to do it," I said.

"Oh, that won't be necessary. I can do it," she responded.

"I think that you'll have plenty to keep you busy looking after the four boys plus me. With them around, cooking will be almost a full time occupation. Besides, if I get someone in to do it you'll only be out of here for a day or at most two while it's being done. I know you need some privacy away from the boys and me," I told her.

"Crane, I think what you are doing for those boys is about the most wonderful thing I have ever seen. I can see why the boys have worked their way into your heart. They are four of the most well behaved I have known. I feel the same way about them as you do. I just have to believe that CPS will let you keep them. It would be a crying shame if they had to go to a group home or orphanage. I cannot see them being split up. TJ especially, he is so dependant on the others. He would probably die of a broken heart if they were separated."

"I couldn't bear that either. That reminds me, I've arranged for a simple memorial service and burial for their mother. I don't know just when yet. Broadmohr is supposed to let me know when they'll have the body in condition to be viewed. Just a few people will be invited. I was thinking the boys, you and I and possibly Jack Hogan and, I suppose, Joyce Gehrig from CPS. I can't think of anyone else. The boys don't know of any relatives, no aunts or uncles, no grandparents or even close friends. They didn't seem to be members of any church so I don't know if we should try to have any clergy there or not. What do you think?"

Hildy thought for a moment before answering, "It might be comforting if we had a minister there. The pastor of my church would probably be willing to say a few words of comfort. He wouldn't know her, of course. Maybe I can find out a little information about her from the boys. I'd hate to have her buried without having a prayer said for her."

"Okay, you talk to your pastor. Tell him to plan on either Friday afternoon or Saturday morning. I think that Broadmohr will have the body ready by that time. I'll let you know as soon as they call me."

I started to turn away to go tuck the boys in but something came to mind, "Have you seen the twins talk to each other? It just hit me. I see them talk to TJ and Joel, but they never seem to converse with each other. Am I seeing this correctly or just not observant enough?"

"Come to think of it, I haven't either. I've often seen them standing side by side staring off in the distance not saying anything. Then, all at once, as if on cue they both take off to do something. I thought it a little strange but had never really thought too much about it. But now that you mention it, it does seem a little odd."

I left to tuck the boys in bed. The twins were asleep when I approached their bed. I brushed the hair off their forehead and kissed them gently not wanting to wake them. They looked so peaceful and angelic.

TJ was still awake when I entered his and Joel's bedroom. I sat down on the bed beside him and leaned over and gave him a kiss on the forehead. Then I did the same for Joel who was asleep. As I started to get up to go to my own bedroom TJ grabbed my hand and held on keeping me from getting up.

"What is it TJ?" I asked.

"Uncle Crane, I wish you was my daddy," he sobbed.

My heart nearly stopped. "I wish I were too my little one. You go to sleep now." I kissed him again and tucked the covers around him before racing out of the bedroom.

I spent the next three hours filling out the paperwork that Joyce had faxed to me earlier in the day. It was hard keeping my attention on them. TJ's words kept coming back to me making my eyes tear up and my mind wandered.

"I have to make this happen!" I swore to myself.

CHAPTER 6

Although I slept more soundly, it was a short night. The forms I had completed last night were faxed to Joyce around 1:45 AM. The faxed forms would continue the process that she had already started but she indicated that until she received the original signed copies she could not do some of the checks like the credit and criminal background. I debated whether I should mail them, give them to Theresa or to drive them to her office but decided that mail was the best option.

Hildy was busy getting breakfast ready when I arrived in the kitchen at around 7:30. Shortly after I had started my first cup of coffee and read the headlines of the newspaper, the boys started to straggle into the kitchen looking starved.

Their hunger appeased, I outlined what was going to happen today. The testing company would be here around 9 o'clock. They would need approximately three hours to complete their evaluation of the boys' educational standing. At 1:30 we had an appointment at the Canyon Lake ISD administration building to get them enrolled in school. If everything went as planned we should be back home around 3 o'clock and have time for a swim. The last comment about a swim brightened the somewhat somber faces they displayed during the earlier part of the day's description.

Just before 9 the testers arrived. Jean and Charles introduced themselves to me and the boys before getting down to business. We decided that my study would be the best place to conduct the written testing. The oral part of the tests would be given individually to the boys either in the study or the family room depending on how quickly each one finished their written parts.

I busied myself at the kitchen table. The telephone in the kitchen allowed me to make a number of calls. I talked to my accountant to tell him about the retainer he was to send to Benjamin Cross and to make sure that the bill he would receive from Broadmohr would be paid.

That reminded me to call Broadmohr to see when the memorial service could be scheduled. They told me that due to the extensive damage done to the face of Mrs. Andersen that it would not be possible to have the service before Saturday morning. We ended up setting the service for 10 o'clock on Saturday with the burial to follow immediately after.

Hildy said that she would contact her pastor to see if he could be present for the service.

I called Joyce to make sure that she received the faxes that I had sent last night. She said that she had all the information she needed to proceed assuming she received the originals in the mail. I assured her that they had already been placed in the mail and she would probably receive them on Friday at the latest. She said if everything went without a hitch that a hearing would probably be scheduled sometime late next week with Judge Frank.

With that knowledge gained from Joyce I called Cross' office to inform them. I didn't get to talk to Benjamin but his secretary said that she would give him the message and he would call me if he thought it necessary.

I just sat back to catch my breath when the phone rang. It was Dr. Sam. He had the results of Joel's tests.

"Crane, I have mostly good news about the test we ran on the urine and blood sample we took from Joel. The sample that you took showed a much higher concentration of blood than the one that I took here in the office on Monday. That indicates that it most likely was caused by trauma such as a beating or a punch or kick to the kidney area. The liver enzymes were slightly outside the normal range. For that reason, I would like to take another blood sample and have another test run to see if it gives the same results. If it does then we can start worrying about the cause. The test for syphilis and gonorrhea came back negative."

"Well, that sounds like good news to me," I said.

"By the way what is your opinion on Joel's yellow complexion? You see him every day, is it getting less noticeable than it was? I thought it was when he was here in the office on Monday," Sam asked.

"Yes, I think there is a noticeable color change. He seems to have almost normal coloring. The eyes are definitely clearer," I responded.

"I agree. Except for the liver enzyme reading, everything else is fine. There is one unknown at this time. I told you there was one test that would take about a week to run and that I would talk to you about it later. That test is the one for HIV or AIDS. Everything else we can handle. If that test comes back positive, there is no cure. I'm not trying to scare you. I just want you to be prepared in case the worst possible results come true," Sam said in his best bedside manner voice.

"Oh god, I almost wish you hadn't told me about that. I don't know what I'd do. I don't know if I could handle it," I choked out.

Sam responded, "Don't worry about it now. I won't have the results until probably next Tuesday. Keep a positive attitude until we know something definite. I'd never have had the test run if it had not been clear that Joel had been repeatedly abused anally. I'll let you know when I get the results. You can call the office to set up a time to get the second blood test. And give me a call if you want to talk about anything, okay?"

"Thanks Sam, I appreciate your frankness. Goodbye."

No sooner had I gotten off the phone with Sam when the twins finished the written part of their evaluation and came into the kitchen. Of course they were hungry and headed for the refrigerator. They emerged with a bowl of white grapes that Hildy had cleaned. Each one took a large bunch and began attacking them. Charles came out of the study and said if I would finish proctoring the written test for Joel and TJ that he and Jean would start the oral parts for the twins.

Jean took Larry into the family room while Charles took Lenny to Hildy's apartment. I went into the study to monitor the other two. TJ soon finished his test. I quietly told him to go get some grapes on the kitchen table and to be real quiet so he didn't disturb Larry. Joel finished his test shortly there after and went to get his snack.

The oral exam for the twins took less than 45 minutes. They finished at almost exactly the same time. TJ was next. The oral part could not be given to Joel. Jean took TJ and gave him the oral test while Charles scored the written exams.

The test results were reassuring. Although the tests that had been administered were only indicators of educational levels achieved, they did show that the boys were all performing at or above grade level. TJ was probably performing at least two grade levels above his placement in first grade. No learning problems were detected in any of the boys.

I thanked Jean and Charles for their help as they left.

"Well boys, that wasn't so bad was it?" I asked.

They all shook their heads no, but I was sure that like most kids they really didn't enjoy taking any test.

"Let's sit down and talk a little. I need to find out more information about your mother if that's alright. I don't even know your mother's full name. Can you tell me what it is?" I asked,

The twins responded in unison, "Her name was Dorothy Marie Andersen."

"How old was she?"

The twins looked at each other, then to Joel and tentatively said, "30."

Joel shook his head in agreement.

"Did she have any brothers or sisters?"

"No," the twins said in unison.

"Do you know what her name was before she married your dad?"

"Our grandma's name was Douglas before she died," TJ piped in.

"Thanks, guys that was a lot of help. I think that Hildy has some sandwiches made. You go get your hands washed before we eat. We have an appointment with the school district at 1:30," I said.

Our visit to the administration office was uneventful. The boys told them what school they had been attending so that their records could be transferred. After filling out enrollment forms, we were invited to visit the school that they would be going to.

I had decided that Joel would be home schooled until he was able to speak so we only had one school to visit. I was unimpressed to say the least by our visit to the elementary school. Although it was reasonably new, it had only, what I would call, the barest essentials for effective teaching. The principal was even less impressive. She was probably the least friendly person that I think I had ever met. I got the distinct impression that she was more interested in maintaining a neat and tidy school facility than educating children. I got a very bad feeling about the school.

I didn't say anything to the boys, but all the way home I debated with myself what I should do. By the time we got back to the house, my mind was made up. I was not going to send the boys to that school. If I could find a good private school somewhere in the vicinity, I would send the boys there. Then the rational side of my brain took over and I realized that I had to get the boys in school if for nothing else but for cosmetics. While they are in school for the rest of the week, I would make it my mission to find a good private school.

As we drove up the driveway, the twins asked in unison, "Can we go swimming?"

"Yes you MAY!" I emphasized. "Go get changed, you have about an hour and a half before Hildy will call us to dinner."

The boys ran off to their bedrooms to change and I went to talk to Hildy. She was in the kitchen fixing the gumbo with the fish the boys had caught. I saw that she had also added some shrimp and andouille sausage. It smelled absolutely wonderful. I hope the boys like it. I knew I would.

"Hildy, do you know of any private school anywhere in the area?" I asked.

Well there are several in San Antonio, of course. But I can only think of one that is close by. I think it is called Corinthian Academy. If I remember correctly they only have grades K through 8, but that'd accommodate all of the boys," she said.

"Do you know anything about their academic standards? Is it co-ed? Is it church related?" I fired back at her.

"I don't know anything about their standards, but I think it's all boys and to the best of my recollection it's non-denominational Christian," she responded.

"As long as it is not a fundamentalist Christian that'd be okay, I guess," I said. "That school I took the boys to today was anything but satisfactory. I got the impression the students were just being warehoused. I didn't get a good feeling at all. I don't want the boys to go there long term but I realize that they have to be in school to satisfy CPS so I'll send them there until I can find a more suitable educational environment. I hope that doesn't sound too snobbish, but I think that education is too important to have them waste away in a place like that."

"I knew that you wouldn't be satisfied with the school. Some friends of mine have kids going there and they've been trying to get rid of the principal for the last couple of years, but she is the wife of a county official so it's an uphill battle. It's unfortunate that political connections are more important than competence especially when it comes to education," she replied.

With that, I went to change into my swim suit so I could play with the boys until dinner was ready.

Dinner was an experience for the boys. They had never eaten gumbo before and didn't really know what to expect. After a few tentative spoonfuls, they devoured the contents of their bowls and begged Hildy for more. It was a good thing that she'd made a huge pot of gumbo the way the boys ate. As it was there was hardly any left by the time they finished. I didn't do too badly in the eating department when it came to the gumbo.

After dinner, the boys were rather lethargic from all the food that they had eaten and all they wanted to do was to sprawl out on the floor in front of the

TV and watch an old western movie starring John Wayne. During one of the commercial breaks, I explained to them the schedule for tomorrow. I would take them to school and get them settled and would also pick them up after school. The next day they would be riding the school bus to and from the school. I didn't tell them anything about my plans for a private school.

The movie ended at 8:30 just in time for them to want a snack. Hildy dished up bowls of ice cream and cookies.

When TJ finished his ice cream, he climbed up on my lap and snuggled into my chest. He looked up with those beautiful azure blue eyes and asked, "When do we getta see momma?"

I was a little taken aback by his question so I said to the boys, "Come here guys and sit down."

When they were settled I continued, "I told you we were going to have a small memorial service for your mother but I didn't tell you exactly when because I didn't know at the time. We have now scheduled the service for 10 o'clock Saturday morning. Is there anyone that you want to invite to be there?"

They thought for a minute before shaking their heads no.

"If you do think of anyone you want to be there let me know and I'll see that they come. But right now it's time to get your showers taken and get to bed. Tomorrow is a school day. I'll be in to tuck you in after while," I said popping TJ on the behind.

He giggled and ran after Joel and grabbed his hand as they took off to the bedroom.

Now that Hildy has her own apartment I should ask TJ if he would like his own room. I think I know the answer but I should give him the option in any case.

I heard the water in the showers stop so I gave it a few minutes before I went to tuck the boys in. The twins were the first. They were just slipping under the covers when I entered the bedroom. I bent over the bed and gave each of then a kiss on the forehead before telling them good night.

"Good night, Uncle Crane, we love you," they both said. I guess that they had all decided that I was to be call that now. TJ was the first to use the uncle title last night.

"Good night, Larry. Good night, Lenny. I love you too," I said.

The scene was repeated with Joel and TJ before I retired to my bedroom for a shower and a good night's sleep.

We arrived at the school at about 8:15 and reported to the principal's office. I wasn't anxious to meet with the principal again. I was afraid I could not hold my tongue and say something I might later regret. Thankfully, the attendance clerk met us and after making out an attendance record for the twins and TJ she took us to the boys' classrooms. The twins' room was first. I had to stifle a laugh when we entered the classroom. You could have heard a pin drop it got so quiet. The mouths of all the little girls gaped open as they saw the twins. As I had mentioned the twins were 'drop dead gorgeous' and the girls all seemed to agree.

The clerk introduced the boys and me to the teacher. Mr. Lansing was young perhaps 26 and quite effeminate. He almost licked his lips as he shook the twins' hands. Chalk up another reason to find that private school.

TJ's first grade teacher was a grandmotherly woman of about 60 years of age. Mrs. Godwin was perhaps the nicest person I had met so far in the school system.

I worked out the details of paying for the boys' lunches and the school dismissal times with the attendance clerk before leaving for home. As I was leaving, I turned around and asked her if she knew of anyone who did tutoring. She handed me a list of people who had registered with the school indicating what subject matter and grade levels in which they were qualified.

"I don't want to put you on the spot, but if you had a seventh grade student is there one person on the list that you would choose first?" I asked.

She leaned over her desk and took the list from my hand and circled a name before handing it back to me. She never said a word, just smiled at me and went back to her work.

"Thanks," I said as I turned to leave.

Joel had stayed with Hildy while I took the other boys to school. I found him in my study looking through the books on my shelves. Reading had been a very important part of my life from the time I could first read. I never threw away or sold any book that I purchased. My study walls were covered by bookshelves crammed with hardback and soft backed books of every subject matter you could imagine. My particular favorites were books by Mark Twain, Conan Doyle and Isaac Asimov. I had all of Twain's books and all of the Sherlock Holmes mysteries. Asimov's *Foundation* series is probably the best science fiction ever written. I have read them many times over.

I walked over to Joel, placed my arm around him and looking into his face, "Do you like to read?"

He nodded and his eyes sparkled indicating to me that he may even like to read as much as I did.

"Well, I tell you what. Have you ever read *Tom Sawyer*?" Receiving a negative response I continued, "Here it is. You take it and spend the morning reading as much of it as you can. After lunch, I want you to write down a summary of what you have read. Also, if you don't understand something, write down any questions that you have and I'll try to answer them. *Tom Sawyer* is one of my favorites. I have read it several times."

Although this was not what I would consider 'home schooling', it at least made an attempt until I could get a tutor in to do the real thing. To that end, I went into the kitchen to call the tutor that the attendance clerk (I never did get her name) had pointed out.

Paul Coulter was a qualified teacher certified by the state to teach grades 7-14. He said that he was comfortable teaching all seventh grade subjects except mathematics. That was fine with me since I was more than equipped to teach it.

I explained Joel's special need to him but it did not seem to bother him at all. We agreed to meet tomorrow morning at around 10 o'clock to discuss more face to face. I gave him directions on how to get to the house before hanging up.

I looked in on Joel a couple of times during the morning. Each time he appeared to be totally consumed by the book. When Hildy asked him if he was ready for a mid-morning snack, she nearly fell over when he shook his head and went back to reading. By lunch time his stomach won the battle for his attention and he stopped briefly to gobble down the sandwich and soup Hildy had fixed for us both.

Joel returned to the study but returned shortly with a notepad on which he had written, "Can I wait to do the writing till I'm done with the hole book?"

I looked at the page and responded, "May I wait…When you are asking permission you use MAY not CAN. We will talk about homonyms later. Of course, we will wait. I'm glad that you are so interested in reading it. I do want to see if you are retaining what you are reading so I want you to write down for me four characters in the story and a two or three sentence description of them. When you have finished the book we will look at those same characters again to see if you would change your description."

He grabbed the pad out of my hand and ran back into the study and furiously began writing. About 15 minutes later he returned beaming at me as he handed the pad back.

"You go back to your reading. I'll discuss this with you later," I told him giving his neck a squeeze.

His descriptions were right on the money indicating to me that his reading retention was good. The sentence structure and some misspelled words show that he had some needs in the English area.

I had made several phone calls during the morning including one to Corinthian Academy. I was very pleased by my talk with the headmaster over the phone but I wanted to visit the campus to see the facilities before I made any commitment to them for the boys' education. We made an appointment for me to visit on Monday morning at 9 o'clock.

Joel was still reading when I went to pick up the boys from school. They never stopped talking from the time they entered the car until we entered the kitchen. The only things that shut them up were the chocolate brownies that Hildy had waiting for them. Hearing the other boys arrive, Joel emerged from the study with the book still in his hand. This time he did not pass up the snack.

Although we put the boys to bed early, it was very difficult getting them up and ready to meet the school bus at 7:40. I drove them to the end of the lane where the bus picked them up. I told the bus driver that I would pick them up from school since I had to go coach the Little League game in San Antonio.

Paul Coulter was right on time for our meeting concerning Joel's home schooling. I was as impressed with him in person as I was over the phone. Joel also seemed to take to him as he sat with me during the interview. By the time the interview was over, we agreed that he would come to the house and tutor Joel for four hours each day in all subject matters except for mathematics. He also agreed to purchase the required textbooks and bill me for them including the math book. He would begin Monday at nine.

Joel read his book the rest of the morning stopping only for a quick lunch. Just before two o'clock he came marching into the study where I was taking care of some ACC business with my office manager over the phone. I could tell by the gleam in his eyes and the broad smile on his face that he had finished the book. As quickly as I could I finished my business with Foster and turned my attention to Joel.

"Have you finished your book?" I asked.

I thought his head would fly off as vigorously as he shook it. His smile seemed to get even broader.

"I think that is wonderful! Come here and let me give you a hug. I'm so proud of you!" I said.

He didn't hesitate and ran to me and jumped up onto my lap throwing his arms around my neck and burying his head in my neck. I gave him a big squeeze and a quick kiss on the back of his head. "If the court allows me to keep you and your brothers, I think we should aim for you to read one book a week. What do you think of that?"

I got another hard squeeze and then he looked up at me with a very quizzical look. I didn't quite understand what he was after until he picked up a pen and pad from my desk and wrote the one word question "court?" on it.

Then I realized what I had said. "You know that I want all of you to stay here but it's not my final say. The judge will have the final say about whether or not you can remain here. I'm doing everything I can to make that happen and I'm hopeful that it will but it's not certain until we go to court. Do you understand?"

He shook his head but I could see just the hint of tears forming in his eyes.

"Do you remember what I asked you to do when you finished your book?" I asked getting a nod from him. "You have about half an hour before we have to go pick up your brothers. Which would you rather do: start your report now or go see if Hildy has a snack for us?" That was probably the stupidest question I had asked in a long time as he grabbed my hand and dragged me to the kitchen.

Hildy was ready for us. She had just finished baking the last batch of snicker doodle cookies. The kitchen smelled wonderful but the cookies tasted even better.

"We had better take some of these to your brothers or they might attack us when they find out we already had some," I said more to Hildy than to Joel. I wasn't surprised when she handed me a plastic zip-lock bag with two dozen cookies in it to take to the boys.

We picked up TJ and the twins at school and then headed for San Antonio to the ball field. We arrived with about 15 minutes to spare before the team started to arrive. That was just enough time to set out the equipment and re-mark the foul lines and batter's box. All of the boys chipped in and made the job go faster. TJ was more of an impediment than a help but he did his best and I loved him for it.

The boys sat on the bench so that I could keep an eye on them and cheered the team on to victory. Our team, the Hornets, won the game by two runs. That brought their record to 4 wins and 3 losses.

This time I asked all of the team to help put away the equipment before giving them their coupon for McDonald's. That way we could all celebrate together. I don't know why I hadn't thought of this sooner. Jack and I herded the bunch of boisterous boys across the street and into McDonald's to get their treat.

It was nearly 9 o'clock by the time we got home. The team wanted to hang around longer than usual it seemed to celebrate the victory.

"Come into the family room and sit down," I said to the boys. "Remember, we're going to say goodbye to your mother tomorrow morning. We'll need to start out at 9AM to be there on time. Hildy will have breakfast ready for us around eight so that we will have time to brush our teeth and get ready. Any questions?"

Getting none, I said "Okay, go get your showers taken and hop into bed. I'll be in to tuck you in a little later."

I was a little apprehensive about how the boys would react tomorrow but I knew from my own experience that long term it would be best for the boys.

CHAPTER 7

I was pleasantly surprised to see that the boys were up early waiting for Hildy to finish breakfast. They seemed to be in good spirits despite what they had in store later. After breakfast, the boys rushed into their bedrooms to brush their teeth, clean up and dress. Hildy had taken the opportunity while the boys were eating to lay out what they were to wear to the service.

They presented a stunning sight as they entered the family room dressed in dark blue slacks and white short sleeve shirts. I was so impressed by their appearance that I insisted on taking several photographs of them including one Polaroid that I had plans for.

Near silence was the order of the day as we drove to the funeral home. The boys rode with me while Hildy took her own car since she was going to pick up her pastor.

I noticed in the rear view mirror that TJ was holding a hand of each of the twins while looking first at one twin then the other. The twins just looked at each other and sort of hummed a barely audible tune. Joel sat in the front passenger seat looking straight ahead.

We finally reached Broadmohr. I'm sure that I was much more nervous than the boys were. When we stepped inside, we were greeted by a handsomely dressed distinguished older gentleman who ushered us into a side room.

Motioning me to one side he said, "The reconstruction came out very well. We have not permitted anyone to enter the viewing area until you and her sons have a chance to pay your respects. How would you like to proceed? Do you all want to view the loved one at once or individually?"

"I think it would be best if they all went together to give each other strength," I replied.

He led us through a door into the main viewing room. The casket which they had picked out was elegant without being flashy. There were three flower arrangements, one at each end of the casket and one draped across the lower portion. Everything was done in a simple but very tasteful manner.

"Take hold of each other's hands," I told the boys. We walked slowly toward the casket almost as if none of us wanted to get there too fast.

Broadmohr had the foresight to place steps near the casket so that it would be possible for the boys to see into it without jumping up and down or pulling up on the side. As we reached the steps I leaned down and picked up TJ. The twins and Joel climbed the two steps to look at their mother.

TJ looked at his mother lying there before saying "She…She's beautiful," Then he broke down and began sobbing uncontrollably. The tears streamed down his cheeks but he did not take his eyes off his mother. "Mommy…Mommy…"

Larry and Lenny reacted much the same as TJ. They stared at their mother as the tears and their sobs joined TJ's.

Joel just looked at his mother and shook his head.

I heard something that was almost like the moan of an animal in pain. At first, I didn't know where it was coming from. Then I realized it was Joel. It kept getting louder until it was almost a howl. The twins and TJ stopped sobbing and looked at Joel through teary eyes.

"Why? Why did you try and stop him? You knew he'd hurt you. I would've let him do it. He always did it to me when he got drunk. You didn't have to do it. I could've took it again. Why'd you do it?" Joel sobbed out the first conscious words he had spoken since that awful day a little over a week ago.

With TJ on one hip I reached out and wrapped my other arm around Joel. The twins were somehow entwined in the group hug. No words came to me. I was so taken aback by Joel's sudden speech and by the gravity of the moment that I was suddenly speechless. I don't think it mattered. The non-verbal communication that was going on among the five of us was enough for the moment.

Several minutes later, the elderly gentleman tapped me on the shoulder to inform me that the other mourners were waiting outside. I reached into my jacket pocket and removed the Polaroid picture of the boys and placed it in the casket on her hands. Her boys would be with her forever.

I led the boys back to the front row of chairs and sat them down. I dried their eyes and had them blow their noses before the others were admitted.

Jack and his wife Carolyn along with their two sons and daughter were the first to enter. Jack Jr. at 15 was almost as tall as his father. Timmy at 13 was more the height of his mother. Sara their daughter was only 5 and was as beautiful as her mother.

Theresa and Joyce were next in line followed closely by Hildy and her pastor. Pastor Rollins was a young man about my age with an engaging smile.

Two couples that I did not know followed. I learned later that they were the Andersen's next door neighbors.

That was it. A total of 18 people were present to mourn the death of Dorothy Marie Andersen.

Pastor Rollins was an excellent speaker. Even though he did not know her, his eulogy was both eloquent and simple. He spoke directly to the boys and told them that she was at peace now and was going to a happier place. The boys smiled at him as he praised them for their courage and the love they had for their mother.

Although the service was short, everyone seemed to be uplifted by it. The procession to the cemetery took less than twenty minutes. Again the burial was simple and short. Pastor Rollins delivered the prayer and benediction before I encouraged each of the boys to approach the casket separately to say goodbye to their mother in their own way.

Joel was the first. He knelt down beside the casket and placed his forehead against it. I couldn't make out much of what he said. I was so elated that he was able to speak again that it really didn't matter. I did make out him say, "I love you" and "Goodbye." He turned to me with tears streaming down his cheeks. I reached out and pulled him to me. At that moment, he just needed physical contact. Nothing but time could take away his grief.

The twins were next. Following Joel's example, they knelt beside their mother's casket. I could not detect any speech from either of them. I did hear that strange humming first from one and then the other. As if on cue, they both reached out and embraced the casket before standing and returning to their seats. Their eyes were also filled with tears.

I held TJ's hand as he approached the casket. "Goodbye mommy. I love you and I miss you," he sobbed.

I placed my hand on the casket and said, "Thank you Mrs. Andersen for the most wonderful boys I have ever met. I wish I had known you in life. You had to be a wonderful person to have raised such exceptional sons. Thank you! I will try to raise them as you would have if I am allowed the honor. You have my word. Goodbye."

I met the next door neighbors and invited then to come to the house for lunch which Hildy was going to prepare for us. They declined saying that they had plans with their own children this afternoon. They expressed sympathy to the boys for their mother's death and then left to go home.

Jack and his family accepted the invitation to come to the house. Theresa and Joyce said that they would stop by later. It wasn't until then that I realized that Dr. Sam was not there. He had indicated earlier in the week that he intended to come. Knowing Sam to be a man of his word, I knew that some medical emergency must have kept him away.

The boys were very quiet all the way back home. Joel only used his newly recovered voice to say "Yes" when I asked him if he was all right.

Hildy had begun fixing lunch by the time the boys and I returned home. I led the boys into my study and closed the door behind us. Indicating to them to sit down on the couch, I pulled up my desk chair and sat down facing them.

"I'm so proud of you for the way that you conducted yourselves today. I know it was not easy for you. I didn't know your mother, but I feel very close to her because I share with her the love she had for you. I know that you feel sad deep down inside. That's natural. With time that hurt will fade. You will always have some of it with you but it won't always be as overpowering as it is today. Do you have any questions about anything today?" I asked.

"Can we go see momma's place again?" TJ asked.

"Of course we can. In fact, we will go again Wednesday evening after school. The headstone is supposed to be in place then and I want you to see it. I hope that you like what I have picked out," going to my desk I retrieved a brochure I got from the monument place and showed them the stone that I had picked out. "Besides your mother's name and the dates, I had them carve 'Beloved Mother of Four' into it."

Getting no more questions I said "Let's go get changed out of these clothes. Our guests will be arriving soon. I'll bet that Timmy and Jack Jr. will want to go swimming. How about you?" They brightened at the suggestion of swimming.

TJ and the twins started out the door to get changed. Joel came over to me, leaned over and kissed me on the cheek and said, "Thank you, Uncle Crane."

I nearly lost it right there but was able to maintain some semblance of composure. Just enough to choke out "You are welcome, son."

My eyes were still wet with tears when I entered the kitchen to talk to Hildy. "Did you notice that Joel can now speak?"

"No! Oh my god, how wonderful! Our prayers have been answered," she said looking to the heavens.

"I don't think we should make too much of a fuss over it, however. I don't want him to feel uncomfortable or too much pressure. He still is not talking a lot. I think that it would be best to let him go at his own pace toward full recovery," I commented.

"Yes, yes. I agree. We don't want him to relapse," she said with tears forming in her eyes. "By the way Crane, I think the arrangements that you made for their mother's funeral were just great. They were perfect. I'm sure the boys will appreciate it later if they don't right now."

"That reminds me, I don't know what the fee is for Reverend Rollins is but I hope this will cover his services," I said handing her a check.

She looked at it and shook her head "This is more than generous. Thank you. I'll give it to him tomorrow after church."

Jack and his family arrived shortly after the boys appeared wearing their swim suits. Jack Jr. and Timmy quickly changed into theirs and were soon splashing around in the pool.

Sara took a shine to TJ and followed him around like a puppy. He didn't quite know how to take her. He didn't mind playing with her but was not inclined to spend all of his time with her. Since she didn't like swimming, TJ found his best chance of escaping her attentions was to stay in the pool as much as possible.

Theresa and Joyce drove up together followed closely behind by Dr. Sam and his wife. He apologized for not being able to attend the funeral, but one of his patients had an attack of appendicitis and had to be operated on immediately.

I introduced Carol Greene to Theresa and Joyce before heading to the house. As we were approaching the house I turned to my guests and informed them of Joel's recovery and how I thought it best not to make too much of it. Dr. Sam was the first to agree.

"I think that's the most prudent course. He has enough pressure on him without anyone applying more," he said. "What triggered his recovery?"

I told him about the incident at the casket.

"Yes, sometimes one traumatic incident will counteract another one. With all that the boy has been through, you should try to find a good psychiatrist. I'm sure that he will need professional help. I know of a couple in the area that I would trust. I'll write down their names as soon as we get inside."

Hildy as usual had prepared a tremendous amount of food. But with six hungry boys along with the rest of us, we put a huge dent in it. Dessert was the lightest angel food cake you could imagine. It literally melted in your mouth. It is a good thing she had made two of them because I think that the boys ate a whole one by themselves.

The afternoon went by quickly. The boys played in the pool. Sara took a nap and the adults sat on the patio watching the kids play. I broke out a couple of bottles of Sam's favorite Merlot which made him very happy. I don't think Carol lets him have it at home. She didn't turn down a glass when I offered it to her though.

Theresa and Joyce were the first to leave after taking the boys aside and expressing their condolences to them. I think they also asked the boys how they liked living here. I didn't hear their answers but I think they were positive. I know that several times during the afternoon they had heard the boys call me "Uncle Crane".

Sam and Carol were the next to go, but only after the wine was gone.

"Jack, the boys and I are going fishing on my boat tomorrow afternoon if the weather holds out. Would you and your family like to go along? We could stop for supper at the restaurant at Turkey Cove before we come home," I said.

"Let me check with Carolyn. I know the boys would enjoy it. They love to fish but don't get to very often," he replied.

Carolyn agreed that it would be nice to go out on the lake. We decided that we should meet at the marina at around 1:30 and then fish until around 5. I told them I would see if Darrell was available to go out with us again to give the boys another fishing lesson.

Soon everyone had gone, even Hildy. She had left us to fend for ourselves for supper. Not that it was such a burden since the pantry and refrigerator were well stocked.

"Okay guys, what do you want to eat tonight?" I asked.

"Can we have waffles like the first day I was here?" Joel asked in the voice that brought joy to my heart.

"Of course we can. How about the rest of you? Would you like waffles too? How about some sausages to go along with them?" I thought I knew what the answer would be and was not disappointed. "You go get cleaned up and I'll have everything ready in about a half an hour."

I got out the big iron skillet and began to brown two pounds of link sausages while I mixed up the waffles. Hildy had bought some blueberry syrup as well as the regular maple syrup which would give the boys a choice. I filled the waffle iron five times and hoped that would be enough to feed them. I place each new batch of waffles into the warming oven, separating each layer with a paper towel. Before everything was finished, I had four hungry faces staring at me wanting food.

"I need you to help me set the table," I said. "TJ, you get the napkins. Larry, you get the silverware. Lenny, you get the glasses. And Joel, you get the plates. I'll get the milk and butter."

I couldn't help but laugh as they scurried around doing their assigned task. But in no time, the table was as perfectly set as when Hildy did it. The boys all laughed and talked when their mouths were not full which was not often. They seemed to stop and listen every time Joel said anything regardless of its importance. We all just enjoyed the sound of his voice.

After we cleaned up the supper table, the boys seemed to need physical contact. I had seated myself on the couch in the family room searching the TV for something to watch when TJ sidled up to me and said "Can I sit on your lap, Uncle Crane?"

"Of course you may," I replied lifting him up onto my lap. "Do you want to talk or do you just want to sit here?"

His only answer was a mumble I couldn't understand as he snuggled into my chest. The other three joined us on the couch. Nobody said anything. We just sat there with our arms around each other.

Maybe twenty minutes later, Joel looked up at me and said "Are we gonna have to live with our dad now? I don't want to."

"No Joel, I promise you. You'll never live with your dad again. The only time that you'll have to even see him is in court. I don't know when, but some day you'll probably have to go to court and tell your story. I hope that you won't but more than likely you'll have to," I said trying to keep as much bitterness out of my voice as possible. "As I told you guys, I am trying to get CPS and the courts to allow you to live here with me. That is, if you want to. I guess I have never asked you directly but do you want to stay here with me?"

"Yes! Please!" Joel almost yelled.

"Yeah!" the twins chimed in.

"Yes, Uncle Crane," TJ said as he lifted his head and kissed me on the chin.

"I sure want you to stay. You have only been here about a week and now I cannot imagine my life without you in it. Now why don't you go get your showers taken and get into your pajamas. I want to talk to Joel for a few minutes. When you finish I'll see if I can't find us a snack. How does that sound to you? TJ if you need help you can take your shower with Larry and Lenny. You can use the big shower in my bedroom. Okay? Now, off you go."

"Oh boy!" and "Yeah!" rang out as they raced to the shower.

I reached over and gave Joel a tight hug before I said "Joel, I am so very happy that you can talk again. I know it's been a very difficult time for you. You've been remarkably brave through all of this and I am so proud of you. Although you have regained your voice, I would still like to have Paul Coulter come here to home school you at least for a while. I don't want you to be put in a bad situation if someone knew what had been done to you. I also want you to talk to a doctor, an adolescent psychiatrist, to see if you need any help."

"I like Mr. Coulter. I think it'll be fun to have him teach me stuff. Can I go get in the shower now?" he asked.

"Run along, I think Hildy left things to make hot fudge sundaes. What do you think of that?"

"Oh, yeah!" he shouted as he ran for my bedroom to shower with the other boys.

As the hot fudge sauce heated up, I set out the finely chopped toasted pecans and the can of Reddi-Wip. I also filled five dishes with vanilla ice cream and put them back in the freezer so they wouldn't melt. I didn't want to risk life or limb dipping up ice cream while four hungry boys looked on.

Everything was ready when four freshly scrubbed pajama clad boys scrambled into the kitchen.

"Joel, I need your help for a minute. The rest of you sit down at the table," I said leading Joel to the freezer. "You take two bowls and put them on the table. I'll bring the others."

I didn't think they were going to wait until I had a chance to pour the hot sauce over their ice cream. The nuts were quickly passed around. I had to laugh at the mounds of nuts they heaped on their bowls. I topped their sundaes with the whipped cream not wanting them to wield the pressurized can. There was too much inherent mischief there that I didn't want to encourage.

I barely got started on my bowl when I heard the spoons scraping the bottom of their bowls.

"Okay guys, put your dishes in the dishwasher and then go check out the TV to see if there is a good movie on tonight. I think I saw there was going to be a Disney film on channel 12," I told them as I tried to finish my sundae before it melted entirely.

The movie helped to keep the boys' minds off the events of the day. I don't even remember what the name of it was but it kept them entertained. They were getting very sleepy by the time the movie was over at 10 o'clock.

"Time to hit the sack. Go brush your teeth and I'll tuck you in shortly," I told them.

I gave them a few minutes before going into the twins' bedroom. The bed was empty when I entered. So was their bathroom. I was a little concerned as I headed to TJ and Joel's bedroom. There were all four of them in the one bed.

I guess I must have frowned a little because the twins in a weak and frightened voice said "Can we sleep in here tonight Uncle Crane? Please!"

"Well, I suppose so as long as you go right to sleep. No talking or giggling, just sleep," I told them smiling. Stretching across the bed, I gave each one of them in turn a kiss on the forehead before saying "Goodnight, angels."

We all slept late on Sunday morning. When I looked in on the boys, they were a tangle of arms and legs all in a pile. I don't know how they slept like that.

I was on my second cup of coffee and third section of the Sunday paper when they came straggling into the kitchen.

"Good morning sleepy heads," I said smiling at them as they rubbed the sleep out of their eyes. "Are you ready for breakfast?" Now that was a stupid question. "Hildy has gone to church so we have to fend for ourselves this morning. It looks like cold cereal, fruit and juice."

I don't think it mattered what they had to eat. It had been at least ten or twelve hours since they had last eaten.

The rest of the day went by more quickly than anyone wanted. The kids had a wonderful time fishing and the adults thoroughly enjoyed watching them have so much fun. Jack Jr. turned out to be a good fisherman. He caught the most fish but I think the others had the most fun. Timmy and Joel seemed to be developing a strong friendship. It was an odd pairing. Timmy was a bit of a scatter-brain while Joel was more serious and reliable. Sara didn't fish. She did constantly watch TJ fish, though. She was always by his side much to his chagrin. The twins were so full of energy that they rarely left their lines in the water long enough to catch any fish.

After a marvelous dinner of fried fish, hushpuppies and cole slaw at Turkey Cove, we took the boat back to the marina just as the sun was setting. We said our goodbyes to Jack and his family and headed home.

"Everybody, get your shower taken and then into bed, you have school tomorrow," I told them.

It was going to be a busy week and I was not looking forward to all of it.

CHAPTER 8

It suddenly dawned on me that I had scheduled two things for the same time. Paul Coulter was due at nine to start tutoring Joel and I was scheduled to meet the headmaster at Corinthian Academy at the same time.

Hildy said that she would explain the conflict to Paul while I met my appointment. This is not at all like me. I am usually schedule driven. All the years managing IT projects has made me acutely aware of time management. I guess the events of the past week have interrupted my usually logical thinking. I can think of four good reasons for it.

Those four good reasons suddenly appeared looking like they were starving as Hildy and I were talking.

"Good morning guys. Did you sleep well?" I asked.

Their only responses were barely audible moans and mumbles. They didn't fully revive until they had consumed the bacon, eggs, hash browns and toast that Hildy had fixed for them and at least a gallon of milk and orange juice.

"Okay guys, go wash up, brush your teeth and get dressed for school. You have twenty minutes before you have to meet the school bus. Joel you need to dress too, just as if you were going to school with your brothers. But while you are waiting for Mr. Coulter, I want you to start writing the summary of *Tom Sawyer* now that you've finished it. If you don't finish your writing before he comes, you can complete it tomorrow morning. Now scoot," I told them.

"Hildy, would you please call Dr. Sam's office to set up an appointment for another blood test for Joel? See if we can get one say around two or two-thirty either today or tomorrow. I think his nurse is in the office at 8:30. Then call my office and leave a message for me. I'm going in to check on things after my meeting at Corinthian. Also, until we get to know Paul Coulter better I would appreciated it if you would remain close by just until we are comfortable with him. Am I being too paranoid?"

"No, any time you bring a stranger into your home it's always best to be cautious. I have laundry to do as well as cleaning the boys' rooms so I'll be around anyway," she responded.

Soon the boys appeared freshly scrubbed and ready for school. I noticed that they all seemed to needed a haircut. It reminded me of all the mundane things that I needed to add to my life now that there were others in it. I'd better call my barber to see if he can get us all in because I could use a trim also.

I drove the three down to the road to catch the school bus. It came about two minutes after we arrived. I told the driver that the boys would be riding the bus home after school and asked him about what time his route took him by here. He told me between 4:20 and 4:30 he usually made it to this stop. I gave all three of the boys a quick hug before they got on the bus and then went back to the house to get ready for my morning appointment.

Although I was generally familiar with the area where Corinthian Academy was I had never been there. I got out my map of the area and decided what route I would take to get there and how much time to allow making the trip. I decided that it should take me about twenty minutes to drive there. I dressed and was ready to go fifteen minutes early so I sought out Joel. He was in my study busily writing his book report for me.

"How's it going, son?" I asked entering the study.

"Good! There is so much I want to write I can't write it fast enough. This is like reading it all over in my head. It's fun, can I read another book when I'm done? Please!" he begged.

"Of course you may. There are several more books by Mark Twain on the shelves if you want more of his books. If you want another one about Tom Sawyer there are a couple more, *Tom Sawyer Abroad* and *Tom Sawyer Detective*. You might also enjoy *Huckleberry Finn*, but you may choose any book you want to read. Mr. Coulter may have you read something for his class, you know.

"Well I better run to my appointment. I'll see you this afternoon. Hildy will be here if you need anything. Goodbye," I said giving his shoulder a squeeze before I left the room.

It took twenty-two minutes to drive to Corinthian Academy from the house. The administration building was an impressive sight. It looked like some sort of Greek temple with six very tall columns across the front. I chuckled as I looked at them. If I remembered correctly from my ancient history class they were Corinthian columns.

I entered the building, found the headmaster's office and introduced myself to the secretary. She said he would be with me shortly. I sat in a comfortable over stuffed chair and took in the rest of the furnishings. They exuded an atmosphere of quality without being opulent. I think the best description would be tastefully elegant.

Before long, just at nine o'clock, a tall thin man of about 50 years of age approached and introduced himself.

"Good morning, Mr. Johnson. I'm Justin Pierce, headmaster here at Corinthian Academy."

"Good morning. It is a pleasure to meet you."

"Please come into my office. Would you like a cup of coffee?"

"No thank you. I had one just before I left to come here."

"Very well. Now, what is your interest in our school?"

"I have four foster children, boys, that I am interested in giving the best education that is available. The county school where three of them are attending is lacking in what I consider the necessary facilities for a proper education. The fourth is being home schooled by a tutor. These children come from an abusive background. I want to give them the opportunity to overcome any handicap they might have brought with them. To that end I am interested in seeing what you have to offer for their education."

"Tell me, what are the ages of your boys?"

"TJ is six. The twins, Larry and Lenny, are 9 and Joel is 12."

"That would make them in first, fourth and seventh grades. Right?"

"Yes."

"Let me explain to you about our program here. We put a very strong emphasis on the basics. Reading and writing English correctly is a specific emphasis. Math and the sciences are stressed as well. That does not mean that the so called soft curriculum is ignored. We believe that the student should be exposed to art and music. Their physical education is also important. We do not have a football program. That may be heresy here in Texas, but we believe that the physical training that we provide should be something that will last a lifetime. We enforce strict discipline, but do not resort to corporal punishment. We rely on our parents to be partners in maintaining an atmosphere where learning can take place. We do not abuse ourselves with the notion that the students will always be perfect little angels. When situations arise, we deal with them immediately and in a manner that serves as a learning experience for the boy.

"This brochure explains in much more detail how the academy is structured and the programs we offer. If, after you have read it, you want any more information I would be happy to provide it to you."

"What about class size and teacher qualifications?"

"Our academic classes are limited to 22 students. The physical education and music classes such as the choir may be twice that size. But the student-teacher ratio is never more than 22 to 1. Teachers must be state certified in the subjects that they teach and are required to take additional college level courses to keep up to date in their area of emphasis."

"This all sounds great. May I have a look around the campus? I am interested in the physical plant also."

"Of course, I'll have my assistant show you around and answer any questions that you might have as you go. His name is Harry Lyle. When you are finished please come back here and I'll explain to you the admissions policy, uniforms and costs. The information is covered in detail in the brochure."

The tour with Harry was quite informative. The physical plant was not new but had been very well maintained. It seemed to be divided into two sections, one for K-4 and the other 5-8. I was impressed with the number of computers I saw in the classrooms. We did meet a couple of teachers on their free period and I was taken by their enthusiasm and positive attitude.

We spent nearly 45 minutes touring the facilities before returning to Mr. Pierce's office.

"Ah, Mr. Johnson, how was your tour? Any questions?"

"No, Mr. Lyle did a good job. You said you would explain the admission policy…"

"Yes, we require that each applicant be tested and interviewed before acceptance. This is mainly to assess their placement in the correct class and to determine if the child understands what is expected of him. We are not equipped to handle children with 'special needs' so we also use these to screen them out. Limited physical handicaps we can deal with but the profoundly handicapped are beyond our current capabilities.

"The school uniforms are what you have observed. The white polo shirt with the Corinthian Academy logo and the tan slacks or walking shorts with white stockings and white athletic shoes," he said.

"What about tuition?" I asked.

"We are not inexpensive. The tuition for each child is $6,500 per school year. That of course is prorated if enrollment is not for the full term."

I did some quick multiplication in my head and came up with the figure $26,000 a year.

"That is a little more than I expected but I think it would be worth it. When could the boys be tested?" I asked.

"Well, we don't accept students in the middle of grading periods. The current grading period ends a week from this Friday. We could set up an appointment for later this week or the first of next which ever would be the most convenient," he offered.

"I think perhaps that next week would be best. We are supposed to have a court hearing this week, I don't know exactly when right now," I said.

"Good, contact my secretary and she will make all of the arrangements. Do you have any more questions?"

"No, I don't think so. Thank you very much for your time. It has been most interesting," I said getting up to leave.

My mind was racing as I drove to the office. Foster was parking his car as I drove into the parking lot.

"Hi Crane, I'm glad you came. I need for you to approve the Latham Oil contract. They are anxious for us to get started. Oh, by the way, how are you and your new family getting along? I don't envy you taking on four active boys. I think they would drive me up the wall," he said as we walked into the office.

"We are doing fine, but I have to admit they are a handful. Thank goodness they are so well behaved. Let me check with Carol to see if I have any messages and then I'll look at the contract," I told him.

Carol had two messages for me. The first from Hildy said we had an appointment with Dr. Sam for Joel's blood test today at 2:15. The second was also from Hildy for me to call Jack Hogan.

I went into my office and glanced through the papers and mail in my in-box but nothing required my immediate attention so I dialed Jack.

"Hi, Jack," I said when he answered. "What can I do for you?"

"Crane, thanks for calling me back. There are two investigations going on right now that involve the boys. One is the result of the 'Suspected Abuse' report that was filed by Dr. Greene and the other is the murder investigation of the boys' mother. Joel is the center of each of them as the star witness. The two investigators both would like to interview him as soon as possible."

"Oh boy, I don't know, Jack. He has just recovered his voice and has just been through the trauma of his mother's funeral. I'm not at all sure that he is stable enough to be interrogated yet. I want him to see a psychiatrist before he has to go through that. How long do you think we can postpone this?"

"Not very long, they want to fast track this as much as possible. The DA wants to get to trial with this before the election. She is running for re-election and thinks this would be a feather in her cap if she can get a quick conviction. Politicians, I think that lady would try her own mother if she thought it would bring her a few extra votes. Anyway, I'll see what I can do, but I'm sure I can't get you too much more time. I'll let you know," he said and hung up.

Something more to worry about. Oh, the joys of fatherhood.

I looked over the contract that Foster had for me and approved it. The contract was worth $650 thousand in gross to the company. About 20% of that would drop to the bottom line. With all the expenses that were piling up associated with my boys, this would be a welcome addition to the company's coffers.

Before leaving the office, I chatted with several of the associates who were not out working on other contracts. As I left, I told Carol that I would try to check in with her two or three times a week until things got settled at home.

When I got home, Hildy had just cleaned up the lunch dishes and had put everything away. I made myself a quick sandwich before going to the study to check on Joel and Paul Coulter. I apologized to Paul for not being there today but had messed up and scheduled something else at the same time. I also told him we would have to cut his time short today because we had a doctor's appointment at 2:15 and would need to leave shortly to make it. Paul responded, "Would it be possible to start Joel's lessons at 8 o'clock? That way we would be done by noon and you would have time to take care of all the things I know you have going on now."

"I think that's a great idea. The other boys have to meet their bus at 7:30 so eight will be no problem," I said. "Let's start tomorrow morning then."

"Oh, and I have looked at the assignment that you gave Joel for the book report and have incorporated it in my lesson plan. I've seen what he has written so far and am impressed at his retention of the salient facts of the book. The spelling and writing style could use some work but we can work on that," Paul said.

Paul left and Joel and I followed shortly. We arrived at Dr. Sam's office right on time. I told the nurse who we were and why we were there. She ushered Joel into an examination room and told me that the doctor wanted to speak with me.

I was just getting settled in the waiting room when Dr. Sam appeared.

"Crane, come in. I have Joel's test results and need to discuss them with you. I didn't think they would be here until tomorrow but I'm glad they are so you won't have to make an extra trip."

My heart was in my throat and was beating twice as fast as normal as I followed him into another examination room. I didn't want to know what he was going to tell me but I had to know no matter what. The results would not change my love for Joel and my intention of giving him a permanent home with me.

I am not a religious man, but I prayed harder than I ever had that the results were negative.

"The results of the test for HIV were negative…" he started.

"Oh thank god!" I exclaimed.

"That's the good news. However, we are not out of the woods yet," he continued.

I guess my face showed my confusion and consternation.

"We will need to repeat this test every month for the next 5 or 6 to be sure that there are no viruses present. Depending upon when or if he has been exposed it could be up to six months before the virus is detectable," he concluded.

"Doc, I don't know if I can take the suspense, the not knowing. This has been eating away at me since our last discussion and now you tell me it is going to go on for another 6 months?" I groaned.

"I know it is not going to be easy for you but you have to be strong for Joel. I don't think it would be wise to tell him why he is going to have to have a blood test every month. There is no reason to worry him. He has enough on his plate right now," Sam advised.

"You're right. I'll worry enough for both of us," I said trying to smile.

Joel was in the waiting room when I came out with Sam.

"Come on, son, let's get home. I bet Hildy will have a snack ready when we get there and your brothers will be getting home soon too," I said as I put my arm around him and led him to the car.

I was right. Hildy had made a jellyroll pan full of lemon squares. Joel and I couldn't wait for the others. We sneaked a couple before they got home.

At 4:15, he and I walked down to the gate to wait for the boys. As we did he asked, "Why do I have to get so many blood tests?"

I decided I would have to tell a little white lie, "Well, I never asked you but I think from looking at your back that you had been beaten and possibly kicked or punched in the back. When you first went to see Dr. Sam, it was discovered that you had some liver damage. The blood tests tell us whether your liver is getting better. It has to be monitored for a while until we know it is back to normal. I know you don't like to have them stick a needle in your arm but it is necessary."

He looked at me with those beautiful eyes that seemed to be searching my soul and said, "Okay."

The school bus arrived and discharged the three rambunctious boys. They waved to their new friends and hollered "Bye" to the driver then ran to the gate. TJ trailed the twins but when he arrived, he jumped up and threw his arms around my neck hugging me tightly.

I was a little surprised at this and said to him. "What's this all about? Are you happy to be home or something?"

"My tummy feels good when I'm here," he said.

"Well, I'll bet your tummy will feel even better when you see what Hildy has for your snack," I snickered as I set him down and swatted him on the behind.

He giggled and ran to catch up with Joel and the twins who had started up the lane to the house. I think that hearing Hildy had a snack for them increased the speed at which they were walking. It didn't take long for them to reach the house, deposit their school books, change out of their school clothes and get to the kitchen ready for their snack.

Even though Joel and I had eaten a couple of the lemon squares earlier, it didn't stop him from enjoying a second helping. They jabbered about their day at school and Joel told them about Mr. Coulter and having to get a needle stuck in his arm at which all the boys cringed.

I had barely entered my study when the phone rang.

"Hello," I said.

"Hello, Crane, this is Joyce Gehrig from CPS."

"Yes, what can I do for you?"

"I just wanted to tell you that most of the preliminary background checks have been completed. We only have to interview two more of your references. They were not available today or we would be pretty much complete."

"That's good," I said with a sigh of relief.

"In fact, we have sufficient information to schedule a hearing before Judge Frank on Thursday afternoon at 1:00. Can you and the boys be there?"

"We will be there. Is there anything I need to be prepared for? I've never done anything like this before."

"No, nothing special. You probably should have in mind a convincing story to tell the judge just why it is you want to continue custody of the boys. He will also want to talk to the boys individually and probably as a group, so you need to prepare them for that. I wouldn't advise you to tell them what to say, just tell them what is going to happen and why this is happening. If you need any more information between now and then you can give me a call and I'll try to help."

"Thanks, Joyce. I know you were not too keen on the idea of me having custody of the boys at first. I hope you have changed your mind."

"Well as a general rule, I am still not convinced it is the best in all cases. I am inclined to believe this might be an exception to the rule. I will not oppose your custody of the boys, but I will not champion your cause either."

"Thank you for your honesty. We'll see you Thursday at one," I said as we hung up.

"I guess I had better call Benjamin," I said to myself as I picked up the phone again.

CHAPTER 9

Before beginning to dial, I looked at my watch. It was nearly 5PM. "No high-priced lawyer is going to be in his office at this time of the evening," I said aloud to myself. But I dialed anyway planning to leave a message to have him call me back. I was surprised to hear a live voice answer the phone.

"Cross, Allison and Brown, how may I help you?" it said.

"Hello, this is Crane Johnson. I would like to leave a message for Mr. Cross if possible."

"Yes, Mr. Johnson, he just returned from court but he may be in conference. Let me see if Mr. Cross is available. Hold please."

At least the "hold music" was good.

"Mr. Johnson, Benjamin Cross here, I'm glad that you called. My associates have nearly completed preparing the brief that we may need to support your position."

"That's why I called. They have scheduled the hearing for one o'clock on Thursday in front of Judge Frank. Will you or one of your associates be available to support me?"

"Let's see…Yes, I have the whole day Thursday. We should meet to discuss the strategy we will take if it's necessary. I always prepare for the worst possible outcome so nothing takes me by surprise. Are you available around ten Thursday morning?"

"Where do you want to meet? If it would be convenient, we could meet here at the house. That way the boys wouldn't have to miss any more than a half a day of school."

"I think that would work. If you could fax me the directions it would be better than me trying to write them down. From my knowledge of the area you are probably close to 60 miles from Austin, right?"

"Yes, I measured it once and it's 65 miles from my gate to the capitol building."

"Oh, by the way, I represented one other client in front of Judge Frank about a year ago. He is a cantankerous old bast…uh, jurist. I think our preparation for the worst case is prudent in this case. He was appointed by our infamous hard drinking, pot smoking former governor. His decisions have been overturned more often than any judge in the state. The only way he stays in office is that he has the backing of the political machine now holding sway in Texas."

"I really didn't need to hear that. The CPS case worker said that although she wouldn't oppose my petition she would not support it either. I'm getting very nervous about all of this."

"Don't worry! I think we will have all the bases covered by Thursday. I'll see you then. Goodbye," he said as he hung up.

I rarely have anything to drink other then a glass of wine, but now I needed a stiff drink. It had been so long since I had mixed myself a drink it took me a few minutes before I remembered where I had put the key to the liquor cabinet. Once I found it, I opened the cabinet and poured a double shot of scotch and took a big sip. Now I remembered why I didn't drink liquor very often. The liquor caused me to choke and cough as if I had swallowed liquid fire. It came spewing out my nose and generally made a mess on the floor.

Well I guess that serves me right. I shouldn't try to solve my problems with alcohol. Look at the trouble it has cause for Joel and the other boys.

I guess the commotion I made attracted the attention of the boys because they all rushed into the study.

"What's the matter, Uncle Crane?" Joel asked with a concerned frown on his face.

"Oh, I choked on some whiskey," I answered.

A look of terror passed across his face. "No!…Don't," he shouted and ran from the study into his bedroom slamming the door shut after him.

"What's the matter with Joel?" I asked the twins.

Larry responded, "Every time daddy drank he'd hurt Joel."

"Oh, my god! How could I be so stupid?" I said rushing to Joel's bedroom door.

"Joel, it's Crane. May I talk to you?" I said knocking softly on his door. "I won't hurt you. I promised you that no one would ever hurt you again. I promised your mother I would take care of you. Please let me in."

I gently turned the knob and slowly opened the door. At first I didn't see him. He was curled up in a tight ball in the corner of the room behind the bed. Those beautiful azure blue eyes showed more pain and terror than I had ever seen. Tears streamed down his cheeks but no sound came from him. No sobbing, no whimpering. I slowly walked to the side of the bed nearest him and sat down.

"Joel, I won't hurt you. I can't hurt you. I love you too much. I want to protect you. Please believe me," I pleaded.

He looked at me with somewhat less terror in his eyes, but it was clear that he didn't quite believe me yet.

"Joel, I know that your dad did things to you when he got drunk. I can't make that go away. It's in the past. No one can change what happened. All I can do is give you my word that what happened in the past will never happen to you again. I love you Joel and I want to protect you." I was very near tears at this point.

I held out my hand to him hoping that he would take it. Most of the terror had gone out of his eyes but there still was a hint of distrust. Finally, after a minute or so he started to reach out his hand to mine. It took a while before he actually made contact. I held onto his hand very gently before slowly drawing him closer to me. He uncoiled from the tight ball he had curled up in and began to crawl toward me.

When he got close enough I gradually, so as not to frighten him, reached out with my other arm and placed it under his other arm. I lifted him up and set him on my lap, wrapping both of my arms around him clutching him to my chest and began to rock him back and forth, cooing soothing words to him.

We continued that way for probably five minutes until the twins and TJ silently crept in and put their six arms around both of us.

Presently, I guess everyone was feeling better because TJ asked, "Can we go swimming?"

I had to laugh but said, "Sure you may. We can always count on you to bring us back to reality, little one. And I love you for that. In fact, I love all of you. Now, let's all get changed and swim until Hildy has supper ready."

We played in the pool until nearly seven o'clock when Hildy called us to get changed for supper.

As we finished eating, I said to everyone, "When you get everything cleaned up and the dishwasher loaded, come into the family room. There is something I need to tell all of you. Hildy, I would like for you to be there as well."

A few minutes later everyone entered the family room. TJ hopped up on my lap, Joel and the twins commandeered the couch leaving the other easy chair for Hildy. "On Thursday," I started, "we have to go to court to see Judge Frank. He will tell us if you will be able to stay here with me a little longer. This is only the first step in what I hope is the eventual adoption of you boys as my sons."

The boys were all paying very close attention to what I was saying. "Judge Frank will want to talk to each of you to see what you want to do. Whether you want to stay with me or be put in another foster home. The choice is really yours. I want you to stay with me but what matters most is what you want and what the judge decides. Do you have any questions about what is going to happen?"

"How come we gotta see a judge? Can't we just stay here?" Joel asked.

"I wish it were that simple, but the law has to be obeyed. That means the judge has to decide what is best for you."

"That's dumb!" he responded.

"It may seem like that, but the law is designed to protect kids from bad people, people who would hurt them and do bad things to them," I said trying to believe what I was telling them.

"When you talk to the judge I want you to be as courteous to him as you are to Hildy and me. Just be the great boys that we have come to love so much. Do you understand that you need to answer all of his questions honestly? Whatever you do, don't tell any lies. That would be very bad. I don't want you to worry about it but I did think that you have a right to know what is coming up that concerns you.

"Hildy, the reason I asked you to come is I need your help on Thursday. I'm meeting with Benjamin Cross, my lawyer handling this matter, at ten on Thursday and would like your help in picking up Larry, Lenny and TJ from school at 11:30 and driving them into San Antonio to the court house. We don't meet with the judge until one but I don't want to be late. I also want you to be present for the proceedings. I will take Joel with me and meet you there sometime around 12:30. I think it best if you take the clothes they are going to wear at the hearing with us so they can change at the court house. If you can think of anything else we need to do between now and then let me know."

"I'll be happy to pick up the boys. I knew this hearing would be coming up sometime soon and I fully intended to be there to support you and the boys.

The judge would have to be an idiot not to let them stay here with you," Hildy stated rather emphatically.

"Okay, guys, go get your home work assignments. You can use the kitchen table for the time being until I can get your rooms fixed up with desks. When you're done I'll check them," I said giving TJ a hug and set him down.

Off they all ran to get their school books. Joel had the most homework and we hadn't even done his math lesson. While the boys did their homework I did mine reviewing the math text book to see just what it was that they taught in seventh grade these days. I was pleasantly surprised at the text that Paul had selected. Not only was it well written and presented the material in a logical and understandable manner, it had a series of cumulative review quizzes every three chapters to test retention of the previous material. I decided to use these quizzes to determine where Joel was in his knowledge of mathematics and to decide where to begin.

As soon as each of the boys finished their home work and I checked it they were allowed to watch TV in the family room. When everyone was finished, we went to find what Hildy had prepared for us to snack on. Tonight it was cranberry nut bread. Earlier she had put out some butter to soften so that it would spread easier. Between the five of us, we ate the whole loaf and a quarter pound of butter. If I don't stop snacking with the boys, I'm going to gain weight. Either that or I'm going to have to get back in the habit of swimming laps every morning. Maybe even do a few more to compensate for all the additional calories I'm consuming.

After the boys had finished their snack, they headed for the bathrooms to shower and put on their pajamas.

I was in the study checking my voice-mail at the office when Joel came in and stood beside me. "What's on your mind, son?" I asked.

"I don't know…What if the judge don't let us stay with you? I don't wanta go no place else. I like it here. Why do we have to go see him? Can't we just stay here and not go?" he almost cried.

"Don't worry, son. That's why I hired a lawyer to help you stay here. He's a really smart lawyer. You go get into bed. I'll be in to tuck you in shortly," I said giving him a big hug before he left.

I finished listening to my voice-mail while at the same time checking my email. There was nothing that required my immediate attention so I went in to check on the boys and tuck them in for the night. It was starting to become a routine. First I would go into the twins' room, give them a kiss on the forehead, arrange their covers and make sure they were all set for the night.

Tonight turned out a little different. Everything went as usual until I was arranging their covers. They both reached up and hugged my neck and gave me a kiss on both cheeks.

"G'night Uncle Crane. We love you," they said in that uncanny way they did in unison. It was like listening to stereo.

"Goodnight my little angels, I love you too," I said giving them an extra squeeze before I left the room.

Joel and TJ were whispering to each other as I entered their room.

"Hey, what are you guys plotting?" I asked humorously.

"Nothing, Uncle Crane," they both said. For a moment I thought I was back in the twins' room.

"Okay, no more talking. You have school tomorrow and I don't want you to fall asleep in class," I said leaning over to give TJ a peck on the forehead. "I love you little man."

As I turned to Joel, I could tell he had something on his mind but didn't know how to get started telling me. "What's on your mind, son? You know you can tell me anything."

"Well…I…ah, well…I'm sorry that I got all scared tonight. I know you won't hit me or nothing. It's just…" he stammered.

"You don't have to explain anything to me. I know you have had some rough times," I said brushing the hair back off his forehead before I leaned over and kissed it. "Goodnight you two. Sleep well."

I retreated to my study to lay out what I needed to get accomplished for the next couple of days. About 10:30 I decided I had identified everything the boys and I had to do to get ready for the hearing and headed to bed.

Although the boys were not what I would call morning people, they didn't complain too much when I called them to get up and come to breakfast. It was probably the breakfast that got them out of bed more than anything else. Hildy had fixed blueberry pancakes and fried ham for us this morning. I couldn't resist having a couple of them despite my resolution to watch my calorie intake.

"Go get ready for school. You have 20 minutes to meet the bus. Hurry!" I told them. "I'll drive you down to the gate to catch it."

Driving to the bus, I informed them that I would pick them up after school and we all were going to get haircuts. I told the driver as the boys boarded that they would not be riding home with him. Now all I needed to do was call my barber and set up the appointment.

Paul Coulter arrived shortly to begin his sessions with Joel. I was sitting at the kitchen table drinking my last cup of coffee before I began the day I had laid out for myself last night. Hildy had let him in just as she left to do her grocery shopping.

"Crane, Joel asked me yesterday when he was going to get to read a book for class. I hadn't planned to assign a book report for another week or so but he seem so anxious that I am considering changing my lesson plans to include him reading a book every week. I see you have quite an extensive library of fiction in the study. Do you have any objections to his using them for his reading assignments?" he asked.

"No, in fact, I would encourage it. He will probably read at least one book a week so I think a written book report would be a little too much to expect, don't you," I replied.

"You're correct. I think that having him give an oral discussion would be a good learning experience. It would teach him to organize his thoughts and to learn how to speak effectively. I think having him speak in a non-threatening environment will also build up his self confidence," Paul said.

"I agree. That's a great idea," I said.

I finished my coffee and went into my bedroom to start making the phone calls on my list. First was to make appointments to get our hair cut. I knew Jose's shop opened at 8:30 so I called right on the dot. I wanted to make sure that we could get in. Jose didn't get in until later but I could set up everything without him being there. I explained to the receptionist that I needed to set up appointments for 5 haircuts for around 4:15. I wanted Jose to cut my hair since he had been my barber for the past 6 years but the boys could have anyone that was available. Since Jose's shop had six chairs it might be possible to have everyone get their hair cut at the same time.

Next, I called my office to take care of some of the voice mails I had received last night. Carol was able to handle most of them and what she couldn't Foster could.

By this time it was 9:30, so I tried the number of the Adolescent Psychiatrist that Dr. Sam had recommended the highest. Owen Adams was well known in the San Antonio area and highly respected for his service on several volunteer organizations. I really didn't expect to be able to get an appointment with him but there was no harm in trying. When his nurse answered, I explained the situation surrounding Joel and the fact that he had witnessed the murder of his mother by his father. I also told her of the physical and sexual abuse he had suffered at the hands of his father.

"If you will hold for a moment I will speak to Dr. Adams," she said.

It seemed like forever, but I'm sure it was only a couple of minutes, before she came back on the line.

"Dr. Adams is interested in speaking to you before he would make a commitment to work with the child. The doctor has a half an hour available this morning. Would you be available at 10:30?" she asked.

"Well it takes about 45 minutes to get from my home in Canyon Lake to downtown San Antonio, but I can try to make it," I said looking at my watch. "What is your address?

"We are located right off of 281 just inside Loop 1604," she said and rattled off the street address.

"I'll be there as soon as I can. It should be about 30 minutes," I said hanging up the phone and rushing for the door.

Hildy was coming in just as I was leaving and I almost bowled her over. "I'll call you and let you know what is going on," I told her as I jumped into the BMW and roared out of the garage.

I was right. It took right at 30 minutes to get to his office. I must admit I pushed the speed limit a bit more that I usually do. Thankfully, the cops were otherwise engaged. Since I had a few minutes before I was to meet Dr. Adams, I took the opportunity to call Hildy and explain where I was and asked her if she would administer Review Test II in Joel's math book if I didn't make it back in time.

Dr. Adams was much younger than I had expected. He was probably in his early 30's. I was impressed that someone so young had developed such a reputation in the community. I repeated much of the information I had given his nurse earlier. He took it all in asking for clarifications when I skipped over some points.

"Have you noticed any unusual behavior other than his inability to speak for a week?" he asked.

"His reaction to my drinking whiskey was unusual. Just the mention that I was having a drink of whiskey was terrifying to him. He became almost catatonic. It certainly frightened me. I don't think I'll ever have another drink without the look in his eyes haunting me" I said.

"I suppose that's to be expected based on what you have told me. Although he seems to be handling the situation fairly well, appearances can be deceiving. The psychological trauma that he has suffered could very well manifest itself later in who knows what way. I think I would like to talk to Joel. I usually keep Friday afternoons open in case an emergency comes up and if not I can get away for a game of golf," he chuckled. If you could have him here at two o'clock I will do a preliminary evaluation of him before we decide what course of treatment he will need."

"Thank you, Dr. Adams. We'll be here Friday at two," I said getting up to leave. "Oh, I guess that all depends on whether the court continues the boys' custody with me. I guess I didn't mention we have a hearing Thursday afternoon for that purpose. I'll inform you if there's a change in plans. I just naturally assume that they'll always be with me. I take it for granted but probably shouldn't. I don't know what I'd do if they took them away from me. They've become such an important part of my life in a very brief period of time."

I rushed back to the house but at a speed more in line with the posted limits. Paul was beginning to wind up his lessons with Joel as I entered the house. Hildy was fixing lunch and I was out of breath. If this is what parenthood is all about, I wonder if I'm up to it. I'm sure that things will settle down once we have the custody issue resolved I silently hoped to myself.

Joel did surprisingly well on the math review test that I gave him after lunch. I decided that we would begin his math instruction with the material covered in Chapter 7 of the text. That could wait until tomorrow. Today I decided he could pick out another book for him to read.

I wasn't surprised when he chose *Tom Sawyer Detective* as the next book he wanted to read. He had about an hour to start the book before we had to go pick up the other boys from school so we could get our hair cut. He used the whole hour and even took the book in the car with us.

The boys were precious at the barber shop. They had never been to one. I guess their mother or father always cut their hair before. When we arrived there were four empty chairs waiting for us. Jose was finishing up with his customer. I put the boys in the chairs with Joel the farthest away from where I would be sitting. The twins were in the next two and TJ was in the chair next to mine. I told the barbers that we wanted to just shape up the cut that they had. Make them look presentable. I didn't have to tell Jose how to cut mine. He knew from cutting it for 6 years exactly how I wanted it to look. I think TJ and the twins giggled the whole time they were getting their hair cut. The barbers sure earned their money on them the way the boys kept twisting and turning trying to see what was going on all around them.

I paid the bill for the hair cuts along with a generous tip for each of the barbers who had suffered through the boys' first experience in a barber shop.

"Guys, we didn't have time for a snack before, do you want to stop at the Dairy Queen and get a cone before we go on home?" I asked knowing that was a stupid question.

"YES!" came the quadraphonic reply.

"Four large cones and one small cone," I told the scratchy voice coming from the speaker.

"Try not to drip any on the seats, but if you do wipe it up with these napkins," I told them as I distributed the large cones and a handful of paper napkins to each of them and kept the small one for me. This was my feeble attempt at controlling my caloric intake.

Our evenings were beginning to be fairly routine. The boys would play or swim until dinner was ready. Then it was time for homework and a little TV before having a snack and getting ready for bed. I looked forward to bedtime for the boys. It was a quiet time, a time to get close to the boys and show them how much they meant to me.

After I tucked them into bed, I went back into my study and nearly broke down. I might have only one more night of this if the judge doesn't approve continuation of my custody. No matter if that happened I would not give up on my efforts to get them permanently. I would spend as much as it took to make it happen or until and if the boys told me they didn't want to stay with me.

Sleep was not easy in coming. It was well after midnight before I fell asleep and then it was not a restful sleep.

I got the boys off to school the next morning telling them I would pick them up from school because we were going to visit their mother's grave this afternoon.

While Joel was involved with his lessons, I took care of some company business that needed my attention. Thankfully, it could be handled over the phone with Foster and my partner.

After lunch, I got my first chance to teach Joel his math lesson. He was really quite good at picking up the new concepts so the lesson went by faster than I had anticipated. He was not disappointed when we finished and I told him he could use the rest of the time to read his book.

TJ, as usual, was excited when he jumped in the car after school. His mouth was going a mile a minute telling Joel and me about everything that had happened in school today.

The twins were dismissed a few minutes after TJ. When they saw the Land Rover, they ran to it waving to their new friends and piled in dumping their school books on the floorboards.

"Hi guys, how was school today?" I asked the standard parent question.

"Okay, I guess," came the reply somewhat tentatively.

That didn't sound quite right so I probed further, "That doesn't sound like it's okay. What's going on that I should know?"

"Oh, it's nothing," started Larry.

"Come on guys, you know you can tell me anything. I really want to know if there is something that is bothering you. Please. It sounds like something is not right," I said.

"It's just that…uh…well…Mr. Lansing sorta…" Lenny stammered.

"Well he is…uh…always putting his…uh…hands on us," Larry continued.

"Yeah, and he rubs our backs all the time," Lenny finished. "I don't like him to do that. It's creepy."

"Thanks for telling me. I'll take care of it," I said trying to keep the anger out of my voice and dropped the subject.

We arrived at the cemetery and found the grave site. As we walked the short distance from the car to it the boys all held hands. TJ grabbed mine to form the final link in the chain. I was carrying the flowers that I had Hildy pick up earlier today.

I didn't know what kind of reaction the boys would have as we approached. We had left the cemetery before the casket had been lowered into the ground.

"Where's momma?" TJ was the first to react.

I tried the best I could to explain that his mother's casket was buried in the ground behind the headstone under that mound of dirt.

"Oh," was the reply he gave with a confused look on his face.

I guess death and burial are strange concepts to a six year old.

Joel and the twins walked up to the headstone and touched it. They didn't say anything. They just looked at it and moved their fingers over the name carved into it.

I place the flower arrangement at the base of the stone and stepped back letting the boys have all the time they needed.

Presently Joel turned around and I could see the tears in his eyes. He walked to me and put his arms around me, looked up and said, "Thanks, Uncle Crane" and started sobbing quietly.

We all had tears in our eyes as we walked back to the car.

CHAPTER 10

The day I dreaded was finally here, Thursday, the day of the hearing to decide the fate of the boys. How did I get myself into this situation? Why couldn't I have just minded my own business instead of reaching out to a boy who needed help? These questions and a thousand more raced through my mind. I knew the answer to all of them. It was because I was a soft touch. I couldn't say no to helping kids, just like I couldn't say no to Jack when he asked me to help with his little league team.

There are times when I wish I could be a calloused bastard and say no, but I can't. It is a character defect that I can't overcome.

I tried to downplay the hearing to the boys as they got ready for school, but I knew they were worried. Hildy reminded the twins and TJ that she would pick them up at 11:30 to take them to San Antonio. As usual, I drove them down to the end of the lane to catch the bus.

It started to rain as they stepped on the bus and waved goodbye to me. I hope this is not an omen of things to come. My mood was dark enough without the weather adding to it.

Paul arrived to start Joel's lessons giving me two hours to fret before Benjamin Cross was due to discuss strategy for the hearing. To fill the time I went over my notes that explained why I thought that the boys should be allowed to stay with me if I was called upon to present my case. I didn't want to forget anything so I made copious notes on three by five cards.

At nine o'clock, Joel got his first break from his tutoring. Paul came into the kitchen to get a glass of water and to talk to me.

"Joel is usually so sharp in class, but today his mind seems to be somewhere else. Is there something going on that would cause this distraction?" he asked.

"Yes, I don't doubt that he's a little bit distracted today," I replied. "We have a hearing this afternoon to determine whether he and his brothers will be able to remain here with me or be returned to CPS and placed lord knows where."

"I'm sure that's it. By the way, is this an open hearing? Can anyone attend?" Paul asked.

"I don't know. My lawyer should be here in an hour and I can ask him. Why do you ask?"

"Oh, I don't know. I thought maybe Joel would like to see another friendly face there. It might make it less stressful if he knew that there were more people who cared what happened to him and were there to support him. You see, I have grown very fond of Joel both as a student and as a wonderful young man. He has great potential and I would hate to see that potential go to waste or be crushed.

"I have personal knowledge of the foster care system in Texas. I was in five different foster homes before I was placed in one where I was loved. In between, I was in their so called 'group home'. No one deserves that. If there is anything that I can do to help, please let me know," he said with a fire in his eyes that I had never seen before.

"Thanks, I appreciate that. I'll ask Benjamin if you can attend the hearing. If you can, it is in court room number 3 in the Bexar County Court House in front of Judge Frank at 1:00," I said.

The gate buzzer sounded a few minutes before ten. The security camera showed a very large black Cadillac waiting to be let in. I activated the electronic gate and the car glided through it toward the house. The only person that this could be was Benjamin.

I stepped out on the front porch as an expensively dressed man who appeared to be about 40 exited the car or more properly limousine.

"I'm Crane Johnson. You must be Benjamin Cross," I said extending my hand to him.

"Yes, it's good to meet you," he said shaking my extended hand in a firm grip. "You have a beautiful place here. I envy you. I live in a high rise condo in downtown Austin."

"Thank you, I enjoy it. This was my parents' vacation home," I told him as we entered the house. "Would you like a cup of coffee? I think Hildy just made a fresh pot."

"Yes, that would be great. Why don't we use the kitchen table? I have a number of papers to show you and to get your signature. That way we can spread them out. Also, may I use your restroom?" he asked.

"Right through there. I'll pour the coffee," I said.

Joel was just coming out of the study on his second break between class sessions when Benjamin returned to the kitchen.

"Joel, I'd like for you to meet Mr. Cross. Mr. Cross this is Joel. Mr. Cross is the lawyer I told you about. He is going to help us," I said.

"Hi, Mr. Cross, are you really going to make the judge let us stay here? Please!" he said as his voice cracked.

"I am sure going to try my best. Do you and your brothers like living here?" Benjamin asked.

"Oh, yes!" he almost yelled. "Uncle Crane is the best! He never hits us or nothing and never locks us up in the closet."

"Okay, Joel, why don't you get a couple of brownies that Hildy made and a glass of milk and take them into the study? Mr. Cross and I have some business to take care of. Maybe you can read a little of your book before Paul starts his next lesson." I knew that food and his book were irresistible temptations for him.

Turning to Benjamin I said "Paul Coulter, Joel's tutor, was asking if the hearing would be open. I told him I would ask you. Is it?"

"That is up to Judge Frank. Most of the time they are open to the public. There are parts that will be closed especially if the children are on the stand. Mr. Coulter would probably be allowed even in those since he is by his position as tutor an interested party. At least I think we could make that case. Again, everything that goes on in that court room is at the sufferance of the judge," he said.

We spent the next hour going over a stack of papers. I had no idea what most of them were. I was paying this guy and awful lot of money and I sure hoped that he knew what they were for. By the time Hildy came in with the boys' change of clothes my head was swimming and I needed a break.

I introduced Hildy as my cook, housekeeper and nanny for the boys as well a surrogate mother for me.

Hildy blushed but said to Benjamin "If that damn judge doesn't let my boys stay here he is an idiot and you can quote me. You just make it happen!"

"I will try my best," he gulped very much taken aback by not only her words but her overpowering presence.

"Wow! Now there goes a woman I would not like to cross," he chuckled as she left to pick up the boys.

"She has a heart of gold and loves the boys as much as I do. They adore her, too," I said.

We went back to work, but this time discussed possible outcomes of the hearing and how we would react. After about an hour I was convinced that we had done a thorough 'threat analysis'. At least that is what we could call it in my business.

I peeked in the study to see how the tutoring was going just as they were breaking. "Paul, I hate to cut you short again but Joel needs to get dressed for the hearing. We have to leave in half an hour to meet his brothers at 12:30. I hope that one of these days things will settle down to a semblance of normalcy."

"That's okay. We are ahead of my lesson plans anyway. It's alright with you if I attend the hearing isn't it? I don't want to butt in. However, I would like to be there," he said.

"No, by all means, you're welcome to be there. We may need another friendly face. Thanks," I replied.

I normally don't wear a suit unless I was making a presentation to client management but thought it would be a good idea to wear one today. Joel looked sharp in his dark blue blazer and tan slacks. He had a tie slipped under the collar of his white shirt but had not tied it.

"Uncle Crane, can you tie this tie? Hildy showed me yesterday but I can't make it do it today," he almost whimpered.

"Yes, come here and let me do it. You look so handsome all dressed up like this," I told him. "Hildy made some sandwiches before she left. I think we have time for some before we leave, that is if you are hungry. Benjamin you are welcome to help yourself. Hildy always makes enough for an army."

He declined saying he was meeting a colleague for a quick bite before court. Joel did not decline. He grabbed the sandwiches out of the refrigerator while I got out the chips and milk and poured him a glass.

Joel was very quiet all the way into San Antonio. Neither one of us had much to say. I tried to make small talk but gave up realizing that he needed to think. The rain we had earlier had nearly stopped by the time we arrived. It was still as dreary as my mood.

That is until we got to the court house and I saw the twins and TJ. My mood brightened immediately as they rushed up and gave Joel and me a group hug.

"Hildy said we had to get our clothes changed," TJ said.

"Well let's go do it. You grab your clothes and we'll find the restroom so you can change," I told him.

They nearly ripped the clothes out of Hildy's hands in their rush. We headed to the restroom for what I knew was going to be a circus. When we got in I tried to settle them down and only succeeded slightly.

"TJ let's start with you. Go into this stall and get undressed. I'll hand you your clothes and help you get dressed," I said. We had taken the last stall away from the door so it was fairly private and the restroom was not very busy.

"Alright, Larry, you go next. I don't think there is room for both you and Lenny in there at the same time.

"Come here TJ let me tie your tie."

"Lenny, it's your turn. Larry let me fix your tie.

"Okay, Lenny, your tie is next.

"You boys look so handsome. I wish I had brought a camera," I said with a lump in my throat. "Take your other clothes to Hildy. She'll put them in the car for you."

Hildy took off with the boys clothes while we found the court room. We had a few minutes to wait before one o'clock so I sat down on the bench outside the door. TJ climbed up on my lap and laid his head on my chest. The twins sat on one side and Joel on the other. I reached out and put my arm around the twins and the other around Joel.

"It's going to be alright, guys. Whatever happens, you know that I will always love you," I said softly.

"We love you too Uncle Crane," Joel whispered.

Benjamin Cross and another man came walking down the hall. "Crane, this is Gary Everett. He is the attorney for CPS."

We exchanged formalities all the while TJ was still sitting on my lap not seeming to want to lose contact with me.

At that moment, the bailiff called us to come into the court room.

"Okay, guys let's go in and get this over with. Remember what I told you. Just be the great boys that Hildy and I love," I said putting on my bravest face and kissing them on the tops of their heads.

Hildy and Paul Coulter arrived almost at the same time. I think Hildy ran to and from the car because she was out of breath as she sat down in the front row behind us. Theresa and Joyce came in right behind them and took their place at the other table with Gary Everett.

The bailiff called the court to order and announced Judge Frank. I was a bit taken aback at the sight of him. The best way to describe him is he could have been a body double for the late actor W.C. Fields. The judge's most distinguishing feature was his large bulbous nose. When he opened his mouth and started to speak, that's where the similarity ended. His "southern accent" was a caricature of the soft mellifluous accent usually associated with this part of Texas.

"Y'all take your seats. I like to run these hearing very informally. For the record will the counsels identify themselves to the court," the judge said.

"Your Honor, I am Gary Everett representing CPS."

"Your Honor, I am Benjamin Cross representing Crane Johnson."

"Yes, I remember you now. You're that fancy lawyer from Austin, ain't you?"

"Very well, let's get started. This hearing is to decide the placement of four minor children identified as: Joel Jay Andersen age 12, Lawrence Jay Andersen age 9, Leonard Jay Andersen also age 9, and Timothy Jay Andersen age 6.

"Bailiff, escort the children into my chambers while we sort out a few details?" he ordered.

The boys looked at me with a slightly frightened expression on their face. "It's alright. Don't worry I'll be right here. Okay?" I said smiling and trying to assuage their fears.

I kept smiling all the time the boys were being led away. My fears did not disappear but I did feel better when I saw a smiling female bailiff as the door opened into the judge's chamber.

"Mr. Everett, please outline for the court the reason these children are under CPS supervision," the judge said.

"Your Honor, the complete details of how the children came under CPS jurisdiction is covered in the brief filed with the court. It boils down to the mother was murdered and the father is in jail charged with robbing a convenience store and is under investigation for the murder of his wife. As far as we can determine there are no close relative with whom the children can be placed. Mr. Johnson has had temporary custody as an emergency certified foster parent of the four youngsters. He has submitted all the required paperwork and references requesting to be permitted to continue custody of the children," Everett said.

"And what is CPS' position on allowing Mr. Johnson to continue custody?" Judge Frank asked.

"Although Mr. Johnson has the financial wherewithal to meet all of the requirements of custody and his references all check out and give him glowing recommendations, it has not been the custom of CPS to place minors in the custody of a single male."

"Does that mean you do not approve of extending the custody arrangement?"

"No, CPS simply does not oppose the request for custody. We also do not support it."

"Mr. Everett, this is highly unusual. This is the first time that CPS has come into this court and not given me a recommendation on custodial arrangements.

"Mr. Johnson, why should this court continue the custody of the boys with you?"

I was about to respond to the judge when the court room door opened and Dr. Sam and Dr. Adams walked in and sat down behind Hildy. I was not too surprised that Sam showed up but I was amazed that Dr. Adams came.

"Your Honor, there are a number of reason that support my request for custody.

"First, as Mr. Everett stated I do have the financial resources necessary to take care of the boys.

"Second, I have a large enough home to comfortably house them.

"Third, I have hired a full time housekeeper-cook-nanny, Mrs. Hildy Ramirez, who is sitting behind me here in court.

"Fourth, I can provide Joel with the psychological help I believe he needs as a result of being physically and sexually abused. To that end, I have engaged Dr. Owen Adams, who is also present in the court room, to do a preliminary evaluation of him tomorrow. Dr. Adams is one of the most highly respected adolescent psychiatrists in this part of the country. Another reason for seeking the help of Dr. Adams is the belief on my part, and confirmed by Joel, that he actually witnessed the murder of his mother.

"Fifth, I can provide for all of the children the best medical care available in the area by way of Dr. Samuel Greene. Dr. Greene is also present today. Joel is already under the care of Dr. Greene for various medical conditions.

"Sixth, it is my intention to enroll the boys in Corinthian Academy at the beginning of their next term. Corinthian is the fifth highest rated private school in the state.

"Seventh, the chances of all four of the boys being placed in the same foster home are infinitesimally small. Only TJ would have a reasonable chance of being adopted if they were put up for adoption. Mr. Paul Coulter, the gentleman sitting here behind me, has related his experience with foster homes to me. He was in five different homes before being placed permanently. His experience in the group homes is something I do not want these youngsters to be exposed to. I offer the chance for all four of the boys to grow up together.

"Eighth and most importantly, I have grown to love them as much as any father could love his own sons and I believe that they love me as well," I said and sat down.

Benjamin Cross stood up and said "Your Honor, I have prepared a number of documents in support of what Mr. Johnson has just told the court. Included in this is a financial statement from his accountant and copies of his tax returns for the last three years. A copy of the latest audit of the company that he is 80% owner of by an independent auditing firm is also here. One other document that might be of interest to the court is the background check done by the best private investigation team in the state."

"Thank you Mr. Cross," the judge responded. "Ms. Gehrig or Ms. Shannon have either of you talked to the boys about where they would prefer to live?"

"Yes, Your Honor we have," Joyce stood up and said. "We both talked with them right after their mother's funeral. They appeared to be happy where they were and expressed no concerns about living with Mr. Johnson. Although the doctor that examined the twins and TJ have not re-examined them it appears that they, and Joel for that matter, have put on weight in the last ten days. They were all somewhat undernourished when they came to my attention."

"You are their case worker, what is your recommendation as to what their placement should be?"

"I would only echo the comments of Mr. Everett. I explained to Mr. Johnson the other day that I would not actively oppose his request for continued custody but I would not support it either," Joyce stated.

"I must say, Ms. Gehrig, I am disappointed with CPS in this matter. Is there some reason that you have not revealed for your reluctance to either support or oppose the placement?" Frank said with a slightly menacing tone in his voice.

"No, Your Honor, the only reason for our stance is that it has never been the custom of CPS to put foster children in the care of a single male," Joyce responded rather timidly.

"I think y'all are scared of that high priced lawyer sitting over there. That's neither here nor there.

"Dr. Greene, Mr. Johnson indicated that you were treating the oldest boy. Would you explain to the court just what it is you are treating him for?"

Sam walked and stood by the table where I was sitting before he said, "When Joel was brought to my attention he had been severely beaten on the back, buttocks and thighs by what looked like a belt. I also observed that he had been sexually abused both anally and orally and have submitted the required paperwork to the police. He was also suffering a jaundice like condition or yellowing of the skin and eyes which was caused in my opinion by blows or kicks to the liver or kidneys or both. As a result of the sexual abuse I have started a series of tests for HIV which will continue for the next six months. At the end of the series we should be able to say definitively whether he has been infected with the virus."

"Thank you, doctor. Dr. Adams, do you have anything to add to this matter?"

Dr. Adams came forward as Sam returned to his seat. "Your Honor, I have not yet assessed the boy's psychological profile. But from talking to Mr. Johnson and taking a brief history of the boy, I would be extremely surprised if he did not need long term psychological support. Having been involved in the assessment of some of the children in CPS' care I am acutely aware of the lack of follow up and psychological support that the majority of those needing it actually receive."

"Thank you, Dr. Adams.

"I'm going to talk to the boys. This hearing will be in recess until I complete my talk," the judge said.

We all stood as he left for his chambers.

The minutes seemed like hours as we waited. It turned out that we only had to wait just over 20 minutes before he returned. While we were waiting, Benjamin talked to both Dr. Sam and Dr. Adams as well as Hildy and Paul Coulter.

As Judge Frank took his seat behind the bench my attorney remained standing after the rest of us had taken our seats.

"Mr. Cross, do you wish to address the court?" he said.

"Yes, Your Honor, I do. To preserve the right of appeal by either party, we request that the information elicited earlier be given under oath," Benjamin said.

"Mr. Everett, how does CPS respond to this suggestion for the court?"

"Your Honor, CPS does not intend to seek an appeal of the decision made by the court no matter what that decision is."

"Well, Mr. Cross, do you still wish to have sworn testimony seeing that CPS will not appeal?"

"Yes, Your Honor, we believe that any evidence upon which the court relies on to assist it in making its decision should be sworn."

"Your request is denied, Mr. Cross. You may sit down. Bailiff, bring in the children," the judge ordered.

"That doesn't look good for our side," I whispered to Benjamin.

"Don't worry, that is exactly what I wanted him to do. He fell for it. I can't believe he is so stupid," he whispered back to me.

Just as I was turning back around the boys entered the court room. TJ looked around taking in everything before running across the room, around the table where I was sitting and jumped up on my lap. The other boys were more controlled and merely walked rapidly to our table and surrounded us.

"We get to stay don't we?" TJ pleaded looking me straight in the eyes.

"I don't know little one. The judge hasn't told us yet," I said trying to keep my voice from quivering.

"Bailiff, escort the boys to that front row bench over there," the judge said.

"It's alright," I said. "Go sit down over there. It's okay."

TJ hopped down off my lap and followed his brothers to the bench the judge had indicated. I wished that I could follow them also but knew that wouldn't be the smart thing to do. However, I was pleased to see that Hildy got up from where she was sitting and went to sit beside TJ.

"Thank you," I mouthed as I caught her eye.

"Let's get this over with," the judge started. "I have talked to the boys and they all say that they want to remain in the custody of Mr. Johnson. The court has to consider that into its decision. It is the courts conclusion that the boys' statements have been bought and paid for by the petitioner and can therefore be ignored. Without the recommendation of CPS as to the fitness of the petitioner to continue as foster parent, the court has no option but to deny Mr. Johnson's petition for custody.

The four minors are remanded to the custody of CPS who will determine the best placement for them until the parental rights of their father has been terminated or are returned to him if that is practicable.

"Are there any motions to be presented to the court before this hearing is terminated?

"Mr. Everett?"

"No, Your Honor."

"Mr. Cross?"

"Yes, Your Honor. We request that it stay its order until the petitioner has the opportunity to appeal the order to a higher court."

"Request denied! Anything else?"

"Yes, Your Honor, with all due respect to the court, I have one of my associates meeting with Justice Yates of the Appellate Court in Austin at this very moment. He has presented all of the documents to her that were presented to this court and has informed me via my digital pager that Judge Yates is prepared to issue a stay in the case that this court will not," Benjamin stated.

I could detect just the hint of a smile on his face as he addressed Judge Frank. The judge's face did not reflect the same. It was getting redder by the minute. His nose, which was already large, seemed to get even larger and took on a glow that would have made Rudolph proud.

As Benjamin was speaking, a man entered the court room, approached our table and handed a note to him.

Opening the note Benjamin continued "I have just been informed that the stay order has been signed by Judge Yates. In a separate decree, she has ordered that a transcript of this hearing be delivered to her in Austin no later than 10:00AM on Monday morning. Copies of her orders are being faxed to your clerk as we speak."

"You son of a bitch," the judge fairly screamed. "One of these days you god damned high priced Austin lawyers will get what's coming to you. This hearing is terminated."

With that, he banged his gavel and stormed out of the court room before anyone even had a chance to stand up.

CHAPTER 11

"That man is toast!" Benjamin said as he broke out laughing. "If that outburst doesn't get him a judicial reprimand I don't know what would."

"I don't care about him. What about the boys? What is going to happen to them?" I asked.

"They get to stay with you for the time being," he started to explain to me.

That is all the farther he got. Hearing that they were going to stay with me, I immediately jumped up and ran to them. They didn't know what was going on when I got there. "You guys want to go home with me?" I asked them.

Almost simultaneously they all yelled "Yes, yes!" TJ jumped up and hugged my neck. The other boys crowded around hugging us both. Hildy even joined in our celebration.

I turned to Benjamin as he walked up to our celebration. "How much time do we have? You said they could stay 'for the time being', what does that really mean?" I asked.

"According to the scant information I have on the stay order, you have custody until Judge Yates has time to review the transcript of the hearing and make her decision. That may take anywhere from a few days to weeks. Knowing Judge Yates as I do, she will probably take no more than a week at the very most," he answered.

"Does that mean we have to have another hearing?"

"Not necessarily. She could simply reverse Judge Frank's ruling which I think she'll do. Or, she could order a new hearing with a different judge. The other possibility which is a very remote one is she will affirm his decision."

"So you mean we will have to sweat this out for another week? God, I don't know if I can handle that. But, I suppose there is nothing that we can do but wait," I said with resignation.

By this time, Dr. Sam and Dr. Adams had joined our little group. "I want to thank both of you for coming today. Dr. Adams, your presence was unexpected but very much appreciated. It looks like we will be able to make that appointment tomorrow," I said shaking his hand. "Sam, I had a sneaking suspicion that you would show up. You're a good friend and I thank you for that."

Turning to the boys and grabbing TJ's hand I said "Let's go get a snack. I know a place that serves some great sopaipillas. Everyone's invited. Come on."

The Mexican restaurant I was thinking of was only a couple of blocks from the court house so we decided to walk. Thankfully, it had cleared up and the sun was shining brightly. Dr. Adams and Gary Everett were the only ones present at the hearing that could not join us. That is except for the judge.

I had to show the boys how to pour the honey on the sopaipillas and eat them. They had never experienced the joy of getting the honey and powdered sugar all over their faces, but they learned quickly. We must have eaten five dozen of the sweet treats among the 11 of us before I had to call a halt to the boys' eating binge. I took the sticky boys to the restroom to wash away the honey from their hands and faces before heading back to the car and home.

It suddenly dawned on me that I didn't have any real toys for the boys to play with. They had never complained about the lack of playthings. I guess they never had much to play with in their home. Since we had to pass close to both a Toys R Us and a Circuit City on the way home I decided to rectify that situation.

Our first stop was at Circuit City where I knew they sold video game machines. I had heard the boys on the little league team talk about all the neat games that they played on them. Frankly, I had never been a fan of computer games. I never saw the purpose in them, but who was I to judge. The boys were awestruck when we walked into the store. I must admit it was quite impressive with all the TV's, VCR's and DVD players on open display. I caught one of the salesperson's eyes and asked him where the PlayStations were. He was happy to show us.

"Do you guys know what a PlayStation is?" I asked.

Joel responded, "I saw one at a friend's house once."

"Have you ever played with one?"

They all shook their heads no.

"Well, I think that we need to correct that," I said turning to the friendly clerk. "I want two complete systems with joysticks or whatever they need. Don't leave anything out that they might need to play any game."

The clerk was delighted and quickly assembled the list of items that he thought was required to meet what I had outlined. He showed me the list on his sales register and suggested that we might need some games to go with the hardware.

"Joel, take your brothers over there to that display of video games. You can each pick out one game. The only requirement is that they are not violent. They should be rated for everyone," I told him.

Turning to the clerk I said, "You probably know more about the games than they do, please steer them to something that is appropriate for their ages."

While the boys were looking at the video games, I went to look at the TV's and at the same time keeping an eye on them. I only had one TV in the house since I mainly watched the news on it, but the boys would need something to hook the PlayStation's up to. I found a 32 inch Sony that had a great picture so when our clerk returned with the boys and their games I told him to add two of the TV's to the list. I check the game that the boys had pick out and was pleased that they heeded my request to pick out the non-violent ones.

When the clerk asked if we wanted to take our purchases with us, I declined requesting that they be delivered tomorrow. He looked at his delivery schedule and said that would not be possible. The delivery to the Canyon Lake area would not be made until Monday.

"Young man," I said looking at his name tag, "…Carl, do you want to make this sale?"

When he said he did I continued, "I don't know what you have to do to get my purchased delivered tomorrow but you better get it done. I can drive over to the other side of this shopping center and get the same thing, maybe even cheaper, and I'm sure that they would be happy to deliver tomorrow. You have two minutes to figure out how to get it delivered or you can start processing a return. Am I making myself clear?"

It took him slightly more than the two minutes I had given him but he came back with the store manager who tried to convince me that he just couldn't make a special trip for this one order.

"Very well," I said. "Would you please process a return of the merchandise I have just charged? I have always liked shopping here and my company has done a considerable amount of business with you. I'm sure that any electronic equipment that we need in the future we will be able to acquire at one of your competitors."

Turning to the boys, I said "Let's go over to Best Buy and see what they can do for us. If they can't, I'm sure Bjorns can."

Realizing that I was serious and he was going to lose a two thousand dollar sale, the manager relented and said that he would arrange a special delivery for us sometime between two and four tomorrow afternoon.

The boys took their games with them as we left the store.

Our next stop was at Toys R Us. I had never been in one so I didn't know what to expect. Thank goodness there were not a lot of people in the store. I guess Thursday afternoon is not prime toy shopping time. Larry, Lenny and TJ were in heaven running from one display to another. There were so many more things for them than there were for Joel. The only thing that he found was another video game for the PlayStation. TJ found a Tonka Truck that he wanted. The twins found a couple of radio controlled cars.

"I think you will have time to play with your new toys for a while when we get home before Hildy has supper fixed for us," I told them. "Joel you will have some time to read your book or even go swimming if you would like."

The day had begun to catch up with the boys by the time we got home. They had not said very much on the way home and I think that TJ took a short nap. I was beginning to feel the strain myself. I needed to get in the pool and swim some laps. It had been almost two weeks since I had done my usual routine. BB, before boys, I swam laps for at least a half an hour every night when I got home from work.

Hildy apologized that she didn't have much time to fix a big meal and that we would have to make do with a tuna casserole. That sounded great to me after all the sweets we had eaten this afternoon. I went to swim. Joel grabbed his book. TJ and the twins unwrapped their new toys.

After we ate, I had the boys get out their homework and get started doing it while I gave Joel an abbreviated math lesson.

Showers completed and pajamas donned the boys gathered in the family room where I was reading the newspaper. I could tell that they had something on their minds. TJ climbed up on my lap brushing the paper out of my hands.

"Okay, guys, what's on your mind? I can tell something is bothering you," I said.

They looked at each other to see who would speak first when TJ spoke up, "Are we going to get to stay here, Uncle Crane? Please!"

"Yeah, are we? Huh?" the twins chimed in.

Joel just nodded his head in agreement.

"Well you see guys it's like this. The answer is yes and maybe. Yes you can stay at least until another judge says yes or no. That should take about a week. Mr. Cross, our lawyer, believes that you will, but even he cannot be certain. I know I'm going to do everything in my power to make it possible for you to stay. I wish I could tell you that you would be here forever but I don't want to tell you a lie. We just have to believe that everything is going to be all right. When I find out anything, I'll let you know," I said trying to keep the emotion out of my voice. I continued to hold TJ as I got up. "I think you need to go to bed. It's been a busy day."

Going through my usual bedtime routine except this time I tucked Joel and TJ in first before doing the same for the twins. I was not far behind in hitting the bed.

Friday was almost normal. I put TJ and the twins on the school bus and Paul Coulter arrived to start tutoring Joel. I called my office and talked to Carol and Foster to see if there was anything that needed my attention. Everything seemed to be running smoothly without me. I didn't know whether to feel good about that or bad that they could run things without me. Foster told me that Eric, my partner in the business, wanted to talk to me when I had time. He wasn't in the office right then so I had Carol put me through to his voice mail. I left him my schedule for the rest of the day and told him he could try to call me on the cell phone, page me or he could try me at home.

I talked to Hildy and asked her if she would be around this afternoon to accept the delivery from Circuit City. I told her what I wanted to have done with the TV's and where they were to be hooked up in the boys' rooms. She could tell the delivery people that all they had to set up were the TV's. I would take care of setting up the PlayStations.

I told her that Joel and I would leave for his appointment with Dr. Adams about 1:15 and probably wouldn't return much before four o'clock.

We even had time for Joel's math lesson before we took off for the doctor's office. I didn't want him to get too concerned about meeting Dr. Adams. As we drove to the appointment, I tried to explain to him what was going to happen. That all Dr. Adams was going to do was talk to him and ask some questions. Joel seemed to be okay with that. I hoped so.

We arrived at Dr. Adams' office a few minutes early. I filled out the paperwork that all doctors require. I didn't have any insurance coverage on Joel and the other boys other than what CPS would pay. I didn't think they would pay

Dr. Adams' fees anyway so I put down 'No' in the question about insurance coverage.

Dr. Adams came into the reception room on the dot of two. I liked punctual people. I really hate waiting especially when I have an appointment.

"Crane, it's good to see you again," he said extending his hand.

"Dr. Adams, this is Joel. You were not properly introduced yesterday and for that I apologize. Things were a little hectic and I was not thinking clearly," I said shaking his hand and then turning to Joel. "Joel, this is Dr. Adams."

"Hello, sir," Joel said and to my surprise he extended his hand to the doctor.

"I am very glad to meet you, Joel. Did your foster father tell you what we were going to do today?"

"Yeah, Uncle Crane said we were going to talk and you were going to ask me questions."

"That's right. Please come with me. Your Uncle Crane will be right out here" he said leading Joel into his office.

Oh, how I wish that I could have been in the office with them. I must have looked at my watch a hundred times while they were in there. I squirmed in my chair, tried to read a magazine and paced the floor but nothing made the time go faster. Finally, the door opened and Joel and the doctor came out. He had his arm on Joel's shoulder and Joel was smiling up at him. At least that was a good sign, I thought.

"Joel why don't you sit down for a minute, I want to talk to your Uncle Crane," Dr. Adams said.

Motioning for me to follow, he went back into his office.

"Sit down, Crane," he said. "From this very preliminary evaluation I believe that Joel will need to have psychological support. However, I don't believe that he needs extensive treatment. He has become very attached to you and the security both emotionally and physically that you provide for him. If for any reason he was removed from your custody it could destroy the amazing progress he had made from the severe trauma that he suffered as a result of seeing his mother murdered. He also seems to be dealing quite well with the sexual and physical abuse that he suffered at the hands of his father. He is a strong young man."

"You said he needs psychological support. What does that mean?" I asked.

"I would like to see him every two weeks for a while to continue monitoring his progress. What he needs most is a lot of physical contact and someone to listen to him. And of course someone to love him, someone who can be a father figure for him," he said.

"God, I love him and his brothers. They couldn't be dearer to me if they were my own flesh and blood," I said with tears welling in my eyes. "On another matter, the police want to interview Joel concerning the sexual and physical abuse. They also want to talk to him about his mother's murder. What do you think? I want to see that asshole of a father disappear from the face of the earth, but to make that happen Joel will have to testify."

"That's a tough call. If you were present when the interview took place and if it was done in a non-threatening environment it would probably be alright. The interview would have to be conducted by someone who is experienced in handling cases like this. I know several of the officers who have such experience. When you find out when they want to do the interview, ask them who is going to do it. Give me a call and I'll let you know if they are ones I would trust to handle it. If they are not, you can ask for someone else.

"I think we have kept Joel waiting long enough," he said showing me out of the office.

"Are you ready to go home?" I asked Joel.

"Yeah, let's go. Goodbye Dr. Adams," Joel said grabbing my hand and pulling me out the door.

We just got to the car and it dawned on me that the little league team had a game today. "Damn," I thought as I reached for my cell phone and dialed Jack.

"Jack, this is Crane. Hey buddy, I'm not going to be able to be there today. I have too many irons in the fire. I hope this doesn't put you in a bind."

"That's alright, Crane. I know the boys will be disappointed but they will get over it. I hope you can make it next week. It's the final game of this season," Jack said.

"I promise you that I will be there. Will you make sure that the boys get their McDonald's treat after the game? I'll reimburse you for the damages. There is a stash of the coupons in that locked box in the equipment shed. The key is on the ring with the key to the shed," I told him.

"I'll take care of it. I hope your life gets simplified soon. Oh, by the way, the two cases that Joel will have to testify at have been consolidated into one. A Detective Silver will be calling you to set up an interview with Joel. She is great with kids and is probably one of the most experienced interviewers of abused children that we have in the department. I'll see you next week," he said as he hung up.

I immediately dialed Dr. Adams' number hoping to catch him before he left the office.

"Hello, this is Crane Johnson. We just left the office a few minutes ago and I was wondering if Dr. Adams is available for a minute."

"Just a moment Mr. Johnson, I'll put you through," she said.

"Crane, what can I do for you?" Dr. Adams asked.

"I just got the name of the person that is going to interview Joel. It's a Detective Silver. Do you know her?" I queried.

"Yes, I know her. She's very competent and a good looking woman to boot. She'll do a good job. Just make sure that you insist on being present at the interview. Good luck!" he responded.

"Thanks, doctor," I said putting my phone away.

We had just turned onto 281 and started toward home when my cell phone rang. It was my business partner, Eric Olsen.

"Eric is it possible for me to call you back in about 35 or 40 minutes? Traffic is getting heavy and I'd rather not be on the phone while I drive," I said.

"Sure, I'll be at the office. Talk to you then. Bye," he said and hung up.

I wondered what Eric wanted. He had been doing a project for us in Dallas for the past three months so I had not seen or talked to him very much except to say "Hi" as we past in the office when he was in town. Eric was one heck of a good project manager. He had been doing consulting work for over 20 years and helped to found ACC about 15 years ago.

We arrived home before the rest of the boys got home from school. Hildy met us at the back door as we came in from the garage.

"The delivery truck left not ten minutes ago. They got everything set up. They even hooked up the PlayStations," she said.

"Great, let's go check them out," I told Joel.

Joel's eyes were like saucers when we entered his bedroom. He didn't realize that he and TJ were getting a TV for their room. "Is this all ours?" he more pleaded than asked.

"Yep, it sure is. There's one just like it in the twins' bedroom," I said.

"Thanks, Uncle Crane, I don't ever want to leave here. Please!" this time there were tears in his eyes.

"Why don't you turn everything on and see if you can figure it all out before your brothers get home. I'm sure they will need you to help them. You're their big brother and that's what big brothers do," I said giving him a hug before I left to call Eric.

I was starting into my study when Hildy stopped me. "A Detective Silver wants you to call her. She said that it was urgent. I put her number on your desk."

"Thanks," I said disappearing into the study.

I called Eric first. "Eric, it's Crane. What can I do for you?"

"Well now that you asked, you can buy my share of the business," he said.

"What? Are you going to retire or what?" I said completely stunned.

"I guess you could say I was going to retire. I told you a couple of months ago that I was having migraine attacks. Well I finally went and had an MRI and they discovered a tumor the size of a golf ball in my brain. It is inoperable and malignant. The prognosis is not good. We are going to try radiation starting next Wednesday. Even with that, they are not giving me much of a chance. That's why I want to liquidate my part of the business. I want my estate as simple and in order as possible so my wife will not have to worry when I'm not around," he finished.

"Oh my god, Eric, I am so sorry! Is there anything I can do?" I asked stupidly.

"No, I've taken care of almost everything. The business is the last detail I need to handle," he said.

"Of course, I will buy your share of the business. You know I have wanted to every since I bought out the other partners four years ago. Do you have a price in mind?" I said.

"The last audit completed two months ago valued the business at $3.54 million. I don't think the value has changed significantly since then. Unless you want another valuation of the business I would settle for 20% of that which comes to $708,000," he concluded.

"No, that sounds fair. Shall we have Carlos draw up the papers? Since he is familiar with us it would probably be easier if he did it," I said.

"Yes, in fact I have already talked to him and he should have everything drawn up late next week. I'm leaving for Houston on Tuesday and won't be back until Friday. I have to stay in the hospital one day for observation after the radiation treatment. My son will drive us back to San Antonio," he said.

"Good, I'll talk to you on Monday to work out how you want the payment scheduled," I said and hung up.

I immediately called my accountant to find out how I could come up with the money with the least impact on my tax bill. He told me he would look over my assets and let me know.

With that taken care of I decided to call Detective Silver.

"Detective Silver, this is Crane Johnson. My housekeeper told me you called. What can I do for you?"

"Thank you for getting back to me so quickly. As you are aware, your foster son, Joel, is a possible witness to his mother's murder by his father. There is also a report filed by Dr. Greene that he has been subjected to physical and sexual abuse by his father and possibly others. I have been assigned to interview him as part of the investigation and to provide a statement from him to the DA to assist in the prosecution of Mr. Andersen," she said.

"Yes, I'm aware of that. Where and when would you like to interview him?"

"We want to do this as soon as possible. Could you bring him to the police headquarters tomorrow at ten?"

"No, that would be much too traumatic for him. His psychiatrist has advised me the interview should be conducted in familiar surroundings where he doesn't feel threatened. I believe that the best place would be here at the house in my study. He is comfortable here and certainly doesn't feel threatened. I will, of course, be present during the interview."

"Oh no, we can't permit you to sit in on the interview..." she started.

"That's what you think Detective Silver. If you want to talk to Joel, you'll do it with me present or you will not see him at all. Save your breath. That's the way it's going to be," I said with as much determination as I could force into my voice.

"Very well, it's highly irregular but if that's the only way I can get to see him we'll do it that way. I need to video tape the interview so I'll have to transport my equipment."

"I have state of the art video equipment here if you care to use it. Bring your own tape. You are using VHS aren't you?"

"Yes, how do I get to your place?"

I gave her directions and told her I would expect her at ten o'clock tomorrow morning.

I had heard the boys come in from school while I was on the phone so I went to see if they had learned how to use their new toy. Joel had the boys hovering over his back as he showed them how to manipulate the figures on the screen.

When they noticed that I was there, Larry and Lenny ran to me and jumped into my arms and gave me hugs and a kiss on each cheek. "Thanks, Uncle Crane, we didn't know we were getting a TV too. Thanks, you're the neatest!"

"Is Joel teaching you how to play the games?" I asked as I set them down. "How about you TJ, do you think you can learn to play the games?"

"I'll try, it looks fun," he said.

"Now that we are all here I want you to know the rule about playing the video games. You can play them for one hour each school day and only after you have finished your homework. On weekends, Saturday and Sunday, you can play them for two hours. School vacation days are the same as weekends. Do you all understand?" I asked.

"Yes, Uncle Crane," they said in unison.

"If you don't obey the rule then you can't play the games for a whole week. These games can become very addictive and that's all you'll want to do. I want you to have fun playing them but I also want you to do other things as well. Now go back to having Joel show you how to play them. We will make an exception to the rule for tonight since you are just learning how to work them, but starting tomorrow it's two hours," I told them.

I went back to my study to set up the video camera for tomorrow's interview. I tried to position the camera so that it was as unobtrusive as possible and still capture the spot where Joel and I would be sitting. Shortly thereafter, Hildy call the boys and told them to get washed up for supper. I think that it was the first time I had ever heard them complain about getting ready for something to eat, but they knew better than to disobey Hildy.

After we ate I guided Joel into the study.

"Joel, tomorrow a lady is going to come here and wants to talk to you about the things that have been done to you. She also wants to talk about the things that you might have seen the day your mother was hurt. Do you think you can do that?" I asked.

"Do I have to, Uncle Crane?" he asked, his lips beginning to quiver.

"I think that you should. I will be with you all the time. You don't want your dad to hurt you any more do you?"

"No," he said as the tears began to flow.

"It's alright," I said cradling him to my chest. "You can tell her everything that happened. You know I'll always love you and I won't ever let anyone hurt you. You know that don't you?" I asked.

I felt his head nod but he didn't say anything. I continued to hold him and stroked his back. The back that had been so badly beaten the first time I saw him without a shirt. I could still feel the old raised welts as I ran my hands over his back.

"God, I would like to get that son of a bitch alone and see how he would like some of his own medicine," I thought.

"Dry your eyes and go see how your brothers are doing with their new game," I said and kissed him on the forehead.

When eight o'clock came around, I stopped in their rooms and told them to put the games away. I was surprised that they didn't put up a fuss but I think the thoughts of one of Hildy's snacks were even a stronger pull than the video games.

After I got the boys in bed, I turned in also. I knew tomorrow was going to be a difficult day for Joel and I wasn't looking forward to it either.

The boys slept in Saturday morning. It was nearly 8:30 before they started straggling into the kitchen for breakfast. They revived quickly as they wolfed down mounds of scrambled eggs, ham, biscuits and jam along with a gallon or so of orange juice.

As their eating slowed down, I said to them, "A lady is going to come here this morning to talk to Joel. While she is here, I want you guys to be real quiet. You can play your video games or watch TV. I think there are cartoons on that you could watch. I don't want you to go swimming until I can be there to watch you. Do you understand? Good! Now go get your teeth brushed and get dressed. The lady will be here in about an hour."

Shortly before ten the gate buzzer sounded. The security camera showed a car with what looked like two women in it. I activated the gate opener and went out the front door to greet our visitors.

As the car approached the house, I observed that there were actually three women in the car. I was not prepared for a crowd to be present for the interview and was beginning to have second thoughts about it.

The driver stepped out of the car and introduced herself, "Mr. Johnson, I'm Barbara Silver. It's a pleasure to meet you."

Dr. Adams was correct. She was definitely a good looking woman. I was slightly taken aback by her appearance but managed to recover without making a fool of myself.

"Let me introduce Sylvia Brown with the DA's office and you already know Joyce," she said as the other women exited the car.

I shook hands with all the women before turning to Barbara, "I didn't realize that there was going to be a crowd for the interview. I'm not very comfortable with all of this. Is it really necessary?"

"Sylvia needs to be here to determine whether additional criminal charges should be filed based on what results from the interview," Barbara replied.

"I can almost understand that, but I'm not entirely convinced that it is absolutely necessary. What's Joyce's role?" I asked.

Before Barbara could respond, Joyce spoke up, "I'm here to protect the interests of Joel…"

"Yeah, I'm sure," I said with as much sarcasm as I could muster. "Just like you tried to protect the boys at the hearing, if you had been successful the boys would be in some awful group home instead of here where they are loved. Don't talk to me about protecting the boys."

Turning back to Barbara, I said "Give me a good reason why Sylvia has to be physically present at the interview. Wouldn't viewing the video tape provide her with the same information?"

"Yes, it's just that we always have the DA's office present when we do one of these interviews," Barbara said.

Joyce interrupted "Mr. Johnson, those boys are under my protection and I am going to be there for the interview."

"Ms. Gehrig, don't you even think of defying me on this. I will not hesitate to get my lawyer, whom I know you remember, to tie you and CPS up in so many knots and lawsuits that it will take you years to untangle. You know I have the resources and Benjamin Cross has the legal know how to do it. Now I will give you a bone of sorts. I'll let you speak to Joel privately after the interview if, and I stress if, he wants to. Take it or leave it, it's your choice," I almost snarled at her.

"Well…well…I…ah…" she stuttered.

"That's settled. Now let's get back to why Ms. Brown needs to be present," I said turning back to Barbara.

She clearly was shocked at my verbal exchange with Joyce and it took her a moment to recover. Glancing over at Sylvia she said, "What do you think? Do you really have to be there? I think that the atmosphere would be better if we did as Mr. Johnson asks."

"Well, I don't know…," she started.

"Look Ms. Brown, I don't want to be a shit about this but I am very protective of Joel and his brothers. This interview is going to be extremely stressful on him as it is. The bigger the crowd the more stress it will put on him. There is no one who wants to see that scumbag father of his put away more than I do. But I don't want to see Joel hurt any more than he already has been. I don't want to interfere with your duties, but if there is no compelling reason for you to be present then I insist that you not be there," I said.

"Okay, I suppose. I don't like it but if that's the way it has to be then I'll go along with it," Sylvia grumbled.

"Now that all of that is settled, please follow me. Barbara, let me show you my video setup. Joyce and Sylvia, you are welcome to go see the boys. I think they are in their bedrooms playing video games. Ask Hildy to show you the way," I said leading Barbara to the study.

Having satisfied herself that she understood the workings of my video setup, she indicated that she was ready to proceed.

I went to Joel's bedroom and asked him to follow me. His eyes betrayed the fear that he was feeling. I gave him a hug and then looked him straight in the eyes and said, "Don't be afraid. I'll be there with you all the time. Please believe me, I love you and I don't want you to be hurt. This is necessary so that your dad can never do anything bad to you or your brothers again. Do you understand?"

He nodded his head, but he clearly was not happy about what he had to do.

"Barbara, this is my son Joel. Joel this is Barbara Silver," I said as we entered the study.

"I'm very pleased to meet you Joel," she said extending her hand to him.

Joel reached out, took her hand and in a barely audible voice said, "Hi."

CHAPTER 12

"Joel, please come over here. Let me show you what we are going to do. This is a video camera," she said pointing it out to him. "We're going to make a video tape of everything that you or I or Mr. Johnson say while I am asking questions. Have you ever been on video tape before?"

"No," he replied somewhat louder than his last response.

"Would you like to see what you look like on tape?" she asked.

Receiving a nod, she turned the camera to record and pointed it at him for a few seconds. Then rewinding it she removed the tape from the camera and put it in the VCR and played it on the TV monitor.

"Is that really me?" he giggled. "I look funny."

Rewinding the tape and putting it back in the camera she said to him, "Now, while we are talking the camera will be taking our pictures. I will ask you some questions and I want you to answer me the best that you can. If you don't know something just tell me. If you do tell me something, I want you to only tell me the truth. I don't want you to make up anything just to give me an answer. This is not a test. There are no right or wrong answers. Do you understand?"

"Yes," he said.

"Good," Barbara said. "Why don't you go take a seat with Mr. Johnson and we'll get started."

Joel took a seat next to me on the small couch while Barbara took the chair at the end of it forming a sort of "L".

After stating the date, time and place of interview, she said, "Persons present in this interview are Joel Jay Anderson, Mr. Crane Johnson, Joel's foster parent, and Detective Barbara Silver. Joel is the person from whom information is sought.

"Joel, do you promise to tell me the truth and only the truth?"

"Yes, ma'am," he said.

"Joel, Dr. Greene has filed a report saying that you have been beaten on your back. Is that true?"

"Yes, ma'am."

"Tell me who beat you on your back."

"My dad."

"Do you know why he did it?"

"No, every time he got drunk he would whip me," he said moving closer to me and grabbed my hand.

"What did he whip you with?"

"Most of the time with his belt. Sometimes with his hands. A few times with a hanger."

"Was that a wire clothes hanger?"

"Yes, ma'am."

"Did he ever hit you?"

"Yes, ma'am."

"What did he hit you with?"

"His fist. Once he hit me with his shoe."

"Was he holding the shoe or was he wearing it?"

"No he had it in his hand and hit me with the heel."

"Did he ever kick you?"

"Yeah, sometimes when it hurt so bad I'd curl up and he would kick me in the back."

I could see the tears starting to form in his eyes so I reached my arm around him and hugged him. He looked up at me with those beautiful eyes as if begging me to stop this. I leaned down and kissed his forehead before whispering, "It's okay."

Barbara had paused a moment while this was going on but then continued, "Did anyone besides your dad ever hit you or whip you?"

"One of his friends slapped me once."

"Why did he do that?"

"He said I didn't get him his beer fast enough."

"What did your dad do when the man slapped you?"

"Nothing, just laughed."

"Do you know the name of the man who slapped you?"

"I think it was Earl something."

"Did your mother know that your father whipped you?"

"Yes, ma'am."

The tears were now beginning to flow down his cheeks. I had prepared for this and had a box of tissues handy. I gave him one and he dried his eyes.

"Did your mother try to stop your dad from whipping you?"

"Yes, ma'am."

"What happened when she tried to stop it?"

"He would hit her and knock her down," he said with anger in his voice.

"Did your mother ever whip you?"

"No! She tried to make him stop, but she couldn't. She tried! She tried!" his body wracked with sobs.

It took several minutes before Barbara could continue.

"Did anyone ever whip or hit your brothers?"

"Sometimes, if I couldn't hide them he would whip them with the belt. When I saw he was that way I would make them go in the garage or up in the attic. I couldn't let him beat them, they're my brothers and I had to protect them. They're too little. I couldn't…Sometimes if he caught them, I would kick and hit him 'till he let them go. Then he would beat me, but I could take it. They're too little. I just couldn't let him hit them, especially TJ. He's too little. He's my brother, I had to protect him."

"How often did you or your brothers get whipped?"

"Every week. Sometimes more. Every time he got paid. He'd get drunk and then beat me."

"Was it always the same?"

"Not always. If he was really drunk, he couldn't hit me as hard or as long. He would fall down on the floor and I could get away from him and he couldn't catch me."

"Did anyone ever do anything to you that you didn't like besides whipping and hitting you?"

Turning his head into my chest he spoke so softly and with as much pain as I had ever heard in a voice, "Yes, ma'am."

"Who did this?"

"My dad," he said so softly that Barbara asked him to say it again.

"My dad," this time he said it with anger.

"What did he do to you that you didn't like?"

This time he looked up into my eyes with the tears streaming down his cheeks as if to ask "Do I have to?"

"It's okay, son. I love you and nothing that you could say would ever make me stop loving you. I know it is hard but you need to tell Detective Silver about it," I said hoping to keep the quiver out of my voice.

"Joel, I know this is unpleasant for you. Please believe me I don't want to cause you any hurt, but I need as much information as I can get. I need you to speak up and to speak clearly so that everything you say will be on the video tape," Barbara said.

Joel nodded, "Okay."

"What did he do to you that you didn't like?"

"Sometimes he would yell at me, 'Come here you little fag, I'm horny' and grab me by the neck. Then he would make me…uh…Do I have to?"

"You're doing fine. It's okay. Just tell us what happened. Remember you did nothing wrong," I said giving him another hug.

"He would make me unzip his pants and…and…" he started sobbing again.

"Take your time," Barbara said softly.

After a minute or so he regained his composure enough to continue. "He would make me rub my hands up and down on his cock. When it would get real hard he would put it in my mouth and make me suck it," he said sobbing but with anger. "He grabbed my ears and jerked me up and down on it. Sometime I would choke. I would gag and throw up. Then he would really get mad."

"What would he do when he got mad?" Barbara asked.

"He'd hit and kick me. He'd take his belt off and whip me. He'd take all my clothes off and whip me. Then he'd…Oh, I can't tell you! It was awful! Please!"

"It's okay. You're doing fine. Just take your time," I said wiping the tears from his cheeks.

"He'd make me sit on his lap and he'd…he'd…put his dick in my butt and bounce me up and down. It hurt. It hurt so bad I would scream but he just did it anyway. If I screamed too loud he would put his hand over my mouth and nose so I couldn't breathe. When he was done he'd lock me in the shed in the back yard."

"Did he do anything else to you that you didn't like?"

"Sometimes when he was doing it to me he would grab and squeeze me as hard as he could."

"What would he squeeze?"

"My…My dick and balls. It hurt really bad. Sometimes I couldn't walk too good after."

"When did this start? How old were you when this started?" Barbara asked.

"I think I was 10 when he did it to me the first time. He didn't do it very often then. But then it started to be almost every week at the end." The tears were flowing down his cheeks now but he was not sobbing. The tears were more of anger than sadness.

"Did he ever do this to your brothers?"

"He tried a couple of times, but I hit and kicked him until he let them go. He would get really mad and was really rough with me then. He would always hurt me worse when I did that. But after a while, he quit trying to do it with them. I had to protect them. I did. I couldn't let him do it to them. They're my brothers!"

"Did your mother know what he was doing to you?"

"Yes, ma'am. She saw him doing it to me a couple of times. She would scream at him and pound him with her fists. Once he hit her with his fist and she fell down and didn't get up all the time he was doing it to me. I think he knocked her out."

"Did he ever beat your mother?"

"Yes, he would hit her all the time. He was always slapping her on the face or hitting her in the stomach. When I seen him do it I would try to get in his way and keep him from doing it to her. Most of the time he would just beat me, but sometimes he'd lock me in the shed and then start beating her again. I tried to make him stop, I really did! I did!" This time the sobs shook his whole body.

"Joel, you are a brave boy. I know you did everything that you could do to stop your mother from being hurt. I know that she loved you very much. You are my hero! I love you even more then I did before you told me this. I didn't think that was possible, but I do," I said as I began to sob along with him.

Barbara waited a few minutes before she asked her next question. "Do you know what happened to your mother?"

"Yes, ma'am."

"Would you tell me about it?"

"He shot her in the face."

"Who shot her in the face?"

"My dad."

"How do you know he shot her?"

"I saw him do it."

"Tell me how it happened."

"I don't know. He came home on Thursday. He was drunk and saying he got fired. He started to beat momma. I tried to stop him. He stopped beating momma and started beating me. Then he did it to me again. This time it hurt really bad. When he was done, he locked me in the shed. He said I was a goddamn fag and he was going to fuck it out of me later. I was scared. I had been digging a hole in the ground at the back of the shed every time he locked me in there. I kept digging most of the night. I didn't have anything to dig with except my hands and a sharp stick. I could hear momma and him arguing. He was screaming and yelling at her. I was almost done with my hole but I was so tired I had to rest. When I woke up I could hear them arguing some more. I think it was almost noon. It was dark in the shed so I couldn't tell. I finished digging my hole and crawled out of the shed. I sneaked into the house through the back door. They were still arguing. I heard her say she was going to go to the police and report him. He said if she did he was going to kill her. I saw him go back into their bedroom and came out with his gun. He said for momma to shut the fuck up or he would shoot her."

He had said all of this almost without taking a breath. It was as if he wanted to get it all out at once so it would be over with. Instead, he broke down again at this point. His sobbing was uncontrollable. I held him to my chest and rocked him as I stroked his back.

Maybe five minutes later, which seemed like an hour, he regained his composure enough that Barbara thought she could continue.

"What happened then?"

"He...He shot the gun a couple of times at her face. She fell down on her back and I saw him shoot her four more times right in the head. There was blood everywhere. I must have screamed because he turned to look at me. He pointed the gun at me and it clicked three times. There were no more bullets in it."

Turning to face me he asked, "Why weren't there any bullet holes in momma's face at the funeral, Uncle Crane?"

I didn't want to go into any gory details so I just answered, "They fixed them at the funeral home."

"Oh."

"Go on Joel, did anything else happen?" Barbara asked.

"When he saw that there wasn't any bullets left in the gun he grabbed me by the throat and said if I ever talked to anybody about what I saw he would rip my throat out so I couldn't talk. He threw me against the wall so hard that he almost knocked me out. Then he ran out the door and I heard the car roar down the street. I think I stood looking at momma down there on the floor and just cried. I remember going outside and screaming at the top of my lungs. I don't remember anything else until Uncle Crane asked me to go to

McDonald's with him. I didn't even know where I was. Every time I tried to talk, nothing came out."

"Thank you Joel. I think that will do it for now," Barbara said as she got up to switch off the camera and remove the tape.

"I am so proud of you, Joel. I know that it was very difficult for you to relive all of this," I said giving him a big hug and kissing the top of his head. Remembering that Joyce wanted to speak to him I said, "Ms. Gehrig would like to talk to you for a few minutes, okay?"

"Do I have to?" he asked.

"No, that is entirely up to you. If you want to talk to her that is fine. If you don't want to talk to her that is also fine. It's your choice," I said.

"I don't want to talk to her. She would have let the judge take us away. I don't like her," he said burying his face in my chest.

"That's okay, I'll tell her. Let's go see if Hildy has started lunch, I'm hungry," I told him.

The thought of food seem to brighten his mood. He jumped up, grabbed my hand and literally dragged me to the door.

Hildy was in the kitchen preparing mountains of ham salad and egg salad sandwiches to go with the big pot of tomato soup that was just coming to a simmer on the stove.

"Hildy," I said "Joel would like to eat a little early. I know it's only 11:30 but he missed his morning snack and I think he might starve if he doesn't get something to eat quickly."

She grinned at my little joke and then said to him, "You go get your hands washed and I'll get a plate set for you."

Joyce came into the kitchen as Joel rushed by her to wash his hands.

"Where is he going? I want to talk to him," she said.

"He is getting cleaned up for lunch to answer your question. As far as the second comment, he doesn't want to talk to you. He said that you would have let the judge take him away. I guess that he can tell a spineless bureaucrat when he sees one," I said with a little more venom in my voice that I had intended.

"I suppose that you have been bad mouthing me to the boys. The twins would hardly talk to me and every time I tried to talk to TJ he would hide behind one of his brothers," she replied.

"No, you are wrong. I have never said anything about you one way or another in front of the boys. For someone who works with children, you seem remarkably out of tune with them. Joel is an extremely bright and perceptive boy. He can read a person very quickly and I think he had you pegged from your first visit. I think that he has shared that read of you with his brothers. Joel protected his brothers from as much physical abuse by their dad as he could and he is still trying to protect them from you and the system that you represent. To you these boys are just another case to be handled. You have no feelings for them as human beings. I do and I'll be damned if I'll let you and the system ruin the lives of four of the most loveable and well behaved boys I have ever known," I said.

"But, I'm responsible for them," she sputtered. "I could have them taken away from you in a minute."

"You just try it. I will have you investigated so thoroughly that by the time I get done with you I will know how much money the Tooth Fairy left under your pillow for your baby teeth. If you think that you can withstand that kind of scrutiny, go ahead, give it your best shot," I said through gritted teeth.

Her blush at the thought of that type of background check told me she wouldn't follow through on her threat.

"Damn, I'm getting to be a pushy bastard," I thought.

Joel bounced back into the room followed by the twins and TJ.

"Can we eat too? We're hungry," TJ asked looking at Hildy.

"Yes, did you wash your hands?" she asked.

Getting a nod from everyone, she started putting plates and bowls on the table. The mountain of sandwiches that she had fixed started to dwindle before our eyes. The soup disappeared almost as quickly.

Turning back to Joyce I said, "If you, Sylvia and Barbara would like to stay for lunch you are more than welcome. I believe that Hildy has made more than enough."

Barbara came into the kitchen as I was making the offer to Joyce. She said, "Thank you so much for the offer, but I have to get back to the office. I have one more interview to do this afternoon."

As I escorted the ladies to the door, Barbara turned to me and said, "Thank you for your support during the interview. Without you displaying your genuine support and affection for Joel, I'm sure that the interview would have been much longer and not as productive. I've got enough information on the tape to charge Mr. Andersen with numerous crimes up to and including premeditated murder. That boy is very remarkable. I can see why you are so attached to him. I don't know many adults who would sacrifice themselves to protect the ones they love like he did. His brothers are very lucky to have him around."

"I am lucky, too. Just having them around has changed my life for the better. Thank you for being so gentle with him in the interview. He is more fragile than he shows. His psychiatrist says that he will need psychological support for some time," I said taking her extended hand and shaking it.

"She is a very good looking woman," I thought to myself still holding her hand. All too soon she gave her hand a tug reminding me that I still had it in my grasp. I hadn't noticed before but she was not wearing a wedding ring. "Hmm."

I activated the gate to let them out before stepping outside. I watched them all the way down the lane and off the property.

As I entered the front door, I was met by Hildy. She walked up to me, put her arms around and gave me a hug.

"Thank you for standing up to her and not letting her take our boys away. They deserve the opportunity that you can give them. They also need to feel safe. They can here," she said giving me another hug.

CHAPTER 13

Joel was quiet the rest of the day. All he seemed to want to do is to sit next to me. It was as though he needed the physical contact. I wished that I could take away the hurt and embarrassment that I'm sure he felt from the interview earlier. All I could do was to put my arms around him and keep him close showing him how much I loved him.

The twins realized that something was different with Joel. They seemed to know instinctively that he needed their love also. In their uncanny mirror image way they came up to him, hugged him and planted a kiss on each of his cheeks, not saying anything. No words were necessary.

TJ was a little confused. He didn't know what to do. He tried to get Joel to go with him and play his video game. When Joel didn't respond, TJ climbed into my lap and said, "Why is Joel sad?"

"He just needs some time to think, little one. He'll be okay tomorrow," I told him. "Give him a kiss and go play with Larry and Lenny."

"Okay," he said kissing Joel on the cheek.

Night came and I sent the boys off to get their showers taken and ready for bed. Soon they were back all freshly scrubbed and dressed in their pajamas. TJ crawled up in my lap and whispered in my ear, "Joel wants to sleep in your bed tonight. Can I too?"

"We'll see, little one," I whispered back to him.

"Joel, come here please," I said.

He shuffled over to the couch where I was sitting with TJ and sat down beside us. "TJ says that you want to sleep in my bed tonight. Is that true?"

"Uh...Yes, can I?" he said in a barely audible voice.

"What about TJ? Do you want him to sleep with us too?" I asked.

"Oh, yeah, he can't sleep alone. He gets scared by himself," Joel answered.

"Alright, I think it would be okay for tonight," I said. "You guys go jump in bed. I'll go get your brothers tucked in and then I'll be in for you."

The twins were very understanding about Joel and TJ sleeping with me tonight.

"Joel is sad today," Larry said.

"He needs somebody to hold him," Lenny added.

"You guys are great. I guess that's why I love you so much," I said kissing each one in turn on the forehead and tucked them in bed.

I was surprised to see Joel in the middle of the bed. I just assumed that TJ would occupy that position. But I guess that he needed the closeness of both TJ and me. I quickly got ready for bed and climbed in. Leaning over I gave TJ a goodnight kiss on the forehead before starting to give Joel the same.

Instead, he threw his arm around my neck and gave me a kiss on the cheek. "I love you, Uncle Crane. Thank you for staying with me today. I never want to leave here," he said emotionally.

"I love you, both of you. I hope that you never have to leave until you go to college which is a long way off," I replied. "Now let's get some sleep." With that, I gave him a kiss, laid down and turned off the light.

No sooner were the lights out then Joel scooted over and wrapped both hands around my bicep and rested his head against my shoulder. Although this was not the most comfortable position for me to sleep in, I knew he needed the closeness of contact with someone he felt safe.

When I woke up it was beginning to get light outside. Joel still had his hands around my bicep and TJ was snuggled up against his back. I gently removed his hands from my arm and began my morning routine.

Hildy entered the kitchen just as I poured my first cup of coffee. "How is he this morning? He seemed so quiet and withdrawn yesterday."

"He was still asleep when I got up. He and TJ slept in my bed last night. Joel held on to me all night long. I hope he recovers today. It kills me to see him like this. He is such a joyful child usually," I said.

"Oh, I'm sure he will. He's a strong youngster. I'm sure he'll snap back," Hildy replied.

The rest of Sunday was fairly normal. Joel seemed to be recovering but was still quieter than usual. The boys wanted to go fishing so after lunch we drove to the marina and took the boat out again. We didn't catch any fish. There were too many jet-skis and noisy motor boats for the fish to bite. They still enjoyed themselves and didn't complain when I sent them to bed shortly after sunset.

After getting the boys sent off on the school bus Monday morning, I took off to the school to have a conference with the twins' teacher. I was disturbed by their report that Mr. Lansing was touching them and making them uncomfortable. I wanted to stop any inappropriate contact before it got out of hand even if I didn't intend for them to be enrolled here very much longer.

It was barely 8 o'clock when I reached the school. I hoped that he would be available before the boys got off the bus. As I entered the building, I saw the attendance clerk that I had met on my previous visit. I inquired of her if Mr. Lansing was available. She called over the intercom and shortly he appeared at the office.

"Mr. Lansing, I'm Crane Johnson, Larry and Lenny Andersen are my foster sons. I would like to talk to you for a moment if possible. Is there some place we can speak privately?" I asked.

"Yes, let's go into the conference room," he replied.

I got right to the point as we sat down at a small table. "Mr. Lansing, Larry and Lenny have told me that they are uncomfortable with the touching they receive from you. I am not implying that there is anything inappropriate going on, at least not yet. These boys come from an abusive home. They were abused physically and possibly sexually. I will not let that happen to them again. Am I making myself clear?"

"Ah…I…Yes," he stammered and blushed a bright red.

"Just so we understand each other. I don't plan to discuss this with anyone else unless I am given a reason to. I hope that Larry and Lenny were misinterpreting your actions. Just don't give me a reason to interpret them otherwise." Standing up I shook his very warm and sweaty hand and left.

I wanted to leave before the school bus with the boys arrived. They would wonder why I didn't drive them to school.

Paul had arrived to start Joel's lesson by the time I returned. I took a seat at the breakfast bar and began making phone calls. The first was to Carlos, our company attorney, to see what kind of payment schedule that Eric had in mind for the purchase of his share of the business.

"Good morning Carlos, it's Crane. How are you doing?" I asked.

"I'm doing great!" he responded exactly the same as he always did when asked.

"I talked to Eric on Friday about his selling the portion of the business that he owns but never discussed what kind of payment schedule he was looking for. If he takes it all in a lump sum the tax bite is going to be horrendous," I said.

"No he wouldn't want to do that. He has set up a trust for the money to be paid into over five years. He wants $208,000 up front and will accept a non-interest bearing note for $500,000 to be paid in $100,000 increments at the end of each of the next five years. That way he relinquishes all interest in running the company and provides for his wife in case his treatment is not successful. Does that sound all right to you?" he finished.

"That's more than fair," I said. "I need to get in touch with my accountant to let him know what he has to plan for. Thanks, Carlos, when do you think you will have everything drawn up for our signatures?"

"I told Eric that I would have everything ready by Friday. I am somewhat skeptical as to whether he will be in any condition to sign a contract then, but I will have the contract ready by that time. I don't think it would hurt to wait until next Monday. It just depends on how he is feeling. My only worry is if he is under some kind of medication whether the contract could be called into question at some later date by his heirs," Carlos said.

Next, I called my accountant to let him know what he needed to prepare for as far as cash I would need to purchase Eric's share of the business. Gerald Cousins was my accountant, financial advisor and tax consultant all rolled into one.

After I explained to him what Eric wanted, he pondered a bit before saying, "Look Crane, I think if we structure this right you could write this off as an expense of the business and not a personal expense. That way it could be deducted from income before taxes were figured, thus lowering ACC's tax bill. Let me work on this a bit. I don't think it will take too much effort and I'll pass it by Carlos just to see what he thinks of it before we actually do it."

"Gerald, you are a sneaky bastard," I chuckled. "I guess that's why I hired you. Go ahead and see what you can work out. I'm in your hands. Just make sure it's legal and above board. Texas prisons are not what I consider prime vacation spots."

Joel came skipping into the kitchen on his break from Paul's tutoring. "Hi, Uncle Crane, you're back."

"Yes I am," I said as he jumped up on the stool with me. "Are you feeling better today?"

"Yeah, I guess I do. Mr. Coulter's classes are always fun. Can I have a cookie and a glass of milk?" he asked hopping down and going to the refrigerator.

"Sure, I think Hildy baked some sugar cookies while we were fishing yesterday. Will a couple do?" I asked foolishly. I knew it would take at least four to fill his bottomless pit.

"Well, maybe a couple more," he said giggling.

It did my heart good to hear him laughing again. I guess I experienced what all parents do when one of their children is not feeling well and there is nothing they can do about it. It's the sense of inadequacy that's so frustrating. All I could do was to show my love for him and hope with all my might that he would pull through his depression quickly.

Joel went back to his classes and I went back to making my phone calls. My next one was to Corinthian Academy to set up an appointment for the boys to be tested and interviewed for possible enrollment there. I reached Mr. Pierce's secretary and the appointment was set for Wednesday morning at nine o'clock. The testing and interviews would take the entire morning.

I had no more than cradled the phone's receiver when it rang. When I pick it up it was Benjamin Cross.

"I just thought I would update you on what is going on in regards to Judge Frank. I have filed complaints with the Texas Bar and the Judicial Review Board concerning his conduct on the bench. I have also convinced four other lawyers who regularly practice before him to file complaints. They were hesitant to do so until I used a little persuasion. I refer a number of cases to them every year and I suggested that gravy train might derail if they didn't report his courtroom conduct with them. I'm not sure it will accomplish anything. These boards are made up of lawyers who are more interested in sweeping dirt under the rug then they are in rooting out unprofessional and unethical conduct. If they choose to do nothing we always have the press," he said with a malicious chuckle.

"Thanks for the info," I responded. "Have you heard whether the transcript has reached Judge Yates as ordered?"

"I haven't heard anything yet. I should know something by noon. We won't have anything from her until Wednesday or Thursday at the earliest. I'll keep you informed," he said and rang off.

I decided that I had taken care of all the business that I need to so I changed into my swim suit and went to do some laps. It had been a few days since I really had a good workout in the pool. I think I have only had one since the boys arrived. I could tell it after the first 15 minutes. I was starting to hurt in places that I hadn't in years. 15 more minutes and I was afraid they would have to drag me out of the pool if I didn't stop. Climbing out of the pool, I toweled off and stretched out in a chaise lounge. I hadn't been there 5 minutes when Paul came to the door to tell me I had an urgent phone call.

"Who in the world could that be?" I wondered aloud.

Picking up the phone in the kitchen, I was greeted by the attendance clerk at the boys' school.

"Mr. Johnson, is it possible for you to pick up your sons from school? They're fine. We had an incident here at the school and are sending all the children home whose parents we can reach," she said.

"Of course, I'll be there in about 20 minutes. What happened? Can you tell me what's going on?" I asked very much worried.

"No, not right now. I'll let your sons know you will be here to pick them up soon. Thanks! Goodbye," she said and hung up.

I grabbed a pair of shorts and polo shirt slipped on a pair of sandals and was out the door in less than a minute. On the way out, I yelled to Paul that I would be back in about 45 minutes. I didn't exactly observe the speed limits as I rushed to the school. Thankfully, the local constabulary was otherwise engaged or I could have faced serious fines. It was just under 15 minutes from the time I got the call until I drove into the parking lot at the school. Jumping out of the car, I raced to the principal's office.

The office was crowded with parents all wanting to know what was going on. The local sheriff was there also trying to calm everyone down and at the same time refusing to say what the problem was that caused the school to shut down. After I gave my name and the names of the boys to one of the parent volunteers who checked me off the parent list, another one went to bring them to the office.

I decided to wait outside the office to avoid the hubbub inside. I had been waiting a couple of minutes when a deputy that I knew from little league approached.

"Hey Jesse, what's going on? What's happened?" I asked.

"Crane, I haven't seen you in a long time. Well, don't tell anyone I said anything but one of the teachers died here at the school," he said.

"Oh?" I more looked the question than asked.

"Yeah, it was kind of messy and we don't want the kids to see. I can't say anymore," he said.

Just then, the parent volunteer returned with the three boys.

TJ broke away from the volunteer, ran to me and jumped up and grabbed me around the neck. "What's up, Uncle Crane?" he asked giving me a hug.

"Yeah," the twins chimed in as they joined our embrace.

"I don't really know guys. Let's go home. Maybe there will be something on the news," I told them leading the way to the car.

After getting everyone safely belted in, we started home at a much more leisurely pace. The twins started to make that strange humming noise that they seem to do every so often.

"Larry, Lenny, what's going on? Did something happen in school today that I should know about?" I asked looking in the rearview mirror.

"Yeah," Larry said. "Mr. Lansing was really strange."

"Yeah strange," Lenny chimed in.

"How do you mean strange?" I asked.

"Well, you know, he was all nervous and couldn't talk right," Lenny said.

"Yeah and he kept dropping things. He even put his head down on the desk," Larry said.

"It looked like he was crying sometimes," Lenny added.

"Anything else?" I asked.

"Well after recess he didn't come back in the class," Larry said.

"The principal came in and she said he was sick," Lenny said.

"Thanks guys, I'll bet that Hildy will have some sugar cookies and milk for you when we get home. How does that sound?" I asked.

"YEA!" they all yelled together and give each other high fives.

Hildy met us at the back door as we arrived. She gave and received a hug from each of the boys before they ran into their bedrooms to change clothes.

"I heard on the local radio station that their school was being let out for the day so I called a friend who works at the administration building," she said stopping to gather herself. "She said that one of the teachers had an accident. Did you find out anything while you were there?"

"I talked to one of the deputy sheriffs. He said that a teacher died and it was messy. He didn't say who or how but I have a good idea who it was," I said.

"Who?" she asked.

"Well, I'm not certain but I think it was the twins' teacher, Mr. Lansing. They said that he didn't come back to class after recess and the principal said he was sick. I think that's a pretty good indication.

"I just had a talk with him this morning about the twins' uneasiness with his touching them. He seemed to be a little shook up about our talk. I told him my suspicions would not be related to anyone else unless I had further cause," I paused as all four of the boys piled into the kitchen. "Oh, I told them they might get some sugar cookies and milk when they got home."

"Okay, little ones, just a couple. Lunch will be ready in about an hour and I don't want to spoil your appetites," she laughed at the thought of anything spoiling their appetites.

I went into the study to talk to Paul to see if he had any connections with either the school or the sheriff's office to get any more information on this morning's events. Since he didn't, I decided to call Jack to see if the SAPD had heard anything. He wasn't available so I left a message for him to call me back.

Joel finished his lessons with Paul while TJ and the twins played with their truck and cars on the patio. After lunch, I gave Joel his math lesson. The boys didn't seem to be too upset about the school situation and I wanted to keep it that way.

Around two o'clock Jack returned my call.

"Crane, what can I do for you? They told me you called," he said.

"Thanks for getting back to me. There was an incident at the elementary school that I would like more information on if you can get it for me," I said. I went on to describe to him what I knew and what I suspected. "Have you heard anything?"

"No, I don't know anything about it. You said that you talked to Jesse and that he seemed to know what was going on. Maybe I can get something out of him that he wouldn't tell you. I'll give him a buzz and see if I can use my powers of persuasion to get the story," he said. "I'll call you back."

The rest of the afternoon was spent with the boys in the pool playing king of the hill again. That is until the hill got tired. I had already swum laps for a half an hour earlier this morning so it didn't take long for the hill to get worn down.

Shortly before Hildy called the boys in to get washed and dressed for supper, Jack called back.

"Crane, this is very disturbing. Jesse didn't want to tell me anything but I was able to persuade him. You had better be sitting down. What I have to tell you is not pretty. Are you ready?" he asked.

"Yes, I think so," I replied. "Go ahead."

CHAPTER 14

"You were right about it being Lansing. Several of the teachers also reported that he was acting strangely this morning. Maybe I should say they said he was acting stranger than usual this morning. Anyway, since he didn't have recess duty today he went to the teachers' lounge during that time period. He chatted with a couple of the other teachers who were also free but seem to be distracted. After a few minutes, he got up and went into the restroom in the lounge. Nobody paid any attention for a while until someone noticed that he hadn't come out and it was time for his class to return from recess.

"One of the teachers knocked on the restroom door and called his name but she got no response. After several tries, she contacted the office via the intercom. The principal arrived and she attempted to get a response. She tried several times with no results so she called on the custodian to open the door with his master key. That's when they discovered what had happened.

"They found him slumped on the floor in a pool of blood. He had slit both wrists and his throat. He bled to death in minutes," Jack concluded.

"Oh, my god!" I groaned. "I can't believe that he did this just because I confronted him with the twins feeling uncomfortable with his touching."

"No, Crane, don't feel like you were the cause of all of this. There's more to the story. When the sheriff went to his apartment, they found even more shocking material. It appears that this guy was a big time pedophile. There were all kinds of child pornography all neatly categorized according to age, sex and sexual activity. There were books, magazines, photos, CD's, DVD's, tapes and disks. Some of the photos and video tapes were of him and various kids who appeared to be anywhere from 5 or 6 to the mid teens. None appeared to be over 15. The sheriff's office is now trying to identify the kids in the pictures.

A couple of them have already been identified and their parents are going to be contacted.

"There is another individual in some of the tapes that they are also trying to identify. They know someone else had to be involved because the camera was being operated by someone while Lansing was sexually assaulting his victims. This guy was one sick puppy," Jack said.

"What should I do? Should I go to the sheriff and report my conversation with him this morning?" I asked.

"Yes, I think that would be wise. They probably already know that you spoke with him this morning. It is probably best if you call them rather than wait for them to call you," he advised.

"Thanks, Jack I'll give them a call as soon as I hang up."

"Hey Crane, are you going to be able to be at practice tomorrow? It's the last one before the final game of the season this Friday."

"I don't know of anything that will prevent me from being there. See you then. Bye," I said hanging up.

I had just dialed the sheriff's office when Hildy announced that supper was ready. "I'll be there in a couple of minutes. I need to talk to the sheriff's office for a minute. If you want, go ahead and get the boys started and I'll be there as soon as I can," I said.

"I'll try to hold them off for a few minutes," she chuckled.

Just then the sheriff's office answered.

"Hi, this is Crane Johnson. I may have some information regarding the suicide at the elementary school today. If possible, I'd like to come in tomorrow morning and relate it," I told the deputy who answered.

"Yes, Mr. Johnson we would like to talk to you. Could you be here around nine?" he asked.

"I will be there," I said.

My next priority was supper.

Afterwards, I call the twins aside. I wanted to try to get any information that they might have about other kids who might have had "contact" with Mr. Lansing.

I started out by asking them how they liked school and got the expected response of "fine". I also asked them if they had made any new friends to which they responded with more information and numbers and names.

"Do any of your new friends dislike Mr. Lansing touching them?" I asked.

They looked at each other before Larry answered "Yeah, a couple of them do. Joey hates it. That's why he stays home sometimes."

"He tells his mother that he don't feel so good and she lets him stay home some," Lenny added.

"How about any of the girls?" I asked.

"Once Sissy said he put his hand on her bottom but she pushed it away," Lenny said.

"Do you know if anyone has ever gone to his apartment?" I asked hoping that they didn't.

"Phil said he did. He's in sixth grade. I don't believe him. He's always bragging," Larry said.

"Thanks guys! Go get your homework done and then you can play your video games if you want. Let me know if you need any help...on your homework, not the video games," I said giving each a hug and a pop on the behind as they left to get their homework started.

I didn't tell the boys but I wasn't going to send them to school tomorrow. I wanted to keep them motivated to do their homework before I told them. Wednesday they wouldn't be going in the morning because of the appointments at Corinthian Academy.

The evenings were becoming fairly routine. After eating, they did their homework. After homework, they played video games or played outside. After play time, they had their snack. After the snack, it was bath time. After the bath, it was time for bed. We were a family with a set routine to follow and it felt good.

Tuesday morning I told the boys at breakfast that they could stay home from school today. In fact, I had seen on the morning news that the school was closed until Wednesday. They were a little startled but accepted the fact that they were going to have a school holiday. It was not really a holiday that I had in mind for them. I was going to speak to Paul when he came about giving attention to their lessons as well as Joel's.

When Paul arrived, I asked him if he could provide a structured environment for TJ and the twins. I told him I didn't expect him to actually teach them their regular classes, but I suggested a reading or possibly a writing assignment that could occupy them while he concentrated on Joel's regular lessons.

I was off to the sheriff's office to give them my statement concerning my meeting with Mr. Lansing on Monday morning. Deputy Jesse Cantu greeted me as I entered.

"Hey Crane, how you doing this morning?" Jesse asked.

"Just fine Jesse. Are you going to take my statement?" I asked.

"Yep, I sure am," he said. "Let's go into the interview room and we can get this over with."

I related to him the brief meeting that I had with Lansing in as much detail as I could remember. I could repeat it almost verbatim since it was so short and I did all of the talking. When I finished the retelling of my meeting with him, I told Jesse what the twins had indicated about Joey and Sissy. He was much more interested in the information that I related about Phil in sixth grade. It wasn't much but I guess it gave them someone to begin with that might have more information.

When I returned home, I found all four of the boys engrossed in a geography lesson that Paul was giving to Joel. I guess the world, its peoples and how it works is fascinating no matter what your age.

I told Paul when he finished the lesson that I would take the other boys off his hands and he could continue with Joel.

"It was kind of fun," he said. "They were perfect gentlemen and I think they were interested in the lesson. They even asked a few questions that I would have expected from kids of Joel's age. I thoroughly enjoyed it."

The boys devoured the last of the sugar cookies along with a gallon of milk for their morning snack. When they finished I asked TJ and the twins if they would like to have me read them a story. I was surprised at the positive reaction from them. In fact, they nearly bowled me over with their enthusiasm.

"Momma used to read us stories," TJ said.

"Yeah!" echoed the twins.

"Well let's see, Joel just finished *Tom Sawyer*, how about I read you that book?" I asked.

"Joel really liked that one," Larry said.

"Okay, you guys go into the family room and I'll get the book and join you," I said.

Settling in on the couch with a twin on either side of me and TJ on my lap, I opened the book and began to read.

Chapter I

"*TOM!*"
No answer.
"*TOM!*"
No answer.
"*What's gone with that boy, I wonder? You TOM!*"
No answer.

> *The old lady pulled her spectacles down and looked over them about the room; then she put them up and looked out under them. She seldom or never looked through them for so small a thing as a boy; they were her state pair, the pride of her heart, and were built for "style", not service—she could have seen through a pair of stove-lids just as well. She looked perplexed for a moment, and then said, not fiercely, but still loud enough for the furniture to hear:*
> *"Well, I lay if I get hold of you I'll—"*
> *She did not finish, for by this time she was bending down and punching under the bed with the broom, and so she needed breath to punctuate the punches with. She resurrected nothing but the cat.*
> *"I never did see the beat of that boy!"* [1]

Reading these words to the boys brought back wonderful memories of the first time I read *Tom Sawyer*. I must have been just a little bit older than Larry and Lenny. We had just moved back to West Texas from Venezuela. Some of the words may have been strange to the boys but they listened intently.

I read to them for about an hour before I detected that they were becoming a little restless. Also, my legs were beginning to go numb from TJ sitting on my lap for so long.

"I think that is enough for right now. My voice is getting a little tired. Let's take a break," I suggested.

Break to the boys meant snack. This time though Hildy was guarding the refrigerator.

"It's getting too close to lunch. You may have a glass of juice," she told them.

Their faces clearly showed the disappointment they were feeling but accepted what they could get and took the offering and went outside to look for the deer.

When Paul finished his tutoring of Joel, I told him about the boys' appointment with Corinthian Academy for the morning.

"Oh, I'm so glad," he said which surprised me. "I didn't know how to tell you but they have asked me to fill in for one of their teachers who will be taking maternity leave for the rest of the year starting Monday. I'm sure from what I have observed that the boys will have no problem passing their entrance exams and interview. I'll be teaching both seventh and eighth grade subjects so I will probably have Joel in a couple of my classes."

"That sounds like a great opportunity for you. I know that Joel has really enjoyed your teaching. He said that you make it fun for him. That's important in making kids want to learn. I hope that the boys will be able to attend Corinthian. This thing with the public school really has me upset. I don't want the boys going back there," I told him.

"Good luck tomorrow," he said as he left. "I'll see you again on Thursday."

After lunch, I gave Joel his math class while the other boys played outside. TJ played with his Tonka truck hauling rocks from the side yard onto the patio. Larry and Lenny played with their radio controlled cars until the batteries ran down. It looks like I had better stock up on batteries the way they are starting to go through them.

"Guys, I have to go to little league practice in about an hour. You can either stay here with Hildy and play or you can come with me to practice," I told them. "Which do you want to do?"

TJ was the first to reply, "I wanta go!"

"Me too!" the twins said in stereo.

"Okay, go put on some shorts, tee shirts and tennies so that you will be ready to go when I am," I said.

They took off like a shot to change. I did too.

When we had practice either Jack or I brought something for the kids to snack on during a break we gave them about halfway through the practice session. Today was my turn. Since I hadn't warned Hildy to prepare anything, I would have to stop at H.E.B. or someplace to pick something up. I'm sure the boys wouldn't mind.

I grabbed my ice chest as we headed out the door so I could ice down some sodas when we got to the ballpark. Shopping for snacks with four excited boys was an experience. They wanted everything that they saw. We settled for several different types of cookies, soft drinks and some bottled water. A couple bags of ice and we were off to practice, but not before adding a couple four packs of batteries.

The boys were excited when we got to the ballpark. They had made friends with some of the team the last time they were here for a game. That seemed like ages ago but it was really less than two weeks. They helped me get the drinks ready by ripping the cartons open and putting the cans in the cooler, while I layered in the ice. It was a good thing we had some time before the drinks were to be consumed because of all the shaking they received by the boys in carrying out their part of the process.

"Thanks, guys. You were a big help," I told them. "Now you can help me get the equipment out of the shed."

They made short work of hauling the equipment out of the shed while I marked the lines and batter's box. Everything was ready by the time Jack and the first kid arrived.

Larry and Lenny were playing catch with each other waiting on the rest of the team to arrive. Jack and I stood there watching as my little left hander threw one wicked pitch after another to his brother.

"That twin has a good arm for a nine year-old," he said.

"That's Lenny. I didn't know he could throw either," I replied.

"We'll have to recruit him next year," he chuckled. "That is if we're still doing this next year. This sure takes a lot of time I could be spending with my kids. Now you with "your four" it's really going to be a struggle. At least I have a wife to help me with my kids."

"Yeah, I'm just beginning to realize how much time they require. And I haven't been working for over two weeks. I hope things settle down after I get them enrolled in Corinthian. With me buying out Eric's share of the business, I'm going to need to spend more time at the office," I said.

When we started practice, my four joined right in with the rest of the team. We did some stretching exercises and ran the bases twice to get warmed up. TJ was pooped by the time he got around the bases the second time and decided he needed to sit down for a while. He was our one man cheering section for the first half of practice.

I think everyone was ready when we took our break. The cookies and soft drinks disappeared faster than the boys ran the bases earlier.

Jack pitched batting practice with four of the team in the outfield to shag the fly balls. After the batter took his eight pitches, he replaced one of the outfielders who then took a place in line to bat. This rotation continued until everyone got to bat twice.

While all this was going on Larry and Lenny were talking to one of the smaller members of the team. Chris Martin was pretty good at the bat and could run like the wind but he had a terrible glove and couldn't throw a ball thirty feet. He was ten years old but was the same height as the twins and they were not tall for their age.

I knew I was in for something when the twins approached me and put their arms around my waist and looked up at me with those beautiful azure eyes.

"Can Chris come home with us and stay all night? Please?" Larry pleaded.

"But, it's a school night. Why don't we wait until Friday after the game? That way he can bring some clothes to change and he can ask his parents," I offered.

"But…But, his mom and dad are gone," Lenny said.

"What do you mean they're gone?" I asked.

"He said that they didn't come home last night and they weren't there when he got home from school," Larry said.

"Please, he's scared to stay there all by himself," Lenny added.

"I'll tell you what. We'll drive Chris to his house and see if there's anyone at home. If there's no one there, we'll decide what we should do. Is that okay?" I asked.

"Okay!" the stereophonic twins answered.

Walking over to Jack I said, "It looks like we might have a little problem. The twins want to take Chris home with them because he tells them his folks have not been home since yesterday."

"What are you going to do?" he asked.

I told him what the twins and I had discussed and then added, "Jack, I really don't need another boy to take care of. I'm not sure I can handle what's on my plate right now. What about his school?"

"Well if he is in SAISD (San Antonio Independent School District) there is a teachers' workshop tomorrow and he won't have to go to school," he said with a grin.

"Thanks Jack, you're a lot of help. I suppose one night won't hurt if his folks are not home. I have to take the kids to Corinthian Academy tomorrow morning and while they're there I can try to find his parents. Will you check to see if they are in jail or dead or whatever?" I asked. "Have you got time to take the team to McDonald's? If you do I'll give you the money to pay the bill and enough to cover last Friday's feeding."

"Yeah, Carolyn is not expecting me until later," he said.

"Good," I said counting out the money. "Then you will have time to put all the equipment away."

Turning to the boys I called to them "Come on guys, let's go. You too Chris!"

All five of them ran to the Land Rover and climbed in and buckled up before I even got there.

"Where do you live Chris?" I asked as I climbed in and started the Land Rover.

He gave me an address that I recognized was about 5 or 6 blocks from the ballpark.

When we got to the house, it did not look good. There was a sheriff's eviction notice posted on the front door and everything was padlocked up tight. That pretty much determined what we were going to do. I got out my cell phone and called Hildy to prepare her for another mouth to feed for supper and then took off for Canyon Lake. I was beginning to feel like I was running a home for strays, very lovable strays.

---

[1] Mark Twain, The Adventures of Tom Sawyer (New York and London: Harper and Brothers, 1903), 16.

CHAPTER 15

The ride home was noisy but uneventful. It seemed like everyone was talking at once and nobody was listening. It was still music to my ears to hear how full of joy their voices were.

The car had barely come to a stop when all five of them hopped out and ran into the house. Hildy was in the kitchen preparing supper and standing guard over the refrigerator.

"Hildy, we're thirsty. Can we have some juice?" Joel almost begged.

"I'll pour you each a glass but go get washed up first," she said giving them that look that said "Don't argue."

"Thanks!" Joel said as all of them scurried to the bathrooms to wash. It didn't take long before they were back waiting for Hildy to finish pouring their juice.

"Hildy, this young man," I said taking hold of Chris' shoulder "is Chris Martin. Chris this is Hildy. She takes care of us."

"Hello Chris, it's very nice to meet you. Do you like Swiss steak with mushroom gravy and mashed potatoes?" Hildy asked.

"Oh yeah, I like just about everthing. It's nice to meet you too," he said taking his juice and following the boys out onto the patio.

"I hope this is not going to be a permanent arrangement, but I just couldn't stand to take him to CPS when we got to his house and found it padlocked and his parents nowhere around. I don't think the twins would let me live it down if I hadn't brought him home with us," I told her. "They have quickly become great friends after two meetings. It's almost like there is empathy between them based on similar family situations."

"You've got a good heart," she said giving me a hug. "Don't ever lose it. You better get washed up. Supper will be ready in about 15 minutes."

Chris seemed to fit right in with the other boys. He certainly did when it came to putting away the food. He filled his plate twice and had thirds on mashed potatoes and gravy. After everyone was full, the boys took their plates to the sink and helped Hildy clear the table. Chris followed the others.

"Thanks Hildy that was the best supper I ever had," he said wrapping his arms around her waist and giving her a squeeze.

"You're welcome Chris. It was a pleasure to see you enjoy it so much," Hildy said with a catch in her voice. "Now you run outside. Have the boys show you the deer."

"Deer? You mean you guys got deer?" he said as he ran out the patio door after the twins.

"Oh Crane, I forgot to tell you. Mr. Cross called and asked if you could call him back. I told him you had little league practice this afternoon. He asked that you call him at home after eight. He gave me a number for you to call. It's on your desk in the study," she said.

"I wonder what he wants. I hope it's good news," I told her as I headed to the study.

Since the boys didn't have any homework tonight, I let them play outside longer than usual. When I did call them in it was time for their snack and then their baths.

"Larry, Lenny will one of you loan Chris a pair of your pajamas? I think they will fit him," I said.

They each grabbed one of Chris' hands and took off for their room.

Shortly after eight, I dialed the number Benjamin had given Hildy. He answered on the second ring.

"Hello Benjamin, it's Crane Johnson. What can I do for you?"

"Crane, I'm glad you called me back. I have some news about Judge Yates. She has issued a bench warrant for Judge Frank. It seems he ignored her order to provide her with the transcript of your hearing. My source said that she was furious with him. I think this time he has crossed the wrong woman."

"That's interesting, but how does it affect the boys' situation?"

"It doesn't directly. It's just good to see him get his. The other piece of news is that she has also ordered the CPS office in San Antonio to provide her with a written recommendation as to your fitness or unfitness to continue custody of the boys. She has made it clear that she expects them to be very specific in their reasoning one way or the other. She has left them with no wiggle room. I love it! God, I wish all judges had her guts and no nonsense attitude."

"That sounds like it might work out for us then, right?"

"I would say that the odds are now in your favor, but I wouldn't get your hopes up too high. There is still a long road ahead if you plan to adopt the boys sometime in the future."

"Benjamin, there is a new development that you should be aware of. It seems that one of the boys on my little league team has been abandoned by his parents. At least that's the way it appears right now."

"How does that affect you? He asks foolishly."

"You're right. I'm a sucker for kids. Anyway, his parents have been gone for a couple of days and the house is posted and padlocked. The twins made friends with him and "convinced" me to let him come home with them and spend the night. I have my friend Jack Hogan with SAPD checking to see if the parents are in jail or dead or whatever."

"And?"

"Well, I don't know. I would like to see him back with his parents if that's possible. I'm taking the other boys to Corinthian Academy tomorrow morning to be tested and interviewed. I thought I would spend that time trying to find his parents. I also plan to talk to him tonight to see if he has any idea where they might be. I would like to find out a little about his home life to see if he has been abused or neglected."

"What if you can't find his parents, then what?"

"I don't know and I don't want to think about that possibility. Maybe there is a close relative that can give him a good home. I'll try to find out all that stuff when I talk to him later."

"Okay, Crane. Let me know if you want me to do anything. Think any action you might take through thoroughly and logically before you commit yourself. I'll give you a call if I hear anything else about your other boys," he said with a smile in his voice.

All five of the freshly scrubbed boys bounced into the family room where I had just settled down to see if there was anything on TV. Larry and Lenny planted themselves on either side of me.

"Can Chris sleep in our room tonight?" Lenny asked.

"Yeah, we'll be good," Larry added.

"Well if he wants to. We do have another bedroom that he could use if he wants to sleep in a bed by himself," I said. "Chris, will you come here for a minute?"

He looked frightened as he came and stood before me. "Did I do something wrong?" he whimpered.

"No, I just wanted to check where you want to sleep tonight. You can have your own bedroom or Larry and Lenny would like to have you sleep in their bed. Which do you want?" I asked.

"You mean I can sleep with them? You mean it?" he asked.

"Yes if that is what you want. No talking and giggling after you go to bed though. The twins have to get up and go to Corinthian Academy tomorrow morning for some testing," I told him.

"Yeah, I'll be real quiet. I promise. I really will," he bubbled.

"Okay, that is settled. Larry, Lenny you guys go watch a little TV. I want to talk to Chris a little bit," I said giving them a push off the couch.

"Come here Chris," I said patting the couch beside me. "I need to get some information from you."

"Okay," he said jumping up on the couch beside me.

"Chris, do you know where your mom and dad went?"

"No."

"Have they ever gone off and left you by yourself before?"

"Once."

"How long were they gone?"

"Two days."

"Why did they leave you alone?"

"Somebody was after them."

"Why were they after them?"

"I don't know."

"What did you do after they came home?"

"We moved to a new house."

"Does your dad work?"

"Sometimes."

"What does he do?"

"I don't know. It's something with cement."

"Does your mom work?"

"Sometimes."

"What does she do?"

"I don't know. She worked at night."

"Do you like living with your mom and dad?"

"Well…I guess it's alright."

"What do you mean 'it's alright'?"

"Well…You know…They don't talk to me or nothing. I don't think they like me."

"Did they ever hurt you in any way?"

"No."

"Did they ever yell at you?"

"Yeah, all the time. I used to go to my room and close the door so they wouldn't yell at me."

"Do you have any relatives around here?"

"No, momma has a sister in Ohio or Iowa or someplace like that. But she is dying momma says."

"Do you know what her name is?"

"Tammy."

"Does Tammy have a last name?"

"I don't know."

"How about a grandmother or grandfather?"

"They're all dead."

"Thank you Chris. You go play with the boys for a few minutes. It's almost time for bed," I said helping him down from the couch.

I gave the boys another 15 minutes before I announced that it was bed time. No one objected and they all made for their bedrooms.

When I got to the twins' room, I found Chris in between Larry and Lenny. It's a good thing they had a queen size bed.

I leaned over and gave Larry a kiss on the forehead and said, "I love you son. Sleep well."

"Goodnight Uncle Crane, I love you," he said.

Next, I gave Lenny a kiss and told him the same thing I told Larry.

"Goodnight Uncle Crane, I love you too," he said.

I turned to Chris and was about to say goodnight to him when he threw his arms around my neck and kissed me on the cheek.

"Thank you Coach Johnson, it's nice to have somebody talk to me and not yell at me. I love you too," he said.

"Goodnight Chris, we all love you too," I said with a lump in my throat.

I went into TJ and Joel's bedroom to say goodnight to them. TJ was nearly asleep when I sat down on the edge of the bed.

"Goodnight little one, I love you," I said and kissed him on the forehead.

"Mmm," was all he replied.

Joel was the last on my goodnight list. Instead of just saying goodnight he asked, "What's gonna happen to Chris? Is he gonna get to stay here?"

"I don't know, son. I don't know. You go to sleep now. I love you and I love you for caring about Chris. Get a good night's sleep. You have to be sharp for your visit to Corinthian Academy tomorrow morning," I said and gave him his kiss.

Morning came all too quickly. My sleep had not been very restful. I guess I had too many things on my mind. I jumped in the shower and got ready for the day before going into the kitchen for my morning coffee. I drank one cup before I went in and woke up the boys. The twins and Chris were all tangled together. I was used to seeing the twins that way but was a little surprised when all three were intertwined.

Five sleepy boys shuffled into the kitchen just as Hildy was finishing the last of 20 pancakes. I got to eat two of them, Hildy didn't eat any and the boys finished them off along with sausages, scrambled eggs, about a gallon of orange juice and about the same amount of milk. They weren't too sleepy to eat, but come to think about it they could probably eat in their sleep.

"I'll have to go back to work pretty soon to pay for all the food this tribe is eating," I told Hildy.

"Doesn't it do your heart good to see them eating like that though? When they came here two and a half weeks ago they were timid and so skinny. Now look at them. They are filling out and they definitely are no longer timid, at least around here. I think they have gotten their self confidence back. And they do love you. You are the father they should have had," she said.

As they finished eating, each one took their plates to the sink and then helped Hildy put everything away in the refrigerator.

"Okay guys, go wash your hands and faces, brush your teeth and get dressed. Hildy laid out what you are to wear today. You have to look special. We want the Academy to like you. Now go!" I said. "Chris, there is a new toothbrush for you and a pair of pants and shirt that you can wear too."

If Chris stays around longer, I'm going to have to get a larger vehicle I mused. The Land Rover seats 5 comfortably, but that back fold down seat is anything but comfortable. The BMW was even worse. It would only seat 5. At least that is all that could be belted in safely.

We left the house at 8:30 so that we would arrive at the academy in time for our nine o'clock appointment. As it turned out, we were about ten minutes early which gave me a chance to see if I could get Chris tested as well as the other boys. Headmaster Pierce was not available but I was able to talk to Harry Lyle his assistant.

"Mr. Lyle, I know you didn't plan on five boys to test, but would it be possible to have another boy done today?" I asked

"Well, it'll take a little scrambling but I think we can squeeze him in. We're doing three children other than yours so it won't be too much of a problem," he answered.

"Good, I don't know for sure if he will be staying with us long term but I want to prepare for that eventuality just in case," I said.

"The testing and interviews will last until around 12:30 at which time the boys will be taken to the cafeteria for lunch and then be given a tour of the facilities. This should all wrap up between 1:30 and 2:00 so if you could plan to be here to pick them up that would be fine," he said.

Returning to the boys, I told Chris that he would be staying with the other boys to be tested also. That provoked a strong positive response from the boys especially the twins.

"I'll be back to pick you up when you are done. I want you all to do the best you can. Remember that I love all of you," I said giving each one a hug before Mr. Lyle led them away.

On the way back to the car, I decided to try to call Jack on my cell phone. This can be an iffy proposition since there are a lot of dead spots for reception here in the hill country. Fortunately, this was a spot with reasonably good reception. I dialed Jack sitting in my car.

It took six rings before he answered the phone. I was just ready to hang up.

"Jack, it's Crane. Have you found out anything about Chris Martin's parents?"

"We don't know where they are, if that's your question. We do know quite a bit about them. He has several warrants out for his arrest ranging from passing bad checks to drunk and disorderly conduct. She also has a few outstanding warrants. Two are for bad checks and another for prostitution."

"Sounds like an ideal family environment," I joked. "What's next?"

"I know you won't like the advice I'm going to give you, but I'm going to give it just the same. You have to contact CPS and report the whereabouts of Chris. I know from your experience with CPS so far that is the last thing that you want to do, but if you don't you could get into a heap of sh…trouble."

"You're right that I've not had a great relationship with CPS. But, I suppose you're right. Do you know anyone there that gives a damn about kids? Everyone seems to be more interested in filling out forms than seeing that kids are placed in loving homes."

"Yeah, there is this one I have come in contact with who really seems dedicated to kids. Her name is Darcie Levin. Ask for her if you decide to contact CPS. She will listen to you and evaluate the situation quickly. She is pretty darn sharp."

"You know, old friend, if you hadn't prevailed on me to help you coach the team I wouldn't be having all of these problems, so all of this is your fault. I'll get even with you someday. Thanks for the advice. If you find out any more about the Martins let me know. I'll see you Friday if not before. Goodbye," I said and hung up.

I retrieved the number for CPS from my Franklin Planner and dialed it. When the receptionist answered, I asked if I could get an appointment to see Ms. Levin sometime this morning and was told she had an available time at 10:15. I told the receptionist to book that slot for me that I was on my way.

I barely made it in time for my appointment with Ms. Levin. It was good that she was running a little behind. About twenty after a very attractive woman of about 30 came into the lobby where I was waiting and introduced herself.

"Mr. Johnson, I'm Darcie Levin. Your reputation has preceded you," she said smiling.

"I don't know if that's a good thing or not but I'm happy to meet you," I replied.

"Well you certainly stirred up a hornet's nest around here with that hearing before Judge Frank," she snickered as she led me into her office. "Now what can I do for you today?"

"I'm not here about the four Andersen boys," I started.

"Oh?" she looked somewhat shocked.

"No there is another boy who spent the night with us that I am concerned about," I said.

I went on to describe the circumstances of Chris staying with us overnight and the information that I had gleaned from Jack about Chris' parents.

"Let me check something," she said turning to her computer terminal. "Do you know the names of the parents and the last known address? I'll check to see if CPS has had any contact with them."

I gave her the information that I had from the form that had been filled out for Chris to play in little league.

"No, I can't find any record that we have had any reason to visit the family. Do you have any reason to suspect that the boy has been abused or neglected in any way?" she asked.

"I didn't see any sign of physical abuse, but from talking to Chris it seems that he was constantly verbally abused by both parents. That can probably be very damaging to a child," I responded.

"Yes, that can leave deep emotional scars that can be very hard to heal. Unfortunately, it's not unlawful conduct. It's bad parenting though," she said with sadness in her voice. "What do you want CPS to do with the child?"

"If I had my preference it would be nothing. I don't want to get into trouble by not letting you all know that I have Chris and that I am willing to take care of him until his future in a good home is assured," I explained.

"Mr. Johnson..," she started.

"Crane, please," I said.

"Okay, Crane, I'll fill out the necessary forms to process him into the system indicating that he is in your temporary custody. I have read the file on your petition to get continued custody of the four boys. I personally believe that the case worker made an error in not supporting your application. Nothing against Joyce, but her thinking is still grounded in the seventies when it comes to the kind of homes to place foster children in. Everything in your file would indicate that you are more than fit to be a foster parent. It's becoming more and more apparent that with the number of children in the system we'll have to look at some of the more non-traditional homes if we're to keep them out of the group home environment," she almost spit out the last statement as if it something bitter in her mouth.

"Thanks, I'm not looking for compensation that CPS provides for the boys in my care. I have more than enough resources to meet their needs. My only concern is that they have a loving home in which to live.

"If you need to visit my home to conduct your evaluation of it or to talk to Chris, here are the directions. It is a little difficult to find if you are not familiar with the area," I said handing her a sheet of paper outlining the way.

"Yes, I'll need to talk to him. Would it be possible to come by this evening?" she asked.

"Certainly, why don't you eat supper with us? We usually eat around six-thirty. We would be pleased if you would join us. It also might be less threatening to Chris," I said.

"Thank you, I think that's a good idea. I'll be there around six if that's alright," she said writing it down in her appointment book.

"We'll be expecting you," I said as I left her office.

Looking at my watch I decided I had just enough time to run by the office before I had to be back to pick up the boys.

Everything was running smoothly at the office thanks to Foster and Carol. Without their help the company would be suffering with me out for the last two and a half weeks and Eric in the hospital. No one had heard anything about the treatment he was undergoing in Houston. It was probably too early.

I took care of a few items that needed my attention and made a mental note to give both Foster and Carol a bonus for the outstanding work they were doing in my and Eric's absences.

I got back to Corinthian Academy before the boys had finished their tour of the campus. The reports on them were ready when I arrived. Mr. Lyle ushered me into his office to go over the results with me.

"I'm very please with the results of the test and interview of all the boys. Christopher will need a little extra help but the potential is there if he applies himself. Although he is 10, he would best be place in the same class as Lawrence and Leonard. He just had his birthday so he will not be much older than the other students in the class. Timothy is very bright but somewhat retarded in his social skills. He also shows signs of lacking self-confidence to the extent that he is very dependent on his oldest sibling.

Lawrence and Leonard appear to be very well adjusted and are well on track academically. Joel is also academically well placed. He is very bright and shows great potential," he wound up his review of the results.

"That's good to hear. In regards to Joel, he's scheduled to have a doctor's appointment every other week for a while. Will that be a problem?" I asked.

"No, it shouldn't be. If we know ahead of time what the schedule is we can make allowances for it and get his assignments and any additional help he needs to make up any work he would miss," he answered.

"That sounds great. It looks like you have five new students," I said getting up to go see if the boys were through.

"Oh by the way Mr. Johnson, it might interest you to know that the board of directors of the school have voted to add an additional grade each year for the next four so that we will be serving grades K through 12 at the end of four years," he said with pride.

"That's a relief. I was wondering what I would do with Joel after next year," I said.

I only had to wait a couple of minutes until the boys returned. They were barely able to contain their excitement.

"Well, do you guys think you would like to go to school here?" I asked.

"Oh yeah!" the twins said excitedly.

"Uh huh, Uncle Crane," TJ said nodding his head.

"This place is neat!" Joel added.

"What about you, Chris? Do you think you would like to go to school here?" I asked the silent member of the crew.

"Yes, but what about my mom and dad? They wouldn't let me go here. It cost too much," he said looking down at his shoes.

"You let me worry about that. Let's go home, guys. I'll bet Hildy has a snack waiting for us," I knew that would get them to the car in nothing flat.

On the way home, I said to the boys, "We're going to have a guest for supper tonight and I want you all to be on your best behavior. Ms. Levin wants to talk to Chris and to look over our house to see if it is suitable for you to live in."

That didn't seem to get much rise out of them. They were probably more concerned about the snack waiting for them then worrying about a supper guest.

The boys rushed into the house and inhaled the wonderful smell coming from the kitchen but were stopped by Hildy and told to go change their clothes and wash up before their snack. She had fixed some of her famous heavenly chocolate brownies.

She was soon besieged by freshly scrubbed and changed boys drooling as she set a huge plate of brownies on the table along with five large glasses of milk. I grabbed one brownie to keep from being left out of the delicacy.

"I hate to spring this on you at the last minute," I said licking the chocolate frosting from my fingers. "But we'll be having a guest for supper from the CPS. Darcie Levin will be here to talk to Chris and I thought it would be less stressful for him if he got to know her informally before she talked to him."

"We're not having anything fancy," she said. "I'm frying chicken and making biscuits and cream gravy and then green beans for vegetable. Apple pie and ice cream is dessert. I hope she's willing to take pot luck."

"I'm sure it will be fine. She seems to be a very nice person and from her accent I would say she's a native Texan," I said.

The boys and I played in the pool until almost 5:30. There was one more to join in the game of king of the hill. That meant it took me even less time to get worn out. I was surprised that Chris was a really good swimmer. I found out later that he spent most of the summer at the pool when it was open to stay out of his parent's wrath.

Shortly after six the gate buzzer sounded. The security camera showed a Toyota Celica waiting to be admitted. I was sure it was Darcie so I released the gate to let her in and went to the front door to greet her.

CHAPTER 16

Darcie was even more striking as she exited her car. I thought that she was an attractive woman when I met with her in her office but now she was something else. At the office she had her hair pulled back making her look like she was in her 30's. Now her hair fell in soft curls down around her shoulders. She looked more like someone in their mid twenties. She was dressed rather informally in slacks and a blouse that showed her figure off nicely.

Thankfully, she had to walk about twenty feet from her car to where I was standing on the front steps, giving me just enough time to recover and to be able to speak coherently.

"Welcome Ms. Levin, I hope you didn't have any trouble finding the place," I said as I shook her outstretched hand.

"No, the directions that you gave me were excellent. Darcie, please. My, this is a beautiful place. I live over on the east side of San Antonio and I certainly don't have a view like this," she said.

"That's why I was unwilling to sell this place after my parents died. Let's go in and meet everyone," I said as I ushered her in the front door.

The boys were playing on the patio and Hildy was in the kitchen. "Hildy this is Darcie Levin, Darcie this is Hildy Ramirez. Hildy takes care of us and keeps us in line," I told her.

They exchanged greetings before I steered Darcie to the patio to meet the boys. The boys saw us as we came out onto the patio and they all rushed up to us interrupting whatever game they were playing. As they lined up I introduced them to Darcie, first Joel, then the twins then TJ.

"And this young man hiding behind the twins is Chris Martin," I said grabbing his hand and gently pulling him around in front of the twins.

"Hi, Chris," she said. "It's a pleasure to meet you. How do you like being here with Mr. Johnson and his boys?"

"It's neat!" he said still holding my hand. "We have lots of fun. I got to swim and play video games and chase deer and Hildy cooks real good and everthing."

"That's great!" Darcie responded. "Chris, I need to talk to you for a few minutes. Crane, could we use your study for a bit?"

"Of course, don't be too long. I think Hildy will have supper ready in about 20 minutes and the boys will need to wash up before they eat," I said.

"We won't be long. I just need some basic information from him. Come along Chris, let's do this quickly. I know you don't want to miss any of Hildy's cooking," she said taking his hand and leading him back inside.

I sent the other boys to get cleaned up and told them to see if Hildy needed any help setting the table. We had to move to the dining room because there was not enough room to seat all of us at the breakfast table.

TJ beamed as he helped. Hildy had assigned him to place the napkins beside all of the plates. You would have thought he had climbed Mt. Everest when Hildy congratulated him on the fine job that he had done. I gave him a hug and told him how helpful he was. As the other boys finished their table setting tasks, I gave them hugs also not wanting them to feel left out.

The boys had just finished when Darcie and Chris came out of the study leading a smiling Chris. He ran to the bathroom at my urging to wash up for supper. I indicated to Darcie where the guest bath was in case she wanted to freshen up.

Darcie sat a one end of the table and I sat at the other. TJ was to my right next to Hildy who was sitting between him and Joel. The twins were across the table with Chris sitting between them. The table fairly groaned with food. There were two large platters piled high with fried chicken, two baskets of steaming hot biscuits, bowls of thick cream gravy and green beans enough to feed an army.

"Joel, would you start the chicken with Ms. Levin? Since she's our guest, please pass her each dish first. Thank you," I told him.

Joel was the consummate gentleman. I was so proud of him it was hard to keep from getting up and giving him a hug. I started passing the duplicate dishes to the twins and Chris. By the time all the dishes had made their way by all of the boys, their plates were heaped with food. I was both surprised and pleased that they waited until everyone had been passed each plate before they looked at me to see if it was alright to begin. I gave them a nod and the feeding frenzy began.

Darcie didn't do too badly in the eating department. Although her plate was not as heaping as the boys' plates, she managed a respectable helping of everything. The boys, as usual were not into conversation while they ate. The three adults did manage to keep conversation alive and avoided any deadly silences.

I was completely taken by Darcie. She was intelligent, articulate, witty and had a smile that could melt Antarctica. All in all, it was a very pleasant meal. And although the boys consumed a mountain of food, their manners had never been better. I was so proud of them.

After everyone finished eating the boys helped Hildy clear the table while Darcie and I took our coffee out onto the patio to enjoy the sun setting over the hills. Soon the boys joined us and pleaded to go swimming. When I told them it was too soon after eating to go in the pool they settled for playing video games on their PlayStations.

"I don't want to sound pushy, but what do you think about Chris staying here until his parents return or until you can find him a suitable foster home?" I asked Darcie. "I should add, if his parents want him back and if CPS finds them fit to have him back."

"It looks like Chris is very happy here and has settled in quite quickly. I need to inspect the rest of the house to see if it meets minimum requirements, but I don't believe there should be any problems. One thing that concerns me is that Chris said that he had to sleep with the twins in their bed. Is that correct?" she asked.

"No not quite. We have a spare bedroom with its own bathroom but he wanted to sleep with Larry and Lenny last night. Long term I don't think that should be the norm but for a few days until he feels comfortable and not so abandoned, I believe it's okay," I replied. "He needed to have the comfort of close contact with the only people he knows who love him."

We inspected the rest of the house including the bedrooms. The boys were totally engrossed in the video games. Joel and Chris were racing Indy cars while TJ cheered them on. The twins were equally glued to their game.

Darcie seemed to be pleased with the amount of space that was available for the boys as we finished the tour. "You know, the state of Texas only allows you to have a total of six foster children at any one time. You can only take in one more before you bump up against that limit," she said with an evil glint in her eyes.

"God, no more please! I love these boys dearly, but thank you I think that I have enough," I sputtered.

She laughed at my embarrassment before adding, "I'll have your temporary foster parent license amended to allow you to have five children in your custody. We will have to wait and see what happens with Chris' parents. Their outstanding warrants will probably keep them out of circulation for some time. You'll also have to have another hearing to extend your custody of Chris if that's what you decide you want. Before you say anything, the hearing will not be before Judge Frank. I try to get all of my hearings scheduled before Judge Riley. She is a no nonsense lady but is one of the most compassionate judges that you could find."

"Let's just see what happens with Chris' parents. Right now, I don't want to make any long term commitments as to keeping him. If you asked the twins what they wanted, I'm sure that he would be here forever," I said.

Darcie said goodbye to the boys giving them a friendly hug and thanked Hildy for the wonderful supper but turned down her offer for apple pie and ice cream before I escorted her to her car. It was a little awkward as we stood at the car. Neither one of us knew exactly what to say.

After several false starts I said, "You are welcome to come back at any time. The boys would enjoy your company and…so would I."

"Thank you, I would like very much to come back sometime…to visit the boys," she hastily added.

"Great! Anytime you want," I said and then screwing up my courage added, "May I call you sometime?"

"Yes, I'd like that," she replied shaking my hand before slipping into her car.

I felt like a schoolboy who had just asked a girl out for his first date. It had been a long time since I had dated anyone. With college and then the job with ACC and then buying into the business, time was not there for a real social life. I stood looking down the lane long after her car had disappeared from view.

Joel was waiting for me as I returned to the house. "She is nice, I like her. You like her too, don't you?" he said with a giggle.

"She is a very nice lady. I invited her to come back sometime. Is that alright with you?" I blushed.

"Yeah, TJ liked her too. Everyone thought she was neat. Are you gonna ask her out on a date?" he asked hiding a smile behind his hand.

"I'm glad that everyone thought she was neat. I think I have more than I can handle with you guys without getting involved with Darcie or any other woman.

"By the way, I was so proud of you at supper for the way that you and the rest of the gang behaved. You guys were super and I love you for that, too," I said squeezing his shoulder.

It was Joel's turn to blush at the praise I had given him.

"Let's go get the others. I'll bet that Hildy has the apple pie and ice cream ready for your snacks," I said.

That was all he needed. He took off like a shot and raced to the bedrooms to corral the others.

Hildy had just finished putting the last piece of pie on a plate when the boys burst into the kitchen.

"Did you wash your hands?" Hildy asked bringing the stampede to a screeching halt and immediately they reversed course to wash up.

Large scoops of cinnamon ice cream had been added to each piece of pie by the time the herd returned looking as though they hadn't eaten in a week, but freshly scrubbed.

"Come here Chris," I said to him as they finished their snacks and put the dishes in the dishwasher. "Do you want to sleep in the other bedroom tonight?"

"Do I have to?" he asked with a quiver in his voice.

"No you don't have to. I just thought it would be more comfortable if you had your own bed and maybe you would sleep better," I answered.

"Okay," he whispered and turned away.

I could see that his eyes were tearing up as he turned.

"Uncle Crane, please! Can't Chris sleep with us again tonight? Please?" the twins begged in unison.

"I don't care as long as you three go right to sleep and no horsing around. Understand?"

I was bowled over by three hugs and kisses on my cheeks. "Thanks, Uncle Crane," all three said. I guess I'm going to be Uncle Crane to Chris now, too.

After the boys took their baths and I tucked them in bed, I turned on the TV to watch the news before going to bed myself. As I was turning through the local channels, I happened on an interview one of the reporters was having with a man and woman who appeared to be in their mid to late thirties. This station is known for two things, its self-promotion to the point of nausea and its tabloid like 'news' coverage. The man being interview bore a striking resemblance to Chris. That was what made me pause and watch because I never watched this channel.

The couple was relating how their son had been missing for three days and they were afraid that he had been kidnapped.

"Please, whoever has our boy bring him back. He is our only son," the woman sobbed, crocodile tears running down her cheeks.

The TV at that moment flashed a picture of the missing child on the screen with the name Christopher Martin at the bottom of the picture.

"Oh, my god! What the hell is going on? They are accusing me of kidnapping Chris. I have to get in touch with Jack," I said aloud to myself.

I grabbed the phone and dialed Jack's home number.

"Jack, it's Crane. Something screwy is going on. I just saw an interview with Chris' parent on TV claiming that he hasn't been home for three days and that they believe he has been kidnapped. What do I do now?" I spewed out not even letting Jack say anything but hello. "How can they do this? They should be arrested for their various activities as well as child abandonment. Something is not kosher here."

"Whoa, Crane. I know you didn't kidnap Chris. If you did, you sure were dumb the way you went about it. Notifying the police and CPS that you had him was not the smartest thing a kidnapper could do," he joked.

"Thanks, Jack! I don't need any hint of scandal right now with the fate of the other four up in the air. This accusation, although not directed at me by name, could adversely affect my petition to keep them. You have to help me get this cleared up. Is there anything you can do tonight? What about the Martins? Can't they be arrested on their outstanding warrants?" I would have gone on but Jack interrupted.

"Calm down, Crane. I'll call headquarters to see if they have filed a missing persons report with us. I don't know if I can do anything until I find out more information. I'll call you back within the hour to let you know what I have found out. Now go have a drink or a beer or hot chocolate or whatever. I'll call you back, I promise," he said before hanging up.

I waited impatiently for Jack to call. It seemed like hours but in reality it was only about thirty minutes.

"Crane, this is what I found out. The Martins have not filed a missing person report concerning Chris. The strange thing is that a case worker with CPS has filed one based on her talking to the Martins. What is even stranger is that the case worker is Joyce Gehrig. How does that grab you? She has to have had access to the information that Darcie entered into the system. I haven't been able to find out how she and the Martins got together but something stinks to high heavens. It looks as though someone is trying to make it appear that you are some kind of pervert before the truth comes out about the whole situation. I think it is pretty apparent who that person is," Jack said.

"Yeah, I guess we do. What can I do? As soon as my name gets associated with this mess, it could ruin me and my chances to get custody of the boys. It won't do my business any good either. Even though it will come out that I am an innocent victim of a smear, the damage will be done. We have to get this cleared up before it goes any further," I snarled. "And you know that the Martins really did abandon Chris. What has changed that they now want him back I wonder? There has to be an explanation besides our CPS friend's vendetta."

"I'm going to make one more phone call before I call it a night. Don't expect any more news tonight. Go to bed. We'll get this all worked out in the morning," Jack advised before he hung up.

I didn't know how I was going to be able to sleep, but I needed to be fresh for the boys. I wasn't going to send them back to school until they started at Corinthian Academy on Monday. Besides, Paul would be here at eight to tutor Joel.

I checked on the boys before retiring. TJ was curled up in a ball against Joel's back. Both were sleeping soundly as I quietly closed their door. The twins and Chris were again in a single mass of arms, legs and heads but they seemed to be sleeping soundly.

After I completed my bedtime ritual, I too climbed into bed knowing that it would probably be a fitful night. To my surprise, I slept rather well. My dreams were of Darcie and not of the other problems that loomed on the horizon.

Thursday morning I woke up surprisingly refreshed. I was sitting at the breakfast table enjoying my first cup of coffee and reading the headlines on the newspaper when the gate alarm went off. I quickly flipped on the gate security cameras to see what was going on. Much to my surprise, the violators were the sheriff's department. There were three cars passing through the now disabled gate. The first two were deputies' cars and the third I recognized as the SUV that belonged to Joyce Gehrig.

This is unreal I thought to myself as I went to the front door to find out what the hell was going on as if I didn't know. I recognized the deputy that stepped out of the first sheriff's car.

"Jesse, what the devil is going on? Why did you have to break my gate? You could have buzzed and I would have let you in, you know that," I questioned the deputy I had given a statement to earlier in the week.

"Crane, it's not my idea but I have my orders. We have a warrant for your arrest on the charge of kidnapping the minor child known as Christopher Martin. Is this person present in the residence?" he asked.

"Of course he is. I am his foster parent as of yesterday and that bit…woman over there knows very well that is the case. Come on in. Chris is still in bed. They are due to be woken up just about now for breakfast," I said bitterly.

"I'm sorry Crane. I'm only doing my job. I know you wouldn't do anything like this but it's my job to obey the law and the courts," Jesse said.

"If that woman steps into my house I will file charges of trespassing on her. In fact, I think I have enough grounds to file just because she is on my land without my permission. Get her off my land now or I will file on her," I threatened.

Joyce blanched but knew she was here on very tenuous grounds so she got back into her SUV and drove down the lane past my gate.

"Let's go see the boys and maybe we can get this straightened out," I said leading the two deputies into the house.

Going directly to the twins' room I tapped gently on the door before I entered followed closely by Jesse and the other deputy.

"Good morning, guys," I said as I gently shook the tangled mass of bodies. "Time to get up. Hildy is fixing breakfast."

I think the mention of breakfast was what penetrated their sleep.

Lenny stretched and yawned before it soaked into his consciousness that there were extra people in the room besides me. "Who are they?" he asked sleepily.

"They are deputy sheriffs. They think that I kidnapped Chris and am holding him here against his will," I said.

"No Uncle Crane," Chris cried. "You didn't kidnap me. That's dumb."

"Alright, you all go get washed up for breakfast and see what Hildy has prepared for you this morning," I told them.

As they all rushed to the bathroom, I told Jesse that I needed to wake up the other two boys. We went into Joel's room and woke him and TJ up and ready for breakfast.

"This sure doesn't look like your typical kidnapping to me," Jesse said to his partner. "Something's not right here."

"Jesse, do you mind if I look at that warrant for my arrest? I just want to make sure what all is covered by it" I requested.

"Sure, here it is," he said.

"Hmm. It looks like this warrant is only for my arrest. It makes no mention of taking Chris into custody and since Hildy is here to supervise the boys there is no reason to take him or the other boys for that matter," I said.

"Well, I don't know," Jesse started at which point Hildy entered the family room.

"Jesse, I have known you since you were in diapers. I know all of your family and all of your friends. If you so much as suggest that these boys be taken from this house, I will personally see to it that you are not welcome anywhere in Comal County. And I can do it and you know it!" she emphatically stated. "These boys have been physically, sexually and even verbally abused until they came to live here. This is the first place in their short lives that they feel safe. They love Crane and he loves them. I do too. I don't know what you have to do but those boys are not leaving here."

With that, she turned around and returned to the kitchen and her boys.

"I'm sorry Crane, but I have to take you in. Since the warrant doesn't mention taking anyone else into custody, we'll leave the boys here at least for now," Jesse said.

"Let me tell the boys that I am leaving and then I'll go with you," I said heading for the kitchen.

"Hey, boys, I have to go with Jesse for a while. I should be back before long. Remember Joel, Mr. Coulter will be here at eight to begin your classes. The rest of you can stay home today. In fact you are on vacation until Monday when you start to school at Corinthian Academy," I told them. "Maybe you can get Hildy to read some more of *Tom Sawyer* to you while I'm gone."

"Yeah, will you Hildy? Please?" the twins pleaded.

"I think that can be arranged," Hildy said.

I gave each one of the boys a kiss on top of their heads before turning to Hildy.

"If Joyce Gehrig comes on the property without a warrant, call the sheriff. Also, will you call Jack and let him know what is happening and call Darcie. Both of their numbers are in my address book on my desk. Thanks!" I said turning to go with Jesse.

Once outside Jesse said, "I don't like doing this, Crane, but I have to handcuff you and advise you of your rights."

CHAPTER 17

The ride to the county jail was less than pleasant. My six foot frame with my long legs did not fit well in the back seat of the deputy's car which was fitted with a barrier between the front and back seats.

Nothing about this whole mess was pleasant. The booking, the finger printing, the strip search, the body cavity search and finally the placement in a cell were all demeaning and degrading particularly when I knew the charges against me were false. I requested to contact my lawyer but was not allowed to do so for nearly two hours. It was almost ten o'clock when I was able to call Benjamin Cross. I didn't know who else to call since I had never had the need for a criminal defense attorney before.

"Crane, I'm glad you called. I was about to call you. Judge Yates' clerk has told my office that the judge will issue her ruling this afternoon," Benjamin said.

"That's great," I said. "However, that's not what I called you about. I have been arrested and booked on the charge of kidnapping."

"You what?" he said. "That is ridiculous! Who were you supposed to have kidnapped?"

"Well, you remember when we talked the other day about the boy whose family had abandoned him, Chris Martin? That's who I am supposed to have kidnapped. What is really weird is that he is known to CPS, they know he has been abandoned and to top it off I have been assigned as his foster parent on a temporary basis. In fact, Darcie Levin, his case worker from CPS, visited my house and talked to Chris last evening. The CPS case worker for the other boys is the one who filed the complaint with the DA's office. What am I to do?" I asked.

"I'm not a criminal defense attorney but one of my partners, John Allison, is. I'll talk to him about your problem and have him or one of his associates come and talk to you. By the way, where are you being held?" he asked.

"I'm in the Comal County Jail. I don't know what the address is, I've never been here before," I said.

"Don't worry. Someone from our office will be there as quickly as they can. In the mean time, I will get in contact with the CPS office there in San Antonio and see what I can find out. Don't make any statements or talk to anyone until one of our lawyers gets there," he said.

The phone call was of little comfort to me. I was more worried about my reputation and the impact that this would have on my business than I was about being found guilty of these blatantly false charges.

Thank goodness, Jimmy Sanchez, my new lawyer, arrived about two hours after I called Benjamin. I was a little surprised at his youth. He looked like he was barely old enough to vote let alone be a member of the bar. I was also surprised at his quick work in gathering statements from Darcie Levin and from Jack Hogan surrounding the circumstances of my having temporary custody of Chris. He had also been able to identify the judge who signed the warrant for my arrest.

I don't know why I was surprised by the fact that the judge ordering my arrest was also the brother-in-law of Judge Frank and cousin of Joyce Gehrig. Here in 1994 the good old boy network was at its peak in Bexar County. The courts served the politically powerful and city council and mayor served only themselves. Corruption was rampant throughout the whole city and county structures. The only way to get something done was to bribe an official.

Another lawyer working with Jimmy had met with the District Attorney's office and explained to them the ramifications of their filing the charges against me based on false allegations and the possibility of a civil suit. After the DA's office checked the statement from Darcie and determined that it was accurate, they concluded that they were in deep trouble if I wanted to file a civil suit for damages against them. They immediately went before another judge and got the indictment quashed.

That is a long way of saying Jimmy had come with all the documentation necessary to have me released from jail. It didn't take me long to get my stuff together and get out of there. Jimmy was kind enough to drive me home. I didn't want another ride in a patrol car.

Since neither Jimmy nor I had eaten lunch, I invited him in for something to eat. We had barely entered the front door when four young boys nearly bowled me over. TJ jumped up and threw his arms around my neck and kissed me on the cheek. The twins and Chris encircled me with their arms so completely that I was unable to move.

"We heard Hildy tell Mr. Coulter that you were in jail. We were scared, Uncle Crane! We thought you'd never come back," he cried into my neck.

"Yeah," the twins echoed.

I could feel the back of my shirt getting wet from Chris sobbing behind me.

"Everything is okay guys. I don't have to go to jail any more. Let's go into the kitchen, I'm hungry. I haven't had my lunch yet," I said knowing that the mention of food would change their focus of attention.

I carried TJ into the kitchen followed by everyone else. I put TJ down and introduced Jimmy to them. They all politely shook his hand as I introduced each one in turn. "Where is Joel?" I asked.

Lenny answered, "He is taking a test that Mr. Coulter gave him. You want me to get him?"

"No let him finish it. Would you guys like a snack while Mr. Sanchez and I have our lunch?" I asked knowing that was a foolish question.

Hildy came in just then and took over the preparation of food for Jimmy and me and a snack for the boys. We had no more started eating when Joel appeared and ran to my side throwing his arms around me giving me a tight squeeze.

"I was afraid that you wouldn't come back," he sobbed.

"It's okay. Everything is going to be just fine. I'm not going anywhere. Why don't you have a snack with your brothers?" I said trying to divert his attention.

After we finished eating and the boys finished their snack which was more than what Jimmy and I had for lunch, I decided to call Benjamin to see if he had any news. Unfortunately he was not available and his secretary did not have any information for me.

I thanked Jimmy profusely as we walked to his car and told him if I ever needed a criminal defense lawyer again, I would definitely call on him. I also thanked my lucky stars that I had hired Benjamin and his law firm. I don't know where I could have turned that would have gotten the results that they achieved for me.

Paul Coulter was getting his things together when I re-entered the house. "Paul, I didn't know you were still here," I said quite surprised.

"I needed to correct the test that I gave Joel and then I wanted to talk to you before I left. By the way, Joel did very well on the achievement test I administered despite being distracted by your predicament. He should do very well at Corinthian. If it is alright with you, I will wrap up today. I have finished all that I planned to do with Joel and will not come back tomorrow, if that's okay. That will give him a day off with the other boys. I know it has been on his mind that they have not had to go to school and he had to so it might make him feel better," Paul said.

"No, that's fine. You've done an outstanding job with him. I appreciate everything that you've done. Joel loves to learn and you are one of the reasons that he does. I wish you well in your new position at the Academy and I'm sure that Joel is looking forward to seeing you there. Good luck!" I told him as I shook his hand and saw him to the door.

"Hildy," I said as I returned to the kitchen, "I think I'll take the boys out for pizza tonight. Do you want to come along?"

"If you think you can handle all of them alone I won't go. I have a meeting at the church tonight that I would like to go to," she replied.

"Go to your meeting. I have to get used to managing all of them by myself. I know we'll be alright. I plan to take them to Chuck E Cheese. They have all sorts of games for them to play and their pizzas are okay, too. I think they should have fun," I said. "What kid could pass up pizza and games? I think I'll wait a while before I tell them. I don't want to set them off this early."

The phone started ringing as I went into my bedroom to change out of my "prison clothes" into my swim trunks. It was Benjamin returning my call from earlier.

"Benjamin, I hope you have good news for me. This has not been the best day I have ever had."

"Yes, I have some good news. Judge Yates has ordered that you continue custody of the Andersen boys until such time that a new hearing decides their ultimate fate. She has also remanded the case to Judge Riley and has prohibited Judge Frank from any further involvement with the case. She has also ordered CPS to assign another case worker to the boys and has issued a stinging rebuke to Ms. Gehrig."

"That's good," I replied.

"Speaking of Ms. Gehrig, I have spoken to the CPS supervisor there in San Antonio about the fiasco that occurred this morning and the distinct probability that you would be seeking some sort of legal redress for the humiliation you were put through. I hinted to him that he and any others involved in the supervision of Ms. Gehrig may well find themselves called to account for her actions as well. But, that you might feel less inclined to include them in any call for redress if Ms. Gehrig were no longer employed there. I hope that I phrased that diplomatically enough that it did not sound like an outright threat but at the same time got my message across loud and clear. My sources have told me that she has been suspended and will face termination proceedings next week. God bless the civil service! They can't just out and out fire someone no matter how egregious their behavior. They have to make sure all the papers are filled out and filed correctly."

"When will the hearing before Judge Riley occur? She's the same judge that will be handling Chris' hearing. Do you think we could combine the two in order to save time?" I asked.

"That sounds like a good idea. I'll contact CPS again and suggest that to them. I think that I've softened them up enough so that they will be amenable. Crane, if you do want to file a civil suit against her and others, you should probably hire someone who specializes in civil law. No one in our office does, but I can give you the names of some very good ones if you want."

"Thanks, Benjamin. I need some time to think it over. It might only bring more publicity to the situation and cause more damage. I'll let you know. Thanks again. I really appreciate what you and your firm have done for me," I told him before we hung up.

I finished changing into my swim trunks and went to find the boys. "Does anyone want to swim with me?" I asked. "If you do, you better get changed."

I was nearly trampled in the rush as they darted back inside to get changed. We ended up swimming and playing the old favorite king of the hill until nearly four o'clock. By that time, I was exhausted and had retired to the sideline while the boys continued to play a game of dunk tag. They took it easy on TJ just keeping him involved enough to think that he was part of the game without picking on him because he was the easiest target.

Finally, I said to them, "Would you guys like to go out for pizza tonight?"

I was overwhelmed by a chorus of "Yea!", "Oh Boy!", "Yes! Yes!"

"Well I guess that's settled. Go get the chlorine washed off in the shower and put on some clean shorts and tee shirts and we'll head out," I said as I got out of the pool followed quickly by a flock of dripping boys. Oh well, as long as they don't slip and fall I thought.

I was reminded again of the limited seating capacity of the Land Rover as I buckled the boys into their seats. TJ wanted the rear fold down seat so that solved the problem at least this time.

The nearest Chuck E Cheese was on the north side of San Antonio so it took us about 30 minutes to get there. Thankfully, we were going against the flow of rush hour traffic. When I had asked the boys earlier if they had ever been to a Chuck E Cheese, they all said they had not. Well they are in for a treat I thought. This could be fun.

The place was not too crowded when we got there so we had our pick of the tables. I shoved a couple together so that all six of us could sit down around them. I ordered three large pizzas and hoped that it would be enough to fill the bottomless pits that masqueraded as boys. I also got a stack of tokens and passed them out to the boys and escorted them to the games and showed them how to put the tokens in and how some of the games worked. It didn't take long before all five of them were playing the games like they had been doing it all of their lives. I had to sit back and enjoy their happy faces and laughter. The only thing that caused them to pause was the need to grab a quick drink of their sodas.

When the pizzas arrived, I almost had to tear them away from the games but finally the smell of the pizzas overcame the attraction of the games. It was a good thing I ordered the pizzas I did because there was only one slice left when they finished. I did get a couple pieces by risking my fingers as I retrieved them.

"Hi Miss Levin! Hi Miss Levin!" the boys shouted. "Uncle Crane, there's Miss Levin."

When I turned around Darcie was standing at a table a couple removed from ours. She started our way when she recognized the boys. Following behind her were a strikingly handsome man and a boy who looked to be about 8 or 9 years of age.

I stood as they approached and reached out to shake her hand when she arrived.

Darcie, it's good to see you again so soon," I said. "This is a coincidence meeting you here like this."

"I didn't know whether you would speak to me again or not after what you went through today because of one of our case workers," she replied.

"I know that was not your fault. Thank you for helping to get it straightened out so quickly," I said.

"Crane, I'd like you to meet my brother Eric Levin. Eric, this is Crane Johnson and these are his foster children," she introduced us. "This young man is Eric's son Eric Junior. He likes to be called JR."

Eric was nearly my height and had an extremely athletic build. It was not a bodybuilder shape. It was more like a gymnast's body. His polo shirt molded to his body as if it had been painted on. His wide shoulders tapered to a narrow waist and hips. He could easily have been a model.

"Please sit down. The boys are itching to go back and play the games again. Would JR like to go with the boys?" I asked Eric trying not to stare at him.

"Yeah, I think that would be a good idea. Let me get some tokens and I'll be right back," he said.

Eric came back shortly and the three of us chatted about nothing in particular as we watched the boys enjoying the games. JR seemed to fit right in with my boys. They were having the time of their lives when Darcie and Eric's pizzas arrived. JR resisted leaving the games but like most boys, the food won out.

While we were talking, I found out that Eric had just recently divorced his wife. It seems that she had run away with another man leaving JR with his dad. I also discovered that he had a small network consulting firm in Houston that he wanted to sell and move to San Antonio. He was in town to scout out the possible employment opportunities and to visit his sister.

When I asked him what type of job he was looking for he reeled off a whole string of computing and computer related jobs that he was qualified for. I was as impressed with his resume as I was with his physique. I explained I owned a consulting firm and we were always looking for talented people and that networking expertise was an area that we didn't have in-house. We always had to sub that out to other groups when we had a project that called for it.

"Look, if you are interested, why don't you call my office manager, Foster Brandt, and set up an interview with him tomorrow. Foster conducts the initial screening of all applicants and then recommends to me whether or not we can use the candidate. I'll leave a message for him that you will be calling. Foster gets in around nine in the morning so you can call him any time after that," I told him as I gave him my card with Foster's number on the back.

"Thanks, Crane. I have heard good things about ACC. I have always heard that you do a quality job. I'll call Foster first thing in the morning," Eric said.

Darcie was sort of left out of our conversation. It seemed that Eric and I were the only ones there. I was quickly brought back to reality when Joel and TJ rushed up. Joel was holding a long string of tickets about two feet long. TJ had a smaller string.

"Can we go trade these in for a prize?" Joel asked.

"Sure, go get the other boys. It's time we started home anyway," I told them.

"It was good to see you again Darcie and very nice to meet you Eric. I hope we meet again," I said as I went to herd the boys to the prize counter.

TJ was the first to reach the prizes and quickly decided which one he wanted. It was a small stuffed replica of a bear, one of the animated characters in the "live" show, which each Chuck E Cheese has.

"I want that one," TJ said looking up at me.

"You don't have enough tickets for that one," I told him gently after looking at his string of tickets and the 'price' of the toy.

"I do," Joel said.

"But you won't be able to get anything for yourself if you use yours for TJ," I said.

"It's okay. TJ and I can share," he responded.

The lump in my throat was so large that I was unable to respond. I just nodded my head as he and TJ pooled their tickets to 'purchase' the stuffed toy. How could any boy who has gone through the hell he has be so caring and unselfish? I wanted to pick him up and give him a big hug but settled for giving his shoulder a squeeze and patting him on the back. I didn't want to embarrass him in public.

Chris and the twins had enough tickets between them combined with the few that Joel had left of his for each to get some small trinkets. Joel left with nothing but my admiration.

When we got home, I called Foster's number at the office and left him a voice mail telling him to expect Eric's call. I told him that I would rely on his judgment as to whether or not to hire Eric. I also took care of some other business that I needed Foster to handle for me.

It wasn't long before the boys began to have hunger pangs and asked what they could have for a snack. After looking to see what Hildy had left, they settled for ice cream and chocolate chip cookies. The five of them completely demolished a half gallon carton of ice cream in one sitting.

I sent the other boys off to get their showers taken but asked Joel to stay behind.

"Did I do something wrong?" he asked with a scared look in his eyes.

"Oh, no son! You did something very right. I just wanted to say how very proud I am of you and how much I love you. You gave up your prize tonight so that TJ could have what he wanted. That was so good of you to do that," I said as I reached out to him. I gave him the big hug that I wanted to give him earlier and kissed his forehead.

"Thank you for being the wonderful boy that you are. Please don't change," I choked out giving him another hug. "Now go get your shower taken."

"But TJ wanted that little bear," he said looking at me with those beautiful azure eyes. "I could never give him anything before. It makes me feel good to give him something. Besides he's little. He needs toys more than me."

TJ was hugging his little bear toy when I said goodnight to Joel and him. Chris was again in bed with the twins. He looked at me with questioning eyes, but when I leaned over and gave each of them a kiss on the forehead he relaxed visibly. This is not going to work long term. We are going to have to come up with more suitable sleeping arrangements.

Finishing my bedtime ritual, I climbed into bed. My thoughts went back to Eric and Darcie. How could I be attracted to both of them? I had never been so turned on by a man before. I was also turned on by Darcie. What's the matter with me? I always considered myself to be completely heterosexual. I was so confused by my conflicting emotions that sleep did not come easily.

CHAPTER 18

Friday was turning out to be busy. The first thing on my agenda was to go to Carlos' office to sign all the necessary contracts to buy out my partner's share of the business. I had asked Gerald Cousins to meet me there to get the financial part of the deal finalized before we signed the final sales contract.

Now don't get me wrong, I'm pretty savvy when it comes to business and finance but between Gerald and Carlos they made me feel like a real dummy when they tried to explain the intricacies of the deal that they had structured. They explained that the company (actually an LLP) was the entity purchasing the share of the business that Eric owned and not me. That way the tax consequences for both the business and me would be considerably less. I was all for that. I had been in the top tax bracket for a long time and anything that would reduce my taxes was welcome. I had only one question when they finished their explanation.

"Is all of this legal?" I asked.

"Yes, it's completely above board," they both assured me. "We consulted with another tax attorney just to make doubly sure."

With their assurance, I signed all of the necessary paperwork. We were sitting around chatting about everything and nothing when my business partner, Eric Olsen, walked in with his son. All of us stood up and greeted him and inquired about his health. Although he seemed to be a little unsteady on his feet, he said that he was fine. His son also assured us that his dad was okay and that his mind was clear and no way impaired by the radiation treatment.

Carlos inquired if he was taking any medication that might impair his judgment and affect the legality of his signature and was told that the only medication he was on was his blood pressure medicine.

All of that taken care of, Eric signed the same papers that I had earlier and took possession of the check for the first part of the purchase.

After we exchanged pleasantries, I excused myself to tackle item number two on my agenda. Rushing back to the house to load up the kids and take them to buy the uniforms that they would need to start school on Monday. Hildy agreed to meet us at the store and help with outfitting the boys before she went grocery shopping to fill the pantry that had a way of emptying very rapidly. With the addition of Chris, the food disappeared even faster.

The shopping went much more smoothly than I had anticipated. Even TJ stayed within sight this time. Using the list of uniforms that Corinthian had given us it only took about an hour to finish outfitting all five boys. With my smoking credit card in my pocket and each boy loaded down with their new clothes, we headed for the car and lunch.

There was a WhatABurger on the way home so I decided to stop there to feed the boys. Of course, they had no objections. They looked like they could eat the leather seat upholstery by the time we got there. Six bacon cheeseburger WhatAMeals, large sized fries and 10 cookies later we were on our way home.

I had the boys unpack all their new uniforms and helped them remove all of the tags so that Hildy could get them laundered before they had to wear them on Monday. I first thought that it would be a good idea to mark each boy's uniform with their names but decided that was not necessary because TJ and Joel's were easy to identify and the twins and Chris could wear each other's interchangeably.

Item three on the agenda was the final little league ballgame of the fall season. We had a couple of hours before we had to leave for the game so I spent some time playing catch with the boys and trying to teach Chris how to throw a ball correctly. Even Lenny tried to help, but it didn't seem to do any good. No matter what we tried Chris could not throw the ball more than 30 feet.

I had no more than set down to take a rest from playing catch with the boys when the phone rang. It was Foster letting me know how the interview with Darcie's brother went.

"Crane, this guy Eric would be a definite asset to the company. We could use him starting Monday if he were available. The Latham contract is going to need someone with his expertise very shortly. I used to do a little networking in my younger days and Eric puts me to shame," Foster said with enthusiasm.

"Did he indicate what he was looking for in terms of compensation?" I asked.

"No, not directly, but I got the impression that he needed something in the $75,000 range. That doesn't seem too far out of line for someone with his level of expertise. It costs us an arm and a leg when we have to sub out the work that he could do in-house. I would suggest that you give him a six month contract with an extension option. Maybe structure his contract to give him a guarantee of 75K with a share of the consultation fees he generates over and above say 125 or 150K he brings to the company. Does that sound okay?" he finished.

"That sounds good to me. I'll call him and set up a meeting to work out the details. Thanks Foster, if you think he will be good for business that's good enough for me," I said before hanging up and dialing Darcie's home number.

I recognized his voice when he answered "Hello."

"Hello, Eric, this is Crane Johnson. Foster just called to tell me about the interview he had with you."

"Hi, Crane, yes it was a very interesting experience. I didn't know that you had so many people working there."

"Yeah, we usually have around 30 on staff at all times. I think the current number is 31. You know how contractors are, they come and go frequently. We do have a core group that has been with the company longer than I have been there. The reason I call is I would like to offer you a position with ACC if you are interested."

"Yes, I am interested."

"Good! I would like to meet with you and work out the details but I'm tied up the rest of the day. I help coach a little league baseball team and we have the final game of the season this afternoon. Would it be possible to meet either tomorrow or Sunday?"

"Tomorrow would be best for me. I need to get back to Houston and was planning on driving back on Sunday."

"Why don't you come to my place for lunch tomorrow and bring JR? Darcie knows the way. If she isn't busy, she is welcome to come also. I know the boys would enjoy seeing her again. Bring your swim wear if you want to go swimming. Plan on making it an afternoon."

"Thanks, that sounds great. I know JR would like to see the boys again. He had a great time with them yesterday. What time should we be there?"

"Let's say some time around eleven. Hildy, my cook, usually likes to serve lunch around noon and believe me she runs the house," I said laughing.

"We'll be there," he said before we hung up.

A short time later, it was time for the boys to grab a snack before we took off for the ball field. Hildy had made a batch of date bars which the boys decimated almost before I got to taste them.

Chris grabbed his baseball equipment and we all took off for San Antonio. We were the first to arrive as usual giving us enough time to get all of the bats, balls, and other equipment ready for the team when they arrived. I marked the batter's box and the foul lines before Jack showed up.

"Hey, Crane. How is the tribe doing?" he asked with a smirk on his face.

"Just fine, thanks, now that I'm out of jail," I said shaking his outstretched hand and laughing.

"I'm really sorry about all of that. Joyce is in a lot of trouble for filing a false police report. She may even face perjury charges because of it. Have you decided whether you are going to file a civil suit against her?" he asked.

"I'm still thinking about it. I'd just like for the whole thing to go away," I replied.

The other team arrived in a beat-up old mini school bus. Their coaches were friends of Jack's and were also police officers. I was a little surprised that they both were in uniform. Jack explained that they had just gotten off their shift and it was just easier for them to come as they were. The kids didn't seem to mind.

Both teams played their hearts out but the score was tied going into the sixth inning. The Hornets were the home team so we would have the last at bat to try to break the tie. We even had a few spectators watching the game from the bleachers where I had found Joel. I didn't pay that much attention to them since they were not being obnoxious like many parents are at their kid's ballgame.

I was standing at the fence near the dugout in the bottom half of the inning with two outs when Chris pushed up against me and started whining.

"What's the matter, Chris?" I asked.

"Don't make me go with them, please!" he begged with his face buried in my side.

"Who?"

"Them," he said pointing into the bleachers.

I followed his finger and saw the man and woman that I had seen on TV saying that their son was missing and they thought had been kidnapped.

"It's alright," I said. "No one is going to take you away. Are they your mom and dad?"

"Yes, but I don't want to go with them. I want to stay with you, Uncle Crane," he whimpered.

"Okay, don't worry. I'll take care of it," I said hoping that I really could.

Calling time out, I motioned for Jack who was coaching first base to come to me. I stopped just in front of home plate and waited for him to get there. I turned so that I was facing the pitcher's mound which put Jack facing the bleachers.

"Jack, be subtle, but see that couple sitting in the second row from the top on the right hand side? They are Chris' parents. I don't know what they are doing here but I would bet they are here to get Chris back for some reason. I'd like to know why since Chris said they were always telling him how much better it would be without him," I said.

"Yeah, I see them. They both have warrants out for their arrest so we shouldn't have any problem keeping them from taking Chris. Besides, you have temporary custody of him anyway," Jack responded. "I'll have one of my two uniformed friends work his way around behind them and place them under arrest. I'll try to have him make as little fuss as possible but I don't know how those two will react."

Jack went back to the first base coaching box near the other team's dugout and strolled over to talk to one of their coaches. In the mean time, I went back to my position near our dugout. The game started up again. Billy, our third baseman, took that moment to hit a towering fly ball. I thought for sure that it was going over the fence for a home run but their center fielder made an heroic effort and caught it just before it cleared the fence for the last out. According to the local rules we played under, any game tied at the end of six innings would stay that way, tied.

In all of the excitement of the near home run, one of Jack's friends was able to work his way around behind the bleachers. He surprised Chris' parents and had placed them under arrest by the time the excitement had calmed down. Jack and the other coach ran to the aid of the arresting officer to see if he needed help. The Martins did not resist but were a little surprised that they were being arrested protesting that they hadn't done anything.

One of the officers used his portable radio to call for a squad car and a female officer to take the two prisoners to jail.

I told the boys to start putting the equipment away in the shed and I went to talk to the Martins to see if they would tell me why I was put through all of that hassle.

"Why did you lie to CPS about Chris being kidnapped?" I asked with more bitterness than I intended.

"We didn't," Mrs. Martin said. "It was all Gehrig's idea. She was mad at you because the judge criticized her work. She said she wanted to get even with you for causing her trouble with her boss. We just wanted to find Chris."

"Why did you want him now? You ran off and left him to fend for himself. If you cared so much about him why did you do that?" I asked angrily.

"My sister died and left all of her money to him. It should be mine! I was her only sister. That damn brat doesn't deserve her money. It's mine! It's mine! I want it!" she screamed.

"You're pathetic," I almost spat and turned my back on her.

"Jack, can you find out more about this? Chris only knows his aunt's name is Tammy. It may not amount to much, but I would rather see him get it than those two," I said.

"Yeah, let me see what information I can get out of them. I'll call you," Jack replied.

The team was just finishing putting all the equipment in the shed when I got back there. The boys from the other team were just standing around not knowing what to do. Both of their coaches were with Chris' parents who were in handcuffs.

"Hey guys, come here a minute," I said to all of the boys. When they all assembled around me I continued, "If you guys like pizza, I'll take you all to CiCi's. How does that sound?"

Hearing no objections from anyone, not even from my boys who had pizza for supper last night, I guess the matter was settled. I got one of the other coaches to drive the old school bus with both teams crowded into it. Thank goodness CiCi's was only about five blocks away. I drove the Land Rover with my four plus Chris.

The manager's face was priceless when he saw 29 young boys and two adults enter all at the same time. I thought he was going to cry. I went to the cashier and told her to put it all on one bill. If you have never been to a CiCi's, it is an all you can eat pizza buffet. They serve all kinds of pizzas including dessert pizzas.

One pass through the buffet line and the pizzas were history. It took the workers a few minutes to try to refill the line but as soon as they brought more the boys inhaled them. After about a half an hour the boys' eating binge subsided. I was very pleasantly surprised at the boys' behavior. They were a little noisy but overall they were very well mannered.

LeRoy, the coach of the other team who had driven the school bus agreed to drive all of the kids to their homes. I'm glad he did because it was getting dark and this side of town was not where I would like to be alone on the street after sundown. It wasn't going to be a big deal because the kids on our team all lived within a miles radius of the ballpark. Most of them lived in the run down apartment complexes that were a feature of this part of town.

By the time we got home Hildy, had all of the boys' uniforms laundered and put away in their closets. I informed her that we would be having company for lunch and possibly dinner tomorrow. She immediately started planning what to have even though I told her not to go to any extra effort.

The rest of the evening was pretty much normal. After the boys' had their showers, Chris came into the family room and climbed into the recliner beside me. He put his head on my chest and put one arm across my body. He didn't say anything for a few minutes, just held on to me.

"What's going to happen to my mom and dad?" he finally asked.

"I really don't know, son. Your mom and dad did some bad things and they will probably be in jail for a while. I don't know for how long," I told him.

"When they get out do I have to go back to them?"

"I don't have an answer for that either. We'll just have to wait and see, but for right now you're going to be staying with us. Is that alright with you?"

"Yes, Uncle Crane. I don't want to go back with them. I want to stay here. Please? They don't like me. They're always yelling at me and telling me I'm bad. I don't do nothing and I try to be good but they still hate me. They wish I'd never been borned," he said looking up at me with tears running down his cheeks.

"We'll have to see what the judge says when we go see her," I said giving him a peck on the nose. "You better go jump in bed. We're going to have company tomorrow. Do you remember JR the boy we met the other night at Chuck E Cheese? He is going to be here and maybe swim with us. How would you like that?" I asked.

"Oh, goody. He's nice," he said.

"Are you going to sleep with the twins again tonight? You know you can have your own bed if you want," I told him.

"I want to sleep with Larry and Lenny. We don't talk or nothing and we're real good and we go to sleep real quick," he said with a pleading tone to his voice.

"Alright, if that's what you want and as long as the three of you behave and get your sleep," I said giving him a hug and a little jab to his ribs eliciting a soft giggle. "You go on to bed and I'll be in to say goodnight in a little bit."

I went to bed shortly after tucking all five boys in. The excitement of the day finally got to me and I fell asleep almost the instant I got in bed.

I don't know how long I had been asleep when I awoke with a start. Something was shaking me trying to rouse me out of a very sound sleep. When my eyes finally were able to focus I saw in the dim light the small outline of TJ.

"What's the matter?" I asked bolting upright in bed.

"Uncle Crane my tummy hurts. I can't sleep," he said pushing his face into my chest. I could feel his hot tears dripping on my bare skin.

I flipped on the bedside lamp and lifted him onto my lap. "Show me where it hurts, son," I told him hoping it wasn't anything serious.

When he pointed to the middle of his stomach, I was much relieved. He had probably just eaten too much pizza, more than likely trying to keep up with the other older boys.

"Let's go see what we have that can make your tummy feel better," I said sliding out of bed and picking him up. I knew I didn't have anything for a stomach ache in my medicine cabinet, but I remembered something my mother gave me to soothe my stomach when I was a kid.

I carried TJ into the kitchen and sat him down at the breakfast bar. Going to the pantry, I retrieved the box of Arm & Hammer baking soda and mixed a teaspoon of it in a half a cup of water and stirred it until it was dissolved. "Here drink this down as quickly as you can. It doesn't taste too good but it is not awful," I said as I handed him the cup. "It'll make you burp too."

"Yuck, that tastes yucky," he grimaced.

"Take a sip of water to rinse your mouth out," I told him. "If you feel like burping, don't hold it in. Just let it go. Let's walk around a bit to help it work."

We hadn't take a dozen steps when he let go with a big burp followed by a high pitched giggle. A couple more burps each one getting smaller and I decided it was okay for him to get back to bed.

"Does your tummy feel better?" I asked.

"Yeah," he said with sleep in his voice.

"You can sleep in my bed so if your tummy starts hurting again we can get it fixed quickly," I told him.

I don't think he knew what bed he was in by the time I pulled the covers up and tucked him in. He had curled up in his usual ball and was fast asleep before I got under the covers.

"Goodnight, little one. I love you so much. I don't know what I would do without you now," I said as I brushed his hair back and kissed his forehead lightly before I turned the light out.

I don't know why I was surprised when I woke up the next morning and found Joel in bed with us on the other side of TJ.

Hildy was already up and in the kitchen when I got there for my first cup of coffee. She was busy planning the menu for lunch since we would have two, maybe three extra mouths to feed. I told her that maybe we should just put something on the grill, either chicken or bratwurst or hamburgers. She took to the idea of bratwursts but suggested some hotdogs in case some of the guests didn't like bratwursts. She would have to drive to New Braunfels to pick up the meat and get some buns, but she had to run an errand over there this morning anyway.

The boys came stumbling into the kitchen with that starved look only a young boy can have. Hildy poured glasses of juice and sat them on the table. TJ surprised me by climbing on my lap and snuggled up against my chest.

"I love you Uncle Crane," he murmured.

"I love you too, little one. How does your tummy feel this morning?" I asked kissing the top of his head. "Are you ready for some breakfast?"

"Yeah!" he said brightening. "It feels good."

Hildy looked at me with a quizzical expression on her face so I had to explain the occurrences of last night. Although she knew that my home remedy treatment of TJ's upset stomach was effective she thought it would be better if we stocked the medicine cabinet with commercially available medicines. We also decided it would be advisable to stock up on treatments for scrapes and cuts and other minor ailments that befall active boys.

Everyone wanted to swim after breakfast. Since we had a couple of hours before our guests were due to arrive, I joined them in our usual game of king of the hill. Actually, I think the game was becoming one of seeing who could dunk Uncle Crane the most times. After a while, I convinced them to play a type of water volleyball which was much easier on me. Chris, TJ and I took on Joel and the twins. With Chris' swimming talent, my reach and TJ cheering us on we were able to hold our own against the other boys.

Around 10:30, I decided to change out of my swim trunks and into some other more appropriate clothes in preparation for our guests to get here. I had just finished changing when the gate buzzer sounded. The security camera showed Darcie's Toyota so I activated the gate to let them in. Thank goodness, the gate maintenance people were able to fix the gate quickly after it had been broken or I would have had to walk down to it to let people in and out.

I had mixed emotions as I opened the front door and went out to greet our guests. I wondered if my attraction to both of these people would still be as strong. As they drove up, I could see JR's head barely visible above the window swiveling around trying to see everything at once. Eric got out of the front seat, opened the back door of the car and released JR from the confines of his seat belt. He fairly bounced out still looking all around.

"Where is everyone?" JR asked.

Eric took hold of his son's shoulder and said, "Where are your manners? You haven't even said hello to Mr. Johnson," Turning to me Eric said, "Please forgive my son's manners. He has been hyper every since I told him we were going to visit your boys. It seems they told him that you had deer running around the place and he's never seen any up close."

"Hello, Mr. Johnson," JR said extend his hand to me.

"Welcome to our home, JR. The boys are around back in the pool. Did you bring your swim suit?" I asked.

"No, my suit is in Houston," he said sadly.

"Well, I'll bet that you could wear one of the twins' suits if you wanted to," I told him.

Eric interrupted our conversation, "That would be great. He has given me all kinds of grief because we wouldn't stop and buy him one on the way up here. Thanks!"

I shook his hand and then turned to Darcie, "I'm glad that you could come. I don't have a suit that I can lend you but you are welcome to put your feet in the water. Eric, you could probably wear one of mine if you feel like it."

Darcie laughed and said, "I'm not very much of a swimmer but I may take you up on the offer to get my feet wet."

"I might take you up on the offer as well," Eric responded.

"Let's get this guy into a suit while we discuss business," I said leading JR and them into the house.

Darcie said hello to Hildy and went out on the patio to see the boys. I introduced Eric and JR to Hildy and then led them to the twins' room to find a swim suit for JR. I was right. Their suit fit him just fine. Maybe it was a little big but not too noticeable.

Eric and I sat down and discussed the terms of his employment. His salary expectations were in line with what Foster and I had discussed so the only thing we had to negotiate was when he would be able to start work. His business in Houston was winding down and he was in the process of negotiating its sale to two of the people who worked for him. We agree to start his contract in two weeks.

All this time I had held my emotions in check. Now that the business was taken care of I could enjoy the company of these two people I was attracted to. Eric and I joined Darcie on the patio to watch the boys enjoying themselves. JR interacted with the other five as if they had been life long friends. I saw Hildy at the barbeque tending the bratwursts and went over to offer my assistance. The grill was covered with enough bratwurst and hotdogs to feed an army or at least six hungry pre-teen boys.

Hildy started laying out the meal on the patio table while I continued tending the grill. I called the boys and told them to dry off and put their shirts on. Hildy is strict about wearing shirts at the table. They had learned that if they wanted to eat they had to be dressed appropriately so they ran into the house drying off but still dripping as they went to get their shirts and one for JR. In a flash the boys returned suitably dressed this time with saliva dripping from their hungry lips.

Hildy put a couple buns on each of their plates and sent them to me at the grill to be filled. They had a choice of either the wieners or the brats. Joel took the brats while the rest of the boys took the hotdogs. After the boys had filled their plates with baked beans, potato salad and chips, the adults got in line to fill their plates. Hildy had fixed sauerkraut to go on the bratwursts. I was in heaven. Bratwursts with sauerkraut and spicy mustard, there is nothing like it.

While we were eating, I mentioned to Darcie the brief conversation that I had with Chris' parents about a possible inheritance. She said that she would check it out with her contacts in the police department to see if they had any information about it. I told her that Jack was also trying to find out as much as he could about it and that he promised to call when he had any information.

All through the meal, I was continually fascinated by both of these individuals. They were bright, charming, friendly, great conversationalists and very attractive physically. I was so wrapped up in my own mental turmoil about my feelings for these two that more than once they had to repeat something they had said to me.

The boys finished their devastation of the hotdogs and bratwursts and came to us pleading to go swimming again. They were a little disappointed when we told them they had to wait for about an hour before they could get back in the water.

"Why don't you go show JR the deer? Be sure to put on some shoes. The rocks are very sharp in the yard. Don't go too far from the house. I'm sure that the deer aren't that far away," I told them.

JR was the first to react positively about getting to see the deer. The other boys were getting used to seeing them so it was not quite as big a deal for them. Still they readily agreed to show him the deer.

Eric said the he would also like to see the deer. "You don't get to see much wildlife around Houston unless you go to the zoo," he said. "I'd also like to go swimming later if the offer of a suit is still good."

"Of course, I'm sure you could wear one of mine. I have a 30 inch waist. You look like maybe 28?" I said. Damn, I could barely wait to see this guy in my trunks.

"Yeah, I've a 28 inch waist. I hope that they have drawstrings," he said.

Darcie joined us as we went looking for the deer. It didn't take long to find some. The boys had already seen them and were slowly approaching them to see how close they could get before the deer would start moving away. There were eight of them grazing in the side yard. TJ was out in front of the group of boys and was able to get within about five feet of a doe before she decided that was too close and moved away causing the rest of the herd to move also. They didn't go far, only about 30 feet before they stopped and started grazing again. This approach/move away pattern repeated itself a couple more time before the deer decided to go some place else where their feeding would not be interrupted.

I took Eric into my bedroom to get him a swim suit. "There are some hangers in the closet over there to hang up your clothes and towels in the linen closet in the bathroom. Make yourself at home," I said hardly able to contain my excitement. I took my suit and changed in TJ and Joel's room.

I know my mouth dropped open when we met in the hall. "Wow, how do you maintain your shape with your business and taking care of JR all by yourself?" I stammered when I regained my senses.

"I have an exercise room set up in my condo with everything you need to keep in shape. Every night after I put JR to bed I work out for 45 minutes to an hour. It helps to relieve stress and to distract me from the loneliness in my life since my wife left me. It has become almost an obsession with me," he said with sadness in his voice.

As we were going out onto the patio, the phone rang and I went to answer it. It was Jack.

"Hi, Jack, what can I do for you?" I asked.

"Crane, I have some information for you concerning Chris and that matter you asked me to look into. It seems that his aunt, Tammy Chandler, was married to an heir of a Midwestern chain of department stores. He died two years ago in a traffic accident in Ohio. She just died of lung cancer last week. From what I have been able to find out, her estate which was left solely to Chris, amounted to over five and a half million dollars. Of course that is before taxes which will probably take a good portion of it but it still should leave him with a sizable chunk of money," he said.

"Good lord, no wonder the Martins wanted to get him back," I mused. "Do you have someone I can contact to get the details of his inheritance? I want to make sure that it is protected from his parents and is available to him when he grows up."

"I don't have that info yet but I should be able to get it the first of the week. I'll give you a call as soon as I find out anything," Jack said before we rang off.

I use to have such a simple and boring life. Now there is too much going on. I hope things settle down pretty soon or I'm really going to need that psychiatrist.

Starting toward the patio, I wondered what more could possibly happen.

CHAPTER 19

I hadn't taken two steps toward the patio when it hit me like the proverbial ton of bricks. Turning I dashed into the study and to my desk. I opened the bottom left hand drawer and removed a large 8" x 11" sealed, padded envelope that I had placed here six years ago when I moved into the house out of college.

The six boys and Eric were splashing around in the pool when I came out of the house. Darcie had retreated to the patio table under the umbrella to escape the hot South Texas sun. I went over and joined her.

"Darcie, there is something that I want to show you. It is something that I have had sealed in here for nearly fifteen years," I told her as I carefully broke the seal on the envelope. I removed the contents and handed them to her.

"What is this?" she asked before she looked at the items.

"Please, just look at them and tell me what you think," I said.

I watched her face change from a curious expression to one of total disbelief. She had in her hands a series of five photographs taken by a professional photographer. One was of my mother. One was of my father. A third one was one of them both together. The fourth one was of me at age 14. The last one was of all three of us.

"Is this who I think it is?" she asked holding up the picture of my mother.

"Yes," I replied.

"I can't believe this. If her hair were styled differently, it would be a picture of me. The resemblance is uncanny. Eric! Eric, come here a minute would you?" she called to him.

Toweling off that buff body as he came, Eric sat down next to his sister.

Darcie handed him the picture of my mother without saying anything.

"When did you get this picture taken? I haven't seen it before. I haven't seen you with your hair combed that way either," he said.

"That's not me. That is Crane's mother," she said.

"You've got to be kidding! I would swear that it's you. Is that really true Crane?" he asked turning to me.

"Yes, that picture was taken on the last home visit by my parents six months before they were killed in a plane accident. It is the last time I ever saw them. I have kept those pictures sealed up for the last 15 years. It just was too painful for me to see them," I told him.

"Darcie, from the first time I met with you at your office, I felt like I had seen you or known you at some other time. It didn't hit me until after I talked to Jack and found out about a sizeable inheritance that Chris has come into. I guess it was because I inherited a sizable amount of money from my parents, something just clicked and I realized where I had seen you before. I'm still a little confused, but I think I understand my feelings toward you more clearly now. You are a very beautiful, bright and highly desirable lady. But I think that you can see the problems that could arise if we pursued a more intimate relationship. I would never know if it were you I was pursuing or if I were trying to regain my mother. I'm sorry," I said with some regret.

"Yes, I see," she said. "I still think that we can be friends and besides I'm still going to be handling Chris' case. And what is this about a sizable inheritance? The last I heard we didn't know if it was big or small."

I explained to her what Jack had told me.

"Well that's good news for Chris. I'll see what resources that we have to find out the terms of his aunt's will now that we know who she is. I hope that she established a trust or some other instrument that will protect the assets from being squandered by his parents when and if they get out of jail," Darcie said. "I can't speak for Judge Riley, but I think that a case can be made for terminating their parental rights based on their abandoning him and their criminal behavior."

"I sincerely hope that something can be done about them. Even if they didn't abuse him physically or sexually, they certainly subjected him to mental and verbal abuse which can be devastating to his self concept and self worth. The scars may not be visible, but they are just as real," I preached to her.

The rest of the afternoon went by more quickly than the boys wanted. They either swam or snacked or chased the deer until nearly dark. Almost as if there were some telepathic signal that pervaded the air the boys in mass rushed up to the three of us on the patio.

"Uncle Crane we're hungry!" all six of them shouted in unison. Even JR joined in calling me Uncle.

"JR, mind your manners. We need to go home," Eric chided his son.

"You all are welcome to stay for supper. I'm sure that Hildy has prepared more than enough to feed us all. In fact she would probably be insulted if you didn't stay," I told Eric. Turning to the boys I said, "Why don't you guys go get the chlorine washed off and put on your shorts? Hildy expects you to be dressed properly for supper. Eric, you and JR can use the shower in my bedroom."

I went to check with Hildy to make sure that she had in fact fixed enough for our guests. I need not have worried. She had prepared one of her late husband's favorite meals. A tamale casserole smothered with chili and topped with cheddar and Monterrey Jack cheese. Spanish rice, refried beans, tortilla chips and salsa rounded out the evening fare. She had even made flan for dessert.

I barely had time to jump in the spare bedroom shower and change my clothes before the boys were lining up at the table. Hildy had put the extra leaf in the table so that it could seat a total of 12. We only had ten but I'm sure that we consumed enough food for twelve.

After supper, we went out to see our guests off.

As I shook Eric's hand, I told him, "Welcome to ACC. We are looking forward to you contributing to the company. I will make sure that you receive your contract by mid week. If there is anything that my secretary Carol or I can do for you to make your move to San Antonio easier, please let us know."

He shook my hand longer than I expected, but I certainly did not complain. As he said goodbye, his eyes seemed to engulf me before he turned away to assist JR into the car and fasten his seatbelt.

Darcie gave me a goodbye hug and whispered in my ear, "Thanks for being honest with me. I think I would have liked our relationship to develop but I can see that it's not possible. Besides, I think that Eric might object," With that, she turned, opened her car door and got in smiling at me.

I think that my face was so red that it lit up the whole area. All I could do was to wave goodbye to them as they drove to the gate.

When I regained my composure I turned to the boys and asked, "How about if we read some more of *Tom Sawyer* before it's bed time?"

A chorus of "Yeah" rang out as they rushed back inside to get the book. I read to them for about an hour before they started to get sleepy. I think TJ had dropped off to sleep a couple of times in my lap before we called it a night. It had been a busy day for all of us.

It rained all day Sunday so the boys didn't get to play outside. The video games, more *Tom Sawyer* and the TV just couldn't tame the boys' restlessness by early afternoon.

When my parents purchased this house, it was part of a bankruptcy sale. The builder went under during some hard times in the home construction business. The house had never been completely finished. My parents completed the ground floor but had never done much to the upstairs. The second floor was one big loft. It wasn't heated or cooled so it was never really used by us on the rare occasions we were in residence at the house. I had not been up there since just after I first moved in permanently.

"I don't think you guys have ever been upstairs," I said.

Joel looked at me strangely, "What upstairs? I didn't know there was an upstairs. Where are the stairs?"

"Follow me, I'll show you," I said leading them to the back entryway to a door that was always kept locked.

Taking a key off the rack beside the back door, I unlocked the door. I reached inside and flipped on the light switch. "Let's see what's up here."

I was nearly trampled by five curious boys as we climbed the stairs.

"What's that?" Joel asked pointing to a rectangular object, partially hidden by a dust cover, with a series of knobs on both sides.

"That is a foosball game," I told him. "Come here, I'll show you how to play."

I retrieved the ball from one of the goals and started to explain the object of the game and how to turn the handles to 'kick' the ball and keep it from going in the goal. The twins and Chris gathered around fascinated at this non-electronic game. TJ had to stand on his tiptoes to see what was going on.

"You can play with two or four players. Joel, why don't you and Chris play Larry and Lenny? TJ and I will watch," I said to them.

I dragged a box from the stack next to the wall to where TJ could stand on it to see all of the action. He and I cheered the boys when they scored and applauded their defensive efforts when they blocked a good try at goal. The twins had an uncanny ability to sense what the other one was doing and were holding their own against their older opponents. All of them were really starting to get the hang of it when their wrists began to get tired from all the twisting.

"That's fun, Uncle Crane," Joel said. "But your hands sure get tired."

"Have any of you ever played table tennis or ping pong?" I asked.

All I got was five boys shaking their heads no.

I pulled the sheet off the table and discovered that four paddles and a ball were still there after all of these years. I had been a pretty fair player in my college days, but hadn't played in a long while. I explained the basics to them and showed them how to serve and how to keep score.

"TJ, I want you to try and hit the ball back across the table when I serve it to you. Remember it has to land on the table to be good," I told him. I served a real slow one to him. He hit it back but he hit it so hard that it flew over my head. "Just hit it easy, it doesn't take much to get it back across."

A couple more serves and he got one back across the net and onto the table. You would have thought that he had won a gold metal he was so happy. I, of course, praised his efforts. The rest of the boys did too. A few more times and a few more successes for him and I suggested that we let the other boys try.

TJ had as much fun running after errant balls as he did playing the game. Chris seemed to have a real talent for the game. Joel probably had the least success with the game other than TJ.

This excursion to the unknown upstairs had occupied the entire afternoon. TJ was the first to come to me and tell me he was hungry. That set off a chain reaction. All of the stomachs seemed to be set to the same clock and the hunger alarm had just gone off.

"Okay, go get washed up and I'll see what Hildy has left us for supper," I told them as we descended the stairs. Hildy lets us fend for ourselves on Sunday evenings while she attended church.

What she had left us was a huge pot of beef stew simmering on the stove made just the way I liked it with lots of potatoes, carrots, corn and green beans. To go with the stew she had buttered a loaf of French bread and left a note telling me to put it in the oven for 15 minutes at 400F (~205C).

The boys were ready before the food was so I set them to the task of preparing the table.

I dished out large bowls of the steaming stew to each of the boys telling them not to burn their tongues. I hardly had time to sit down to my own bowl before they were ready for seconds. We pretty much finished off the stew and the French bread. I got to eat the end pieces of the loaf. The hard crusty ends are my favorite pieces and the boys gladly let me have them.

After the supper dishes were put into the dishwasher, I turned on the TV to a National Geographic special that I thought the boys would enjoy. It was all about deep sea diving and all of the strange and beautiful animals that were found at the bottom of the ocean. I was right they were enthralled by the fantastic photography and the sense of adventure.

When the program ended, it was time for a snack before they took their showers and got ready for bed.

"Remember tomorrow you start school at Corinthian Academy so you need to get a good night's sleep. I'll take you to school in the morning and then you can ride the school van home tomorrow afternoon," I told them.

I was about to go tuck the boys into bed when Joel came into the family room where I was still watching TV. He surprised me by climbing into the recliner with me. He hadn't sat on my lap for quite a while.

"I love you Uncle Crane," he whispered.

"I love you too, Joel, more than I can say," I said giving him a hug.

"I didn't know grown ups could be so nice before you found me. I don't ever want to leave. You won't send us away, will you?" he pleaded.

"No, never! My life would be empty without all of you here."

"How 'bout Chris? Is he gonna stay too?"

"That is up to the judge. I hope that he will be able to stay with us. Now let's get you into bed. I don't want you to fall asleep in class tomorrow. You know Mr. Coulter may be one of your teachers, don't you?"

"Really? He's nice, I like him."

"Yes, he starts teaching there tomorrow just like you guys are starting there," I said as I led him to his bedroom and tucked him and TJ in for the night.

The boys were all excited the next morning about starting their new school. They looked so handsome in their matching uniforms that I had to take a picture of them before we piled into the Land Rover to go to school.

When we got to the school, I parked the car and escorted them into the administration office to get them properly registered and pick up their room assignments and class schedules. With all the paperwork taken care of, I gathered them all together to give them some last minute instructions.

"Now after school all of you are to wait for Joel right here and get on the van together. Joel, you are to get on van number 7. Remember that's van number 7. Okay? I'm depending on you to take care of your brothers and Chris. I know you can do it," I said. "You boys be good and pay attention in class."

I gave each one a hug and sent them off to their classrooms. My heart was in my throat as they walked away. They were off on a new adventure and I was suffering from separation anxiety.

Going to the office seemed strange. I hadn't been there in several weeks to spend a full day working and never since I bought out my partner Eric. Even though Carol and Foster had done a remarkable job running the place in Eric and my absence there was still a lot of paperwork and other odds and ends to take care of. I spent the entire morning catching up first with Carol and then Foster on the status of each contract that we had ongoing.

After instructing Carol on the details of Eric Levin's contract, she typed it up and gave it to me for my signature and then put it in the outgoing mail.

We didn't stop working until almost one o'clock when my stomach reminded me that we hadn't eaten lunch. "Carol, if you and Foster don't have any plans I would like to take you both to lunch. Would you see if we can get reservations at Texas Land & Cattle Steak House over on I-10?"

They both agreed they were free and hungry. Carol made our reservations for 1:30 so we had to leave almost immediately to get there on time.

I had a voice mail from Jack to call him as soon as I returned to the office. It sounded urgent so I immediately dialed his number.

"Jack Hogan, how can I help you?"

"Jack, it's Crane. You called earlier."

"Yes, Billy Joe Slocum the detective working Joel's dad's case wanted me to get in touch with you to see if Joel would be available for a preliminary hearing on the murder charge tomorrow afternoon. The DA hasn't issued a subpoena for him but I'm sure she will if she thinks it necessary."

"He just started to school today, but I suppose I can have him there. What time is the hearing?"

"It starts at two o'clock in Judge Farley's courtroom. I'm not sure which room that is so look it up on the directory inside the courthouse. Oh, you might consider having a lawyer there to represent Joel. I know the defense attorney and he can be, let's say, rather aggressive in his questioning of witnesses."

"Thanks Jack, I'll call Benjamin to see if he can recommend someone."

As soon as we hung up I called Benjamin's office to arrange for a lawyer to be with us at the hearing. He told me that Jimmy Sanchez who was my attorney when I was put in jail would represent Joel. That made me feel a lot better.

I also called Dr. Adams to see what he recommended I do to prepare Joel for the hearing. His advice was to explain to Joel in as unemotional manner as possible what was going to happen and to make sure I gave him extra attention, love and support before he had to get on the stand.

Giving him love and support was the easy part. Telling him what was going to happen would be the hardest thing so I called Jimmy to see if he could give me an idea as to what Joel might expect when he testified. He wasn't an awful lot of help other than to say that he would do everything he could to protect Joel from being traumatized by the defense attorney's examination. His only suggestion was to tell Joel to answer the questions as completely as he could and not to embellish anything.

I wanted to get home to make sure that the boys got on the right van to get home so I left early. I was waiting at the gate when van number 7 pulled up and five active boys hopped out yelling goodbye to their van driver and their new friends.

TJ ran to me and jumped up into my arms. "Did you have a good time today?" I asked.

"It was the best," he said. "Mrs. Cowen is fun. She reads to us if we're good. I like her."

"That's great," I told him. "How about the rest of you? How was your day?"

Joel was the first to reply, "I have Mr. Coulter for Geography and home room. Everybody is so nice. Thanks for letting us go to school there Uncle Crane."

The twins and Chris all talked at the same time but they too seemed to like the school. "We played dodge ball at recess and we had to tell everybody our names and everybody shook our hands and we ate lunch in the cafeteria and everything."

"So you want to go back to school there tomorrow?" I said jokingly.

"Yes!" everyone yelled and took off to the house to see if Hildy had a snack for them.

Later that evening I took Joel to one side and told him about the hearing tomorrow and what was going to happen as much as I knew. I put my arm around him as I was talking to him and hugged him tightly to my side.

"I'll be there all the time. All you have to do is tell the truth exactly as you remember. Jimmy Sanchez will be there too. You remember him don't you? He's the one that got me out of jail and then ate lunch here. He's going to help you too," I told him giving him another hug.

He seemed comfortable with going to court tomorrow, but I'm sure that he would have preferred to stay in school instead.

I was not comfortable with him having to testify against his father. I remember the interview with Detective Silver and the effect that it had on him. He wasn't even cross examined then and she was very gentle with him. I was afraid that this experience would be even more traumatic.

As we waited for the school van to arrive to pick up the boys I told them, "Joel will not be there this afternoon to see that you get on the right van. Be sure that you see the number 7 on the van. That is the one you are to get on to bring you home."

The van arrived as we were talking. "Now see that 7 on the van, that is the one you are to get on and only that one. Be good and study hard," I told them as I gave them a group hug and sent them on their way.

I picked Joel up from school at noon and drove to San Antonio to meet with Jimmy Sanchez before Joel's court appearance. We met Jimmy at a small cafe about six blocks from the court house. He was waiting outside when we got there.

While we were waiting for our food order to be delivered, Jimmy explained to Joel and me what to expect and impressed on Joel how important it was to tell the truth when he was asked questions. He explained that he would be there with Joel to protect him and his rights.

Our food came but I was too nervous to eat much. Joel on the other hand had no problems eating his lunch and even had part of mine.

We reported to the court bailiff at 1:45 and were told to wait in the witness room adjacent to the courtroom and not to talk about the case with any other witness. There were no other witnesses in the room when we entered, but within five minutes an older distinguished Hispanic gentleman and a young lady entered. They appeared to know each other. Finally, a police officer in uniform and what I assumed was a plain clothes detective arrived.

At about ten after two, the Hispanic man was called by the bailiff. I learned he was the coroner from listening to the young lady. She was next to be called approximately 20 minutes later. I think she was the forensic lab tech because the policeman asked her if she had received a gun that need to be tested. The policeman was next followed by the detective. We had been sitting in the room now for about an hour and a half with nothing to do but sit there. Joel was beginning to get restless. I tried to keep him occupied by asking him all kinds of questions about Corinthian Academy and the new boys that he had met and so on.

Finally, Joel was called by the bailiff to go into the courtroom. Jimmy and I stood up and went with him. As we entered the courtroom, Joel pushed back against me and hid his face in my side.

"It's alright, son. No one is going to hurt you. I promise," I whispered to him.

"But that's my dad," he whimpered.

"Don't be afraid. He can't hurt you any more," I said.

Jimmy stepped in front of us and addressed the court, "Your Honor, my name is James Sanchez. I am the attorney for Joel Andersen. If it pleases the court, I request that the court instruct both the prosecution and defense to question my client with the greatest restraint. He is in a fragile emotional state and is under the care of a child psychiatrist, Dr. Owen Adams."

"Thank you Mr. Sanchez. The court takes note of your request and agrees that this witness should not be subjected to unduly harsh questioning from either the prosecution or the defense. This is a preliminary hearing. We are here only to decide if there is enough evidence to bind the defendant over for trial. Gentlemen, I am instructing you to tread lightly in your questioning. The court will not tolerate any badgering of the witness," Judge Farley said.

With that, the bailiff led Joel to the witness chair and asked him to raise his right hand and swear to tell the truth.

"I will, I promise," Joel responded nervously.

"Tell us what your full name is," the prosecutor said.

"Joel Jay Andersen."

"What is your father's name?"

"Harry Andersen."

"Do you see him in the courtroom?"

"Yes."

"Would you describe where he is and what he is wearing?"

"He's over there wearing orange coveralls."

"Let the record reflect that the witness has identified the defendant."

"It is so ordered," the judge said.

"What is your mother's name?"

"Dorothy Marie Andersen."

"Do you know what happened to her?"

"Yes."

"Tell us what happened."

"He shot her."

"Who shot her?"

"My dad."

"How do you know he shot her?"

"I saw him do it."

"Where were you when you saw him shoot her?"

"In the door between the kitchen and living room."

"How far away from you was your dad?"

"Oh…I guess 'bout as far as you."

"Do you think that is about 10 feet?"

"Yeah, I guess."

"How many times did you see your dad shoot your mother?"

"I think six. I know it was a lot. He shot her two times in the face before she fell down and then four more times."

Tears were beginning to flow down Joel's cheeks. I wanted to rush to him and hold him but knew that I couldn't.

"What happened then?"

"I think I screamed or something 'cause he ran to me and pulled the trigger on the gun a couple more times but there were no bullets in it."

"Did he say anything to you?"

"Yes, he grabbed my throat and said he'd rip it out if I ever told anyone."

"What happened then?"

"He ran out the front door and drove away real fast."

"What did you do?"

"I think I went out the front door too. I remember screaming something."

"What happened then?"

"I don't remember anything until Uncle Crane found me."

"Who is Uncle Crane?"

"That's him over there. He takes care of all of us. He's like our new dad."

My heart nearly exploded when he said I was like a "new dad," Nothing would make me happier than to be his dad. If Jimmy hadn't placed a restraining arm on mine, I probably would have rushed up and hugged him. All I could do was to give him my biggest smile as the tears of joy flowed down my cheeks.

"That's all the questions I have your Honor," the prosecutor said and sat down.

"Mr. Lane, do you wish to cross examine?" the judge asked.

"Yes, Your Honor.

"Joel, why weren't you in school the day your mother died?"

"The day before when he got home he started beating momma. I tried to stop him and he whipped me when I tried to get him to stop hitting momma. Then he fucked me and locked me in the shed all night, but I dug my way out the next day. Then I went in the house and saw him do it. That's why I wasn't in school."

This time there was fire in his eyes. Also, it was only the second time I had ever heard him say fuck.

"Your Honor, I move to strike that answer."

"Denied, counselor, you knew the answer before you asked and you asked it anyway."

"No further questions."

"Does the prosecution have any re-direct?"

"No, Your Honor."

"The witness is excused. That means you can go son," the judge said.

Joel fairly ran to me and jumped into my arms. I squeezed him so tight I was afraid that I might hurt him but I didn't put him down until we were out of the courtroom.

"I'm so proud of you, Joel. I know it was very hard for you to do that but you were so brave. I love you!" I told him now clutching his hand.

"Jimmy thanks for being here. I'm sure if you hadn't the defense would have been very aggressive with Joel and I probably would have gotten into trouble," I said shaking his hand as we parted company.

"Come on son, let's go home. I'll bet your brothers are wondering where we are," I said and pulled him under my arm and led him out of the courthouse.

CHAPTER 20

Joel and I started for the car when my pager started vibrating. I had shut off the beep during the court proceeding. When I looked at the number, I saw that it was my home phone. We hurried to the car where I had left my cell phone locked up in the console. I immediately dial my home number as soon as we got into the car.

"Hello," I could tell it was Hildy.

"Hildy, this is Crane. What do you need?" I queried.

Her voice was frantic when she replied, "TJ didn't get on the school van. He's not home. I don't know where he is."

"How about the twins and Chris, are they home?"

"Yes, they're here, but they don't know where he is," she almost sobbed. "They didn't notice he wasn't on the van until they were almost home. They were talking to their new friends and didn't pay any attention when they got on the van."

"Oh, my god! This can't be happening. How could they not miss their own brother? We will be home as soon as possible. I just hope that the cops are not out this afternoon because I might not pay any attention to the speed limits."

I punched the off button and pulled the car out of the parking garage giving the attendant a 20 dollar bill not waiting for my change. I wanted to get home fast even though I didn't know what I was going to do.

The trip which would normally take at least 45 minutes was accomplished in just under 25. I was extremely thankful that the evening rush hour traffic had not yet begun in earnest.

As Joel and I walked into the house, the phone was ringing. Hildy answered it before I could reach it.

"Oh thank god," she said as tears began streaming down her cheeks. "Thank you, thank you so much. Let me have you talk to Mr. Johnson."

"Who is it?" I asked as she handed me the phone.

"They have TJ at their house. I don't know who they are. I just know that he's safe," she sobbed.

"Hello, this is Crane Johnson," I said taking the phone from Hildy.

"Good evening, my name is Harold Nicholas. Your son seems to have gotten on the wrong van at school this afternoon and came home with my son Joey," the voice on the other end of the line said.

"You don't know how glad I am to hear that. I was beside myself. This was only the second day that he has been attending Corinthian. I guess he just got confused as to what van he was supposed to get on. Where do you live? I will come get him as soon as I can," I said with the relief showing in my voice.

"We live just about a half a mile north of 306. Do you know where the Conoco station is on 306?" he asked.

"Yes, I do."

"If you turn north at that intersection we are the second house on the right. As I said, it is about a half a mile up the road. You will see our name on the mail box."

"Thanks, I'll be there in about 15 minutes. I appreciate you calling us."

I grabbed Joel and headed for the car. "Come on let's go get your brother."

We made record time getting to the Nicholas' home. I skidded to a halt in front of a very impressive home set back about two hundred yards from the road. I think Joel and I were both out of the car a split second after it came to a halt. As we ran up to the door it opened and TJ came out.

I fell to my knees and grabbed him in a tight hug. For a moment I couldn't say anything I was so overwhelmed with emotion. I didn't know whether to be angry with him or to be happy that he was safe. The latter emotion won out.

"Oh TJ, TJ! You had us so worried. I'm so happy that you're okay. I love you so much. I couldn't bear to be without you. Please don't scare us like this again," I sobbed with tears streaming down my cheeks.

"I'm sorry, Uncle Crane. I really am. I didn't mean to worry you. Really I didn't. You're not going to whip me are you?" he cried.

"Oh, no! I would never whip you. You know that don't you? How come you got on the wrong van?" I asked.

"I guess I was playing with Joey and followed him to the van. I didn't think until we started going that Larry and Lenny were not on it. I started getting scared, but Joey said it was okay that I could come to his house. I'm sorry. I'm sorry," he whimpered into my ear.

Joel had joined in our hug at some point and was kissing his brother on the cheek. "I didn't think I'd ever see you again and it scared me. Don't ever do that again, I need you."

I stood up and as I did I picked up TJ and held him in my arms as tightly as I could and still allowed him to breathe. It was then that I noticed a tall thin man standing there with a boy about TJ's age.

"You must be Mr. Nicholas," I said as I extended a free hand to him.

"Harold, please and this is my son Joey," he said shaking my hand.

"I'm very pleased to meet both of you. I don't know how to thank you for looking after my foster son. He and his brothers have given me a new reason for living," I said bringing Joel into our hug. "This young man is Joel. He is also my foster son."

"You mean that you have two foster children living with you?" he asked.

"Actually, I have five. It's a long story but TJ and Joel have twin brothers that are also my foster sons and then there is a fifth boy that lives with us at least temporarily," I said as TJ and Joel gave me strange looks.

"God bless you! You and your wife are truly good people to take in so many unfortunate children."

"I'm not married," I responded.

"You're not? I assumed that the lady I talked to on the phone was your wife."

"No, that was my housekeeper, cook and nanny for the boys. She is the only reason that I have been able to take care of these wonderful boys," I said. "She pretty much runs the household."

Harold and I exchanged pleasantries and some personal information before I decided it was time that we got back home. I did learn that Harold was a single father, that his wife had died last year in a car crash on 281 just north of San Antonio at Stone Oak Parkway.

"If you and Joey are not busy this weekend, why don't you join us? We are going to go fishing on Saturday and you are most welcome to come along. I know that TJ would really like to have Joey come," I told him.

"Thank you that would be great. What time are you going?" he asked.

"Why don't you meet us at the marina at 10 o'clock? I'll have Hildy pack us a lunch and we can make a day of it," I told him.

"We'll be there, won't we Joey?" he said as he put his arm around his son and pulled him against his hip.

The three of us climbed into the car. Joel and TJ got in the back seat and fastened their seat belts. We all waved goodbye and we drove out of their long driveway.

As we drove home, I could see in the rearview mirror that Joel was whispering something in TJ's ear. I would have loved to hear what he was saying but didn't want to interfere. It looked serious.

Hildy exploded out of the house as we drove up the driveway. With tears streaming down her cheeks, she grabbed TJ and squeezed him to her breasts. "Don't you ever do that again young man. You nearly scared me to death. What would I do without my little TJ?"

"I'm sorry Hildy. I won't do it again. I promise, really I do," he said.

"Okay, you remember that," she said and kissed him on both cheeks before she put him down and gave him a swat on the seat of his pants. "Go get your clothes changed. It will be time for supper soon."

The boys and Hildy went into the house. I sat down on the front steps and began sobbing uncontrollably. I sat there for a few minutes before I felt a pair of arms around my shoulders. As I raised my head, I looked into those beautiful azure eyes of Joel.

"What's wrong, Uncle Crane?" he asked.

"Joel, you and your brothers and Chris have become such an important part of my life that when TJ was missing a part of my heart felt like it had been ripped out. I love you guys with all of my heart and soul. If anything happened to any of you, I don't know how I could stand it. You all are the most important things in my life. Do you understand that?"

"I think so. For the first time that I can remember, I feel safe. I don't have to think about anybody beating me or making me do other things. I love you, Uncle Crane. So do Larry and Lenny and TJ too. And Chris does too. Please don't cry," Joel told me and kissed me lightly on the cheek.

"You're a very special boy, Joel," I said and returned the kiss on his cheek. "Now let's go get washed up. Hildy will have supper ready soon."

The twins and Chris were unusually quiet during supper. They were not their usual lively and outgoing selves. I thought I knew what was bothering them but did not want to discuss it at the table.

After the dishes were rinsed and placed in the dishwasher, I called all of the boys into the study. "Please sit down," I said. "I think we need to talk about what happened today. I want us all to understand how we can prevent this from ever happening again.

"TJ, can you tell me what you think you did that made you get on the wrong van?"

"Uh…I don't know. I was just playing and talking with Joey," he said.

"Do you know what van number you are supposed to get on?"

"Aah…seven."

"What was the number of the van that you got on?"

"I thought it was seven 'cause a boy was standing by the van and he hid part of the number. When we got to Joey's I saw it was a one."

"Thank you, TJ. Now then Larry, Lenny and Chris what do you think that you should have done to prevent TJ from making that mistake?" I asked turning to them.

Three pairs of eyes were diligently studying their shoes but no one spoke up.

"Well, let me tell you what I think and you can tell me if I'm wrong, okay? I think that the three of you were having fun and talking and not paying much attention to what was going on around you. Am I right so far?"

Three heads nodded but their eyes were still studying their shoes.

"I want you to know that I'm not mad at you, but I do want to emphasize to you that you all have to look out for each other. How would you have felt if something bad had happened to TJ?

Three pair of eyes looked up at me. All of them had tears in them.

"We're sorry, Uncle Crane," Larry sobbed.

"Yeah, it won't happen again," Lenny added.

"What are you going to do to us?" Chris asked.

"I think I'll give you all a big hug and a kiss and send you off to do your homework," I said as I gathered the three of them in a group hug and kissed each of them on top of their heads. "That goes for you too, TJ. Come here!"

Not to be left out, Joel joined the mass hug.

Shortly after eight, the boys began straggling into the study to have me check their homework. Chris was the last to finish his and he had made the most errors. I decided that tomorrow night I would sit down with him while he did his homework to see if I could help him learn his lessons.

The boys had eaten their snack and were taking their showers and getting ready for bed when the phone rang. It was Jack Hogan.

"Hi, Jack. What's on your mind?"

"Just called to give you some good news."

"Great, I could use some good news. What is it?"

"I got a call from Billy Joe Slocum, the detective handling the Andersen murder case. He informed me that the DA has worked out a plea agreement with Harry Andersen. He has agreed to plead guilty to first degree murder in return for the DA not seeking the death penalty. Instead they will ask the judge for a life sentence."

"Does that mean Joel will not have to testify again?"

"Yes, at least not on the murder charge. I don't know for sure but the sexual assault of a child will probably be dropped to save Joel from any further trauma."

"Thanks, Jack. I appreciate the call. I'll phone you later in the week and maybe we can go to lunch. I'll buy if that wouldn't be considered bribing a police officer."

"That's the kind of bribe I like," he laughed and hung up.

The rest of the week went by without any more crises. I was able to get back into running the business and the boys settled into the school. They were very conscientious about looking out for one another and there were no more problems with wrong vans. Darcie called me on Friday at the office and informed me that we had a custody hearing scheduled for Monday afternoon at 1:30 before Judge Riley. The hearing for all of the boys had been consolidated to Judge Riley's court and Darcie was handling them for CPS. Every evening I spent with Chris helping him to learn his lessons and get his homework done correctly. He responded quite well to my help and I saw an improvement in just one week.

Since it was also time for Joel to have another blood test, I decided to pick the boys up at eleven on Monday so we would have time to have the test done and eat lunch before the court hearing.

Friday evening after supper, I noticed that Joel was unusually quiet. I tried to draw him out several times but he seemed to be deep in thought and didn't really respond to my efforts. I was becoming more worried by the time the boys took their showers and were ready for bed. After I tucked the others into bed, I asked Joel to come with me into the family room. I steered him to the couch and sat him down beside me.

"Joel, I can tell that something is bothering you. Is there something that I can do?" I asked.

"No...ah...I don't know," he said staring down at the carpet and shaking his head.

"You know that you can tell me anything. I won't be mad at you. I just want to help," I said giving his shoulder a squeeze for emphasis.

"Well...you'll hate me if I tell," he sobbed.

"Oh, Joel, I could never hate you. Please believe me all I could ever do is love you. Nothing you could possibly tell me would ever change that," I choked out.

"Okay, you promise you won't hate me?"

"I promise, cross my heart."

"Well…there is this boy at school…ah…and he…ah…kissed me."

"How did you feel about that?"

"Kinda funny."

"What did you do when he kissed you?"

"I…well…I kissed him back."

"How did that make you feel?"

"I liked it. I felt real funny like I was out of breath and my face felt hot."

"Do you like this boy?"

"Yeah."

"Is he in your grade at school?"

"Uh-huh."

"Where did this happen?"

"In the locker room after gym class."

"Do you think that you did anything wrong?"

"No."

"I don't think that you did either."

"Thanks, Uncle Crane. You're the greatest," he said and threw his arms around my neck.

"Even though you didn't do anything wrong, it would be better if you didn't do this again at school. Some people might not understand and could cause you some problems. I think that you and I had better sit down Sunday afternoon and talk about some things. Now it's time for you to get to bed. Remember, we are going fishing tomorrow with TJ's new friend Joey," I told him as we walked back to his bedroom.

TJ was asleep when Joel slipped into bed. I whispered to Joel as I tucked him in, "Goodnight, son. I love you. Sleep well."

Our fishing trip on the lake was a great success. Joey and his father, Harold, were perfect guests. Joey and TJ had a ball. They didn't catch many fish but that didn't seem to bother them. I don't know which one of the boys caught the most fish but by the time it started to cloud up and threaten rain around two o'clock we had enough for a fish fry that evening. I convinced our guests to join us. I called Hildy and told her what I was planning for this evening. She agreed to fix all the side dishes but insisted that we had to clean our own fish.

When we got home, I showed the boys how to clean the fish. I didn't let the two young boys handle the cleaning knives and I watched the others very carefully to see that they handled the knives safely.

The rain had quit so we were able to put the fish on the grill when it came time for supper. Harold and I enjoyed a glass of white wine while the fish cooked. As we talked, I learned that he had a small construction business specializing in building custom homes and remodeling.

"After supper, I'd like for you to take a look at my upstairs. Right now, it is not really useful. I would like to do something with it and make it more accessible from the first floor," I said.

"Sure, if you're not in a hurry to have anything done. I have all of my crews tied up on projects right now. It could be a month or so before I would be able to do anything," he replied.

"I'm not in any great hurry. Whatever I have done I want it to enhance the house. I'm interested in creating a good traffic flow between all areas of the house," I told him.

Supper was wonderful. There is nothing better than fresh caught fish grilled over a mesquite fire.

Over another glass of wine, Harold and I discussed the possible remodeling of the second floor and better access to it. He suggested that I might consider a "grand staircase" leading to the second floor. He said there was the perfect spot for it in a line with the front door. One of the men that worked for him was a draftsman/designer and could probably draw it up for me. It sounded great but I told him I would need to see the drawings before I could make up my mind. He told me that he would send his man over in about a week to look and take some measurement before he could make the drawings.

It wasn't long after Harold and Joey left that the boys were showing signs of sleepiness so I sent them off to the showers to get ready for bed. They didn't complain a bit. They had quite a busy day.

I tucked them in and decided that I should also go to bed. As I tried to settle down and get to sleep, I kept thinking about what I was going to discuss with Joel tomorrow. How do you explain the facts of life to a boy who has been sexually abused and make it something that can and should be a beautiful thing? What can I tell him about the feelings he is having for the boy in his class without making him feel guilty? What do I know about gay sex? I don't even know how to explain my own feelings about Eric. God I hope I don't make a mess of this with Joel.

Sunday afternoon came much sooner than I was prepared for but my session with Joel went better that I had any reason to expect. I knew that Joel was bright but I was really impressed with his mature attitude and the direct questions that he asked. I was prepared for most of them. Some of them I told him I would find the answers and get back to him.

"Can I…I mean, may I invite John over to visit some time?" he asked when we finished. (John was the boy in question.)

"Of course, your friends are always welcome. Why don't you invite him to visit next Saturday?" I said.

Monday morning I reminded the boys that I would pick them up at eleven o'clock so we could get Joel to Doctor Sam's office for his blood test. Then we would have time to have lunch before the custody hearing. I had made them wear long pants to school over their protests. I also hung their jackets in the Land Rover as I took off for a couple of hours at the office.

They were all lined up waiting for me as I drove up to the administration building at the school. Getting everyone situated in the Land Rover was getting to be a hassle. I have got to get a vehicle that holds at least six comfortably.

Dr. Sam's office was within walking distance of the court house so I parked the car and we trooped into his office so Joel could get some blood drawn. It only took a couple of minutes and we were off to find a place to eat. I wanted something that was not too messy. I didn't want to have the boys go into court with food stains all over them. They dragged me into a small Tex-Mex place about a block from Dr. Sam's office. I had never eaten there before but I was pleasantly surprised at the quality and the boys were impressed with the quantity of the food. I made the boys wear their napkins around their necks to avoid splashing salsa on their shirt fronts. We made it through the meal without any major spots. Even those came out with a little dabbing with the wet corner of a napkin.

Benjamin was unable to attend our hearing but he did send one of his associates to assist us in case we needed any help. Karen Lin was young and very business like.

I was not very happy when I saw Gary Everett approaching with Darcie. The boys all rushed up to Darcie and surrounded her. Each one received a hug in turn from her. Darcie turned to me and shook my hand.

"It's good to see you again Crane. You know Gary don't you?" she asked gesturing to Everett.

"Yes, I do. I can't say that I'm glad to see him again," I said trying not to let the bitterness show.

"Don't worry, I think that Judge Yates has had an impact on the thinking in the office," she chuckled.

Hildy and Jack Hogan arrived at the same time just as we were starting for the courtroom.

It took a little doing but we got the seven of us seated at one of the tables. Hildy and Jack sat in the first row behind us.

The bailiff called the court to order as the judge entered. Judge Riley was a large middle aged black woman who reminded me of a younger black Hildy. My first impression would later prove to be accurate.

"Alright, let's get this started. Ms. Levin, which case would you like to start with?" Judge Riley asked.

CHAPTER 21

"Your Honor," Darcie started "I think it would be easiest to start with the Andersen children. It is clearest as to terminating parental rights."

"I agree," Judge Riley responded. Turning toward our table she continued, "Are you Ms. Ramirez?"

Hildy stood up before she answered, "Yes, I am Your Honor."

"Would you be so kind and escort the children into my chambers? The bailiff will show you the way."

Hildy gathered all five of the boys around her and herded them after the bailiff.

"Now that's taken care of we can get down to business. Ms. Lin it is good to see you again. I presume that you are representing Mr. Johnson?" she asked more rhetorically than wanting an answer. "And you must be Mr. Johnson," she said looking straight at me or I should say looking straight through me as if she had x-ray vision.

"Ye…yes, ma'am," I stammered.

"Ms. Levin, I have read your brief concerning the incarceration of Mr. Andersen for the rest of his natural life without the possibility of parole and have prepared an order severing all of his parental rights effective immediately. He will be informed by the sheriff's office and will have thirty days to protest the order.

"Now as to the disposition of the children, Mr. Johnson are you seeking permanent custody of the four Andersen siblings or do you only want to provide foster care for them?"

"I want permanent custody and if the court sees fit I would like to adopt them as soon as I can. I believe that I can provide for all of their physical and emotional needs. You have a financial statement of my net worth and can see that I have the resources to do that. The most important thing is that I love them as if they were my own sons and I want them to be my sons. I believe that they love me as well," I said.

"Ms. Levin, what is CPS' position on the placement of the boys?" the judge asked.

"Your Honor, of the four boys, the only one who would have a reasonable chance of being adopted would be TJ, the youngest. The other three would probably remain in foster homes or a group home until they turned 18 or ran away. I believe that the only way that all four of them could remain together is if they were placed with Mr. Johnson. That is my recommendation. I realize that this is a departure from standard operating procedure for CPS. For once, I think it is best that we take the interest of the children and place them first before the bureaucratic red tape and outdated policies of the department. It is for that reason that I believe the boys should be allowed to grow up as a family in a household where they are loved and where they can be given every opportunity to reach their potential," Darcie said.

"Mr. Everett, I noticed in the hearing before Judge Frank that you did not reject or recommend that Mr. Johnson be given custody of the boys. Have you now formed an opinion?"

"Yes, Your Honor I have. I cannot support Ms. Levin in her recommendation," he responded.

"Are their legal issues that support your position?"

"Precedence, Your Honor. In the five years I have been working for CPS, there have been only two occasions when children were placed with a single male and in both of those cases that person was related to the children in some way either by marriage or blood. Neither of the cases involved this many children."

"Let me get this straight," Judge Riley said sternly. "You are saying that you would rather have these boys split up and put in foster homes or group homes than have them remain together as a family with a single male?"

"That is not how I think of it. I just don't believe that we should endanger four young boys by placing them with him. Lord knows what goes on out there in the sticks where he lives. I shudder to think. We have to protect the children from the temptations of Satan. They need God fearing families to raise them in the way of the Lord. We need to find them families where they will learn strict discipline. Where they will learn to respect their elders and do as they are told.

My information is that Mr. Johnson has never taken them to church even once since they have been in his custody," he said staring at me.

I could see the fire start up in the judge's eyes when she said "This opinion of yours couldn't have been affected by the stinging rebuke that Judge Yates gave both to you and Ms. Gehrig as the result of the last hearing would it?"

"No...I..," he sputtered.

"Sit down Mr. Everett. Don't make a fool of yourself. I don't want to hear that 'religious' claptrap from you again. In my time on the bench I have seen what your so-called 'religious' families can do and believe me it is not always a pleasant sight.

"Mr. Johnson is there a reason why you have not taken the children to a church?" she asked turning to me.

"No, Your Honor, I am not a religious person in the sense that I am a church going person. My parents raised me to believe that to be a good person you did not need to attend a church or believe in any particular religious document or dogma. What made a good person was when you believed in the worth of the individual and rights of others. This idea is embodied in the writings of all three major religions. The so called 'golden rule' probably expresses it as succinctly as any.

"I have never denied the boys the opportunity to attend church with Hildy. In fact, she asks the boys every Sunday if they want to attend church with her. So far, they have not accepted her invitation. If they wanted to go I would encourage them. If they don't want to go, I will not force them. I believe that it is more important to provide a good role model for them than to force some religious dogma on them. However, if the court ordered me to take them to church as a requirement for keeping them I would do so," I said.

"No, this court would never do that. I think that would overstep the boundary that separates church from state although some of my colleagues have differing views. I agree that a positive role model is far more important. I'm going to talk to the children. We will be in recess until I have finished," she said and quickly strode to her chambers.

I wish that I could have been in the room with the boys. The wait was agonizingly long. At least it seemed to be. Darcie, Karen Lin, Jack and I sat around and talked. Gary Everett sat by himself sulking at the other table.

It wasn't forever, it just seemed that way before Judge Riley and Hildy entered the courtroom surrounded by the five boys. The boys rushed to our table and sat down but not before we had a six way hug.

Judge Riley took her place and the bailiff called the court to order. It took a minute or so to get the boys calmed down before she started speaking.

"I have talked to all of the boys. I have read all of the briefs submitted to the court by all parties. I have listened to the parties involved. I have also spoken to Ms. Ramirez whose opinion I give great weight. Now as to the matter of the four minor Andersen children, it is the order of this court that they remain in the custody of Mr. Johnson on a permanent basis. If at the end of 90 days from today Mr. Johnson is still willing to adopt them, this court will entertain a petition for their adoption and will consider it favorably. My clerk will prepare all the necessary paperwork for my signature to make the custody arrangements permanent. Are there any questions?"

No one spoke up but I could see that Gary was getting much redder in the face. I was ecstatic over her announcement but what she had said did not seem to sink in on the boys. I had hoped so hard and had done things like enrolling the boys in Corinthian Academy in the belief that things would work out that now I was overcome with relief. But we were not finished. Chris' custody arrangement was still to be determined.

"Ms. Ramirez I think that the boys would enjoy a snack about this time. Would you please take them to the snack bar and get them some ice cream?"

"Of course I will. Come along boys. Let's get your snack," Hildy said.

She hardly had the words out of her mouth when the boys were literally pushing her out the courtroom door.

"Now in the matter of Christopher Mathew Martin, the parental rights issue is not as clear cut. Although both of his parents are currently in jail, it is not the judgment of this court that the offences are of such gravity that their rights can automatically be revoked. I am aware that they did desert the child and seemingly only returned for him when it was discovered that he was a beneficiary of his aunt's will.

"The papers filed with this court do not spell out just how much the inheritance is for Christopher. Is there any information on the exact terms of the will of his aunt?" she asked.

"Your Honor, I received some preliminary information just before I came to court that I have not had time to prepare for the court. The information that I have learned from contacts in Ohio is that the estate is worth between $5.5 and $6.0 million before taxes and other fees. His aunt was prepared for her own death and was also acutely aware of her sister and brother in-law's attitude and treatment of Chris. She placed most of her liquid assets in a trust fund for Chris with the provision that her sister or her husband never have any control over it. As I understand it the executor has the authority to appoint the trustee to oversee the trust. Also, any monies left over after the sale of the real property and payment of the duties and fees is to be placed in the trust. I have the name of the executor and his contact information and will provide it to the court."

"Yes, please give that name to my clerk and thank you for that information."

"Ms. Levin, what is your recommendation for the custody of Chris Martin?"

"Although I do have some concerns about placing Chris with Mr. Johnson, it is not because I feel Mr. Johnson would not make a good foster parent for Chris. On the contrary, I believe that he would be an excellent foster parent. My concern is only the number of children that he is taking on," she said.

"Have you talked to Chris about his feelings?"

"Yes I have."

"And?"

"He is adamant about wanting to stay where he is. He told me that it is the only place he has ever been where nobody yelled at him all the time. He has strongly indicated that he was verbally abused and harassed by his parents for as long as he can remember. The other boys love him as if he were one of their brothers and I know that he loves them in return."

"Mr. Johnson, how do you feel about taking on a fifth child?"

"I really didn't notice that much difference when he first came to live with us. I was just getting used to the other four and it didn't seem like there was that much more impact between having four boys than there was with five. He fits in well with the others. The only real difference I notice is in the grocery bills," I said.

"Are you saying that you are willing to take responsibility for raising him at least temporarily?"

"Yes, Your Honor I am."

"From my speaking with him I believe that removing him from your home would be a traumatic experience for him that I would not like to inflict. This court orders that Christopher Mathew Martin remain in your custody until such time as the rights of his parents are terminated or their custodial rights are reinstated. I sincerely doubt that will happen in this court. I will also have the executor of his aunt's estate informed that you are to be named as the trustee for his trust fund with the additional stipulation that all monies expended from it be reported to this court monthly. You are ordered by this court to expend the money in a fiscally responsible manner. I will not hesitate to hold you in contempt if I believe that the money is being mishandled. Is that understood?"

"Yes, Your Honor. As far as I am concerned there will be no money taken out of the trust until he starts college or goes out on his own. I will raise him and pay his expenses the same way I plan to pay for the other boys," I told her. "I will have my accountant provide you with the status of the trust monthly. I will actively manage the assets with the intention of increasing the value of it over time as I do my own money."

"Good luck, Mr. Johnson, I will see you in 90 days if you are still intent on adopting the Andersen boys," Judge Riley said. "If there are no other matters to bring before this court we will stand adjourned."

Everyone shook hands except for Everett. He stormed out of the courtroom like he had been shot out of a cannon. When I enquired of Darcie how Eric was coming along with his move to San Antonio, she responded that he would be in town on Wednesday to begin looking for a place to live. In the mean time, he would be living with her.

"He really liked the country atmosphere at your place and wondered if you knew of any property that was for sale in the area," she said.

"As a matter of fact the property one place removed from mine just went up for sale over the weekend. I think the property is around five acres but I don't know the condition of the house or the asking price. I met the owners a year or so ago. They were an older couple in their late 70's or early 80's who were talking of moving into San Antonio to an assisted living housing project when I met them. I'm sure there are others in the area also. He should contact one of the local realtors if he's interested in moving to the lake area," I said not wanting to sound too anxious.

We left the courtroom and had started down the hall toward the snack bar when I spotted Hildy and the boys. They saw us at the same time and broke into a run and all five of them tried to jump into my arms at once.

"Do we really get to stay with you forever and ever?" TJ asked excitedly.

"Yeah?" came a chorus from the others.

"Hildy said we did. Didn't she?" TJ continued.

"Yes she did," Joel said.

"Okay, let me explain what the judge said. She said that Joel, Larry, Lenny and you, TJ, are now officially and permanently my foster sons. Chris you are my foster son also. I don't like it but someday, maybe, when your parents get out of jail you might have to go back to them. I will do everything I can to prevent that from happening. But that won't happen for several years, so don't you worry. You are all my sons now," I said with pride.

I gathered all of them into a big hug and kissed each one of them on the tops of their head. Hildy was standing several feet from us with tears flooding down her cheeks.

"Are you our dad now? Really?" Lenny asked.

"Yes, I guess I am," I replied.

"Can we call you daddy?" Larry asked.

"Yeah, can we?" the rest chimed in.

My eyes were clouded with tears and my voice failed me. All I could do was nod my head.

We spent the afternoon after we got home going over the lessons that the boys had missed at school that day. Since there were three in the same grade it wasn't all that bad but I was pooped by the time we were finished. I was more than relieved when Hildy called us and told the boys to get washed up for supper. She apologized for not having one of her usual feasts prepared for us. I thought it was great and so did the boys from the way they devoured the pork chops, dressing with brown gravy and baked beans. Dessert was a peach cobbler topped with whipped cream.

After their showers, I went to tuck the boys into bed. Chris and the twins were first. As usual, they were all in the same bed.

"Chris, are you sure that you don't want your own bed? We do have that spare bedroom," I said.

"No, I like sleeping with Larry and Lenny," he replied.

"What about if you guys each had your own bed but were in the same room. How would you like that?" I asked.

"But how would we get three beds in this room?" Larry asked.

"I wasn't thinking about this room. You know that I am going to have the upstairs remodeled and there is plenty of room to make a big room where you could each have a bed. You would still be together but you would each have your own space," I said trying to make it sound as good as I could. I really thought that it would allow them to have a better night's sleep if they were not all in the same bed. Whenever I would check on them after they had gone to sleep they would be a mass of arms and legs all intertwined. I know I could never be comfortable that way. What if you had to get up to go to the bathroom in the middle of the night? How would you get untangled before you had an accident?

"Okay," Lenny said not totally convinced.

"We'll talk about it some more later," I said and gave each of them their goodnight kiss and tucked them in.

I went into TJ and Joel's room to say goodnight to them. I wanted to see if they would like separate bedrooms but really didn't know how to approach the subject knowing how dependent TJ was on Joel. I knew at sometime Joel would want his own space. All teenagers do. Anyway, I chickened out and didn't bring up the subject. I just said goodnight, gave them a kiss on the forehead and tucked them in.

The rest of the week went by rather quickly. I talked briefly with Eric on Wednesday when he got into town. He was curious about the place down the road that was for sale. I gave him the realtor's number that was on the sign and offered him any assistance I could to make his transition to San Antonio go smoothly. Friday evening I received a call from Bruce Gordinier, the father of Joel's friend John. He wanted to make sure that I was aware that Joel had invited John to visit on Saturday. When I confirmed that I was he was much relieved.

"John doesn't have many friends," he said hesitantly. "He's very shy, but every since Joel has started going to Corinthian he seems to be coming out of his shell. I'm glad that he has found a friend."

"I am too. Joel doesn't have many friends either. He and his brothers have just recently been placed in my custody so he hasn't had much of a chance to make friends," I said. "I don't know what time Joel said for John to come, but I think if he were here around 9:30 or 10:00 that would be about right. If you don't have any other plans I will bring him home after we have supper. That would probably be around 8:00. Does that sound alright?"

"Yes, that's fine. I hope he'll not be any trouble," he said.

"No, I'm sure he won't. With five other boys, counting Joel, I'm sure he'll have a great time. Be sure to send his swim suit. The boys, I know, will want to go swimming at least part of the day. Do you know how to get here?" I asked.

When he said he did not, I gave him directions and told him we would see them tomorrow around 9:30 or so.

Saturday morning Joel was nervously waiting for John to show up. At nine-thirty, he turned on the security cameras at the gate and didn't take his eyes off the screen until a car drove up at ten minutes to ten. He was out of the house like a shot after he hit the gate release. He hardly waited until the car came to rest before he had his hand on the door latch trying to open John's door. When the door opened, he grabbed his friend by the arm and started toward the house.

"Joel, haven't you forgotten something?" I asked.

"Oh, I'm sorry Uncle Cra...I mean dad. This is my friend John. This is my new dad," he said to John.

"Hi, Mr. Andersen. That's my dad, too," John said to Joel pointing to the man getting out of the driver's side of the car.

"Hi, Mr. Gordinier," Joel said and again grabbed John's arm and headed toward the house.

I just shook my head at the two as they ran. Turning back to John's dad I said, "Mr. Gordinier, I'm Crane Johnson. It's nice to meet you. Would you like to come in for a cup of coffee?"

"It's good to meet you also. It's Bruce. I don't want to pry but is Joel your step-son?" he asked looking confused. "I noticed that John called you Mr. Andersen."

"No, Joel and his brothers are my foster sons. Their last name is Andersen. I also have another foster son, Chris Martin. It's a long story. Let's go have a cup of coffee and I'll tell you about," I said as I led him into the house.

I found out that Bruce and his wife had four children, one boy, John, and three girls. John was the oldest at 13. The girls were 10, 8 and 7 years old. We talked for nearly an hour before he excused himself to go back to his house. I got directions from him on how to get to their place and told him I would have John home by eight.

All six of the boys were outside playing a game of softball (of sorts). Lenny was pitching and the other boys were trying to hit his pitches without much success. TJ was content to chase any foul balls that the others managed to hit. I decided it would be more fun for them if I pitched and at least gave them the satisfaction of hitting a ball. I think that we all enjoyed the game but were just as happy when Hildy called us to get washed up for lunch. She didn't need to call twice.

After lunch, Joel took John to see the video games that he had begun to accumulate. Of course, the rest of the boys followed and kibitzed from the back as they played. This soon lost their interest and they drifted away to play with other toys. This gave me the opportunity to talk to Joel and John alone.

I made small talk with the boys for a while before broaching the topic that I really wanted to talk to them about. Finally, I thought that John was comfortable with me so I dove right in.

"John, Joel has told me that you and he kissed each other the other day. Is that right?" I asked.

The reaction that I got was not one that I expected although I should have been prepared for it. John broke down in tears and curled up in a ball not unlike what Joel did when he discovered me drinking whiskey. I had been sitting on Joel's bed talking to the boys who were sitting on the floor.

Responding to John's reaction, I joined them on the floor and cradled him in my arm. "It's alright. Don't be afraid. Nothing is going to happen to you. There's nothing to be afraid of."

Joel joined in holding John. "My dad said we didn't do anything wrong. Please don't cry, Please."

"Joel's right, John. You didn't do anything wrong but I do want to talk to both of you about it. Is that alright?" I asked as his crying slowed down and he uncurled slightly. "That's better. Now then, kissing each other is not wrong! Having said that there are a lot of people who would not understand when two boys kiss. Do you understand what I'm saying?"

Getting two nods I continued, "It's very important for boys of your age to be like every other boy your age. That is called peer pressure. Most boys of your age do not kiss another boy. Am I right?"

Again I received two nods. "If some of the other boys at school saw you kiss each other, what do you think they might do? Would they tease you or make fun of you?"

This time John responded, "Yeah, I guess."

"Would you like that?" I asked.

"No," John said.

"Well, what do you two think you should do if you don't want to be teased or made fun of?"

Joel responded this time, "I guess, maybe we shouldn't do it at school."

"How do you feel about what Joel said?" I asked.

"Okay, I guess. Other boys tease me anyway 'cause I don't talk much and some times have a hard time making the words come out of my mouth," he said. "We can still be friends, can't we?"

"Of course you can be friends. You are welcome in our home any time. I'm glad that Joel has made a friend at school and I'm glad that it is you. Now, why don't you guys get into your swim suits and let's get in the pool," I said getting up from the floor.

"You won't tell my dad, will you?" John pleaded.

"No, but you might want to talk to your mom or dad about the way you feel toward Joel. But that is your business," I told him.

All of the boys seemed to enjoy the rest of the afternoon. We swam and played water tag and generally wore ourselves out in the water. Hildy fixed ice cream with sliced peaches for their afternoon snack. My boys were used to getting hugs from me any time and for no particular reason. John first thought it was a little strange but before the day was over he too was receptive to the hugs I gave him.

"Thanks Mr. Ander…I mean Mr. Johnson my dad hardly ever gives me a hug. I know he loves me. He just doesn't hug me. I wish he would," John said the last time I gave him a hug.

"Maybe if you gave him a hug he would feel comfortable hugging you. Do you think that might work?" I suggested more than asked. "You know some boys your age don't want their parents to show affection toward them, especially in public. They think it makes them look like sissies. I don't agree with that. I think it feels good to give hugs and even better to get them."

The boys stuffed themselves on Hildy's supper. It's a good thing we didn't have a dog that depended on table scraps because there were very few that were ever left after a meal.

Joel and I took John and started for his house shortly after 7:30. They were as animated as they were when John first arrived. I was very pleased that Joel had found a friend outside of his brothers. I wasn't sure that I was completely pleased with all aspects of the friendship but that was only because I didn't want to see Joel hurt in any way. He had been hurt enough in his short life. I knew I couldn't always protect him from everything but I sure wanted to protect him from as much as I could.

John and his family lived not to far from Rebecca Creek Golf Course in a very nice neighborhood. It only took us about 15 minutes to get there from our house. It was starting to get dark as we drove up and the front porch light was on. Bruce and a woman I assumed was his wife came out of the house as we exited the car.

John ran and threw his arms around a very surprised father, "I had the greatest time. Can I go again?"

"Whoa, John don't you think you should wait to be invited?" Bruce said.

"But, Joel asked me. He really did," John said.

Bruce looked up at me still a little surprised and then realized that he had not introduced his wife, "Crane this is my wife, Pauline. Honey, this is Crane Johnson—Joel's foster dad."

We exchanged pleasantries before I responded to John's request of his dad to visit us again, "We would be happy to have John visit us again. Maybe next time we could go out on the boat and do a little fishing. My boys love the lake and think it's great fun to fish. They're actually getting pretty good at it."

"That's very kind of you," Pauline said. "We'd like for Joel to visit us also. With three sisters, Johnny doesn't get to do boy things very often. And there are no other families near us that have children his age."

"We'll have to do that" I said. "Joel, say goodbye to John. We need to get back home. It was nice meeting you, Pauline."

"Thank you Mr. Johnson," John said as he threw his arms around me. "I had a great time."

"I enjoyed your visit. You're welcome to come back any time," I said as I gave him a hug.

We waved goodbye to the speechless Gordiniers as we drove out of the driveway. Joel reached over and squeezed my arm. "Thanks for being nice to John. He really likes you 'cause you talk to him like he's not a baby. You're a great dad. I love you."

"I love you too, son. I'm glad that you have a new friend," I said and gave his shoulder a pat.

CHAPTER 22

Sunday was one of those really dreary days that come to San Antonio in mid November. It was a foggy, drizzly, damp and chilly day. It had a depressing effect on the boys even though I tried to keep them entertained by getting them involved in table tennis and foosball. That did help for a couple of hours but even their video games could not keep them occupied for long.

After lunch, I suggested that I finish reading *Tom Sawyer* to them. We had stopped reading after Chapter 29 and there were not that many chapters left to read. That perked up their interest at least for the time being.

Joel retrieved the book while the twins and Chris claimed their places on the couch. The twins were on my right side while Joel and Chris sat on my left and, of course, TJ claimed my lap. I smiled as I was reading Chapter 34. It reminded me of Chris' good fortune and his unknown riches.

> "Huck's got money. Maybe you don't believe it, but he's got lots of it. Oh, you needn't smile—I reckon I can show you. You just wait a minute," Tom ran out of doors. The company looked at each other with a perplexed interest—and inquiringly at Huck, who was tongue-tied.
>
> "Sid, what ails Tom?" said Aunt Polly. "He—well, there ain't ever any making of that boy out. I never—"
>
> Tom entered, struggling with the weight of his sacks, and Aunt Polly did not finish her sentence. Tom poured the mass of yellow coin upon the table and said:
>
> "There—what did I tell you? Half of it's Huck's and half of it's mine!"
>
> The spectacle took the general breath away. All gazed, nobody spoke for a moment. Then there was a unanimous call for an explanation. Tom said he could furnish it, and he did. The tale was long, but brimful of interest. There

was scarcely an interruption from any one to break the charm of its flow. When he had finished, Mr. Jones said:

"*I thought I had fixed up a little surprise for this occasion, but it don't amount to anything now. This one makes it sing mighty small, I'm willing to allow.*"

The money was counted. The sum amounted to a little over twelve thousand dollars. It was more than any one present had ever seen at one time before, though several persons were there who were worth considerably more than that in property.[2]

"Boy, I wish I had that much money," Joel said.

"Me too," the twins echoed.

"Is that a lot of money?" TJ asked.

"Yes, that's a lot of money even now. Back when this story was written, it was an awful lot of money. It was a fortune," I told them.

It took only a few more minutes to finish the book. I sensed the boys were sorry that it was finished. "We'll have to start another book next weekend. There will be lots of time to read over the Thanksgiving holiday coming up week after next. Now, how would you guys like to go to a movie this afternoon? 'The Swiss Family Robinson' is showing in New Braunfels and I think we have time to get there before it starts."

I had no more gotten that out of my mouth then they were off the couch like a shot to their bedrooms to get their shoes on. By the time I had retrieved my wallet and car keys, they were waiting impatiently by the back door. As it turned out, we got to the theater about 15 minutes before the show began. That gave us enough time to get a couple of tubs of deliciously and sinfully buttered popcorn and large sodas. Thankfully, the theater seats were equipped with cup holders. There would have been no way for the boys to balance their drinks and those huge tubs of popcorn without spilling something.

The boys were thoroughly enjoying the movie, but about half way through TJ leaned over and whispered to me that he had to go to the bathroom. I got Joel's attention and told him I was going to take TJ to the bathroom and for him to watch the other boys. Chris said that he had to go too, so the three of us headed to the back of the theater to the restrooms.

The restroom was empty except for a man about my age standing at one of the urinals. He looked up as we entered but I ushered the boys back to one of the stalls not paying any attention to him. The boys did their thing and then I had them wash their hands. As we walked out I noticed that the man was still standing at the urinal. I didn't think too much of it at the time. I know some men have "bashful bladder" and can't go if there is anyone about.

We got back to our seats without having missed too much of the movie. I guess it was the power of suggestion but soon the twins and Joel decided that they needed to go also. I didn't want to leave TJ and Chris there by themselves so I told Joel to watch out for his brothers and sent them off to the restroom. I kept looking back to see if they were coming. They hadn't been gone two minutes. It just seemed like more before I saw them coming down the aisle. They were trying to cover their mouths to stifle their giggling but without much success.

As Joel went by me on his way to his seat I asked, "What's so funny? What happened?"

He leaned over and whispered in my ear, "The man in the bathroom unzipped his pants and started playing with himself. We just laughed and ran out."

"You did the right thing. I want you to stay here with your brothers. I'll be right back," I said and got up to go see if I could find the manager.

The manager was in a little office off to the side of the theater. When I got there, I explained the situation to him and told him the man was probably still in the restroom. He nearly bowled me over as he bolted out of his office toward the restrooms. I was following close on his heels. He did slow down as we got to the door. He pushed the door open very slowly so as not to make any noise and quietly entered with me close behind. As we came around the corner, I could see the man who had been there when I brought TJ and Chris here. He was standing there with his genitals exposed masturbating.

I thought that the manager was going to kill him. He knocked the man to the floor like an NFL tackle.

"Go have the ticket seller call the police!" he almost screamed at me.

I did as I was asked and then went to sit with the boys. I didn't want any more involvement if I could help it.

The rest of the movie went by without any further interruptions. As we were leaving the theater however, the manager spotted me and pulled us aside. After thanking me for my assistance in nabbing the pervert, he handed me six passes to the theater for any movie that we wanted to see. I thanked him and we left to go home. It was getting to be time for supper and I knew the boys would be getting hungry.

Hildy had gone to church as was her usual routine on Sunday evening so we were left to my culinary expertise to scrounge up supper. I looked in the pantry and refrigerator to see what I could whip up in a hurry.

"Hey guys, how about chili-dogs for supper?" I asked.

I got a chorus of "Yeah!"

That settled it. I took out two packages of wieners and a couple large cans of chili without beans and started to prepare our repast. I didn't know if the boys liked chopped onions on theirs but I did so I prepared some. The boys set the table while the chili and hot dogs were heating up.

They inhaled the chili-dogs like human vacuum cleaners. Of the 16 wieners I had prepared there was only one left and no chili.

"Okay, guys. It's time to get your homework done. Tomorrow is a school day," I said as I started the dishwasher so Hildy wouldn't think we were complete savages when she got home. "Chris, if you need any help I will be in the study."

Since I had given the boys their Friday afternoon lessons, they didn't have a lot of homework to do so it wasn't long before they were bringing it to me to check. I was beginning to see a noticeable improvement in Chris' work. There was no question that he had the intelligence required, it was always a question of motivation. I think him seeing the twins excel at their lessons was motivating him to succeed as well. Also just knowing that someone really cared about him and that he learned was a motivating factor. I could not have been happier.

Monday morning I got the boys off to school and I went to work. Eric Levin reported in and between Carol and me, with some help from Foster, we got him signed up for all his benefits and oriented to the office routines. Foster had a project all lined up for him to begin working on. He cornered him after all the paperwork was finished and began to describe what the client wanted and who he would be working with from the office. I had wanted to take Eric out to lunch at noon like we did for all new employees but Foster took him off to visit the client and the other members of the consulting team. We would have to postpone the lunch until some other day.

I was about ready to go to lunch when I got a call from the executor handling the estate of Chris' aunt. He wanted some information about me and my relationship with Chris. Judge Riley's clerk had been in touch with him as to my being named as the trustee of the trust fund for Chris. After I explained my intentions for leaving the funds untouched until he was off to college or decided to go out on his own, he was satisfied that I would be acceptable as the trustee. When I asked him how much the trust was going to be worth after all expenses, he replied that the best he could give was $2.35 million. The inheritance taxes both state and federal amounted to 58% of the gross value of the estate. He informed me that it would be about 60 days before the will made it out of probate.

The discussion with the executor sowed some seeds of an idea in my head. I needed to flesh them out before I acted but I made a note to myself to follow through.

By this time, I was really getting hungry and I didn't want to eat alone so on the off chance that Jack had not eaten I gave him a call.

"Jack, it's Crane. I'd like to bribe you with lunch. How about it?"

"That sounds great. I haven't had my daily bribe yet today. Where can I meet you?"

"How about that Chinese place over on Zarzamora? You know the one that has that great egg drop soup you liked so well. I'll meet you in about twenty minutes," I said.

Jack replied, "I'll be there even if I have to use the lights and siren."

Jack drove in at the same time I was parking the car.

Since it was late, we didn't have to wait for a table. Jack and I had eaten here several times. The food was excellent. The place was always impeccably clean and the atmosphere was peaceful and relaxing.

"Have you heard anything more about Chris' parents?" I asked as we sat sipping a final cup of hot tea.

"As a matter of fact I have. We did a check of the NCIC computer and found two outstanding warrants from Louisiana for both of them. It seems that they were accused of being involved in a string of burglaries. In one of them, a man died of a heart attack while being robbed. In Louisiana that makes them eligible for a charge of murder even though they did not actually inflict any physical injury that caused his death. Naturally they are fighting extradition so it may be a while before they go on trial," Jack said.

"Is there any reason to believe that Chris knows anything about this?" I asked.

"No, there is no mention of him in the information we just received from Plaquemine Parish. These events occurred almost five years ago so I doubt that Chris has any knowledge of any of this."

"Thank goodness. I know he never had a loving relationship with his parents but I don't want to foul his image of them any more than it already is.

Although, this information might be important for Judge Riley to have," I mused deviously.

"I knew you were a sucker. That boy has wormed his way into your heart the same way the others have, hasn't he?" Jack laughed.

"Yeah, it looks like I've opened a home for stray boys and it's all your fault. But seriously, I think I should let Darcie know about this. This could be added ammunition for terminating the Martins' parental rights," I said.

I paid the bill and we left for the parking lot. As we did, I offered an open invitation to Jack to bring the family and visit us during the upcoming Thanksgiving holidays. We would probably take the boat out if the weather was nice. Considering the time of year, it might be the last time until spring.

I got back to the office and made several phone calls. The first was to Darcie to inform her of the information that Jack had related to me. The second was to Benjamin Cross' office to see if it would make sense to seek another hearing before Judge Riley concerning Chris. Benjamin was not in his office but his secretary said that she would give him the information and that he would probably call me later this evening since he was tied up in court all day.

The third call was one that I really didn't want to make but felt an obligation to make it. It was to Eric Olsen, my former partner, to see how he was coming along. The news was not what I wanted to hear. I didn't get to speak to him. I did get to talk to his wife. She told me that Eric was not well at all. In addition to the brain tumor, he had suffered a stroke and could no longer speak. He had also lost the use of his left arm and leg. She broke down and cried as she told me that he appeared to have lost the will to live. I tried to comfort her as much as I could but I knew that at this point it was impossible for her to be consoled.

Foster and Eric Levin returned from the client site around three o'clock. I had a chance to talk to Eric and find out about how his house hunting was coming along. He said that he had looked at the house down the road from me but was not too impressed with it. He thought he would have to spend a lot of money on it to bring it up to date. The location was great but the view was not as good as mine and he thought the asking price was way too high. There were a couple of others a mile or so away that offered more promise. He wanted Darcie to go with him this weekend to see what she thought of them.

"What do you think of the project that Foster has lined up for you?" I asked him.

"It's going to be a challenge to do it in the time frame that they want it, but it's not anything out of the ordinary. I think that the real challenge is going to be getting the hardware in to meet the schedule. I know a few people who might be able to pull a few strings and get some of the routers ahead of other people's orders. I can't promise anything but some of them owe me favors. We'll see," he said.

"How about school for JR? Have you decided where you are going to enroll him?"

"No not yet, I would like to put him in a private school. I have not heard that many good things about SAISD. If we do move to Comal County, I may look into the school you are sending your boys to. What's the name of it again?"

"Corinthian Academy," I answered. "They don't take mid-term enrollments. If I remember correctly, the next term begins the second week of January. It's the beginning of the second semester. That would probably be a good time to get him in if you move to the area.

"If you're in the area this weekend feel free to stop by. I know that the boys would enjoy seeing JR again," I told him.

We chatted for a few more minutes before I decided that it was time for me to head home.

It always feels good to get home, but something didn't seem right when I got there. Joel, Chris and TJ came running to greet me as I entered the back door. The twins were not with them.

"Hi guys, how was school?" I asked giving each of them a hug.

"It's great," TJ said. "Joey and me got to be on the same team at recess. He hit a really long ball and almost got a home run. I only got to first base."

"I got an A on my spelling test," Joel said with pride.

"Congratulations son, that's great. I'm very proud of you," I said giving him an extra hug. "How about you, Chris? How was your day?"

"Okay, I guess. We got to see a movie about Alaska. There were polar bears and seals and walruses and whales and all kinds of animals. They said it got really cold and it stayed dark all winter. Hardly no sun. I wouldn't like that," he said shaking his head.

"Where are Larry and Lenny?" I asked them.

They looked at each other for several second before Joel said, "They're in your study waiting for you. Hildy told them to stay there until you got home to talk to them."

"Okay, let me talk to Hildy. You go play and I'll find out what's going on," I told them.

Hildy was waiting for me when I entered the kitchen.

"What's going on with the twins?" I asked putting down my briefcase.

"The school called and said that they were sending a note home with them about an incident that happened today," she said handing me the note.

I read the note which said that the boys had been involved in a fight with another student during afternoon recess and that I needed to come to school with the boys to meet with the headmaster at 8:30 tomorrow morning.

"Well I guess I'd better go talk to the twins," I said. "Did they say anything to you about this?"

"No, they didn't. I can't imagine them doing that. They have never shown any violent tendencies before," she said.

I walked into the study and saw the twins. They looked like they had lost their best friend. I'd never seen them look so sad.

"Come here guys," I said reaching out to them. "Give me a hug and then tell me what happened. You know that I love you and always will, but I want you to tell me the truth about what happened today at school that got you in trouble."

"We didn't do anything," they said with their faces buried in my chest in that uncanny stereophonic way they had of talking.

"Well then, tell me why Mr. Pierce sent a note home with you. You know I'm not going to spank or beat you. I would never do that. But I do expect you to tell me the truth," I told them.

"Well..," Larry started.

"Go on," I said.

"Billy Sutton was picking on Jerry Lane and making him cry. He was shoving him and calling him names," Lenny said.

"And?" I asked.

"Well…Jerry is our friend and we didn't like Billy doing that," Larry said.

"So?" I queried.

"Ah…we sort of sat on Billy and told him not to pick on Jerry," Lenny said. "We didn't hurt him. We just made him stop picking on Jerry. We promise that's all that happened."

"What you did, stopping Billy from picking on Jerry was a good thing. The way you chose to do it was probably not the best way to do it, however. Can you think of another way you might have stopped Billy without sitting on him?" I asked.

I waited but neither one of them seemed to have an answer so I asked another question, "Okay, why do you think that Billy picks on Jerry?"

"Jerry's the littlest boy in the class," Larry said.

"Does Billy pick on anyone else?" I asked.

"Yeah, he tries to pick on everyone," Lenny answered.

"Does he have any friends?" I asked.

"Nobody likes him," they answered in unison.

I asked them, "Do you think he might pick on people because he doesn't have any friends?"

"I guess, maybe," Larry whispered.

"Do you think if he had a friend he would pick on everybody?" I asked.

"Maybe…he might not," Lenny said with not too much conviction.

"Tomorrow I have to go with you to school and we have to meet with Mr. Pierce and Billy's parents to see how we can resolve this matter. I know it is not going to be easy, but I want you guys to shake Billy's hand and apologize to him for sitting on him. Okay?"

"Do we have to?" they asked.

"I would really like for you to. I would also like for you to invite Billy to come to the house on Saturday for a visit. My mother used to tell me when I was a little boy that the best way to turn an enemy into a friend was with kindness. I think she knew what she was talking about.

"Most bullies are just looking for attention. They don't know how to be friends, so we have to show them how," I said.

"Okay," they said barely above a whisper.

"Now I want you to remember, I don't want you to fight at school. Always try to think of a better way than fighting. That is always the last resort. You can always protect yourself, but fighting is never a good way to solve problems. It usually causes more problems than it solves," I lectured them.

"Okay, give me a hug and go play. You have about an hour before Hildy will have supper ready."

"I love you dad," they said.

"I love you too," I said with a lump in my throat giving each one a peck on the top of their heads and a swat on the behind as they ran out of the room to join the other boys.

"You didn't get a spanking or nothing?" Chris inquired.

I chuckled as I heard them say, "No, it's worse. We have to invite Billy over here on Saturday."

The rest of the evening was uneventful and very routine.

In the morning after everyone had eaten breakfast and brushed their teeth we took off for the school in the Land Rover shortly after eight o'clock. We arrived at the school about five minutes early. I told Joel, Chris and TJ to go play while I took the twins into the building to meet with Mr. Pierce.

---

[2] Ibid. 318-319.

CHAPTER 23

Mr. Pierce's secretary ushered us into his office and said that he would be with us shortly. It wasn't long before Billy and his parents arrived. I introduce myself to them. Mr. and Mrs. Sutton appeared to be very nervous as they chatted with me. Billy was silent and hardly looked up as we waited for Mr. Pierce.

"Good morning," Mr. Pierce said as he entered the room. "Mr. Johnson, it's good to see you again."

I shook his hand before he turned to the Suttons.

"Mr. Sutton, Mrs. Sutton we meet again," he said with a slight frown on his face.

"Lawrence, Leonard, William, I want you to tell me exactly what happened. Don't fib to me. I want to hear your side of the incident on Friday. Who wants to start first or should I pick on one of you?"

There was a moment of silence before Lenny spoke up, "We were trying to stop Billy from picking on Jerry. We didn't hit Billy, really we didn't. We just pushed him down on the ground and sat on him to get him to stop."

"Yeah, that's all we did, we didn't try to hurt him. It's not nice for him to pick on someone littler than him," Larry added.

"Billy, were you picking on Jerry?" Mr. Pierce asked.

"No, I..," he started but stopped as he saw Mr. Pierce staring at him.

"Well...I guess I might have been. He's such a little twerp..," Billy began before he thought better of it.

"Do any of you boys have anything to add to this?" Pierce asked as he waited a minute. "Well, since no one had anything more, this is what is going to happen. For the next two days, the three of you will not have any recess privileges. You will report to Room D instead of going to recess. Do you understand?" he looked at each one in turn and got a nod of confirmation from each. "Resorting to any kind of fighting or violence will not be tolerated. If there are any further incidents, the punishment will be much different. That's all for you boys. You may go to class."

I gave the boys a hug and whispered in their ears, "Do you remember what I told you?"

They nodded and went to Billy and stuck out their hands to him. He was taken aback but automatically put out his hand and shook first Larry and then Lenny's hand.

"Billy, if your parents don't mind," Larry said looking at Billy's parents, "we would like to have you come to our house on Saturday."

"Yes, we would," Lenny echoed.

Billy was completely taken by surprise. His mouth opened but nothing came out. Finally, he regained his speech and senses enough to look to his parents, "Okay?"

They were equally surprised at the twins offer. They looked at me and I nodded. "Yes, you can go if you want to," Mrs. Sutton said.

The boys filed out, a twin on each side of a very mystified Billy.

Mr. Pierce looked at me, "That is rather unusual, Mr. Johnson."

"I suppose that it is. I don't want the boys fighting and the best way I thought to prevent it was to try to get them to be friends with the person they had a problem with." Turning to the Suttons I said, "I hope you don't mind my saying this, but I think the reason that Billy picks on the other kids is that he really doesn't have a friend he can be with."

"Billy doesn't make friends easily and it's been hard on him that we have moved so often. This is the third school he has attended in the last two years. My husbands old job caused us to move much too often for Billy to form any lasting attachments," Billy's mom said. "That's in the past now and we hope to be here for a good long time."

"If it's convenient, why don't you bring Billy by around 9:30 or 10 on Saturday? Bring his swim suit. If it's warm enough the boys always like to swim on the weekends. I would also like to invite you to dinner that evening. We usually eat around seven."

"Thanks, we would be pleased to come for dinner," Mr. Sutton replied.

"Mr. Johnson, thank you for your unique solution to this problem. I just wish all of our parents were as innovative in trying to eliminate violent behavior. I sincerely hope that your efforts are successful. I'm sure that it will be with both sets of parents cooperating," Mr. Pierce said. "I think we are finished unless anyone has anything else."

On the way out, I gave the Suttons directions to the house.

When I got to the office, I had several messages to return calls. Two of them took priority. Number one was a call to Dr. Sam. I quickly dialed his number even though I was apprehensive about what he would tell me. I knew it was probably about Joel's last blood test. I wanted to know but I was so afraid that the results would be a death sentence for Joel. His receptionist answered and said she would put me through to the doctor.

"Crane, I'm glad that you called back so soon. I wanted to let you know that everything is still fine. No antibodies to HIV are detectable in his blood sample. I do have one concern though, his liver function has still not returned to a level I'm comfortable with for someone of his age. It is not as abnormal as it was when I first tested him, but it still concerns me. I don't think it is anything to be overly worried about but I think we should keep an eye on it though."

"Thanks for the good and bad news, Sam," I said very much relieved. "Is there anything I should look for? His color is as normal as his brothers. They all have gotten tans from being outside, mostly in the swimming pool. It's a little harder to tell if his skin has that yellow tinge it had when he first came to me."

Sam replied, "Just keep an eye on him to see if you notice any changes in his activities. Complaints of pain in the back and side or lethargy or that yellowing of the whites of his eyes would all be things that might indicate a more serious problem. I don't want you to obsess over this. I just want you to be aware that there is the possibility of a problem.

"Well, I have patients waiting. I will talk to you later. Bye."

"Bye, Sam and thanks," I said.

Call number two was to another doctor, Dr. Adams. His office nurse put me on hold, telling me that the doctor would be with me in a minute.

"Mr. Johnson, Owen Adams here, I'm glad you called. I just wanted you to know that I have an opening when I could see Joel if you are still interested."

"Yes, I think it would be best if we did have him talk to you. Although in my non-professional observation, I can see no indications that he is anything other than a normal pre-teenage boy. I don't know how that is possible knowing everything that he's been through," I said.

"The time that I have available is at 3:00 on Monday starting next week. I think we discussed having Joel come in every other week until we can assess his situation. Is that still your thinking?" he asked.

"I believe that will be acceptable. The three o'clock time will prevent him from missing too much of the school day.

"Something that you probably should be aware of is that Joel has formed an attachment to one of the boys in his class. I think the best way to describe it is a crush. They have exchanged kisses. I don't believe that it has gone any farther. I talked to him and the other boy about how others might look at their relationship from the standpoint of them being teased or ridiculed. I don't want him to be hurt and I don't want him to feel guilty about the relationship," I said.

"That's interesting. I work a lot with young people who are gay or confused as to their sexuality. I do not try to change their orientation. I do try to have them think through their emotions to help them understand themselves and to be comfortable with whatever they are. I'm pleased that you did not freak out when you learned of Joel's interest in this other boy.

"I am somewhat heartened by it though. Not the fact that he may be homosexual but that he is able to form a relationship whether it is a sexual or a loving one outside the family unit. Very interesting, thanks for letting me know. This could be very important in his treatment," he said.

"I'll have Joel at your office at three on Monday," I said. "Thanks, doc, for finding time to see him."

The remaining calls were more routine business but they took up the rest of the morning. I did finish in time for Foster and me to take Eric to lunch. We went to Ruth's Chris Steak House. They serve probably the best steaks in San Antonio, maybe even Texas.

My attraction to Eric was still as strong as ever. I knew that I could not act on my attraction even though Darcie had hinted that it might be reciprocated. But as employer/employee it did complicate the situation. It could negatively impact the office morale if it were known that I was involved with one of the staff. Another thought also surfaced that I did not need any more complications in my life right now with the status of the boys still not fully resolved. I did not want the courts to have any reason, no matter how flimsy, to reject my petition for adoption of the boys.

I decided to try to make it home every evening as near as possible to the time the boys got home. That meant I had to leave the office around 3:30 because their van dropped them off just after four. Today I followed their van down the road to our gate. The boys didn't notice my car until Joel was about to punch in the gate code when I opened it with my remote. They turned around as a single unit and launched themselves at the car. The BMW was not meant to carry five boys with backpacks and a grown man but we did all get crammed in after each one of them got their hug. I didn't insist that they buckle-up since we were only going to the house.

"How did you guys get along with Billy today?" I asked the twins.

"He was kinda weird. He didn't pick on nobody today. He just looked kinda weird," Larry said.

"Yeah," Lenny added, "he just kept looking at us with that really weird look on his face."

As I parked the car in the garage, the boys exploded out of it to change their clothes and wash up so that Hildy would give them their after school snack. They were fully aware of the routine required if they wanted a snack.

We had just finished supper when the phone rang. When I answered it, I was surprised to find it was Bruce Gordinier, the father of Joel's friend John.

"Bruce, what can I do for you?" I asked.

"Well this may be a little forward, but could I come over and talk to you?" he asked.

"Sure, all I have planned for this evening is to check the boys' homework. I'll have Hildy put on a pot of coffee. See you in a bit," I said as we hung up.

I wondered what he wanted to talk about, but I had a sneaking suspicion as to what it was. He showed up about thirty minutes later. I activated the gate and went out front to greet him. Joel saw Bruce as we entered the front door.

"Hi Mr. Gordinier, did John come with you?" Joel asked.

"No son, he had to do his homework," he said. "How have you been?"

"I'm fine, thanks," Joel said and went back to his room to finish his homework.

"Could we go someplace where we can talk privately?"

"Of course, let's go into my study. I'll have Hildy bring the coffee in there," I said showing him the way and then went to ask Hildy to bring us the coffee.

Bruce was looking at the book lined walls of my study, "Man, you have a lot of books. It's like a mini-library."

"I can't bear to part with a book after I've read it, so I have almost every book I've ever read since I was a boy. Please sit down and make yourself comfortable," I said.

After Hildy served the coffee he began, "I can't tell you the change that has come over John since he was here. He was never one for wanting to be hugged or touched before. I guess that he thought he was too big for all of that. Now he will come up to me or his mother and just put his arms around us and hug us."

There were tears in Bruce's eyes as he continued, "I don't know what happened while he was here, but whatever it was I want to thank you."

"I don't think that we did anything special. I think that I told you when you brought John to visit that all five of my boys had been in abusive homes before they came to live with me. I try to show them that they are safe and loved. I guess we do a lot of hugging and touching and showing our love for each other. John didn't quite know what to make of it at first. I think that he realized that the boys didn't think they were too old to be hugged and then he realized that it felt good to get hugged. It didn't take him long before he was in line to get his share of the loving. I'm a hugger. Hildy is a hugger. You can't be in this house for long without getting a hug. That's just the way it is," I said.

"I love my son more than life but I was never able to show him before. Now I feel that we are so much closer. He even crawls up in my chair with me before bed and just sits there with his arms around me," The tears were really flowing down his cheeks now.

I handed him a box of tissues and allowed him to dry his eyes before I said, "It gets to you doesn't it? It happens to me all of the time. With five of them getting and giving hugs and sharing their love with me, I go through a lot of tissues."

Bruce recovered shortly and continued, "There is another matter I want to discuss with you but I don't quite know how to start."

"I think I know what you want to say and I'm sure that it's difficult for you. Am I right?" I asked.

"Yes, it is difficult. I guess the best way is to be as forthright as possible. It's about John and Joel. John says they are more than friends. Do you know anything about that?" he asked with a very pained look in his eyes.

"I know," I said. "I knew about it before John came to visit. I talked to both of them together and tried to explain that outward display of affection at school or around their friends would probably cause them to be teased at least and more likely ridiculed.

"When I first broached the subject with John, he reacted as if he thought that I was going to hit him. It took a while before he realized that I only wanted to talk to him and Joel about the consequences of them openly displaying their affection.

"I don't want Joel to be gay. Not because I think it is a sin or anything like that, I just want to protect him from the discrimination he would face. Texas is not the most tolerant state when it comes to alternative lifestyles. I think it's too soon to tell if this is going to be his sexual preference. He is, after all, only twelve going on thirteen. Many boys his age experiment with other boys but later turn out to be hetero.

"If he does turn out to be gay, I will love him just as much. He will need extra love and understanding to make up for the harsh realities that he'll face outside our home."

"When I talked to John about him and Joel, he was very much afraid that I would tell you. Although I told him I would not, I urged him to talk to you and Pauline about it," I said.

Bruce looked a little bewildered. I think that my reaction to the possibility that Joel might be gay confused him. "Do you mean to say that you would approve if Joel were gay?" he asked.

"I don't think that it would make any difference to me. My only concern is about protecting Joel from being hurt until he is old enough to handle it on his own. Whether he's gay or straight is not a choice he can make. He either is or is not gay. I repeat, I will love him no matter what," I told him.

"I wish that I could believe as you do but I have always been told that homosexuality is a sin against God. A gay person is to be shunned and condemned as unclean. Our pastor is always preaching against them. It has been that way all my life. My religion is a very important part of my life and my family's lives. How can I reconcile my faith with the possibility that my son, my…my only son, could be condemned to hell?" he sobbed out this last question.

"I can't answer your theological question, and I won't try. I know most Christian religions teach that man is made in the image of God. If that is so, isn't it unthinkable that we could hate and condemn anyone made in the image of God? To me that would be a sin against God. That has always bothered me and I guess that's why I'm not a church going man," I told him.

"How can I cure him if he does turn out to be gay," he asked.

"You can't. It's not a disease. All you can do is love him. You don't have to approve of his preference but if you do love him don't force him away. You could easily lose him forever. The suicide rate among gay teens is alarmingly high. I'm sure that is not something that you want for your son. Try to understand him and above all let him know by word and deed that you love him," I said.

Bruce sat there for a minute or so before he stood up. "I don't know what to think. This is something that I never thought I'd have to face. I know John has never been happier than he has been since he met Joel. I don't want him to revert back to the way he was before. We still want Joel to come visit. Maybe next week during the boys' holiday if you don't have any plans."

As we opened the study door to leave, the boys were waiting for me to check their homework. They gathered around me for their hugs which I gladly gave them. Joel even gave Bruce a hug and asked "Can John come over and visit again?"

"Why don't you come to visit John? Your dad and I discussed maybe next week. Would that be okay with you?" Bruce asked.

"Yeah," he said and then led the rest of the boys into the study to wait for me to check their work.

"Thanks, Crane, I don't know that I feel any better but at least you have given me some things to think about. I believe that Pauline and I have a lot of things to think through together. If it's convenient for you, maybe Joel could come over on Tuesday. The girls will still be in school since they don't start their holiday until Wednesday so John will be at home with nobody to play with."

"That sounds fine," I said. "I'll call you to confirm."

I began checking the boys' homework when the phone rang. It was Harold Nicholas. He said that his designer could come tomorrow to begin making sketches of what the remodeling of the upstairs and the grand staircase would look like. Harold said that he could bring him by around nine if that was convenient. He wanted to meet with both of us to discuss exactly what I had in mind for the upstairs. I agreed that nine would be just fine and went back to checking homework.

Each of the boys had taken to sitting on my lap as I checked their homework assignments. When it was Chris' turn, he climbed into my lap. His work was showing noticeable improvement. I finished checking it and as I gave him a hug, he looked up at me.

"How come I never got to sleep in your bed? Larry and Lenny said they did. Do you like them better than me?" He asked, his lower lip quivering.

"Oh no, son, I love you all the same. I didn't know you even wanted to sleep in my bed. I thought that you wanted to sleep with the twins," I said giving him an extra squeeze. "I tell you what, if you want to, how about tonight? Are you sure that you won't miss sleeping with Larry and Lenny?"

"Yeah, but…I want to sleep with you tonight," he said brightening.

"Okay, now why don't you go see what Hildy has for your snack? I smelled something really yummy a while ago," I said. I no more than got the words out of my mouth when they were off like a shot to put their homework away and wash their hands.

Hildy had fixed gingerbread and whipped some cream for their (and my) snack. Warm gingerbread and whipped cream are food for the gods. The melding of ginger and spices along with the cool smooth sweetness of the cream is to die for.

After the boys showered and got ready for bed, I followed my regular routine of tucking them in but this time Chris followed me. We started with Joel and TJ. I tucked them in and kissed them on the forehead as I always did. Chris decided he had to give them a kiss also.

Next, we went into the twins' room. The scene was the same. I tucked the twins in and kissed them goodnight followed by Chris giving them his kiss.

"We're going to miss you," Larry said.

"Yeah, it's gonna be strange with you not here," Lenny added.

"Yeah, but..," Chris started and then walked out of the room toward mine.

I tucked Chris in my bed and gave him his kiss. "I'll be back in a little while. I have some work I have to do before I come to bed. I won't be long."

It was almost an hour before I finished answering my email and taking all the voicemail messages. When I finally crawled into bed, Chris was sound asleep. I leaned over brushed the hair off his forehead and kissed him before I settled down to sleep.

I woke once in the night with the urge to go to the bathroom. This always happens when I drink coffee in the evening. Chris had moved over in the bed and had one leg draped over one of mine and his face resting on my shoulder. I slowly untangle myself from him and went to take care of my business. I crawled back into bed on the opposite side and went back to sleep.

The alarm rudely interrupted my sound sleep at 6 AM. As I struggled out of bed, I looked over to where Chris should have been. Not only was he there, but the twins were too. Their characteristic pile of arms and legs were in that impossible sleeping position. I don't know why I was surprised that the twins joined us during the night. They had become so used to sleeping together that it probably seemed unnatural to them not to. I just shook my head, smiled and went to take my shower.

"Wake up guys," I said shaking the mass of bodies. "Time to get up."

The twins looked up with a sleepy but sheepish grin on their faces. "Morning, dad. We got lonely last night."

"Me too," Chris said. "I missed them too."

"Okay, get your hands and faces washed. Hildy will have breakfast ready pretty soon. I'll go wake your brothers," I said as they untangled and piled out of bed.

Joel was awake when I went in to get him and TJ up. "You are up early. Couldn't you sleep?" I asked.

"I was just thinking about how lucky we are to have you for a dad," he said.

My heart nearly burst, I got a lump in my throat and tears clouded my eyes. When I was able to speak I said, "Thank you son, but I think I am the lucky one to have five of the most wonderful boys I have ever known. I love each and every one of you with all my heart and soul. My life is so much more meaningful since you have entered it."

I hugged him to me and said, "You are such a special boy. I treasure the day you came into my life. Now, wake TJ up and get ready for breakfast,"

Chapter 24

After breakfast, I walked with the boys down the lane to wait for the van's arrival to take them to school.

"Remember," I told the twins, "you still have to go to Room D instead of recess today. Tomorrow you'll be back to normal."

As the van arrived, I gave each of them a quick hug and sent them on their way. I returned to the house to await Harold Nicholas and his designer. They arrived a few minutes before nine.

It took about an hour to discuss with them my ideas and to merge them with what Konrad, Harold's designer, suggested. I was extremely satisfied and excited at the prospects of the new space when we finished.

The rest of the day went by quickly and without any major crises. I did invite Eric to bring Darcie and JR to Thanksgiving dinner next week. I was sure that the boys would enjoy seeing JR again. He accepted and said that he was sure that Darcie would be able to come also.

I got home just before the van dropped off the boys. They were their usual exuberant selves as they ran toward the house. That is except for TJ. He seemed to be more reserved than usual. After they deposited their books, washed their hands and had their after school snack, TJ climbed into my lap. He didn't say anything, he just sat there leaning against my chest and sighed every so often.

"What's the matter, little one?" I asked as I brushed the hair back off his forehead.

"Nothin'," he mumbled.

"Come on now, you can tell dad what's wrong. You know I love you."

"Well…we…ah..," he started. "We are supposed to invite our mommas and daddies to the Thanksgiving play we are going to have on Friday."

"You know that I will come, don't you?"

"Yeah, but...but...I don't have a...a momma," he forced out as the tears and the sobs started to wrack his little body.

I hugged him tighter to me and rocked him back and forth. "Your momma has gone to heaven to be with the angels. She may not be able to be there in person but I'm sure that she'll be there with you. As long as you remember her and love her, she'll always be with you. Your mother would be very proud of you for being the fine young boy that you are.

"You know that my mother is in heaven also. I'll bet that your mom and mine are watching over us both. Since your mom can't be there in person, how would it be if Hildy came instead? I know that she loves you the same as she would if you were her own son."

TJ paused his sobbing and thought for a moment. "I love her too. Do you think she'll come?"

"I'm sure she will, if you ask her," I told him as I hugged him again and gave him a peck on the forehead. "Why don't you go ask her?"

"Thanks, daddy you're the best," he said as he squirmed down off my lap wiping his eyes on his sleeve. "Can you come with me?"

When TJ asked her, tears came to Hildy's eyes. "Of course, I will be honored to go to your play. I wouldn't miss it for the world. Now go play while I finish fixing supper."

Hildy turned away wiping the tears from her eyes with her apron. "Crane, I want to thank you for giving me a new life. Before these boys came into your life and mine, I just existed. I had my late husband's pension which provided for my basic needs, but I had no real purpose to my life. Now I have five wonderful boys to love and care for. I can't imagine my world without them. They have given meaning to my life again. I didn't think that was possible after my husband died," She turned back to me and paused before she said, "You are the luckiest man in the world to have them in your life. You are truly blessed."

"I know...I know," I said.

Wednesday was a fairly easy day. Things at the office were quiet as most of the consultants were out on projects. The most exciting thing that happened was the conversion van company called and told me that the van I had ordered was ready and that they could deliver it this afternoon around two o'clock. I had kept the van a secret from the boys. I wanted it to be a surprise. The van had seating for nine. There had to be enough so that we would have room for all of us and a friend or two of the boys to ride comfortably. There were six comfortable captain's chairs arranged two across with a bench seat at the back that would accommodate three. All seats were equipped with lap and shoulder seat belts.

I had the cabin reinforced with roll bars, discreetly hidden, for added protection. The engine was a gas guzzling V-eight which produced something over 400 horsepower. It was fully air conditioned with a unit for the front and one for the rear seats. Good air conditioning is a necessity in South Texas. A good six speaker sound system rounded out the van's interior. The exterior of the van was painted a pearlescent gold. Very appropriate, I thought, considering how much it cost.

That reminded me I needed to talk to my accountant, Gerald Cousins. After we exchanged the usual pleasantries, I got down to what I called for.

"Gerald, I need for you to prepare a statement of my net worth. I'm not worried about the house and cars being included. The main things I am interested in are stocks, bonds, other investments such as the business and of course cash. How long do you think that it will take to prepare that?" I asked.

"Well, if I use the figure for the business that we used for the sale of Eric's portion it shouldn't take too long. I have most of your assets set up in a spreadsheet so all I have to do is to wait until the market closes to update the value of your stocks. The bonds are automatically updated based on their interest rates and the assumption that they will be redeemed at face value. Given those conditions, I should be able to fax or email the results by around four o'clock," Gerald replied.

"Gerald, you are amazing! Fax the results to my home fax if you would. I'll review it tonight and let you know what I want done in the next few weeks. Thanks, friend," I said as we hung up.

I left the office around one so that I would be home to take delivery of the van. Hildy was surprised when I arrived. She thought that I must be sick to be coming home that early. I had no more than started to explain why I was home early when the gate buzzer sounded with the reason.

"Is that yours?" Hildy asked. "What a beautiful color."

"Yes, it's ours. At least now we can all ride comfortably and safely," I answered. "I think I will call the school and tell them I will be picking up the boys instead of them riding the school van."

I arrived at the school before the classes were let out. TJ's class was first to be released. I was waiting next to the van that they usually rode home. When he saw me, he ran and jumped up and threw his arms around my neck giving me a big hug.

"I didn't know you were gonna pick us up," he said. "I gotta learn my lines for the play. Will you help me? I gotta learn them all. I just gotta."

"Whoa, of course I'll help you. So will your brothers," I told him as I set him down.

The three musketeers were next to be released. They were so engrossed in their own conversation that they didn't see me until they were almost to the van. When they noticed TJ and me standing there they launched themselves at us but then stopped dead in their tracks.

"We didn't do anything. Honest we didn't," Larry said

I couldn't let this opportunity slip by. "Are you sure? I'll bet that you three have been up to something," I tried to keep a straight face but when TJ started giggling I broke up too.

"That was mean, dad," Lenny said.

"Yeah," echoed Chris. "You scared us bad."

"How come you're here to pick us up?" asked Lenny looking up from our group hug.

"I'll let you know in a minute when Joel gets here," I answered.

We only had to wait a couple of minutes before Joel and John appeared around the corner of the building. He saw us almost immediately and they both took off running toward us.

"Hi dad," he said as he wrapped his arms around me for his hug.

"Hi son," I said. "And hi to you John, it's good to see you again. Are you looking forward to your vacation next week?"

"Yeah, I guess," he answered looking down at his shoes.

I was a little confused but continued, "I know that Joel is looking forward to visiting you on Tuesday." That seemed to brighten him a little. At least he looked up and smiled. I gave him a quick hug before telling him, "You had better go get on your van. You don't want to miss it. I'll see you next week when I bring Joel over."

As John left to catch his van I said, "Grab your backpacks, guys. Let's go home."

"Where's your car?" Joel asked as we approached the parking area.

"That's why I came to pick you up. I have a surprise for you. Remember how crowded the Land Rover was for all of us to ride in? Well I have fixed that. This is our new van," I said as we approached it.

"WOW!" all five of the boys said in unison.

"Is this really yours?" Joel asked.

"It's ours," I corrected.

"This is so cool," Chris said as I opened the sliding side door.

"Each of you can have your own big chair to sit in when there is just the six of us. There is also room for three more to sit in the back. Now hop in and let's go home. Be sure to buckle up your seat belts," I told them. I made sure that they did before we took off for home.

I thought they would jerk those seat belts out of the anchors the way they tried to take in everything in the van. It looked like the van was going to be a hit.

Later in the evening TJ came to me holding a piece of paper, "Dad, I can't remember this."

"Okay, let me look at what you have to memorize. Hmm. Let me show you a trick one of my teachers taught me when I had to memorize something.

"First, I want for you to read this to me three times out loud," I told him.

I handed the paper back to him and he did what I said. It was only about seventy-five or so words, but I'm sure to him is seemed like a whole book.

When he finished reading it for the third time I said, "Now read the first sentence out loud again and then repeat it without looking at the paper."

He did.

"Now read the first two sentences out loud and then repeat them without looking."

We kept this up until he had read and repeated the four sentences that he had to memorize.

"That's great. Let's try reading it all the way through and then repeat it without looking three more times."

He did it perfectly.

"I think that you have it memorized, don't you? Now you need to do it in front of an audience. Go ask your brothers to come in here. I'll get Hildy," I said.

TJ was a little nervous when everyone was assembled but he performed flawlessly. In fact with each repetition he became more and more confident. I had him run through it three times without looking at the paper. My old teacher always told me that three was the magic number for memorizing. I don't know if it really was or that it made you concentrate more on what you were doing. Whatever, it seemed to work.

TJ got congratulatory hugs from everyone before I told the boys that they had homework to complete.

We got a recitation of TJ's part at the breakfast table the next morning. He got through it without a hitch. He fairly beamed with pride. When I hugged him he whispered in my ear, "Thanks dad, I love you."

"I love you too little one," I whispered back.

Friday afternoon Hildy and I drove to the school to watch the school play. The first, second and third graders each had twenty minutes for their part of the program. The other elementary grades were not involved in the program, but were allowed to watch.

We watched Indians, Pilgrims, the landing at Plymouth Rock, assorted pumpkins and turkeys all parts of the varied program. TJ's part came close to the end of the program. He walked onto the stage as if he owned it and delivered his lines clearly and projected them like a pro. Of course, I was prejudiced, but he really did a very good job. I was so proud of him and so was Hildy. I saw her wipe a tear from her eye when he finished.

When it was over and each class had taken their bows, we met TJ outside the auditorium. It was just starting to rain very lightly, just a sprinkle really.

As usual, he launched himself into my arms and put his arms around my neck. "You did really well! You didn't forget your lines and we were able to hear everything you said."

"The teacher said I did the best," he said proudly.

"Your teacher is a smart lady," Hildy said.

"I'm glad you came, Hildy. I wish my momma could've been here, but you're like my grandma," TJ said.

"Thank you my little one. I wish I were your grandma," she responded. "I'm sure she is watching over you. The rain is probably her tears of joy for you."

"You think so?" he asked.

"I'm sure of it honey," Hildy said.

"TJ, you were great," Larry said as the three inseparable ones appeared. "See, I told you."

The three surrounded him telling him how good he had done as Joel joined the group. "What's going on?"

"TJ did a really good job remembering his lines," I told him. "Let's go home. Remember Billy is coming to visit tomorrow."

Right at 9:30 Saturday morning the Suttons buzzed the gate announcing their arrival. I think that Larry and Lenny were actually looking forward to Billy's visit. They had said that he had been acting differently this week and was even playing with Jerry and them at recess.

The six of us were standing on the front steps as the Sutton's drove up. It must have been a little intimidating because the first thing Mrs. Sutton said was, "You really have a crew there. Are you sure that you want another one to take care of today?"

I laughed at her comment, "Of course, one more is no trouble. I hope you brought Billy's swim suit. The weather is supposed to be great today and I know my troop will be itching to get in the pool this afternoon. Please come in. Hildy has coffee and pastries fixed for us. That is if the boys didn't eat them all."

"Thank you, Mr. Johnson," Mr. Sutton said.

"Crane, please. Why don't we take our coffee out on the patio? It is so nice out there in the morning."

"That would be fine. And I'm Max and my wife is Janet. You have a beautiful home here. I can't wait until our home is complete. I'm so tired of living in an apartment. We've been there since last spring."

The boys had disappeared into the house, probably to show Billy their PlayStations. Soon they joined us on the patio looking longingly at the pastries that Hildy has set out for the Suttons and me.

"Go tell Hildy I said that you could have some," I said. They were gone back into the house before I had completed my sentence.

"Are your boys always hungry too?" Janet asked. "I think that one of ours has a bottomless pit for a stomach. He never seems to get full."

"Yes, it is a fulltime job for Hildy to keep them supplied with food," I chuckled.

Max spoke up, "I don't want to be nosey but all five of your boys have last names different from yours…"

"It's a long story. Joel, Larry, Lenny and TJ are brothers. I am in the process of trying to adopt them. My petition should go before the court sometime in January. Right now the court has granted me permanent custody of them. Chris is my foster son. I only have temporary custody of him but I will be seeking a permanent arrangement for him with the intention of adopting him also. All of the boys come from abusive backgrounds."

"That's wonderful," Janet said. "I don't envy you the job of raising them. One seems to be more than I can handle at times. Billy has always been so rebellious and hard to handle. I hope he grows out of it. He has seemed to be less so recently. I hope that it's a good sign. I think that your boys befriending him has had a positive effect on his behavior."

We chatted for about forty-five minutes drinking our coffee before they took off for home. Before they left they gave me their home number in case Billy got into anything. They also reminded Billy to behave himself and to mind what I said.

It turned out that all of the boys had a great time. Billy was really very funny. He was full of wisecracks and could turn almost anything that you said into something funny. He had us in stitches most of the day. He was a little afraid of the pool. He went in with the rest of the boys and me but you could tell he wasn't comfortable. Chris took him aside and showed him some basic swimming strokes and how to float. After that he was a bit more comfortable but he stayed in the shallow end of the pool most of the time. I kept a close eye on him to see that he didn't get himself in trouble.

Janet had warned me that he was a first class eater and he was. I thought my boys could put away the grub, but he more than held his own in the eating department. Hildy fussed over him like he was one of the family. He also got his share of hugs.

Max and Janet returned shortly before seven. Hildy was just in the process of finishing her cooking. We did her proud. I think every plate was licked clean and no one left the table hungry.

The Suttons were a little surprised when my boys started clearing the table and taking everything into the kitchen for Hildy. Janet was even more surprised when Billy joined in the clean-up. "Do they always do that?" she asked.

"Yes, that's one of their chores. I don't even have to remind them anymore. With five of them everyone has to do their share," I said.

"I hope this rubs off on Billy," Max added.

We sat in the family room drinking coffee while the boys lay out on their stomachs in front of the TV watching The Flintstones special. By the time the program was over at nine o'clock, the boys were beginning to get sleepy. It had been an active day.

Lenny came up to me and whispered in my ear, "Can Billy stay all night?"

"I don't care, but you will have to ask his mom and dad," I whispered back.

He turned to the Suttons and stammered "Can...ah...can Billy...ah...stay all night?"

"I'm afraid not, son. We have to get up in the morning and drive to Dallas to visit his grandmother. We are going to spend Thanksgiving with her. Maybe some other time. Is that alright?" Janet replied.

"Okay," Chris said.

With that, the Suttons took their leave. Billy got hugs from everyone including Hildy.

TJ followed Hildy back into the kitchen. "Can I go to church with you tomorrow?" he asked.

"Yes, of course you may, little one," she answered.

"Thanks, I want to talk to momma," he said and ran off to join his brothers in the showers.

When he came back from church the next morning, I asked him how he liked it. His only comment was that he liked the singing, nothing about talking to his mother. I didn't press but I was dying to know more.

I decided to take the week off since the boys would be off from school. I knew Hildy had things she need to do during the week so I would be needed to watch the boys some of the time. Monday was spent shopping for cool weather clothes for the boys. Everything that they had to wear was for summer. I guess I never thought that they would be around to need anything else. Chris had been making do with the twins' clothes since they were the same size, but now he got to pick out his own. The new van came in handy when it came time to haul all of the clothes the five of them loaded up on.

Tuesday morning when I went in to wake Joel so that he would be ready to go to John's house he was already up and dressed.

"My you're eager this morning, but it is a couple of hours before we are going to leave for John's house," I said. "Do you still feel the same way about John?"

"Yeah, I guess," he said. "He is my best friend and I like to be around him. Is that wrong?"

"No, of course it's not. Whoever gave you that idea?"

"Well, John's mom and dad said it's not right for us to like each other that much."

"How does John feel about that?"

"He wants to do what they say but he still wants to be my friend."

"I'm glad that you and he are such good friends. Just remember what I told you before about showing your affection for each other around people who wouldn't understand," I told him and gave him a hug. "Let's get some breakfast. We'll let your brothers sleep."

I dropped Joel off at the Gordinier's house just after 9:30. John was waiting on the front steps as we drove up. I got out briefly and talked to Bruce. I told him I would pick Joel up around five o'clock if that was alright. He agreed that would be fine and I left after giving Joel and John a hug since they were standing there together.

It was too cool to swim so the boys entertained themselves chasing the deer and throwing rocks down the steep path leading to the lake. I finally got around to reviewing the information that Gerald had faxed me the other night concerning my financial status. I must admit that since the boys came into my life I had not been as actively involved in buying and selling stocks as I had previously. It looked like that was a good idea. My investments had increased in value as a result of my inattention. It confirmed that I had sufficient funds to do what I had in the back of my mind but I wanted Gerald's accounting to prove it before I did anything.

It was nearly 1:30 when the phone rang. We were sitting on the patio enjoying the warm afternoon sun as I picked up the receiver. I was surprised when I recognized Joel's voice on the other end.

"Daddy can you come and get me?" he sobbed.

"What's the matter? Are you hurt?" I asked frantically.

"I want to come home, please," he begged.

"I'll be there as soon as I possibly can," I told him.

Turning to the other boys I said, "Dad has to go get Joel. Stay away from the pool while I'm gone and be good for Hildy."

I told Hildy that I had to leave as I passed her in the kitchen on the way to the car and asked her to watch the boys.

The BMW and I made record time getting to the Gordinier's house. I was out of the car almost before it stopped. I hardly noticed the brand new Mercedes sitting in the driveway. My focus was on finding out what was wrong with Joel. I knocked furiously on the front door and rang the bell at the same time. Bruce answered it almost immediately.

"What's wrong? Where's Joel" I almost demanded.

"He's in John's room and won't come out," Bruce said pointing down the hall toward a closed door.

My manners left me as I brushed Bruce aside and ignored the expensively dressed man sitting on their couch as I rushed to the closed door.

"Joel, it's dad. May I come in?"

I didn't hear anything for a few seconds until the door started to open. Joel's beautiful eyes peeked through the crack. He was still sobbing as he opened the door fully and lunged into my arms. I held him for what seemed to be several minutes until his sobbing let up. I led him to the bed and lifted him up on my lap.

"Tell me what's wrong. Why are you crying? Are you hurt?"

"I…I…don't want to go to hell," he sobbed.

"Who told you that you were going to hell?" I tried to ask calmly as I felt the anger rising in me.

"That man out there. He said that John and I were bad and God would punish us. I didn't do anything bad, did I?"

"No, you're a good boy. You've done nothing wrong. Who's that man?"

"He…he's their preacher. I think his name is Reverend Fullwell."

"Here's what I want you to do. I want you to find John and then go outside and play until I come to get you. I need to have a talk with Reverend Fullwell. Will you do that for me?" I asked.

"Okay" he said crawling off my lap and going to the closet door and opening it. "Come on John, let's go outside and play."

I tucked both of the boys under my arms and led them to the back door and let them out before returning to the living room.

Turning to the man I had ignored on my way in I asked, "Are you Reverend Fullwell?"

The man stood up and offered his hand to me, "Yes I am. It is a pleasure to meet you Mr. uh…"

"It's Johnson," I said ignoring his outstretched hand. "Did you tell my foster son that he was bad and that God would punish him and that he would go to hell?"

"I…uh…yes I guess I did."

"What in God's name made you do such a stupid thing? And who gave you the right to judge anyone?"

"He and John have sinned against the word of God. It is God's judgment that he be condemned to spend eternity in hell to pay for the sin of homosexuality."

"And I suppose that God himself relayed this to you personally?"

"Well…no…But it's written in the Bible."

"And just how do you know that Joel and John are homosexual?" I asked barely able to control my increasing anger.

"I have been told that they kissed."

"So, just because they kissed each other that means they are gay and are condemned. Is that what you are saying?"

"Yes, that's God's law."

What I did next shocked even me. I did it strictly on impulse. I put my hands on both sides of the reverend's head and leaned forward and kissed him full on the lips. The good reverend was so surprised that he just stood there speechless.

"There, you have been kissed by a man. Does that make you gay? Are you condemned to hell with John and Joel?"

"Nnn...no, that's not the same. You're twisting the word of God."

"No reverend, and I use that title advisedly, you are the one that is twisting the word of God. What I think you are is a sanctimonious hypocrite who gets his jollies by intimidating others with his selective use of the writings in the Bible.

"The God I know is a loving God. You say that you are a Christian. Well I'm not an expert in theology but from what I have been taught, Christ died for our sins. That all of our sins can be forgiven if we believe in Him.

"Now let me tell you what is going to happen, and it will happen the way I tell you. You are never to speak to Joel again. If you see him on the street, you are to cross to the other side. I don't care if you have to cross Interstate 35 at rush hour, you will do it. You will never speak to anyone else about what you imagine John and Joel's relationship is.

"Do you know why you are going to do as I say? Because I will spend my entire fortune to investigate your background and dig up all the dirt in your past and publish it to your parish if you don't. I will make it my life's work to see that your reputation follows you wherever you go. Knowing your type, I'm sure that finding the dirt will not be hard for my private investigators. They would probably start with how you got that Mercedes sitting out front.

"Have I made myself clear, reverend?" I asked as my anger subsided to a manageable level.

The good reverend's face was as white as a sheet. I knew that I had struck a nerve. "I...I...I understand. If you will excuse me I'll be going," he almost whispered as he rushed to the door.

All the time I was talking to Fullwell, the Gordiniers were standing there not saying anything. They were still speechless after he fled out the front door.

"Bruce, Pauline please forgive me, but I am very protective when it comes to Joel. I simply will not let him be hurt again, if there is any way I can prevent it. I'm usually not the confrontational type but that SOB got my dander up," I said apologetically.

Bruce replied, "No, we were wrong to allow that man in the house. I think he has seen the last of us in his church. We had gone to him for counseling when we feared that John might be gay. I mentioned in that session that Joel would be visiting today. I never expected that he would show up uninvited."

"I think it would be best if Joel left with me now. I'm sure he needs to talk about this and I want to be available for him. He was very shaken up by Fullwell's comments.

CHAPTER 25

"You seem to have a very open relationship with Joel," Pauline said. "You seem to be able to talk to him freely about his and John's feelings. How do you do it? Every time we have tried to talk to John about his relationship with Joel it just seems to make things worse."

"That may be your problem. Don't talk to him, listen to him. Don't let your revulsion at the thought that he may be gay cloud your love for him. Don't judge him. Try to understand him. Don't drive him away from you by criticizing him. You don't have to approve of his feelings for Joel. But for now at least, he has these feelings. They may last and again they may not. I'm not at expert at this but I know I love Joel and I will no matter if he is gay," I told them.

Bruce looked like he was deep in thought before he said, "Would you consider talking with John at the same time you speak with Joel? We don't want to lose our son."

I studied both of them for several seconds before I answered. Their faces showed the desperation that they were feeling. I had ambivalent feelings about doing it but I feared that the fundamentalist Southern Baptist theology that they had been brainwashed in would prevent them from maintaining a reasonably open mind with John.

"Very well," I said. "I don't know that I'm qualified for this. I'm new at all this parenting stuff. I guess I don't have all of the baggage that comes with being one for several years."

I went to the door leading out to their patio and called for the boys to come into the house. As they entered both of them peered into the room and looked around before coming inside.

"Is he gone?" Joel asked.

"Yes," I said hugging him with one arm and John with the other. "He is gone and is not going to come back to see you ever, I promise."

Looking down at both boys I said, "I want you both to tell me and John's parents about how you felt when Mr. Fullwell talked to you. Please sit down on the couch with me and make yourselves comfortable. Let's start by you telling me what he said to you. John, I know your parents were present when he talked to you but I wasn't and I need to understand what he said."

John hesitated, ducked his head down and pushed his face into my side.

"Well…ah…John and I were tossing his football around in the back yard when that man asked us to come in the house," Joel said.

"Yeah, we were getting thirsty anyway," John added.

"Mrs. Gordinier got us a glass of juice before we talked to him. He asked me if I went to church every Sunday," Joel said. "When I told him no, he seemed to get all upset and everything. He said I was a sinner and would have to pay for that. What did he mean, dad? Is not going to church a sin?"

"No, son it is not. You know that Hildy goes to church every Sunday and she doesn't think you are a sinner and neither do I. Many people get comfort from going to church and that's fine, but many people do not attend church. Who is the better person? There are many good people who go to church. There are many good people who do not go to church. There are many bad people who go to church. There are many bad people who do not go to church. You cannot tell whether someone is good just because they attend or don't attend church."

"What else did he say?"

"He asked us if Joel and me were friends," John said.

"And?" I prompted.

"I said that we were," John responded.

Joel looked up at the Gordiniers and said, "Then he looked real serious and asked if we had…ah…you know…ah…kissed."

"And what did you tell him?" I asked.

"I said yes," Joel replied. "You said it wasn't bad."

"What did he say?" I asked.

"He got all red in the face and started saying all kinds of things I couldn't understand. He waved his arms and his voice got real loud. He seemed to talk for a long time, maybe ten minutes," Joel said.

"I know that some of what he was saying was bible verses 'cause I heard him say them in church," John added.

There was a pause of a minute or so before I asked, "Did he say anything else?"

"Yes," Joel pushed his face into my chest before he continued. "He said that God hated us for what we did and He would punish us. He said that we would be…ah…condemned to hell forever," With this he began quietly sobbing into my chest.

When I looked at John sitting on my other side, he was beginning to cry also. I hugged him tighter to my side and let them both cry for a few minutes. I looked over at Bruce and Pauline, they were just sitting there. Their faces were blank, no emotions showing.

When the crying had pretty much stopped, I asked "What happened then?"

"He…he started yelling at us again," Joel said. "Then John got up and ran to his room. So did I. When I got there, I couldn't find him. I looked all around even under the bed 'till I heard him in the closet. He wouldn't let me in. He was crying. Me too. That's when I called you to come and get me. Can we go home dad? Please?"

"In a minute, son," I said. "Now I want both of you to look at me. Okay?"

"There now, I asked you this when both of you were at our house but I want to ask you again. Do you think that you have done anything wrong?"

They both shook their heads no as they looked into my eyes.

"How do you feel about Mr. Fullwell and what he said?" I asked.

The only response I got was a shrug from each boy.

"Well, did you think he was right?"

"No!" Joel said forcefully. "He was tryin' to make us feel bad 'cause he didn't like what we did."

"What do you think, John?" I asked.

"I didn't like it. His words hurt me in my stomach," John said.

"Do you think what he said was true?" I asked both of them.

"NO!" came a simultaneous response from both of the boys.

"I don't either," I said. "Fullwell is a narrow minded man. He distorts the very book he professes to believe in to suit his set of prejudices. He sees evil in everyone except himself and yet he is probably more evil than anyone else. He spouts bible verses or more accurately shouts them to drown out the voices of reason and sensibility. Anyone who disagrees with him he automatically brands as a sinner. He is a small man. His rantings are not worth causing you concern. You are both good boys and are certainly not going to be punished by God. God loves you both and so do I.

"Do either of you have any questions or want to say anything?"

"What if he comes back?" Joel asked.

"He will never, ever, say anything to you again. I can almost guarantee that. If he even so much as says hi to you, I want you to tell me. Understand?" I said.

John looked at me and said, "What if he tells everyone that we're going to hell?"

"If you hear that he is doing that, you tell me also. I will handle Mr. Fullwell and do it with great relish," I said.

"Are you guys feeling better?" I asked after a minute or so when it appeared they didn't have any more questions.

I felt both of their heads moving in the positive against my sides. "Joel, I think we should go home. John and his mom and dad need to talk and so do we. Are you ready?"

"Yeah, dad, let me get my ball glove in his bedroom. Come on John, help me find it," he said.

They both took off for John's bedroom.

"How can you be so calm?" Bruce asked when they were gone. "I had a thousand questions I wanted to ask them."

"Do you think they would have been able to answer them? They don't really understand all of this that is going on with their feelings. If you establish an atmosphere where John feels that he is not threatened, he will probably open up and talk to you about his feelings. I don't think it would be helpful to interrogate him. Love him and show him your love by your words and by your deeds. He is very vulnerable right now," I preached to them as if I really knew what I was doing. But, it sounded right.

Joel was quiet all the way home. As we got out of the car and started into the house he wrapped his arms around my waist just as he had when I brought him home the very first time.

"What's the matter, son?"

"Are you sure that Reverend Fullwell won't yell at us any more?"

"Yes, I am positive that he won't ever bother you again. I have made sure of that. Don't you worry about that man again," I told him as I gave him a squeeze and kissed the top of his head. "You let me worry about the Reverend Fullwell. I'll bet that Hildy has a snack fixed and if we don't get in there your brothers will have it all eaten up."

The other boys had not heard us drive up. They were too busy inhaling their afternoon snack as we walked in. They didn't stop when we walked in but did look up and mumble a greeting through mouthfuls of fruit salad and whipped cream. Joel joined them after running to his room to wash his hands.

"Crane, Dr. Adams called and left a message. He apologized again for having to cancel Joel's appointment Monday. He said he would be able to see him at nine tomorrow morning and asked that you call him to confirm that you would be able to make it. His number is on your desk," Hildy said.

I was almost glad that Joel's appointment with Dr. Adams had been postponed seeing as what happened today with Fullwell.

We were at Dr. Adams office a few minutes before nine. Joel was a little nervous but did not seem to be unduly so as he went with the nurse into the treatment area. I'm sure that I was more nervous than Joel was.

About forty minutes later Joel and Dr. Adams walked into the waiting room. "Joel, I'd like to talk to your dad for a few minutes. Will you wait here?"

I followed Dr. Adams into his office and sat down in a chair that he indicated. "Crane, I want to tell you I have never come across a situation like this. Joel is an amazing young man. With all of the things that he has gone through in his young life, his mental health appears to be in fine shape. I can detect no apparent psychological effects of the abuse he has suffered. I would like to do a battery of tests on him the next time he comes. I think we should be able to go back to the Monday afternoon time. That is if one of my patients doesn't pull another dumb stunt like one did this Monday.

"I believe that your interaction with Joel has had a very positive effect on his mental health. He thinks the sun rises and sets in you. Your outward expressions of love for him have had a remarkably healing impact on him. As Dr. Carl Rogers would say, your 'unconditional positive regard' for Joel has helped him to develop a 'positive self-regard' and move him toward a 'fully functioning person who is open to experience' and 'able to live existentially'.

"That is a longwinded way of saying that you are doing a hell of a good job with him."

"Thanks, he has embedded himself in my heart as have his brothers. After you run the tests on him, what do you think his treatment schedule will be?" I asked.

"If the tests turn out as I believe they will, I don't think he will need as much support from me as I had originally anticipated. Let's wait for the test results before we change the current schedule," he said.

Joel grabbed my arm as I exited Dr. Adams' office and pulled me toward the door. "Let's go, I'm hungry. Hildy was gonna bake some pies."

"I guess we're going. Doctor, we will see you a week from Monday," I chuckled as Joel dragged me through the door.

He was right, Hildy had been cooking all morning getting ready for tomorrows big dinner. Although there were only going to be ten of us, it looked like she was preparing enough for all of Canyon Lake. Three pumpkin and three pecan pies were cooling on the counter as well as two apple pies that she indicated were for our supper.

When Joel asked her what he could have for a snack she told him to get his hands washed and she would find something for him. It seemed that the other boys had their snack before we got back. As Joel ran to his bathroom to wash up, she uncovered a platter of butterscotch brownies and placed a couple of them on a plate then poured a large glass of milk.

The boys were hyper all day in anticipation of all the food that Hildy was preparing and that JR would be coming with his dad and Darcie.

Our guests arrived just after ten, Thanksgiving Day. The boys quickly took JR in tow after all the greetings were taken care of. They disappeared into the house, presumably to play with the PlayStation video games. It was still a little chilly to go swimming this early in the morning. Before long, six starving boys reappeared looking for a snack.

"I don't want you to spoil your appetites," Hildy said. "You may have a piece of fruit. We have apples, pears and bananas, take your choice."

Although they looked a little disappointed, they took what they could get and went back to their play. When I looked into TJ and Joel's room later, Lenny and JR were playing video games while Joel read his latest book to TJ. Larry and Chris were playing videogames in the other bedroom.

Dinner was an experience for the boys. I don't think that mine had ever celebrated Thanksgiving before. Their eyes nearly popped out of their heads when they saw all of the food that Hildy loaded the table down with. The turkey, which was the center piece, had to be at least twenty-five pounds. There were sweet potatoes, mashed potatoes, green bean casserole, oyster dressing, cornbread dressing, cranberry salad, giblet gravy, hot rolls and butter and white wine for the adults. The boys had apple juice so that their glasses looked like ours.

I carved the turkey, or at least started to, before Hildy suggested that she might be better at it. I had never carved one before and I was making a real mess of it. The boys were even laughing at my efforts. Hildy quickly sliced the turkey and placed some on each plate before passing them to each of us. I didn't think that Hildy was going to get anything to eat because by the time she had served each of us some turkey, the boys were ready for second helpings. She did get to sit down and eat as the boys started to slow down their eating. I was amazed at the amount of food that we consumed. There were not an awful lot of side dishes left. The turkey had shrunk considerably from its original size. Everyone seemed to be completely full. In fact the very thought of dessert caused everyone to groan when Hildy asked us if we wanted a piece of pie.

After we helped Hildy clean up the table, I suggested to the boys and Eric that it might be a good idea if we went for a walk to work off all of the food we had consumed. Darcie declined my offer and said that she would stay and help Hildy with the rest of the clean-up.

I decided to take everyone down the steep steps leading to the lake front. I wouldn't let the boys go down there by themselves because the incline was so steep. The steps had been carved out of the rock hillside and were irregular in width and height so they could be dangerous to traverse.

I led the way with TJ holding onto my belt behind me followed by Joel, the twins with Chris between them, and finally JR and Eric. The boys thought this was a real treat since I had never taken them down to the water before. At the bottom of the steps, the slope became much less steep. In fact, it was almost flat. There was an area that probably measured thirty yards long and at its widest ten yards. It was not smooth or sandy. It was rocky with stones ranging in size from one to six inches or so. These were just the right size to throw into the lake.

While the boys were throwing stones or trying to skip them across the water, Eric and I sat on an outcropping that gave us total overview of the area where the boys were playing. We talked of many things but mostly about our boys.

"How do you do it?" Eric asked. "I think I have my hands full with JR. I can't imagine having five at the same time."

I laughed before I answered, "I sometimes wonder myself. I consider myself to be an 'accidental' father. I always wanted children, but I never thought it would be this way or this many. I thought I would have them the usual way. Now, I doubt that is going to be a possibility. There are not too many women that would be willing to take on an instant family of five growing boys. I'm not sure that I would be willing to share them either. I guess my fate is sealed to being a bachelor."

"It is not all bad being a single father. I think it is better for JR that my ex-wife and I are no longer married. He is beginning to come out of his shell now. I didn't realize how much the tension between Simone and I was affecting him," he said. "You know he really loves to come here to visit your boys. It seems that he had formed a bond with all of them. I like it here also. It's so quiet and peaceful and you have such a magnificent view. I envy you."

"I know, this place is my sanity. I can forget everything about the hustle and bustle of the city and the office and just kick back and relax," I said. "That reminds me, have you found anything that interests you in the area yet?"

"Yes, I guess I haven't told you. There is a place that is probably two miles further on 306 that I have made an offer on. It is not a lakefront lot but it has a really nice view of the lake. Not like yours, but it is only two and a half acres. The house is in fairly decent shape so I won't have to do too many changes to it. They haven't accepted my offer yet. I expect to hear something by Monday."

"That's great!" I said. "JR could start to school at Corinthian second semester then."

"Yeah, I really want to get him out of the San Antonio schools," he sighed. "If we get the house, I'll need to hire someone to be there when he gets home from school. Do you think Hildy would know of anyone who is available?"

"I don't know, but we can ask," I replied.

Eric remained quiet for several minutes. He looked like he was deep in thought. He also looked as if whatever it was that he was thinking was disturbing to him.

Finally, I said, "What's troubling you, Eric?"

"I have been trying to decide how to tell you this or even if I should tell you," he started but stopped as if he didn't know how to continue.

"Eric, whatever you want to tell me will go no further. I realize I'm your employer, but I also know that you could get another job in a minute with your job skills. If it is about your employment, I'm sure we can work whatever it is out. If it is personal, I'm a good listener and I don't judge," I said putting my hand on his shoulder.

"Crane, it's a little of both. I've indicated to you that my marriage was not working for quite a while. Both of us were to blame for its break-up. Simone wanted something that I could no longer give her and I wanted something that she could not provide for me. She acted on her wants. I didn't. She satisfied her wants and needs with another man. I repressed my wants for the sake, I thought, of JR. Now I'm not so sure," he said quietly. "JR is my life. I fought hard to get sole custody of him. If anything happened that he got taken away from me my life would be pointless. Her adultery was the prime reason that I was able to get him. I had never cheated on Simone.

"I know I'm rambling, but what I have to say is not easy. What Simone wanted from me was sex. She was a beautiful and desirable woman, yet I could no longer make love to her. I went to a number of doctors to see if there was anything wrong with me. They could find nothing that would explain my lack of interest in sex. It was not until after the divorce that I slowly began to realize that it was not just Simone that no longer attracted me sexually. Simone had been my only sex partner and I really thought that I loved her when I married her. Looking back on it with all the advantages of hindsight, I know that I never really loved her. I married her because I was expected to marry her.

"I have come to the conclusion, after analyzing my emotions and my troubles with Simone, that I am gay," he said with a quiver in his voice. "I hope that you are not offended. I just thought that you ought to know. I hope this will not influence my employment because I really enjoy the work I'm doing and the people I work with."

"Eric, the fact that you are gay has no bearing on your job. You were hired because you are extremely talented and we needed your skill set," I said as my mind raced. "Does Darcie know?"

"I haven't told her in so many words. I think that she suspects though," he answered. "The main reason that I told you is because I find myself attracted to you and have since we first met at the Chuck E Cheese."

Before I could answer, I saw TJ trip and fall into the lake. The lake bottom dropped off rather sharply about a yard off the shore. Although he can swim a little, he is not a strong swimmer. I jumped off the outcropping and raced toward where he fell in. I was still about 20 feet from the lake when Chris, without hesitation, jumped in behind TJ. Chris grabbed a frightened TJ like a professional lifeguard and slowly swam with him toward the shore. When I got there, they were only a couple of feet from the shore. I reached out and grabbed them both and dragged them onto the bank.

CHAPTER 26

TJ was sputtering but did not appear to be in any distress physically. He hadn't been in the water that long before Chris got to him. He was more frightened than anything. I sat on the rocky shore and hugged both TJ and Chris to me while the other boys including JR gathered around.

"Are you okay TJ?" I asked more to break the tension than anything.

He shook his head to indicate what I had seen that he was not hurt before leaning over and hugged Chris and kissed him on the cheek. "Thanks Chris, I was scared," he said before leaning back into my chest.

"Let's get you guys into some dry clothes," I said as I tried to get up with them both in my arms. Thankfully, Eric took Chris from me and started back up toward the steps leading to the house. The rest of the boys followed closely behind as we made our way to the house.

"Come here, Chris," I said as he came out of his bedroom showered and dressed in dry clothes.

He walked over to me as if he thought he was going to be punished or something. When he got to where I was sitting, I reached out and picked him up and kissed him on both cheeks and forehead.

"What you did for TJ was a very brave thing. I'm very proud of you and I want you to know that. Your quick thinking may have saved TJ from being hurt. I love you, Chris," I told him with tears in my eyes.

TJ soon joined us and sat on my other knee. He buried his face in my chest and whimpered. "What are you going to do to me?" he asked.

"How about if I give you a big hug?" I said as I pulled him into a tight squeeze.

"Ain't you mad at me?"

"Why should I be mad at you? I was worried that you might be hurt, but I'm not mad," I said.

"But…but, I got my clothes all wet and everthing."

"Don't you worry about that. I'm just glad that my little TJ is safe. Next time I want you to promise me that you'll try to be more careful. Can you do that for me?" I asked still hugging them both.

"Now, why don't you guys go outside and play for a while. I'm sure that Hildy will have a snack after while," I said and pushed both of the boys gently off my lap but not before I gave each of them another kiss on the forehead and a swat on the seat of the pants. They ran off to join their brothers and JR who were already outside playing as if nothing had happened.

I now had to deal with the revelation that Eric had dropped on me only seconds before TJ's unplanned swim.

"Eric, I think we need to talk. Would you join me in my study?" I said as I led the way.

As I closed the door Eric said, "You really love those boys don't you?"

"Yes, I do with all of my heart and soul. They're the most important things in the world to me. I can't let anyone or anything stand in my way of being able to keep them forever. That's what makes what I have to tell you so hard," I started.

"They love you too. It shows in their eyes every time they see you and the way they come up to you and hug you for no apparent reason," Eric said. "Darcie's told me a little bit about their backgrounds and it's amazing to me that they have formed such an attachment to you in the short time you have had them with you. I would have thought that they would have had a hard time becoming close to anyone after what they have all been through, especially Joel. He appears to be as normal as any kid could be."

"That's part of the problem. I can't let them be taken from me if there is any way in the world to prevent it. Eric, you said that you are attracted to me. Well…," I paused trying to get the right words to tell him what I had to. "I also feel a strong attraction to you. I've never felt this way about anyone before, especially a man. I always believed myself to be completely heterosexual, but my feelings for you tell me that's not the case. That's the other part of the problem.

"What do you think my chances of being able to keep the boys if it were even rumored that I was gay? In Texas, I would have about the same chance of keeping them as I would of building a snowman in July in San Antonio."

"But, why should anyone know if we were involve?" he asked.

"Eric, I have a family court judge, a CPS attorney and an ex-CPS case worker who would like nothing better than to see the boys taken away from me. Just the hint of scandal and it would give them ammunition to take them. Oh, I might be able to win custody of them in court after a couple of years, but what would happen to them in the mean time? They are still fragile and not totally certain of their status with me. At times, they revert back to the frightened little boys that they were when they first came. You could see that in the way that both Chris and TJ reacted after they changed their clothes. They fully believed that they would be punished. Thankfully this behavior does not last for long and it is getting less often, but they are not totally convinced that they will always be here."

Eric thought for a while before he said, "What does that mean for us?"

"It means that until after I adopt the boys that we can only be friends and colleagues. After that happens we'll have to see what develops," I said.

All this time Eric was standing several feet from me looking into my face, when I finished he turned and looked out the window onto the patio where the boys and Darcie were playing. He stood there for a minute or two before turning back to me. "I understand, Crane. I don't like it, but I understand. I didn't really know what to expect when I told you about my feelings. I could have accepted it if you had thrown me out of your house or fired me. I guess I wasn't prepared to be put on hold and I think it'll take a while before I fully comprehend it."

There was just a hint of moisture in his eyes as he spoke.

I put my arm around his shoulder and said, "Let's go relieve Darcie. It looks like the boys are wearing her out playing ball."

The rest of the day was without incident. JR fit right in with the rest of the boys as if he had known them all of his life. By seven, they had worn themselves out as well as the adults. Eric announced that it was time for them to pack up and leave. JR started to complain but when he saw the stern look on his fathers face quickly started gathering his things.

There were hugs all around as our guests prepared to leave. Chris turned to me and asked, "Can JR come back again?"

"I'm sure that he can, son. He's welcome to come back anytime," I said aiming my last comment at Eric.

"I tell you what, Chris," Eric said. "We have to come back up here on Saturday to look at the house we are trying to buy and if we have time we'll stop by for a while so you guys can play. How does that sound?"

"Super!" Chris responded.

I read to the boys for about 30 minutes before I could tell that their busy day had gotten to them so I sent them off to bed about an hour earlier than normal for a non-school night. They didn't complain so I knew that they were tired. I soon followed them. My day was more emotionally draining than physically tiring.

Sleep did not come easily. Eric's revelation about his feelings for me weighed heavily on my mind. Were it not for the boys, my response to him would have been much different. I tried to conceive of a scenario that would allow us to explore a relationship without jeopardizing the boys' adoption. After an hour or so, I gave up trying and attempted to go to sleep.

I don't know how long I had been sleeping when I felt someone shaking me.

"Dad! Dad, wake up," I heard Joel's voice saying through my sleep induced haze.

"What's the matter Joel?" I said sleepily.

"TJ's crying and I can't get him to stop."

Throwing back my covers, I managed to clear my head enough to swing my legs out of bed and start toward their bedroom. "Did he tell you what the matter was?"

"No, he just started crying and wouldn't stop."

I sat on the side of their bed and gently lifted TJ onto my lap. "What's the matter son? There's nothing to be afraid of, dad is here."

His sobbing did not let up even though he buried his face in my chest. The tears ran down his cheeks and down my bare chest. I rocked him back and forth and kept telling him he was safe and there was nothing to be afraid of for maybe five minutes. Slowly his sobbing began to subside and the tears stopped flowing as freely.

"Can you tell dad what the matter is?" I asked.

"I...I...had a bad dream. I thought I was in the water and...and...I couldn't get out. I didn't want to drown. I...I didn't want to die and be put in a big box," he said and started sobbing again.

"I know you had a scare today, but there is nothing to be afraid of now. You're safe and there are a house full of people who love you. You know that don't you?" I asked.

I felt his head nodding.

"Why don't you come sleep with me tonight, you'll feel safe there. Come on, let's get you tucked in," I said as I carried him into my room.

Usually he curled up in a ball with his back toward me when he had slept in my bed. Tonight he snuggled up against my side and leaned his head against my shoulder. He sniffled a few times before he dropped off to sleep. His sleep was restless as was mine. I think I was awake at least every hour checking on him. Sometime during the night, Joel joined us and he snuggled up to TJ on the other side.

After my morning shower, I went to the kitchen to greet Hildy and get my first cup of coffee. Hildy was starting to fill the syrup dispenser as I walked in. I stopped and stared at the unexpected gift we were to be treated with this morning. The syrup that she was pouring was pure maple syrup from a half-gallon jug.

"Where did you get that?" I somehow gasped out.

"Oh, a friend who lives up in Vermont sends me a jug every fall. I got it the other day and thought that the boys might like it with their pancakes this morning for a change," she said matter-of-factly.

"I haven't had any of the real stuff since I was in boarding school in New England. I'm sure the boys will like it and I am positive that I will," I said.

"Breakfast will be ready in about ten minutes if you want to get the boys up. I've almost got enough pancakes ready for the hungry horde," she laughed.

"This is really good, Hildy," Joel said between mouthfuls of pancakes. "It tastes different but better."

There followed what appeared to be sounds of agreement from the other boys, but their mouths were never empty long enough for words to be formed.

The rain started to come down in buckets right after breakfast so the boys had to entertain themselves inside the house. Joel went to my study and selected a new book to read. This time it was "A Study in Scarlet" by Sir Arthur Conan Doyle. It was the first Sherlock Holmes mystery published in 1887. The volume was well worn from many readings. I remember my dad reading it to me when I was about the twins' age. I was pleased to see that TJ asked Joel to read it to him. I think he just wanted to be close to his brother to erase the memory of the previous night.

I busied my self by calling my private investigator to have him start a thorough investigation of Rev. Fullwell. I wanted to be prepared in case the bigot decided that I hadn't meant what I told him.

Jack called later in the morning to tell me that the extradition hearing for the Martins had been held on Wednesday and they were ordered to Louisiana to stand trial for the death of the man that resulted from the robbery that they were accused of. I thanked him for the information and again invited him and his family to visit during the holidays.

When the twins and Chris came to me complaining that they were bored, I suggested that they get one of the *Hardy Boys* mysteries and read it. I think I had maybe 35 or 40 of the stories and some of the earlier books were easy enough for them to be able to read. I was happy that each of them took one and began reading them. There is nothing that stimulates the imagination like reading a book.

The nasty weather put a damper on the moods of all of us the rest of the day. The only times when the boys were unaffected by it was when they were eating which for those little eating machines was quite often.

Saturday's weather was just the opposite of Friday's. It was clear, not a cloud in the skies, and warm. The ground was still wet and there were puddles of water all over. There is a strange affinity between puddles of water and young boys. They found every puddle and waded or stomped their way through each and every one. They were having so much fun that I didn't have the heart to interfere with the mess they were creating. Their screams of joy and laughter brought Hildy out onto the patio to see what was going on. When she saw, she simply shook her head and went back into the house with a broad smile on her face.

When every puddle had been explored at least once, five wet and muddy boys came up to where I was sitting on the patio with sheepish grins on their faces.

"Hi, dad," Joel said. "Can we get something to drink?"

"Yes, you may have something to drink, but I don't think Hildy would like for you to be trooping through her clean house with those muddy shoes and clothes on. Do you?" I asked.

"No," he said getting unanimous agreement from the other four.

"Well, I tell you what. You go over there to the outdoor shower and take off your muddy shoes and clothes and I'll go get some towels," I said. "Wash the mud off and then you can go into the house and have something to drink and a snack."

When I returned to the patio, I was greeted by five naked boys frolicking under the shower. I had not expected them to be so uninhibited out in the open, but then again there were no close by neighbors to see them. I had to laugh at the five little bubble butts bouncing around, each trying to get under the single shower head. I stood there enjoying their play until they noticed that I had returned with the towels.

"Okay, dry off and then wrap the towels around you and get some dry clothes from your bedrooms before you go to the kitchen for your snack. I'm sure that Hildy doesn't want you running around the house with no clothes on," I chuckled.

Joel helped TJ dry off and wrap up in his towel before he attended to himself. I wondered if he ever would stop seeing himself as the protector of his brothers. It can be a burden for a twelve year old to always put others before yourself. I wonder what Dr. Adams would have to say about that. I must remember to ask next time we have an appointment.

Shortly after lunch Eric and JR stopped by. JR was all excited as he bolted out of the car and ran to the boys.

"We got a new house. It's just over there," he shouted excitedly pointing somewhere to the east of the house which wasn't all that helpful in determining where it was.

"So you must have come to an agreement on the house," I said shaking Eric's hand.

"Yes, they agreed with my last offer and if everything goes right we could be moving in just before Christmas," he said. "The owners have already moved to Arizona, so as soon as the survey is completed and they can give me clear title we can move in. There is no problem with a mortgage since I'll be paying cash thanks to the sale of my business in Houston.

"If you're interested, I know JR would like to show your boys the house. My agent said she would leave the house unlocked for an hour or so in case we wanted to come back to see it again. She has an open house just down the road so it won't be a problem for her."

"Sure, I'd like to see it and I'm also sure the boys would too," I said. "Hey, guys, do you want to go see JR's new house?"

As I expected there was a chorus of 'Yeah' followed by a stampede to the van.

"I guess we are going," I laughed. "The van will hold all of us. All you have to do is navigate."

The house turned out to be about five minutes from our house. It was a good looking Spanish style stucco with a red tile roof. It was not large, only about 2200 square feet, but it was well laid out and in very good condition. The lot was just under two acres and had a lot of live oak trees so the setting was very nice.

The boys ran from room to room investigating every nook and cranny before they went outside to investigate the yard. JR told them that it didn't have a pool yet but his dad said they would put one in.

"Let me show you around," Eric said indicating that I should follow him. "We have two large bedrooms and a smaller one. This is going to be my bedroom. It has its own bathroom and sitting area that I think I'll use as a place for my computer."

I was admiring the view out of his sliding glass doors when he came up behind me and put his arm on my shoulder. When I turned to face him, he pulled me close and kissed me passionately. I felt my body responding to him even though I tried to overcome it.

"Eric, we can't do this. As much as I would like to, my responsibilities to the boys is paramount in my life right now," I said catching my breath and trying very hard to control my emotions.

"I just had to see if my feelings were based on reality or just my imagination. I'm sorry, I know you told me that there was no way we could become involved. I think I understand my emotions better now and although I hate the thought, I'll wait until your adoption of the boys is consummated before I pursue a relationship further," he said with a sad look in his eyes.

CHAPTER 27

The rest of the weekend was rather uneventful. Jack and his family visited on Sunday much to the chagrin of TJ. Sara again followed him around like a puppy. His patience wore thin after about 45 minutes of her undivided attention. Some day, I thought to myself you will relish the attention that she is giving you. His brothers and Jack's boys saved him by involving him in their baseball game.

Monday the boys went back to school and I went back to work. I was just beginning to see the end of all of the paperwork that had accumulated on my desk when Darcie called.

"Judge Riley has scheduled a hearing on Chris' custody arrangement for Wednesday at 1:00," she said. "Do you think you and your lawyer will be able to be there?"

"I'm sure that Benjamin or one of his associates will be able to be there. Do the other boys need to attend?" I asked.

"No, not at this one, but she has tentatively scheduled an adoption hearing for them on January 23rd. That is if you are still interested in adoption," she almost giggled knowing what my answer would be.

"Thanks, Darcie, I think I'd better call Benjamin to see what he can do for me," I told her before we hung up.

Benjamin was not in when I called but his secretary said that she would have him call when he returned from court.

I had just sat down at my desk after returning from lunch when Benjamin called. I explained the situation with Chris and his parents' problems.

"Hmm," he started. "I wonder if the Martins would be willing to voluntarily give up their parental rights to Chris now that they know there is no way they will ever be able to get their hands on his inheritance?

"You say they've been returned to Plaquemine Parish?" he asked.

"That's what I've been told by Jack Hogan."

"I have an old school buddy that practices there. Let me contact him to see if he will return a favor he owes me. If we can get them to relinquish their parental rights, it would smooth the way for you to ultimately adopt him also. You've never said so in so many words, but I'd have to be rather naive if I didn't know that's what you intend to do."

"Yeah, you're right. I sometimes think I have rocks in my head but I do love those boys."

"Karen Lin will be able to attend the hearing with you. It should be fairly routine and she's a very bright young lady with a great future in family law. I'll be getting back to you as soon as I hear from my friend in Louisiana," he said before hanging up.

I didn't get my hopes up about the Martins giving up their rights to Chris so I was surprised Tuesday afternoon when Benjamin called and told me he had a signed and notarized release from them. I was both happy and sad at the event. I was happy for me and for Chris but at the same time I was sad that any parent would think so little of their own flesh and blood to simply cast him off so easily.

I waited until Tuesday evening to tell Chris that we had a hearing the following day. I explained as best I could what I thought was going to happen trying to make it as routine as I could.

His reaction was nonplussed until he asked, "Are Larry and Lenny gonna come too?"

"No, son, they have to stay in school. It's just you and me and of course Darcie will be there," I said trying to make him feel more comfortable about it.

"But, that man Mr. Everest said I shouldn't be here. He wanted to take me away," he said with tears starting to form in his eyes. "Please, can't they come with me? Please?"

"That's Mr. Everett, and he is not going to take you away. Darcie, our lawyer and I are going to make sure that he doesn't," I said although I was weakening.

Chris got up from the couch where we were sitting and ran into his and the twins' bedroom sobbing as he went. I felt like a first class heel realizing when we had been to court before there was always comfort in numbers having all of the other boys there. It dawned on me that if I didn't address his fears of being alone and of being taken away from us, he would be a basket case tomorrow.

I followed him to their bedroom and knocked on the door, "May I come in?"

I waited a few seconds with no response before I opened the door slowly and looked in. Chris was sitting on the edge of the bed with a twin on each side of him. He was sobbing uncontrollably. The twins had their arms around him and were doing that humming thing that they did. I knelt down in front of him and took his hands in mine. He tried to pull them away but I held onto them.

"I'm sorry, Chris. I didn't think about your feelings when I said that these guys couldn't come with you. I know that you'll feel much more comfortable if they're with you," I said.

"You mean they can come?" he sniffed.

"Yes, Chris. Sometimes dads aren't as sensitive as they should be. I'm pretty new to this dad business and I don't always look at you as a boy. I'm more used to dealing with adults. I promise that I'll try to be more aware of your feelings in the future. Is that alright? Come on, let's see if Hildy has a snack ready for us," I told him as I stood up still holding his hands.

"Thanks, dad!" Larry said as he and Lenny wrapped their arms around my waist and hugged me.

The lump in my throat kept me from saying anything. I could only nod.

I picked my 'Three Musketeers' up at eleven o'clock so that we would have time for lunch before we had to be in court. The boys were dressed in their regular school uniforms. I brought their school blazers along so that they would be more formally dressed for the proceedings. I am still amazed at the amount of food that three nine and ten year old boys can put away. I'm sure that the 'all you can eat' buffet that we stopped at lost their days profits by the time we finished.

We met Karen Lin at the court house. She had all the paperwork that the Martins had signed giving up Chris. "This should be fairly easy," she said. "I can see no way that there can be any roadblock to you getting permanent custody."

"Great!" I said.

The court room was called to order and Judge Riley took her place on the bench. Ignoring the rest of us, she looked at the trio of boys sitting with us at the table.

"Well, I wasn't expecting to see so many handsome young men here today. Let's see…you two must be Lawrence and Leonard. I can't say which is which but I remember you two," she said with a smile and getting one in return from the twins.

"Christopher, please follow that man in the uniform to my room," she said.

Chris and the twins got up and started to follow the bailiff one twin on each side of him.

"Lawrence, Leonard you don't need to go," Judge Riley said.

Chris looked up at her with a look in his eyes of abject fear. "But…but…" was all that he could get out.

Realizing that he needed the support of the twins she said, "Go ahead, you can all go."

The rest of the hearing was relatively straightforward as Karen had predicted. With Darcie's recommendation and the Martins' documents presented to the court it only took about fifteen minutes before the judge said that she was going to talk to Chris. Gary Everett did not say anything and was not asked for his opinion by Judge Riley.

A few minutes after she entered her chambers the twins came out and stood right outside the door as if guarding it. Ten minutes later a smiling Chris came out with Judge Riley's arm around him. The twins immediately commandeered him and escorted him to our table.

"That is some threesome you have there Mr. Johnson," she said laughing at the boys.

"Yes, it is," I responded with pride.

Taking her place on the bench she began, "I can see no reason not to grant Mr. Johnson permanent custody of Christopher Mathew Martin. It is so ordered. My clerk will prepare the necessary order and it should be delivered to you no later than end of business on Thursday.

"Mr. Johnson, if you intend to adopt Christopher, I will entertain a petition to that effect at the same time as your other petitions are considered in January."

The entire hearing lasted less than an hour and it had been less that two since the boys had eaten but that didn't stop the twins from asking if we could stop for something to eat. We stopped at the Marble Slab for some of their marvelous ice cream. I settled for a single dip while the boys had triple dips, each dip a different custom blended mix done right in front of their eyes on the store's marble slab.

We enjoyed our treat in the store. I was not anxious to have the ice cream dripping on the leather seats of the BMW. We still arrived home about an hour before Joel and TJ got there.

TJ was walking on air when he got home. He could hardly wait until he got off the van before he started telling me about his day.

"We had a fire drill and I got to lead everyone out to our place and the teacher said I did a great job and I got to wear a fireman's cap and I got to shake the fireman's hand and everthing," he bubbled.

"That's great! I'm so proud of you," I said as I picked him up and hugged him as we walked back up the lane to the house.

When we got to the house, he ran to tell Hildy about the fire drill. She also beamed with pride as he told her all about it.

Later in the evening as I was sitting in my lounge chair reading the paper, Chris came in and crawled into my lap.

"What's the matter Chris?"

"Well…What's going to happen to me now? Do I get to stay here with Larry and Lenny?"

"Yes, Chris, you get to stay here just like all the other boys do. The judge said that you are my son now and if you want me to be in January you will be my son forever," I told him.

His answer was to snuggle into my chest putting his head under my chin and purred almost like a cat. I held him tight for several minutes before the twins came in and insisted that he go with them. Before he went, he kissed my cheek and whispered in my ear, "Thanks for being my dad."

With Christmas approaching, things seemed to get more hectic around the house. None of the boys had ever had a real Christmas and I was determined that this one would be special for them. I had each of them make a list of the things that they thought they would like to have. I helped TJ write his list.

Hildy, the boys and I went to the 'Christmas Tree farm' on Saturday and selected a beautiful six foot tree. The man there cut it down, bound it up and tied it to the luggage rack on top of our van. I thought that the van would bounce off the road the boys were so excited about getting it home to decorate.

I don't know where Hildy found all of the decorations that she came up with, but when she brought them out the boys' eyes were as big as saucers. They were very attentive to her instructions on how she wanted the tree to be decorated. For the most part they did as she instructed. TJ could only reach about half way up on the tree so his job was to decorate the lower branches. I helped a little but most of the decorations were put on by the boys. Hildy could have done the job in half the time but everyone was having so much fun it didn't make any difference. Besides, they were so proud of their work when it was done it was worth the extra time and effort that it took.

When the job was complete and everyone was standing back admiring their handiwork, Hildy brought out one more small box and handed it to TJ.

"In my family the youngest one was given the honor of putting what's in that box on the tree," Hildy said. "Open it little one."

TJ carefully opened the lid of the box and looked inside. The other boys crowded around trying to get a look at the treasure inside. TJ reached in and took out an object wrapped in tissue paper and handed the box to Joel. He carefully removed the paper to reveal a beautiful white angel with gold tipped wings that was clearly meant to top the tree.

"That's so pretty, Hildy. Where do I put it?" TJ asked.

"It goes on the very top of the tree. Your dad will have to lift you up so that you can put it up there," she replied.

I dutifully complied and after the second attempt, TJ got the angel securely in its place on the top of the tree.

When Hildy plugged in the lights, there was a collective "Ooooh!" from the boys.

"Now all we need are presents under the tree," I said. "In the next couple of weeks I'll take each of you to the mall so that you can pick out a present for each of your brothers and then we'll put them under the tree.

"Since Joel has an appointment with Dr. Adams on Monday we will start with his shopping first."

It was hard to get the boys settled down the rest of the weekend. A few firm reminders that they had school on Monday and that their homework had to be done before they could have their Sunday evening snack finally succeeded in calming them somewhat.

While Joel was taking the battery of test that Dr. Adams was having administered by his staff I talked to the doctor about Joel's very protective attitude towards TJ.

"Does this protective attitude go so far as to exclude his other brothers?" he asked.

"No, but he seems to protect or do for TJ to the extent of ignoring his own comfort and needs."

"I don't think that I'd worry too much about it unless he begins to exclude the others from his care. He's the big brother and naturally feels a need to protect his siblings. Since he was placed in a position, because of his father's brutish behavior, to protect his brothers, he probably finds it difficult to give up that role. TJ being the weakest of the boys has probably reinforced that role for him. I'm sure that as he becomes more and more sure of the security that you are providing he'll begin to relinquish that role. It would be unhealthy if he ever completely abdicated that role and began to reject his brothers," Dr. Adams said. "Keep an eye on his actions toward TJ and the others to see if there are any significant changes and let me know if there is and I'll try to explore them with him."

Joel's test took longer than his normal appointment so we didn't get away from the doctor's office until almost five o'clock. We went to the mall to start the round of Christmas shopping. When we got there, I reminded him that he could spend around $25 each on presents for his brothers. But before we started, we had to stop at the food court for the afternoon snack that he had missed because of the doctor's appointment.

I was surprised at how well organized Joel was when it came to shopping for the presents. He had given a lot of thought to each gift that he wanted to purchase and what store he thought where he could buy them. I wish that some of my project managers at work were as well organized I mused.

We finished shopping for all of the present in less than an hour and were on our way home at the height of the rush hour traffic. Despite the traffic, we arrived home before Hildy had supper ready. The other boys were really wound up when the presents were placed under the tree. I had to warn them that they were not to handle the presents once they went under the tree. I was sure that I would have to administer that admonition several more times before Christmas arrived.

I had planned to spread the present buying out over a week or so but that didn't fly. I was coerced into taking one boy each night until all had finished their shopping and the floor under the tree was piled high with presents. I decided that the best way to select who got to go which evening was to do it by age. That meant that Chris went next, then Larry (he was 15 minutes older), Lenny and finally TJ. I figured that it would take TJ longer to buy his presents and it did. All of them did a good job of picking out presents with a little help from me. Several of the present were duplicated from boy to boy since they had similar interests.

Saturday I took all of the boys shopping to buy something for Hildy. After much discussion we decided that we would buy a new TV for her since her old one was almost as old as Joel. I had to caution the boys to keep the TV a secret so that it would be a surprise to her on Christmas. We were walking through the mall when we passed a store that was displaying an apron that caught TJ's eye.

"Can we get that for Hildy, too?" he asked with his nose pressed against the display window.

I took a closer look at the apron. It was very nice, but the thing that caught my eye was the fact that they could embroider a message on it. We went into the store and purchased it and waited while they stitched the message that we requested and wrapped it.

As we left the store, Joel whispered in my ear, "May I buy a present for John? Please?"

"Of course you may. That is a very good idea. Each of you may buy a present for a friend you have at school," I announced to all of them. "TJ if you want to buy a present for Joey, you may. Larry, Lenny, Chris you may also if you have someone you would like to give a present. The present that you select should be a token of your friendship and should not be very expensive. It should tell the person that you are giving it to that you value them as a friend."

Joel bought a present for John. Larry bought one for a boy named Craig. Lenny bought one for Billy. Chris bought one for JR and TJ bought one for Joey.

Now that the boys had finished all of their shopping, I had to start thinking about what I would get for them. I still had their lists of things that they said they would like to have. The lists were rather meager. They had never been given a lot of gifts for Christmas, mostly clothes and maybe a small toy. I was determined that this year would be different for them.

Being new at this father thing, I decided to ask some of the consultants that worked for me who had children for some ideas. I got a lot of advice, some of it good and some not so good. It did give me enough ideas that I decided on the major gift that each would receive.

I must say that after I started shopping for the boys I got almost as excited as TJ had been. I just didn't hop around and run from display to display. The harried store clerks were very helpful once they realized the amount of money that I was going to spend. It was a good thing that I had driven the van to work the day I went shopping because I doubt that the BMW would have held all the packages I ended up with. I still had to buy the major presents.

However, due to requirements of the business it was several days before I could stop at the Bike Shoppe to make the final purchases. I wanted to give each of them a bike that they could ride around the property and would be rugged enough to stand up to the rough terrain. The salesperson was very knowledgeable and helpful in helping me select the right bikes for the terrain and the right size for the boys. I arranged for the delivery to take place while the boys were at school.

Hiding the bikes until Christmas should not be a problem since the third garage bay was separately enclosed from the other two car space. The van was too long to fit in any of the spaces and it sat out all of the time so that space was never used and could be locked.

The closer it got to Christmas the more excited the boys got. It was hard to get them to concentrate on their school homework, but threats of withholding their evening snack seemed to work fairly well. Since Christmas was on Sunday, the last day of school for them was on the Wednesday before.

Eric closed on his house and got moved in on the Monday before Christmas. The boys insisted on going to see JR on their first day off from school. I didn't object and phoned Eric to see if it was okay to bring the boys over. He said that things were still a bit messy but that he could use a reason to take a break.

"I need Darcie to help me arrange furniture," he said when we arrived. "She has a knack for decorating and making things look homey and inviting. I'm a klutz when it comes to this stuff. Unfortunately she has been in a conference in Austin all week and hasn't been able to help me."

"Don't ask me. I'm as big a klutz as you are," I said laughing. "When does she get back?"

"She'll be back this evening. I know that she will throw up her hands in frustration. Every time my ex-wife and I moved into a new place, Darcie would come help us decorate and try to explain how to arrange things. I heard what she said and they made sense at the time, but I can't translate what she told me to a new situation," he said shaking his head. "I guess it just goes to show that not all gay guys are interior decorators."

We chatted awhile before I told the boys it was time to go home. As we were leaving I told Eric that if they didn't have plans that they were invited to the house Saturday evening, Christmas Eve, to have some wassail and cookies. He agreed that they were available and was sure that JR would be happy to come.

It was all Hildy and I could do to keep the boys away from the mountain of presents around the tree. We did succeed in keeping the presents from being shaken to pieces. TJ was beside himself wanting to believe in Santa Claus but at the same time not sure there was such a person. He still hung up his stocking on the fireplace mantle as did the other boys, even Joel.

Eric and JR arrived around eight. The six of them were having a great time playing and talking about all the presents under the tree. The only thing that calmed them down was when Hildy served the wassail (the non-alcoholic kind) and cookies to the boys. TJ turned up his nose at the drink after his first sip and asked Hildy if he could have a glass of milk instead. The others seemed to like it but the cookies went faster than the wassail did. They did leave a few cookies along with a glass of the wassail for Santa when he came down the chimney.

When our guests left about 9:30 I suggested to the boys that they get their showers taken and get ready for bed so that Santa would have time to come while they were sleeping. It was still about an hour later that I finally got them to bed, tucked in and kissed goodnight.

Every so often, I would listen at their doors to see if they had quieted down and gone to sleep. For a little while I thought I was going to have to go in and settle the twins and Chris down, but eventually there were no sounds coming from either of the rooms.

Santa Hildy and Santa Crane spent the better part of the next two hours laying out the presents that Santa was leaving and filling the stockings with candy, fruit and small toys. This was the most fun that I had had since I was a small boy at Christmas time. Hildy was like a teenage girl. She was having as much fun as I was. It looked like a toy store exploded and all the toys dropped into our family room.

Although it was nearly 2:00AM when I got to bed, I was up at six to set the bikes out on the patio for the boys to find when they went outside. I needed my coffee badly to try to keep my eyes open. Two cups later, I was ready for the boys as they straggled into the kitchen. TJ was the first to see all of the stuff in the family room.

He grabbed Joel's hand and dragged him in there. "Santa did come. See! See!" he shouted but stopped in the middle of the room and just stared. "Is all of that for us, dad?"

"Yes, son, Santa said that you all had been very good boys this year so he left a lot of presents for you," I said giving him a hug. "Now why don't you go see which gift that Santa brought is yours. Then we'll open the other presents."

That's all it took and they were off to claim their prizes. After each one had claimed their presents from Santa, I had them sit down and passed out a wrapped present to each from under the tree. The whole procedure took about an hour before the entire floor of the family room was covered with wrapping paper remains.

"Okay, guys, listen up," I said trying to get their attention. "Now you all got a lot of toys and they belong to you. They are yours to play with, but I also want you to share. If you want to play with one of your brother's toys, you first have to ask if he cares. I expect that he'll say yes most of the time if he isn't playing with it. Do you understand what I'm saying?"

"Yes, dad," Joel said. "But what if they break it?"

"Well, that depends. If they broke it on purpose, then they would have to use part of their allowance each week to pay for a new one. If they didn't then I'll buy you a new one to replace it. Is that fair?" I asked.

"Let's get this place cleaned up. Joel, if you will get a couple garbage bags from under the sink, the rest of us will start picking up the wrappings," I told him.

Displaying a mischievous grin on his face Joel said, "Just a minute, we got a present for you."

Hildy had retrieved a package from somewhere and handed it to Joel who then handed it to me.

I had not expected them to get me anything and I don't know how they did it but I suspect that Hildy had a hand in it. My hands trembled a little as I carefully slipped the bow off the package and removed the paper. Inside the box was a beautiful silk dressing gown in a royal purple. I took it out of the box and slipped it on. It fit perfectly and felt absolutely fabulous.

"Thank you, this is so nice," I said with a lump in my throat. I went to each of the boys and gave them a hug. "I love you so very much."

We started the clean-up process and before long the family room looked livable again. I whispered in TJ's ear and he ran to his room and came back with another package.

"Hildy," he said. "We got something for you too."

She opened the package and held up the apron that TJ had picked out for her. When she saw the words embroidered on it, tears filled her eyes. The words read "We Love You Hildy" and then each of the boys' names was stitched below.

"I love you too, boys!" she said as she went to each giving them a hug and a kiss on the cheek.

"We also have another present for you, Hildy," I said. "Joel if you will help me bring it in from the garage."

We went into the garage and took the TV box out of the back of the Land Rover and carried it into the house and presented it to Hildy. I could probably have carried it in by myself but I wanted Joel to be part of the presentation.

"Hildy, we know that your old set is as old as me so we thought you could use a new one," Joel said in a very adult manner. "If you will lead the way dad and I will set it up for you."

This surprised me but I was very proud of him for his thoughtfulness. So we did. I was also surprised that Joel was able to hook up the TV and her VCR and cable box without my help.

"I have one more thing to show you all. If you will follow me to the patio," I said leading the way.

I opened the curtains and then the sliding glass door to the patio. I was nearly crushed in the mass rush of the boys when they saw what was waiting for them outside. Each one ran to the appropriately sized bike for them. TJ was so thrilled he was jumping up and down yelling "Oh boy! Oh boy!"

Joel was rubbing his hand over his new bike but there were tears flowing down his cheeks. I walked up to him, put my arms around him and asked, "What's the matter son? Don't you like it?"

He turned around and buried his face in my chest still sobbing loudly. I just held him not knowing what else to do. The other boys gathered around trying to soothe Joel and to find out what the matter was. It took a few minutes before he regained his composure enough to try to answer my questions.

"When we were in our old home and my old dad was beating me or doing other things to me, I always thought that someday I would run away and live someplace where nobody would hurt me. As long as I could think about that, I was able to stand what he did to me. When he hit me hard it was hard to keep my thinking on it and sometimes it was so bad I couldn't think about it, but when it was over I could remember and start thinking about it again. I knew I couldn't run away because he would just hurt my brothers. I had to stay and protect them.

"Now we have you as our dad and everything I used to think about is real. I'm so happy about our new life but I'm so sad about our old one. How can I be happy and sad at the same time?"

"Joel, I don't know. I can't answer that question. I just want you and your brothers to have your new life and to always be happy. You are a remarkable boy, Joel. So are your brothers. I thought that my life before you guys came into it was full. I thought that I was happy. Now I know that my life was really empty and I was just going through the motions. My job was my life and it was boring, now that I look back on it. The five of you have made my life complete. You have made me happier that I even knew was possible," I told all of them as we gathered in a group hug.

After a minute I continued, "Let's go have breakfast and then I'll get my bike out and we'll go for a ride."

CHAPTER 28

The thought of breakfast had a remarkably brightening effect on the boys as they rushed into the house to wash their hands. Hildy again had outdone herself preparing breakfast. She had fruit, scrambled eggs, sausage, home fried potatoes, cinnamon sweet rolls with caramel topping, milk and of course orange juice. I don't know how she had time to prepare all of it but the boys didn't care. They just enjoyed it.

When they finished and had taken their plates to the sink, Joel went to Hildy and wrapped his arms around her waist and said, "Thanks, Hildy, we love you. I'm glad that you're here. You're like a grandma to us. Merry Christmas!"

"Thank you, Joel. I would be proud to have all five of you as my grandsons. Now scoot! Get dressed, your dad wants to take you bike riding," she said wiping her eyes with the tail of her new apron.

It had never dawned on me that the boys had never ridden a bike before. Chris, it turned out, was the only one who knew how to ride. The only reason that he did was one of the kids in his old neighborhood let him learn to ride on his bike. He never had a bike of his own. TJ would be no problem since his bike was equipped with training wheels, the other boys would have to be taught the basics.

TJ got on his bike and started riding around the patio before I could get a helmet on him. I did snag him on his first time around and got the helmet adjusted to his head.

"There's something I want to tell all of you and it's very important. I want you to wear your helmets anytime that you ride your bikes. This is a hard and fast rule. If you don't wear it there will be no riding your bike for a week. Is everybody clear on that?" I asked and getting nods of affirmation, I continued.

"Joel and Chris I want you to help me with Larry and Lenny. I want you to get on either side of Larry and hold him up while he learns to balance on his bike while I do the same with Lenny. Watch what I do and then try it with Larry."

For the next forty-five minutes, we worked with Larry and Lenny in an attempt to get them comfortable balancing on the bikes as we slowly pushed them around the patio. I was really surprised that they were able to get the hang of it as quickly as they did. It seemed as soon as one of them learned something the other one knew how to do it immediately after.

I took a break before I started working with Joel. Being the big brother, he had not complained that the others were getting to learn how to ride while all he got to do was help steady them as they learned. When I did start working with him he knew all the right things to do to make his learning process go quickly. In less than a half hour he was riding his bike on his own, He was still a little unsteady but had made remarkable progress. All of the boys were now able to ride on their own, but were not ready to get out on the road.

After lunch, I took the boys around to the front of the house and we rode down the lane to the gate and back so that they could gain confidence in their abilities. Before the afternoon was over (taking time out for a snack) they were all able to control their bikes fairly well. TJ was a regular speed demon with his training wheels. He had no fear of falling over and after a while, he didn't realize that he was riding without the training wheels touching the ground.

By supper time, the boys were thoroughly worn out and were ready to put the bikes away. I showed them where they could put them in the third garage bay. I told them that I expected the bikes to be put away after they finished riding them each day.

While we were riding bikes, Hildy had fixed one of her fabulous meals. Tonight it centered on a baked ham and all of the trimmings. Pumpkin pie and whipped cream ended our Christmas feast.

Hildy rushed to clear what was left of the food from the table as the boys cleared the dishes. She told us that she had to get to her church to take part in the caroling that they were going to do in Old Square in New Braunfels. It seems that the city closes down the square to traffic and a couple of churches and two choral groups put on a concert there starting at eight o'clock. Her church was to perform first. The boys were all excited and asked if we could go and watch Hildy sing. How could I refuse?

We bundled up because it was forecast to get down into the thirties. It took us a while to find a parking place close to where the concert was to be, but we finally found one about four blocks from the square.

"Okay, guys, listen up. Remember where the van is parked. This street is South Academy and the street up there at the corner is San Antonio Street. If for any reason that you get separated from the rest of your brothers, you are to find your way back here. That's only in case of emergency. I want all of you to stay close to each other so that you won't get lost. Now pay attention to the way we go to see Hildy sing," I told them.

As we walked down San Antonio Street toward the square, TJ was so excited that I could hardly control him. The street was all decked out with Christmas decorations which I had not thought to bring the boys to see. This being a father thing is going to take a lot more thought than I realized. I certainly have a lot to learn. We arrived early enough that we got a relatively good spot to watch the concert.

The boys loved the music and sang along to the carols that they knew. They were awestruck when Hildy sang a solo part to "Oh Holy Night." I was just as surprised that Hildy had such a pure voice. It seemed strange that such a beautiful sound was coming from this large woman that I had known for some nine years. I had never heard her so much as hum a tune around the house.

The concert lasted until nearly ten o'clock and by that time I had a bunch of sleepy boys on my hands. TJ could hardly keep his eyes open. I ended up carrying him the last couple of blocks to the van. Joel took over when we got to the van and saw to it that TJ was securely buckled in his seat before we took off for home. We hadn't gotten very far before I noticed in the rear view mirror that TJ was sound asleep. It had been a long and exciting day for all of us.

I decided not to go into the office on Monday. Most of the staff were off on holiday so nothing much would be happening anyway. Beside I wanted to enjoy the boys' company and watch them play with the new stash of toys that were still covering the family room floor. We also needed to deliver the presents that they each had picked out for a friend.

A still sleepy TJ wandered into the kitchen while I was having my second cup of coffee. When he saw Hildy fixing breakfast for them he ran up and threw his arms around her. "Hildy, you were wonderful," he said looking up at her.

"Thank you, little one," she said giving him a squeeze. "Now go get your hands and face washed and by that time breakfast will be ready. And get your brothers up while you're at it."

At around ten, I received a call from the private detective agency I had hired to look into Fullwell's background.

"Mr. Johnson, this is Collin Cupp with Independent Investigators. I have the preliminary report on Gerald Fullwell that you asked for. We still have a couple of leads to run down but for the most part our investigation is essentially complete. Would you like me to fax it to you now or first give you a summary over the phone," he asked.

"Give me the summary and then fax what you have so far to me."

"Very well, this is what we have so far. He left high school suddenly and without notice in the middle of his junior year. No one could give a definitive reason for it but it was rumored that he was found with a seven year old boy in what was known at the time as a 'compromising position'.

"He next shows up as a seminary student studying to be a Catholic priest. Again, he left before finishing his training without explanation. The seminary would not provide any information about the reasons for his leaving but a fellow seminarian suggested that Fullwell was not living up to the order's precepts of 'piety, purity and prayer'. This time it seems that the object of his ardor was a twelve year old girl.

"Then there is a two year gap that we can find no record of him although one of the leads we are following suggests that he spent that time in Canada. We should have some information on that in the next week.

"He suddenly appears as a preacher in a small town Southern Baptist church in Oklahoma. He leaves just as suddenly less than two years later under a cloud of suspicion that he diverted the funds for the overseas outreach effort into his own pockets. The congregation became suspicious when his lifestyle far outstripped the meager salary that he was receiving from the church. There was also some indication that he was far too friendly toward some members of the Cub Scout troop that he was Scout Master of.

"We have never been able to determine where or if he received any theological training other than the brief stint in the Catholic seminary. The credentials that he used to obtain the pastor's job in Oklahoma are bogus. The schools and references that he used to get the job do not check out. In fact the references do not exist and the school he claims to have attended has never heard of him. The church just accepted his credentials without actually checking them for accuracy. I guess that this is common in small congregations who don't have the resources to do a thorough background check.

"Although he has never been convicted of any offense, other than a couple of traffic violations, he has been detained by police on various morals charges.

One was in Pryor, Oklahoma where he was picked up in a public restroom and charged with indecent exposure. It seems that he exposed himself to two eight year old boys. The Justice of the Peace dismissed the charge on the condition that Fullwell leave town and never return according to a police officer involved in the arrest. A second arrest occurred in Little Rock where he was accused of masturbating in front of an eleven year old girl. This charge was also dropped because the girl's parents would not allow her to be put through the ordeal of testifying. One of the police officers was reported to have threatened Fullwell if he ever came back to Little Rock.

"He next shows up in Topeka, Kansas parading with the homophobic Fred Phelps and his band of bible thumping bigots. I guess this is where he got his ideas for hating gays even though he has at times displayed homosexual tendencies. He stayed with this group of lunatics for about eight months before coming to Comal County and his present job with Shepherd of the Lake Baptist Church. Again, the church accepted his resume as genuine without checking it out.

"Looking at his lifestyle with the fancy new car and expensive clothes, it is not realistic that these are being paid for out of his salary of around $12,000. It would take an audit of the church's finances to determine whether there is any hanky panky going on. I would not be surprised to find that he has been dipping into the kitty," Collin finished.

"Wow, this guy has been around," I said. "It doesn't sound like he's stuck around anyplace very long. I guess it's hard to hit a moving target."

"Do you want me to fax the preliminary report to you or do you want to wait for the final one?" he asked. "It is about thirty pages long."

"Yes, fax it to me now if you can. I want to see the whole report. I would like to share some of this information with some of his church goers."

The report turned out to be 29 pages and much more graphic than what Collin described over the phone concerning the various sexual escapades of Fullwell. It did make interesting reading and guaranteed that should I want to get rid of the man I would not have any trouble.

After lunch, I asked the boys if they wanted to deliver to their friends the presents they had purchased. Of course, they were excited and quickly put on their coats and grabbed the presents and were waiting for me when I came out of my bedroom.

I decided that we would stop at Joel's friend John first. It was the farthest away from our house but I wanted to visit with Bruce and Pauline about Fullwell.

Driving into the Gordinier's driveway, I saw that the entire family was in the front yard. Bruce and John were playing with a Frisbee while Pauline and the girls were starting to remove some of the Christmas decorations. As we approached the house, John recognized the van and came running to meet us.

Joel grabbed his present and was out of the van's door before anyone else had time to remove their seatbelts. He ran up to John and presented him with the gift. I don't think I had seen a happier look on Joel's face since I met him. John was a little startled and didn't quite know what to say. He just stood there looking at Joel with a smile on his face.

Joel was the first to speak. "Dad said we could give a present to a friend so I got one for you."

"Thanks, but I didn't get you anything," John said with the smile draining from his face.

"That's okay, I got more presents than I ever had in my entire life," Joel bubbled.

The boys wandered off to be by themselves while the rest of us disembarked and paid our respects to Bruce and Pauline.

"I'm sorry that we didn't call before coming but I didn't want you to feel obligated to get a present for Joel. He wanted to give a friend a present because he had never been able to before," I told them.

"Thank you, Crane. I know that John appreciates it," Bruce said. "You haven't met our daughters have you? Come here girls, I want you to meet Mr. Johnson. Crane, these are our girls. This is Rachel our oldest, she's 10. Then Linda is our middle one, she's 8. And the baby of the family Cassie has just turned 7."

"It's very nice to meet you young ladies," I said to them. "These are my boys. Closest to me is TJ, then Lenny, Chris and finally Larry. Oh and that is Joel over there with your brother."

Larry and Lenny looked like they had swallowed their tongues when I introduced them to the girls. I had never seen them as quiet as they were. TJ and Chris walked over to the Frisbee which was lying on the ground, picked it up and started tossing it. Rachel went over and joined them in their play.

I noticed that Linda and Cassie were very attractive girls and I think that the twins did too. I don't think that they had ever looked on girls as anything but pests to be avoided.

"You want to see the Christmas presents we got," Linda asked to the twins.

Two heads nodded in unison, then looked up at me with a bewildered look on their faces. I shook my head in approval trying very hard to keep the grin I was feeling inside off my face. "You go ahead I want to talk to Mr. and Mrs. Gordinier."

Off the four of them went. The boys looked like lambs being led off to slaughter. When they were far enough away, I had to let out the snicker that I had been so desperately suppressing. The Gordiniers joined in my mirth.

"I did want to talk to you. That's the other reason that we came by today. I got the preliminary report from the detective agency I hired to look into Fullwell's background. I think that you will find it very interesting. I've made a copy of it for you to read. It's nearly 30 pages long and reveals the rather sleazy past of the 'Reverend Fullwell'. What may be of more interest to you is the suspicion that he quite possibly is pilfering the church's funds. According to what they were able to discover, there is no way he could support his life style on the salary that your parish pays him and there is no other source of income that they have been able to discover."

Bruce took the stack of papers that I handed him and said, "Several members of the church besides Pauline and I have also been wondering how he can drive a fancy new car and dress in expensively tailored clothes. We've been discussing the possibility of having an audit done of the church's books."

"If I were you, I would do it quickly and without Fullwell knowing. He has been known to skip town not to be seen again," I said.

We chatted a few more minutes before TJ walked over to me and pulled on my sleeve. When I bent down to him, he whispered in my ear, "Can we go to Joey's now?"

I gave him a hug and said, "Sure, go get Joel and the twins and we'll go see Joey."

The twins came out of the house having a very animated conversation with their two new friends. TJ was holding on to Joel's hand and pulling him toward the van.

Our next stop was at Craig's house. He and his family were not at home, so we went on to Billy's apartment. Our stop there was brief. Billy it seemed had come down with the flu. I certainly did not want that to get started in our house. Then on to Joey's place. TJ was about to jerk the seatbelts out of their anchors by the time we got there. He was so excited about being able to give someone a present for the very first time that he could barely contain himself.

Joey was riding what appeared to be a new bicycle on their front drive as we drove up. Harold was sitting on the front steps watching with pride as his son raced around the circle drive. Joey looked up at the van, not recognizing who these strange people were until TJ jumped out the sliding side door. Then he rode his bike as quickly as he could to greet TJ. As the boys greeted each other, I went to visit with Harold.

"TJ wanted to give Joey a present," I explained the reason for our visit to Harold. "He has never had the chance to do anything like this before. He was so excited."

"That is so nice of him. I'm sure that Joey appreciates the thought. He had the same thought and has a small gift for TJ also," Harold said smiling toward the boys.

"Oh, by the way, we should be able to start the construction on your upstairs right after the New Year. It will be either Monday or Tuesday. I'll let you know. The only thing that could hold us up is if the materials don't arrive on time. In order to minimize the mess, we will complete as much of the upstairs as possible before we break into the first floor to build the staircase. I'm having it custom made in a shop in Wisconsin so it is going to take some time before it will be ready. If things go as planned that should be sometime in the middle of March."

"That sounds great. I just wish it could be done quicker, but I understand that things take time. Even in my business, doubling the number of people on a project does not translate into getting it done in half the time. Most of my clients do not understand that. They just want it done yesterday," I said laughing.

About twenty minutes later, I gathered the boys into the van and we started toward our last stop after saying our goodbyes.

Darcie was at Eric's when we got there. I had not planned to stay long because it was getting on in the afternoon. Chris gave the gift to JR and then all the boys started playing with the mountain of toys that JR had gotten for his Christmas. Darcie, Eric and I sat drinking coffee while the boys enjoyed themselves. It was amazing the way all six of the boys interacted as if they were one big family. If only they could be I mused to myself.

Soon it was time for us to be getting back home. We bade them farewell and loaded into the van for the last leg of our journey, the home stretch. We were just about to turn into our drive when Joel hollered, "Dad, stop!"

"What's the matter, son?" I asked as I slammed on the brakes bringing the van to an abrupt halt.

"There's a dog in the ditch. He looks like he's been hit by a car. We gotta help him!"

Before I could get the van turned off, Joel was out the door and running back to where he had seen the dog.

"Be careful, Joel! He might bite you if he's been hurt. Watch yourself!"

Joel slowed down and slowly approached the dog who was whimpering almost as if it was crying. Joel knelt down close to the dog and slowly held out his hand and started to caress the head. I walked up slowly behind Joel and saw the dog clearly for the first time. He had definitely been struck by something. His hind leg was twisted at an unnatural angle. He was also very undernourished. You could see his ribs through the short scruffy fur on his sides. When I tried to pet him, he growled at me but only whimpered softly when Joel did the same.

"We gotta help him, dad," Joel said looking at me with tears running down his cheeks, "He's hurt bad. We gotta!"

"Okay, you stay here with him and I'll go get the box Hildy's TV came in and some blankets to make him a comfortable bed and then we'll take him to the emergency vet clinic. Keep an eye out for cars and I'll be back as soon as I can."

I ran back to the van and drove the other boys back to the house. I explained what we were going to do to Hildy and the boys before I grabbed the blankets and box. The box looked like it was too big so I also picked up a box cutter from my tool box in the garage. I didn't want to leave Joel by himself down there by the road too long so I didn't take time to cut down the box.

Joel was still sitting with the injured dog when I returned. The dog's whimpering was much less frequent and barely audible now. Joel's ministrations seemed to have lessened the dog's fear if not the hurt that he had suffered. I now took time to cut the box down to a convenient size to put the dog in. After I had arranged the blankets in the bottom of the box, I reached toward the dog to pick him up. He snapped at me and wouldn't let me touch him, yet he still allowed Joel to pet him. It was as if there was a bond between two beings who had suffered abuse from their 'masters'.

"Try to slip your hands under his body and then lift him into the box, son. Be careful, it may cause him some pain and he might try to bite you. Do it very slowly and see how he reacts. If he does I might have to put a blanket over his head and then try to lift him up."

Joel whispered encouraging words to the dog as he started to slip one hand under his upper body and when there was no reaction slipped the other hand under the dog's injured hind quarter. The dog's whimpering became much louder but he allowed Joel to pick him up and place him in the box.

"Good boy, good boy," Joel kept repeating to him. "You're gonna be okay. I'm gonna take care of you."

I helped Joel put the box in the back seat of the BMW I decided to take instead of the van we had been using earlier. Joel climbed in beside the box and buckled his seat belt.

The nearest emergency animal clinic was in San Antonio. It was going to take us at least a half an hour to get there. The only reason that I even knew there were such things as and ER for animals was we did a project for a large banking company on the north side of the city and there was one just down the street from where we did the work.

Thank goodness the place was not crowded when we got there. Joel insisted that he carry the box into the clinic. The vet was able to see us just ten minutes after we arrived. He took one look at the dog and shook his head. I'm sure that the obviously broken hind leg, malnourished body and the scruffy look of his coat did not look good to the vet.

After examining the dog for a couple of minutes he said, "Son, the dog is probably not going to live. I think it would be best if we put him to sleep to put him out of his pain."

"What does that mean?" Joel asked.

"It means that we give him a shot and he won't wake up. All his pain will be gone," the vet answered.

"No, dad! Please, you can't let them kill him. Please?" he begged.

I looked at the vet, "Is there any way that you can save him?"

"There is probably less than a 50% chance that he would survive what we need to do to fix his leg. He'll need surgery to set the bone. It appears to be broken in at least two places. It's going to be an expensive proposition and he's not a valuable animal."

"I don't care what the costs will be if there is anything that you need to do, do it. It's important for my son. Please do what you have to do to save 'our' dog."

"Very well, it should take about an hour to fix his leg and he'll be out for probably another half hour. You can wait in the lobby if you like."

"Thanks, dad, we can't let him die. He needs someone to take care of him. Can we keep him? Please?" Joel asked.

"Let's let the doctor do his work and them we will see what happens, okay?" I responded.

Joel sat on the couch in the lobby leaning up against me, seeming to need to be in contact with me. He didn't say anything but I did notice a few tears run down his cheeks every so often. It was the longest fifty minutes before the vet emerged from the surgery.

"Mr. Johnson, Joel, the dog came through the surgery as well as could be expected. The leg should be fine if he survives his other injuries. He has been badly beaten and may have internal injuries. We will just have to wait and see. He is too weak for any more surgery. The x-rays that we took do show that two of his ribs are cracked. We have diagnosed a case of heart worms in him but giving him medicine to eliminate the infestation would probably kill him in his current condition. We will have to wait until he has gained weight before we start treatment. The mange on his skin we can treat now and we have already started that."

"You mean that he wasn't hit by a car?" I asked.

"No, the injuries he sustained are consistent with being beaten by some type of rod, possibly a stick or bat. Something like that."

"Can I go see him, please?" Joel asked in a small voice.

"He's still sleeping from the anesthetic, son," the doctor said. Seeing the need in Joel's eyes, the doctor relented, "Just for a few minutes. He needs his rest to recover."

We followed the doctor back to a kennel area where the dog was. He was in a wire cage with an IV suspended from the top with the tube running to his front paw. As the cage was opened, the doctor said, "You can pet him if you want but don't disturb the IV. He will need to remain here over night at the least. Depending on his condition tomorrow he may be able to go home if you think you can care for him."

"I'll take care of him. I'll take care of him real good," Joel said. "Can't I dad?"

"Yes, Joel, I think you could," I said getting a smile from Joel.

CHAPTER 29

The vet let Joel stay with the dog for about ten minutes before he suggested that we go home and come back tomorrow. Joel was not at all pleased with the suggestion but relented after I reminded him we would come back and bring his brothers tomorrow and besides he hadn't eaten supper yet. I think the latter was the more persuasive. He was quiet all the way home and didn't say much even after he had eaten his supper.

It had been several months since one of the boys needed the comfort of sleeping in my bed but I was not surprised when Joel climbed in with me at about one o'clock.

"What's the matter son?" I asked as he snuggled up against me.

"He's not gonna die is he? Please, he can't, he needs me to take care of him. I gotta help him, I just gotta," he cried.

"I don't know son. The doctor is going to do everything he can to make him well. We will go see him right after breakfast in the morning. Try to get some sleep," I said and kissed his forehead.

It wasn't long before another little body crawled in to bed with us and snuggled up against Joel.

Morning came with two of my angels sleeping soundly in my bed. I slipped on my new dressing gown after finishing in the bathroom and headed to the kitchen for a cup of coffee.

"Good morning, Hildy."

"How's Joel this morning? He seemed upset last night."

"He climbed in bed with me early this morning so I know he was worried about that dog. It looks like we'll have an addition to the family. That is if he lives. The vet didn't give him all that much of a chance of making it. For Joel's sake, I hope he does pull through. He's formed such a strong attachment to that dog that I hate to think what would happen if it died."

Shortly after my first cup of coffee, I heard activity in the boys' bedrooms before all five of them appeared fully dressed and scrubbed. I got my morning hug from each of the boys before they sat down at the table for breakfast.

"Well, I see that everyone is ready to go see the dog so I had better get ready while you guys eat," I chuckled and went to take my shower and get ready.

By the time I was ready they all had their coats in hand and were waiting for me outside my bedroom door.

"Okay, put your coats on and get into the van," I said. "I guess it's time to go see the dog."

There was a nervous excitement as we drove into San Antonio. It took longer to get there this morning due to the rush of people going to work. It wasn't as bad as it could have been because a lot of people were still on holiday until after New Year's. I was surprised when we got to the clinic that Joel didn't rush in. Instead, he held back and walked with the rest of us. I suspected that although he wanted to see his new friend, he was afraid that his friend might be dead.

The vet we had spoken with the previous night was not there, but the young vet that we did speak with quickly alleviated Joel's concerns.

"Your dog is doing fine this morning. He's eating a little and seems to be getting along fine. Would you like to go see him?" he asked.

Five heads nodded in unison. The young vet led us back to the kennel that the dog was now in. The IV had been removed from his front paw and he was standing up and trying to hobble around the enclosure. The splint on his back leg made walking difficult. When he saw Joel, he made a valiant effort to get to the kennel gate. His route was anything but a straight line. He did finally navigate to where we were all standing.

"Can I go in?" Joel asked.

"Yes, just don't let him get too excited. He's still very weak," the vet answered.

The kennel that he was in probably measured six by four feet at most. But soon it was holding five boys and one happy dog judging from the speed of his wagging tail.

I turned to the vet and asked, "Is he well enough to be taken home?"

"He probably should stay here another 24 hours for observation...," he began.

"Ah, but...," I started to interrupt.

"But," he said holding up his hand "I can see that he'll be much happier and I think I can be assured that he'll be well taken care of. I'll need to send some medicines home with you. Let me get them and I'll write out the instructions for their usage."

"Joel, if you will go bring the box in from the car, the doctor is going to let us take the dog home."

Joel looked back and forth between me and the dog several times before he made up his mind to leave the dog and get the box. It was not an easy decision for him to make and I don't think the dog liked it very well either. I handed Joel the keys to the van as he headed toward the front door of the clinic.

Joel was back before the vet returned with the medicine and instruction. He also included a feeding schedule for the dog and a recommendation for the brand of dog food to buy. We checked out, paid the bill, set up a time to bring the dog back for a check up and headed to the nearest PetsMart to get the dog food.

On the way home, I broached the subject of the dog's name. "We can't just keep calling him 'the dog', so what are we going to call him? What do you think? Any ideas?"

There was silence for a moment and then they all started talking at once. They must have come up with two or three dozen names. None seemed just right until Joel came up with "Samson."

"Yeah!" came a chorus from all the other boys.

Samson gave an approving bark which made the selection unanimous.

When we got home and introduced Samson to Hildy, I went over the vet's instruction for taking care of Samson and when to give him his medications. Joel took the instructions from me and grabbed the tablet from under the kitchen telephone and began developing a timetable for Samson's medications. There were two different pills that he was to take. One was to be given every twelve hours and the other every four hours during the day and they were not to be given at the same time.

A few minutes later Joel came to me with a worried look on his face, "Is this right? I don't want it to be wrong. Will you check it, please?"

After looking over the schedules that Joel had prepared, one for today and one for the rest of the week, I could not find anything to change. The schedules were meticulously done and easy to follow with the name of the medication clearly written beside each time starting at eight in the morning until eight at night. There was one time when I would have to administer the second dose of one medicine at 10 PM. The boys, I hoped, would be in bed at that time.

The rest of the day was spent playing with Samson, riding their bikes, eating and playing with Samson. The medication was delivered on schedule by Joel under the close supervision of the rest of the brothers. Samson seemed to thrive on the attention that the boys were giving him. He was still a little unsteady walking due to the splint but was getting better at walking a straight line.

By Friday when it was time to take Samson back to the vet he seem to be much improved. His coat was now clear of any signs of the mange he had when we first found him. There were still spots where the hair was gone but with any luck and time, they would fill in. The vet that had originally worked on Samson was amazed at the change in the dog that he had recommended to be put to sleep. The x-rays showed that the leg was healing nicely and the cracked ribs were also healing to the vet's satisfaction.

"I want you to bring him in again at the end of next week and I'll replace the cast with one that will not interfere so much with his walking. He'll still have to wear one for probably five more weeks. After that, we'll see how the leg has healed. Next time he's in, we'll make a decision whether to start the heart worm eradication program or put it off a little longer. As soon as the supply of the medicines you were given runs out, you will not need to get any more. I'll give you a list of supplements that you can get at any pet supply that would be beneficial in speeding his recovery. Do you have any questions?" he said directing the last at Joel and the boys.

"Can we give him a bath?" asked Joel. "He's getting a little stinky."

"Sure you can. Just cover his splint in some plastic wrap so that it doesn't get wet. I would recommend that you not put him in a tub of water. Instead, give him a sponge bath with warm soapy water."

Saturday night the boys wanted to stay up and see the New Year in. I consented knowing that they probably would be asleep long before midnight. We turned on the TV and watched the celebrations going on around the country. We built a fire in the fireplace. We popped popcorn. Samson curled up in his new basket and wondered what all the fuss was about.

About ten o'clock TJ curled up in my lap trying desperately to stay awake. He was not successful. He was sound asleep by ten-thirty. Chris was the next to succumb followed shortly by the twins. Joel made it long enough to see the ball drop in Time Square in New York before he decided it was time for him to go to bed.

I carefully carried TJ into his bedroom and tucked him in. "Happy New Year little one."

Three trips later, I had all the boys in their beds.

Monday came quicker than the boys wanted, but they didn't complain when they had to get up early to be ready to catch the van to school. I reminded Joel that I would pick him up for his appointment with Dr. Adams. The last time we had seen Dr. Adams, Joel's appointments were reduced to the first Monday of every month.

The office was getting back to normal with most of the staff back from their Christmas vacations. I sat down with Carol and Foster to discuss the business opportunities for the coming year. Foster's assessment of anticipated consulting contracts based on the number of contacts from companies in the fourth quarter of last year exceeded my most optimistic hopes. If he were correct, we would need to hire at least eight to ten more consultants to handle the work load.

The planning meeting took all morning and through lunch. I barely had time to get to Corinthian to pick up Joel so that he could get to his appointment with Dr. Adams.

Dr. Adams was very pleased with the progress that Joel had made in coming to grips with the past abuse that he had suffered. In fact, his assessment was that after a couple more sessions he would probably release him to an occasional session to evaluate his ongoing mental health.

"We have an adoption hearing coming up on the 23rd of this month and I would appreciate a written assessment of Joel that I could present to the court in case they should have any questions," I told him. "I'm sure that Joel told you about the dog, Samson, that we have taken in. He has become very attached to it and it to him. The dog was also abused. Is this a healthy sign?"

"I would say that it's healthy. If the dog survives, and from what Joel told me Samson was badly served, it will demonstrate to Joel that there can be good outcomes. If he truly loves the dog, he will come to realize that he can be loved just as he loves the dog. I'm sure that he knows that you love him, but he doesn't really know why you do. He hasn't done any thing for him to 'earn' your love. This will help him to realize that he can be loved for no other reason than he is Joel. I don't know if I'm making myself clear. What I'm trying to say is that he will realize that there is such a thing as unconditional love."

Eric called after supper and wanted to know if Hildy or I knew of a housekeeper that would be able to be at his house to sit with JR until he got home from work. Neither Hildy nor I could think of anyone right off hand. He said that JR was going to start at the boys' school next week with the start of the second semester and he needed someone to start Monday.

"Why doesn't JR ride the van home with the boys and stay here until Eric can get here to pick him up?" she suggested more than asked.

When I put the suggestion to Eric, he was taken by surprised but then offered the standard excuses about not wanting to take advantage of our friendship and so forth but finally relented when JR heard about the possibility. He did insist on paying Hildy for her babysitting duties.

When the boys heard that JR was starting to go to their school and that he would come home with them every evening after school they could hardly contain their excitement.

I was a little surprised on Tuesday when I got a call from Bruce Gordinier inviting me to a 'prayer meeting' that night. He laughed when I hemmed and hawed around trying to think of a way to politely decline when he rescued me.

"We are calling it a 'prayer meeting' to get Fullwell to come. In reality it is a meeting to confront him with the information that you provided to me and the results of the preliminary audit of the church's books. The meeting will start at eight and we would like for you to be there to thank you for your bringing this information to our attention. I think that you will enjoy the surprise we have in store for him," he said with a smile in his voice.

"Now that is the kind of 'prayer meeting' I like," I said as we hung up.

I decided to call Collin Cupp, the private investigator, to see if he had any more details that I could add to the information we already had on Fullwell. Thankfully, he was in when I called. He said that the report on Fullwell was complete and that he was in the process of printing it out and would fax it to me as soon as it was through printing.

The completed report contained several more salacious tidbits about the 'Reverend Fullwell' that were not in the original including the time he spent in Canada.

I called Hildy to check if she would be available to watch the boys tonight while I went to the 'prayer meeting'. She was happy to when I explained what was going to happen to Fullwell. She was only sorry that she would not be there to witness the proceedings.

I made another call to add to the surprise for the 'prayer meeting'.

Waiting until time to go to the meeting was almost agonizing. Time seemed to crawl by. Since I wanted to be there early, I left thirty minutes before the start of the meeting. I wanted to share the new data that I had received on Fullwell with Bruce before everyone else arrived.

I was still huddling with Bruce when the rest of the people attending the 'prayer meeting' started to arrive. Bruce simply shook his head at the new revelations in the report. The parishioners arrived in small groups of two or three until the house was filled with fifteen guests not counting the Gordiniers and myself. Fullwell had not yet made his appearance.

As his car drove into the driveway, I stepped into Bruce's study and closed the door all but a crack so that I could observe the proceeding without being seen. I didn't want to give away what was about to happen. Pauline let him in and ushered him into the family room where everyone else was assembled. After he shook hands with everyone, she strategically guided him to the middle spot on the couch between two very large, strong looking men.

Bruce stood up and started to speak. "Thank you all for coming tonight. Pauline will be serving coffee and cookies after the meeting. Reverend Fullwell it's good that you could join us this evening for this very special event. You came to our church a little over a year ago so we thought we would give you a little surprise. We thought we'd do a take off on the old TV program 'This is Your Life'."

The color in Fullwell's face seemed to drain away as Bruce picked up the final report I had given him on Fullwell. Fullwell started to move off the couch but found himself being restrained by the large men on both sides of him.

Bruce began ticking off the items that were in the report from the high school incident, the Catholic seminary through his coming to Shepherd of the Lake Baptist Church. The two years in Canada were most enlightening. It seemed that Fullwell had been arrested at the Calgary Stampede for performing oral sex on an eleven year old boy in one of the restrooms. He was convicted of that offense and sentenced to six years in prison. He served a little over a year before he walked away from a work detail and fled the country.

By the time Bruce had finished with the private investigator's report, Fullwell had all but disappeared into the couch.

"Now Mr. Fullwell," Bruce said emphasizing the mister, "That takes your life up to the present. It seems that some of us, in the congregation, have been wondering how you have been able to afford the fancy car and fancy clothes on the small salary we are paying you as our preacher? So, we engaged a CPA to analyze the books of the church and guess what? He found that the building fund for our proposed new church has been completely drained of the $138,000 that is supposed to be in there. He also found that the mission fund is empty. He is willing to testify that you are the one responsible for the shortages. The methods you used for embezzling were so amateurish that it was easy to find where and how the funds were diverted.

"The last surprise we have for you is our special guest, Deputy Sheriff Jesse Cantu, who has a warrant for your arrest for embezzling the church's funds. Jesse has notified the Canadian authorities, thanks to an interested friend, that you were going to be arrested. They informed him that they are very interested in returning you to Canada.

"Jesse, he is all yours!"

Jesse appeared out of the kitchen and with the help of the men restraining Fullwell put him in handcuffs before leading the sobbing, protesting Fullwell out the front door to the waiting sheriff's car.

"Before we have coffee, I would like to introduce to you all the man responsible for bringing these matters to my attention. Crane, would you come out now?

"Friends, this is Crane Johnson. Crane's foster son Joel and my son John attend the same school. He first became suspicious of Fullwell after an incident at our house. He spent his own money to acquire the information that I read to you tonight. If it had not been for him we might not have found out about Fullwell's financial shenanigans until after he skipped town.

"Thank you Crane, we owe you more than we will ever be able to repay."

"Bruce, what I did, I did for purely selfish reasons," I said to him before turning to the assembled group. "Fullwell berated my son and made him feel like he was bad. The 'reverend' told Joel that he was going to go to hell because the 'reverend' assumed that Joel was gay."

I stopped and looked around at the shocked and somewhat disapproving looks on many of their faces before I continued. "I don't know if Joel is gay or not but what I do know is that I love that boy and his brothers more than life and I will do everything in my power to see that he is not hurt by Fullwell or anyone else. Let me repeat I will not let anyone hurt my son. That includes present company. That is not a threat but a fact of life."

"But the bible says that homosexuality is an abomination," one of the men said.

"It also says to love one another. I don't want to get into a theological discussion with you. What I have observed is that the most rabid homophobes are usually using their prejudice to hide a part of them that they cannot accept and then use the bible as a club. There is a line in one of Shakespeare's plays that goes something like 'Me thinks thou doth protest too much' which may apply to many situations. Beware of extreme positions. They might be hiding someone's real feelings."

I turned to Bruce and began to say my goodbyes, declining an invitation to stay for coffee. I told him I wanted to get home in time to say goodnight to the boys and tuck them into bed.

At breakfast the next morning, Joel informed me that they had their semester tests on Thursday and Friday and asked me if I could help him study this evening. Of course, I agreed and said that I would be home about the time they got off the school's van. I had no doubt that he would do well. All of his tests to this point had been excellent getting scores in the high nineties when they weren't a hundred. In fact all of the boys were doing great. On the rare occasions that I couldn't check their homework, Hildy did. We always set aside a study time every day so that the boys would not fall behind in their school work.

The day was going by quickly now that the office was pretty much back to normal. I did arrange to fly into Houston next Tuesday to meet with a potential client. If we got the contract, it looked like it would be worth about one and a quarter million. I don't usually visit our clients routinely, leaving that up to Foster or one of the senior project managers, but for that size contract, I felt the personal touch would be appropriate.

I was just clearing off my desk getting ready to go home when Carol told me I had a call concerning Chris' inheritance.

"Mr. Johnson, this is Jim Harrington, we talked a couple of months ago about Christopher's inheritance. The will has made it through the morass of probate and can now be distributed. Are you still willing to be the trustee of his estate?"

"Yes, I am. In fact if everything goes as planned, Chris will be my legally adopted son by the end of the month."

"That is good news. He deserves to have a family that cares for him. There are some papers that you need to sign in my presence so that I can turn everything over to you. I have a flight into San Antonio that arrives at 11:40 AM. Would you be able to meet me so that we can get this finalized?"

"Yes, I can fit that into my schedule. How long are you going to be in town?" I asked.

"I'll be leaving on Saturday. I have some other business to take care of in San Antonio and plan to visit a friend I went to law school with."

I got the information that I would need to meet his plane before we hung up and then quickly left the office to try to get home around the time the boys got there. I wanted to be available if Joel needed me to help him study for his semester tests.

The boys were home when I got there. Hildy said that the first thing that they did was to check on Samson and make sure that he had gotten his medication on time. After changing out of their school uniforms the next thing on their agenda was a snack before going back to playing with Samson.

It was easy to tell that Samson was beginning to thrive on the boys love and attention. His coat was taking on a healthy shine and he was gaining weight. He still seemed to tire easily but that was probably due to the heart worms.

For two hours after supper, I worked with Joel helping him to prepare for his tests tomorrow. The only breaks we took were for me to check the other boys' homework. They didn't have semester tests in their grades. I was continually amazed at the organization the Joel brought to everything that he did. He had all of his homework for the previous grading period arranged by date. His interim tests were done likewise. As I quizzed him on the three subjects that he had tests in tomorrow, I was positive that he would do well.

I met Jim Harrington at the airport Thursday morning. His plane was about fifteen minutes late so by the time he got his luggage it was nearly half past twelve. We decided to sign the paperwork over lunch. As he went to get his rental car, I went to the parking garage to get the BMW. He followed me to a Tex-Mex restaurant that I knew was good since he expressed a desire for Mexican food.

"The Mexican food we get in Ohio sucks," he said dipping another chip into the salsa. "This green stuff is great, but I like the hot stuff better."

As we waited for our meal to be delivered, he produced a small stack of papers which he handed to me for my signature. There were two copies of each. One was for my record and the other was to be delivered to the probate judge. I signed all of them after briefly skimming them for anything unusual. The last document was the trustee agreement for Chris' inheritance. The sum was about what he had indicated that it would be $2,335,486.22.

"That amount is what the total was as of yesterday. The funds are currently invested in money markets. You, of course, can invest them in any way that you see fit. I understand that the family court judge, a lady named Riley, I believe, is requiring you to submit an accounting to her periodically. Correct?"

"Yes, I have set that up with my accountant to submit the reports as required by the court. I don't know how my adoption of him will affect that," I said as I handed him his copies of the documents that I had signed.

When I got back to the office, I immediately called Gerald Cousins to see if he had been able to come up with a scheme that would allow me to set up trusts for the other boys and avoid any serious tax consequences.

"Crane, I'm glad that you called. I just now got off the phone with Carlos and I believe we have come up with a strategy that will allow you to do what you want and still minimize your tax bill."

"Great, I hate giving the government any more money than I absolutely have to. I want you to set up each of the boys with $2.5 million trusts. Chris' trust will have to have some monies added to it. I don't imagine that I can avoid taxes on that but it shouldn't be to onerous," I said.

"Let me work on that. I may be able to do something with your tax-free government bonds," Gerald said.

The transfer of the almost $12.7 million out of my accounts would not impoverish me in any way. My liquid assets would still be in the neighborhood of $70 million. I had not touched any of the assets that I had accumulated after I left college. In fact, I had added to them and lived off my income from the business. They had compounded very nicely over the last few years so that I had more money than I would ever be able to spend in my lifetime unless I drastically changed my lifestyle.

I remember back in 1986 when grandpa bought 10,000 shares of Microsoft for my account and how it had grown since then. With the additional shares I had purchased the now 100,000 shares were worth, as of Wednesday, $8.25 million. That $250,000 investment had really paid off due to grandpa's foresight. A number of his other stocks had done as well or better for me over the years.

Hoping to catch Benjamin Cross in, I dialed his office in Austin. His secretary said that he was in but on another call. I decided not to hold on the line, electing to have him return my call.

It was only about ten minutes later when he called back.

"I just wanted to confirm that someone would be able to represent me at the adoption hearing for the boys on the 23rd," I said. "I don't want anything to go wrong at the last minute."

"No problem," he responded. "I have you on my calendar. I plan to be there myself to witness the happy event. In my job, the outcomes are not always as pleasant as this one."

"I'll let you know what time the hearing is scheduled for as soon as I find out," I told him before hanging up.

This day had certainly been an unproductive one from the standpoint of the business. I had been able to get very little real work done due to the other distractions. It's a good thing I own it or I would probably get fired.

Joel was in high spirits when I got home.

"I think I got a hundred on two of my tests. The geography test was hard and I think I missed one question," he said.

"That's great, son," I said as I gave him a hug. "I'm so proud of you."

"I got the easy tests tomorrow, math and Texas history. But I still gotta study. Can you help me again tonight?" he asked.

"Of course I can help you," I said. "Now go play for a while, I'll help you after supper."

The next morning as I was going to get my coffee I noticed a third lump in Joel and TJ's bed. On closer inspection, I saw that it was Samson. "Hmm, I wonder how he got in there," I said to myself as if I didn't know. "I think we'll need to talk about this tonight."

CHAPTER 30

❁

"Good morning, Hildy," I said as I walked into the kitchen and poured myself a cup of coffee. "Have you checked on the construction upstairs?"

"No, but I wish they were finished. After a while that hammering and sawing gets on my nerves. The back hallway is a mess when they get done for the day with all the coming and going and hauling materials up those stairs. I know it's going to be a great addition for the boys to play in when the weather is bad, but it can't get finished fast enough for me," she said.

"Did you notice that Samson was not in his own bed this morning?" I asked.

"No, I hadn't checked yet."

"He ended up sleeping in bed with Joel and TJ. I know that many people let their pets sleep in bed with them, but I never thought it was a good idea. I never told them that he couldn't so I can't scold them for it. It's just something I want to stop before it becomes a habit."

After reading the first section of the paper and finishing my first cup of coffee I went to wake the boys for breakfast. Before long, they straggled to the breakfast table followed closely by our hobbling dog. I decided that I would not bring up Samson's sleeping arrangements until this evening.

I drove the boys down to the gate to wait for the school van because I needed to get to work early to take care of some business. Giving each of them a hug, I wished Joel good luck on his tests today. As they drove off in the van, I drove off to work.

I got to the office in plenty of time to prepare for the conference call that Foster and I were to have with one of our clients in Dallas at 9:30. Foster and I went over our contract with them and discussed between us what resources we could bring to the project to do the additional work that they wanted us to do. After running through several scenarios, we concluded that the only way we could do what they wanted was to negotiate the delivery dates. We would only be able to add one more analyst to the project until the end of January when one more would become available.

The negotiations went very well with the client. They ended up satisfied with the delivery dates and we were satisfied with the additional quarter million in revenues we would derive from the additional work.

Since part of that additional work we were going to perform for the client involved designing and installing a large computer network, I called Eric at his project and asked him to drop by the office. When I told him about the work that they wanted done, he was very excited about it. Having to be gone from home for two days a week for several months, he was less enthusiastic about. He didn't like leaving JR but he knew that Darcie would be able to care for him while he was gone. Actually, he would only be gone one night because he would fly out early one morning and fly back the following night. His part of the project would not start until the first of February.

Dr. Greene called in the afternoon to inform me that the latest test for HIV that he had done on Joel still showed no sign of the antibodies and the liver enzymes were now at normal levels.

"Crane, I think we are out of the woods as far as HIV is concerned, but I would like to do another test in six months. I know Joel won't mind not getting a needle stuck in his arm every month. He has been very good about this, much more so than a lot of my patients."

"Thanks, Sam. I know that he'll appreciate that. You and Carol should come over some weekend so that I can introduce you to the newest member of the clan."

"My god Crane, you haven't taken in another kid have you?"

"No, nothing so drastic, we now have a dog," I said laughing. I had to explain the circumstances surrounding Samson becoming a member of the family.

"Crane, one of these days they are going to take you away to the funny farm. You are what, 29 years old, raising five boys and a dog as a single parent and running a multi-million dollar business all at the same time. You are either going to kill yourself or they WILL carry you away to the funny farm."

"Sam, I've never been happier in my life. If all of this becomes too much for me, I'll sell the business to one of the big five consulting firms. A couple of them have already approached me to buy it. They have offered me over three times what I have valued it at. Right now I'm having too much fun to give it up."

After we hung up, I spent the rest of the day catching up on paperwork that needed to be completed before I left the office for the weekend. Even so, I was able to get home before the school van arrived with the boys, but only by a couple of minutes.

The boys hurried into the house and went straight to Samson's basket to check on him before they gave Hildy and me our usual hugs. When they went to change out of their school clothes I turned to Hildy, "I guess I know where we rate."

"We want to ride our bikes," Joel said as they finished their snacks.

"Sure, just be careful. The workmen will be here for about another half hour, so watch for their trucks and be sure to wear your helmets," I told them as they raced to get their coats.

I decided to go outside and watch them to see how well they were learning to ride the bikes. I noticed that Lenny was having a hard time keeping his helmet on. It kept slipping down over his eyes when he leaned forward.

"Come here Lenny and let me fix your helmet. You can't see with it over your eyes," I said.

I took his helmet off and looked it over and discovered the problem. One of the straps had been twisted and wouldn't let the chinstrap fit correctly. I started to fix the problem when Lenny said loudly, "Ouch."

I looked at him, "What's the matter? What happened?"

"Larry hurt himself," he replied.

I looked around and couldn't see Larry. "How do you know that he hurt himself?"

"Don't know, just do."

"Here, your helmet's fixed. Let's go find your brother."

Sure enough as we rounded the workmen's truck, Larry was sitting on the ground holding his left arm and tears were starting to run down his cheeks.

"What's the matter, son? What happened?"

"I fell off my bike," Larry sniffled.

"Did you hurt it bad?"

"Don't think so. I scraped my hand on the ground and banged my elbow, but it hurts."

"Let's see if you can move your arm," I said as I gently flexed his arm. "Does that hurt?"

"A little bit," he said.

"I don't think anything's broken, but we need to get that scrape on your hand cleaned and put some antiseptic on it. Let's go see where Hildy keeps the first aid kit," I said helping Larry to his feet. "Lenny will you put Larry's bike and helmet away, please?"

"Hildy, where do you keep the first aid kit?" I asked as we entered the back door. "Larry scraped up his hand when he fell off his bike."

"Come here, baby, let me look," she said to Larry. "Oh, that doesn't look too bad. Let me get a wash cloth while you take your coat off."

She took Larry to the kitchen sink and ran cool water over the scrape and then carefully took the soapy wash cloth and cleaned the scrape."

"Oh, oh…that stings," Larry said trying to pull his hand away.

"I know honey, but we have to wash the germs off. We don't want it to get infected," she cooed.

What little blood there had been had stopped by the time Hildy finished washing the scrape and rinsing it thoroughly. After she had dried his hand, she opened a jar of an antiseptic salve. "Hold still now while I put this on your hand."

"Will it hurt?" Larry asked.

"No, it will just make it feel cool and it'll stop all of the hurt," she said as she applied the salve and then the square Band-Aid patch to cover the scrape.

By this time, all the other boys had crowded around to see their brother being ministered to. Satisfied that he was going to live they went to hang up their coats in preparation for supper.

"Did you put your bikes away where they are supposed to be?" I asked.

Chris and TJ looked at each other and then ran back out to put their bikes in the garage. Well, maybe they will remember next time I thought to myself.

As they came back into the family room I said, "Larry, Lenny, come here a minute. I'd like to talk to you."

"Did we do somethin' wrong?" Larry asked.

"No, I just want to talk to you and ask a few questions that have been on my mind for a while. Sit here on the couch beside me," I said indicating a spot on each side of me where I expected them to sit.

I gave each of them a hug before saying, "Lenny, today when Larry got hurt you said that you felt it, is that right?"

"Yeah," he said. "Is that bad?"

"No son, it's not bad. I just wanted to know how you can tell when your twin is hurt or whatever."

"We just feel it sometimes. I don't know how it just happens, don't it Lenny?"

"Can you tell what the other one is thinking?" I asked looking first at one then the other.

"No," they both said.

"I've noticed that you guys sometimes seem to be humming to each other. I have been meaning to ask why you do that."

"When we were little, dad always yelled at us to shut up or hit us when we talked so we hummed to hide our words and he didn't yell at us no more," Larry said.

"Very clever, but I couldn't hear any words when you were humming. How do you hum and talk at the same time?"

"We do the talking real soft. I don't know how, we just do," Lenny added.

"Thanks guys! I love you," I said giving each another hug and a kiss on top of their heads. "Now go play, Hildy will have supper ready in about thirty minutes."

After they were gone, I tried to hum and say something at the same time and found that there was no way I could do it. I just shook my head and wondered at the ingenuity of those two.

Before bedtime, I sat down with all of the boys and discussed the sleeping arrangements for Samson. Although what I told them was not met with universal appreciation, they agreed that Samson would sleep in his basket. I did relent and let Joel take the basket into his bedroom at night as long as he promised that Samson would remain in it all night.

Larry's arm was a little sore for the rest of the weekend but it didn't seem to slow him down too much. By Monday, the scrape on his hand was sufficiently healed that Hildy didn't put a new bandage on it.

"Remember, guys," I told them as we waited for their ride to school, "JR will be riding the van home with you this evening. I want you to make sure that he gets on the van with you. Okay?"

Joel's "Yes, dad," was echoed by the other four.

I got a call from Eric Olsen's son about mid-morning with the sad news that his dad had died late Sunday afternoon. I had not visited Eric for several weeks with all the things going on with the boys and Christmas. He informed me that the funeral for his father was scheduled for two o'clock Wednesday afternoon at Good Samaritan Chapel in Boerne. After I had given my condolences to him and we hung up, I informed Foster and Carol of Eric's death. They had both worked closely with Eric while he was part owner of the firm.

The rest of the day, I spent preparing for my trip to Houston tomorrow. I was not particularly looking forward to the trip. Houston's population had grown so fast in the late 70's and 80's that its infrastructure had not had time to catch up and it seemed like it was in a perpetual traffic jam. I was, however, looking forward to the business that the trip would bring in.

I met most of the afternoon with Amanda Karnes who would be the supervising project manager for the Houston project. She was an extremely capable manager and I had every confidence that she would do an excellent job for us and our client.

We agreed to meet at the airport around half past six tomorrow morning to catch the plane to Houston.

I rushed home to be there when the boys arrived, all six of them. Thank goodness they all piled off the van. Of course, I got the usual hugs from my boys and JR decided he needed a hug too which I gladly gave.

JR was in a grade behind the twins and Chris. He was almost a year younger than Larry and Lenny and about a year and a half younger than Chris. Despite the larger age gap between Chris and JR, they seemed to gravitate to each other whenever they played. Chris was still very attached to the twins when JR was not around but acted almost the way Joel acted toward TJ when JR was there.

"JR, how was school today? Did you like it?" I asked.

"It was fun. It's a lot better than that old school. I like Miss Judson. She's nice," he announced.

It wasn't long after the boys had their afternoon snack when Eric showed up to collect JR. This met with much disapproval from the others.

"Come on JR. Dad has to fix your supper," he told his young son. "Get your school books and say goodbye to your friends and let's go.

"Hildy I hope he wasn't any problem. I really appreciate you doing this for me. I don't know what I would have done. I have to think of so many more things being a working single parent."

Later that evening after the boys had finished their homework, which was very light being the first day of the new term, I sat down with all of them to explain my trip to Houston.

"I want you guys to know that I will not be here when you wake up in the morning. I have to leave early so that I can catch a plane to Houston to meet with one of our customers there. I will not be back until after suppertime tomorrow night. I know that you will be good for Hildy until I return.

"Joel, you are going to be the man of the house while I'm gone so you look after your brothers, okay?"

I gave each of them an extra hug and a kiss before I tucked them into bed for the night. This was going to be the longest period of time that I had been away from them since they had come to live with me and I was already regretting having to go.

The trip to Houston went very well from a business stand point. The client was very impressed with the presentation that Amanda gave outlining how the work that they had hired us for was going to be accomplished. My job was to glad-hand the big wigs. I would have loved to manage the project myself but now with my new family that was not possible. I resigned myself to simply overseeing the company's operations.

When the meeting was over, Amanda went to visit her sister who lived in Sugar Land and I went to the Galleria to do some shopping for souvenirs for the boys. We decided to meet at Hobby airport at 5:30 to catch our plane back to San Antonio.

We didn't get back to San Antonio until shortly after seven. By that time I was anxious to get home to see how the boys were. "My god," I thought, "I'm getting to be an old mother hen." I don't think I was ever as happy to see my gate come into view. It was nearly eight o'clock when I punched the remote control to let me in.

I was taking the packages out of the car when I was nearly knocked off my feet by my five precious angels. "Hi guys, did you miss me?"

This was greeted by a chorus of "Yeah!" I could feel TJ's head nodding against my mid section. "I was scared you weren't gonna come back," TJ mumbled.

There were tears in his eyes as I squatted down to look him in the eyes. "You know I would never leave you, but sometimes dad has to go away on business. You're my little TJ and I can't live without you. I love you and I love your brothers," I said picking him up in my arms. "Will the rest of you bring my briefcase and those packages into the house? Don't look in them. They are a surprise."

Hildy met us at the back door as we entered the house. "I swear I thought they were going to wear out the carpet running back and forth to the windows to see if you were coming," she said.

Setting TJ down, I picked up the packages that the others had brought in from the car. "Let's see what I have in here," I withdrew from the large sack six Astro's shirts and ball caps and started handing them out to everyone. "There is one here for JR also. You can give it to him tomorrow when he comes home with you."

From a smaller sack, I withdrew a box of See's candy which I handed to Hildy. "It's not much, but I wanted to get you something for looking after the boys for me."

"Oh, thank you. You know my weakness for sweets, but I'll bet I have help with this though," she said.

She was right about the help. As soon as the boys saw the box, you could almost see the saliva starting to drip. Hildy opened the two pound box and told the boys that they could each have one piece. There were so many choices in the box it was like making a life and death decision for them to pick which piece they wanted.

"Okay guys, how is the homework coming along?" I asked after they had eaten their candy.

"It's all done," Joel volunteered. "Hildy checked it for us."

"Great! Then I guess it's bath time. Run along now while dad gets out of this monkey suit," I told them as I ushered them toward the bedrooms. I stripped out of my suit and tie and got into my pajama bottoms and then donned what was now becoming my favorite garment, my dressing gown.

As I sat on the couch reading, the morning paper that I hadn't gotten the chance this morning I heard a pair of bare feet running down the hall toward the family room. A pajama clad TJ crawled into my lap brushing aside the newspaper.

"My you smell clean," I said as he tucked his head under my chin. "Did Joel shampoo your hair?"

"Uh huh," was the reply. "Don't leave me again, please."

"I wish I could promise you that, little one. Dad has to earn a living so once in a while I will have to go someplace. But I promise you, I will always come back. I promise. Nothing could keep me away from my TJ."

While we were talking, the other boys joined us on the couch. "And nothing could keep me away from you all either," I said looking at each one in turn.

It was cold and rainy at the funeral for my former business partner on Wednesday. Although funerals are usually real downers, the eulogy for Eric however was uplifting and positive stressing all the good things in his life. The whole thing turned out to be a celebration of his life and not the mourning of his death. Of course his family and friends were saddened by his death but rejoiced in his life and their being part of it. "What a wonderful way of remembering a friend," I told the minister as we left the chapel.

It seemed like the rest of the week was spent discussing with potential clients what we could and could not do for them. Foster was right in his assessment of expected business for the coming year. We didn't have sufficient staff to do all of the work that was being requested from us. I instructed Foster to begin headhunting. (A process of raiding other company's employees.)

One more week until the hearing for adoption I told myself when I got to work the following Monday. Darcie called and informed me that the hearing was scheduled for 10 AM on the 23rd. I was glad to finally hear what time the hearing was scheduled for so that I could begin to lay out the plan to have everything ready.

I first called Benjamin Cross to let him know the time of the hearing and to see if he would have all the papers ready by that time. He assured me that he had all the necessary filings ready for all five of the boys and didn't expect that there would be any problems that he could foresee.

Next, I called Gerald to see that he had everything ready for the trust funds to be put in place on Monday. He said that the final papers were being scrutinized by a tax attorney to make sure that everything was entirely legal and air tight.

I made out lists of reasons why I should be given the rights to adopt all five of the boys despite being a single male. I tried to think of a defense to every point that could be raised against me and by the end of the day I believed that I was prepared for the hearing.

Although the rest of the week seemed to drag on the business kept me busy. Foster and I interviewed five possible additions to the company and made offers to two of them. At least it kept my mind off the upcoming hearing most of the time.

I didn't want to upset the boys unnecessarily so I waited until Saturday evening to tell them about the hearing on Monday. I assembled them all in the family room after supper to tell them what was going to happen.

When we had all settled in, I began, "On Monday we have to go see Judge Riley again so you won't be going to school in the morning."

"Why do we have to go see her again?" Joel asked.

"She is going to decide if you guys get to stay here with me permanently, that is if you want to."

"Yeah, but I thought she said we could last time," Joel said as TJ climbed into my lap.

"I want to stay here," TJ said.

"This hearing before Judge Riley is called an adoption hearing. Do you know what adoption means?"

Joel replied, "Yeah, I think so."

The rest of the boys just looked at me and shook their heads.

"If Judge Riley says it is okay, you will become my sons legally. That means that you are my sons forever and ever. No one can ever take you away. This will always be your home. You can even change your names to Johnson if you want to. Would you like to be TJ Johnson?"

"Uh huh," replied TJ giving me a tight squeeze.

"That'd be neat," Chris said. "Everone always asks me why my brothers' last names is different than mine."

"Chris, are you sure that you want me to be your dad forever? What about your real mom and dad? Do you ever think that you might want to live with them?"

"NO! They hated me," he said with tears forming in his eyes. "I tried to be good, but they hated me. They told me they wished I was dead. They did! They did!"

"Come here son," I said making room on my lap for him. "Everyone here loves you and always will."

Joel and the twins joined us on the couch in a group hug trying to soothe the now sobbing Chris. We sat like that for about fifteen minutes before I said, "Hey guys I love having you sit on my lap but dad's legs are going to sleep. How about if we go upstairs to see how the construction is coming along?" I hadn't let them go up there to see because I knew that it would probably be a mess and I didn't want to chance the possibility that they might get hurt.

This suggestion met with immediate approval so we trooped to the back stairs. Everything was pretty much in disarray when we got up there. Some of the side walls had been framed and a ceiling had been installed in about half of the attic. The two dormers that were going in on both side of the large space had been marked out but the roof had not been cut through to allow them to be finished.

Our trip upstairs seemed to take the boys' minds off our earlier discussion about adoption. The rest of the weekend went fairly normally. The boys played their video games, played with Samson, rode their bikes, fed and chased the deer and of course ate what seemed to be huge amounts of food.

When Monday morning finally arrived, I was a basket case. I knew we had done everything humanly possible to make the outcome of the hearing be in my favor, I was still nervous. Something kept insinuating doubt in my mind. Even though I knew better I still questioned if there was something that we had overlooked. I just could not put the doubt out of my mind.

CHAPTER 31

I gathered up the boys at 8:30 and got them loaded in the van. We had a meeting at 9:30 with Benjamin and I didn't want to be late for it. The traffic was heavy going into San Antonio but we got to the court house in plenty of time. In fact, we got there before Benjamin. We only had to wait for about ten minutes before he showed up. He wanted to discuss the various filings that he had prepared to present to the court so we headed for the snack bar to have a place to sit down. This immediately met with the approval of the boys. Although they had eaten less that two hours before you would have sworn that they hadn't eaten in a week.

Benjamin found a couple of tables where he could use one to spread out his papers while I took the boys through the serving line to get them a snack. The workers were just bringing out a pan of fresh cinnamon rolls as we started through the line. These had that gooey white icing dripping off the tops of the rolls. The boys each had to have one. I agreed if they promised to try not to get any of the frosting on their clothes. They all had one plus a pint of milk. I was tempted to get one they looked so good but settled for a cup of coffee. I also got a cup for Benjamin.

The boys sat at one table eating their rolls while Benjamin and I sat at another one next to them. He went over the various papers and did his best to explain to me exactly what each one was for. He might as well have been trying to explain nuclear physics to me for all that I understood. What I did understand was that he had prepared a petition to the court for me to adopt all five of the boys. That was all I was concerned about.

"Is there anything that we've forgotten?" I asked. "I have this terrible feeling that we've not done everything to assure that everything goes right."

"Look Crane, I have been at this a long time and I have an exceptional staff to look after the details that you are afraid we overlooked. I can assure you that from the standpoint of having all of our ducks in a row they are standing in rigid military formation.

"What I am about to ask you may sound a little strange but I want you to put a dollar bill in this envelope."

"All I have is a five. Will that do?" I asked.

"Yes, that will do fine," he said as he placed the bill in the envelope which I saw was labeled 'Retainer'.

"What's that for?" I asked.

"Just a little insurance," he said. "You have just retained a civil attorney in case it becomes necessary. There will be a colleague of mine who practices civil law who will be sitting in the gallery."

"Why do I need a civil attorney?" I asked. "I'm not suing anyone that I know of."

"Let's just say that my contacts suggest that there may be need for someone to advise you about civil matters," he replied.

I just looked at him with a bewildered expression on my face. "Okay, I trust that you know what you are doing."

As it was approaching ten o'clock, I started to get the boys' faces cleaned of all traces of their encounters with the gooey cinnamon rolls so that they would be presentable to the court. Thankfully, they had heeded my admonition not to get any frosting on their clothes.

The bailiff outside Judge Riley's courtroom told us to go on in that we were first on her docket. We took our seats at the table dragging chairs up so that all seven of us could sit at it. Darcie came in right after we were seated. The boys ran to her and gave her a group hug. They hadn't seen her in a couple of weeks. She gave each one of the boys a hug and a smile before she came over to Benjamin and me. She shook our hands and chatted for a few minutes before Gary Everett entered the courtroom and sat down at the other table without even acknowledging either Benjamin or me.

It wasn't long before the court was called to order as Judge Riley entered the room. The bailiff read the particulars of the case for the record before the Judge spoke.

"Miss Levin, Mr. Everett it's good to see you again," she said before turning to our table. "Mr. Cross it's a pleasure to see you also. How's that talented wife of yours? I saw some of her paintings displayed at a private showing a couple of weeks ago. I wish that I could afford to buy one of them but a judge's salary doesn't permit that," The last was said with a twinkle in her eyes.

"Thank you Your Honor, I will tell Linda that you remembered her and appreciate her work," Benjamin said.

"Good! Let's get to this matter before us. I assume that you have prepared the adoption petitions for the boys, Mr. Cross," the judge stated more than asked.

"Yes ma'am, I have all five of them here. They are the standard petitions with added addenda containing the financial statement of Mr. Johnson and his business. There are also a number of letters of reference from several well known members of the community. Statements from the boys' school, their doctor and Joel's psychiatrist have been provided," Benjamin concluded.

"Miss Levin, what is the position of CPS in relation to these petitions for adoption?"

"Your Honor, as their case worker I have no problem with or opposition to the petitions. That is not the position of Mr. Everett, however. I will let him speak to his opposition," Darcie replied.

Judge Riley looked sternly at Gary Everett as he stood up to speak. "I hope that you are not going off on one of your religious tirades again, Mr. Everett. If you are, you might as well sit down right now and not waste the court's time. I have had it up to here," she indicated with her hand raised over her head, "with using religion to bolster untenable positions. If you have some legal reason why these petitions should not be granted I will listen to your arguments. Otherwise sit down and save your breath."

Gary stood there staring at the judge. His mouth was trying to form words but nothing came out. After a moment or two, he sat down knowing that she had shot down his arguments before he could make them.

"Very well," Judge Riley started. "I need to speak with the children individually. Ms. Ramirez, it's good to see you again also. Would you be so kind as to help me with the boys while I talk to them?"

"Yes ma'am," I heard Hildy reply. I hadn't noticed when she entered the courtroom but was glad that she was here.

Hildy rounded up the boys and led them into the judge's chambers followed closely by the judge and her court reporter.

The courtroom was quiet for a while after the judge left. Benjamin looked briefly at his pager and then excused himself to make a phone call. I looked around the gallery to see who was present. There was one well dressed gentleman sitting a couple of rows back behind us who I suspected was the civil attorney I supposedly retained earlier. To my surprise, Joyce Gehrig and another rather rotund man were sitting directly behind Gary Everett and whispering to him. Darcie was not participating in the conversation.

"Darcie, how long do you think the judge is going to take talking to the boys?" I asked.

She got up from her table and came over to ours before she answered. "That's not easy to answer. I have seen her take as little as ten minutes or as long as half an hour. I don't know whether she is talking to each one individually or all at once. I would guess it will be at least half an hour."

"Oh, I hope it doesn't take too long. By the way, what do you think about Eric working on that project in Dallas?"

"He knew that he would probably have to travel when he took the job. I think I will enjoy watching JR occasionally. He's such a great kid. Of course, I'm prejudiced," she said laughing.

"No you're right. The boys really like having him to play with after school every day. I hope that works out for you as well when you look after him. I never asked Eric, but I just assumed that you would be staying at his house the days he was out of town."

"I think that makes the most sense rather than having to get JR up an hour or so earlier just to get him to school," she said. "I'm not an early bird myself and having to drive him all the way from my house to his school even if it's only one day a week is not something I would look forward to doing."

Benjamin came back shortly and stopped to talk to the man I presumed to be the civil attorney before he joined Darcie and me at our table. We chatted a while before I started getting worried. It had been almost an hour since the judge took the boys to talk with them. My mind conceived of all sorts of horrible things that were happening or about to happen. Darcie and Benjamin tried to allay my fears but to no avail.

Fifteen minutes and several fingernails later Hildy and the boys came back into the courtroom. I almost collapsed from the relief that I felt. I had time to give the boys a group hug before the court was called to order and the judge took her place at the bench.

"Mr. Johnson," Judge Riley began "those are five of the most delightful young men I've met in a long time. They seemed to have grown and matured so much since the last time they were here three months ago."

"Thank you Your Honor," I replied. "They are the light of my life."

"I'm going to ask Ms. Ramirez to take the boys to the snack bar while we discuss the petitions before the court. I'm quite sure that the boys will not mind that," the judge laughed.

"Can I have another cinny roll?" TJ asked as they left the courtroom.

I just shook my head in disbelief as the five bottomless pits hurried toward the snack bar.

"Now then, let's see if we can get this matter settled quickly. Mr. Cross, I have reviewed the petitions that you filed with the court and find them to be in order. Do you have anything further to add?" she asked looking at Benjamin.

"No, Your Honor," he answered.

"Mr. Everett or Ms. Levin does CPS have anything to add to these proceedings before the court grants the petitions?"

"No, Your Honor," Darcie answered.

"Yes, Your Honor," Gary spoke up.

"Mr. Everett, you have been cautioned by this court. I hope that whatever you have in mind is germane to this hearing."

"It is, Your Honor. I have just been given information that directly bears on Mr. Johnson's fitness to adopt the children."

"Tread lightly Mr. Everett. Whatever information you have had better be factual and able to be corroborated," Judge Riley said with an almost evil grin.

"Ahh…ahh…," he stammered. "I received this information from sources that I believe to be very reliable but I have not had sufficient time to verify it personally."

"And just who are these sources?" she interrupted.

"I would rather not divulge them at this time Your Honor."

"Mr. Everett, I don't have time to mess with you. If you want to introduce derogatory information concerning Mr. Johnson's character, I want to hear it from the 'horse's mouth'. Now either put up or shut up."

"But Your Honor these are allegations of sexual abuse of the children in question. Isn't it worth the courts time to make sure that Mr. Johnson is a fit parent before he is granted custody of them?"

"Mr. Everett, you will reveal the source of these allegations or I will hold you in contempt of court and have you held in the county jail until you reveal them. Do I make myself clear?"

"Yes, Ma'am," he barely whispered. Gary turned to Joyce and the fat man sitting behind him before turning back to the judge. "My sources are the two people sitting behind me…"

"Ah, yes I see. Ms. Gehrig and Judge Clinton I believe. I want to get this on record. Ms. Gehrig, would you take the witness chair please?"

Joyce looked like a deer trapped in the headlights of a car. I don't think that she had expected to have to testify to any allegations.

Judge Riley's bailiff administered the oath to Joyce. Then the judge began, "Ms. Gehrig it's the understanding of this court that you have information that is of a derogatory nature with respect to Mr. Johnson. Is that correct?"

"Yes Your Honor."

"Tell this court what that information is and the source of it."

"One of the boys had made an outcry of being sexually abused by Mr. Johnson. The outcry was made in my presence."

"And what type of abuse was it and which one of the boys made this allegation?"

"It was the oldest, Joel. He reported that he was repeatedly raped by Mr. Johnson."

"Tell me, Ms. Gehrig, are you still employed by CPS?"

"No, Your Honor, I left CPS about three months ago."

"Hmm. Mr. Cross would you like to question Ms. Gehrig?"

"No, Your Honor, not at this time."

"Thank you. Ms. Gehrig, the court will give the information that you provided all the consideration that it deserves. Judge Clinton, would you please take the witness stand?"

After he took the chair in the witness box, the bailiff administered the oath to Judge Clinton.

"It's a rare occurrence indeed when I have a member of the bench as a witness in a proceeding before this court," Judge Riley said. "Now what information do you have that bears on the fitness of Mr. Johnson to be granted custody of these boys?"

"Thank you Judge Riley. It's a pleasure to be in your court. I was also present when the child made his outcry of molestation and I couldn't in good conscience permit it to continue."

"Then you corroborate Ms. Gehrig's statement?"

"Yes."

"Mr. Cross, do you have any questions?" Judge Riley said with a broad smile.

I was sitting there not believing what I was hearing. These people were obviously lying. I was totally floored by what was going on but too stunned to do anything except sit there with my mouth open in disbelief.

"Yes, I do have a question or two for Judge Clinton," Benjamin said turning to me and giving me a wink. "Judge Clinton, have you or are you willing to give a sworn statement elaborating on the time and place and the exact nature of the outcry that you allege that Joel gave?"

"I have not put the details to paper but I am prepared to do so."

"I assume that you have medical evidence of this abuse. Is that true?"

"We have not yet received the medical records from the examining physician."

"What is the name of the examining physician and when did the examination take place?"

"Dr. Lewinski was the physician and I'll have to check my diary for the exact date," At this point Judge Clinton was beginning to squirm slightly in his seat and a sheen of sweat droplets were showing on his brow.

"That's very interesting. Didn't Dr. Lewinski appear before you charged with lewd and lascivious acts in public?"

"That's possible."

"What was the outcome of those proceedings?"

"Ahh…I don't recall. I see so many cases that I can't be expected to remember every verdict."

"Very well, you allege this abuse has been going on for the last three months. Is that correct?"

"Yes."

"Sir, are you sure that everything that you have told this court is truthful?"

"Mr. Cross, that is an insulting question. I am a respected member of the judiciary."

"I'll take that as a yes. As far as being a 'respected member of the judiciary', were you not given a verbal reprimand from the senior presiding judge for issuing a warrant for Mr. Johnson's arrest based on what you knew to be a false accusation?"

"That is outrageous. Mr. Cross, you have stepped over the line. You are in contempt…"

"Just a minute, Judge Clinton, this is my courtroom and I will decide if anyone is in contempt," Judge Riley spoke sternly. "You are a witness in this matter. You left your robe behind when you entered the witness stand."

"Judge Clinton do you see that gentleman behind Mr. Johnson?" Benjamin asked as he indicated for the man to stand.

"Yes."

"You may not know who he is so I will tell you. His name is Ezra Bernstein. He is Mr. Johnson's civil attorney. He is prepared to file a civil suit on behalf of Mr. Johnson based on information that we became aware of several weeks ago that you and Ms. Gehrig were going to make false allegations against Mr. Johnson. I am sure that you did not expect to have to testify under oath and for that I am grateful to Judge Riley for going along with our plan.

"Thank you Judge Riley. I have no further questions," Benjamin said and sat down beside me and gave me a pat on the back.

Clinton seemed to shrink as he sat in the witness box. He knew that he had been caught in a lie and that his false testimony under oath would probably cause him his judgeship.

Judge Riley broke the silence, "Judge Clinton, is there anything that you would like to say before I dismiss you as a witness?"

"No, Your Honor," he said barely audible.

"You are dismissed. For the record, this court finds that the testimony of Ms. Gehrig and Judge Clinton is not credible. Furthermore, this court will forward the transcript of this hearing and other information that the court has to the District Attorney's office with a recommendation that they pursue possible perjury charges against both of them.

"Now, as for the petitions of adoption before this court they are granted. Congratulations Mr. Johnson you are now the father of five boys. And I might add good luck. You are surely going to need it.

"There is only one matter to be resolved and for that we need the boys here. Bailiff, will you bring Ms. Ramirez and the boys back into the courtroom?"

Benjamin shook my hand and congratulated me on my official parenthood. I was in a state of near shock with all that had gone on in the last couple of hours.

The boys hurried back in with as much decorum as they could muster and quickly took there seats at the table. Hildy was beaming, her eyes clearly starting to show tears forming in them.

Judge Riley cleared her throat which brought everyone's attention back to her. "Joel, Chris, Larry, Lenny and TJ, I have good news for you. Crane Johnson is now officially and forever your father…"

All the boys jumped up from their chairs and they all landed on me nearly knocking me and the chair over backwards. After a round of hugs and kisses, I was able to urge them back to their own chairs.

"There is one more matter that you boys must decide before you leave here. That is; do you wish to have your last names changed to Johnson from Andersen and Martin?"

"YES!" came a loud chorus from all of the boys at once.

"I take that to be unanimous," the judge chuckled. "It's a great day for this court when I can keep siblings together in a single unit and not have them split into various homes with the probability that they will lose track of each other as the years pass. It's also a happy occasion when I can place a youngster in a home where he will have brothers who love him and a father who loves him and is able to provide a quality of life undreamed of in his previous home. I congratulate you again Mr. Johnson on your new family. The court also lifts the requirement that you provide it with an accounting of the trust fund for your son."

"Thank you, Your Honor. For the courts information I have set up identical irrevocable trust funds for all of the boys in the amount of $2.5 million. The monies will be made available to them for college expenses upon their enrollment in an accredited college. They will gain unrestricted access to the trust upon graduation from college or when they reach age 25 whichever comes first."

"Ms. Ramirez," Judge Riley said, "these boys love you as much as they would love their own grandmothers and I know that love is returned by you. If it were in my power, I would let you adopt them as your grandchildren. Unfortunately the law does not allow for that."

A few minutes later after all of the legal niceties were wrapped up we got up and started out of the courtroom. Hildy was surrounded by the boys as we left.

"Did she say you were our grandma?" Joel asked Hildy.

"Not exactly, honey. But I think of you as my grandsons, all five of you," she said putting her arms around all of the boys.

"Come on guys, let's go home," I said.

978-0-595-36378-0
0-595-36378-4

Printed in the United Kingdom
by Lightning Source UK Ltd.
132354UK00001B/322/A